# STAR TREK®
## STRANGE NEW WORLDS 10

# STAR TREK®
# STRANGE NEW WORLDS 10

Edited by
Dean Wesley Smith
with Paula M. Block

Based upon *Star Trek* and
*Star Trek: The Next Generation*®
created by Gene Roddenberry,
*Star Trek: Deep Space Nine*®
created by Rick Berman & Michael Piller,
*Star Trek: Voyager*®
created by Rick Berman and Michael Piller & Jeri Taylor,
*Star Trek: Enterprise*®
created by Rick Berman & Brannon Braga

Pocket Books
New York    London    Toronto    Sydney

Pocket Books
A Division of Simon & Schuster, Inc.
1230 Avenue of the Americas
New York, NY 10020

This book is published by Pocket Books, a division of Simon & Schuster, Inc.,
under exclusive license from CBS Studios Inc.

First Pocket Books trade paperback edition July 2007

POCKET and colophon are registered trademarks of Simon & Schuster, Inc.

Manufactured in the United States of America

10  9  8  7  6  5  4  3  2  1

For information about special discounts for bulk purchases,
please contact Simon & Schuster Special Sales
at 1-800-456-6798 or business@simonandschuster.com.

ISBN-13: 978-1-4165-4438-8
ISBN-10:     1-4165-4438-0

# Contents

## STAR TREK: VOYAGER

## STAR TREK: ENTERPRISE

## SPECULATIONS

# Introduction

## Ten Years of Great Adventure

Ten years! Wow, that is nothing short of fantastic. This anthology series has lasted three years longer than any of the shows did. Ten years of the fans taking *Star Trek* in hundreds of new directions, from the ancestors of the characters to a million years into *Star Trek*'s future. And everything in between. The existence of this book shows the power of *Star Trek* fans.

For the tenth year in a row, I get to welcome you to a book filled with wonderful, original *Star Trek* fiction. It has been a pleasure, year after year, to read the stories, help pick the winners, and see fans contribute to the *Star Trek* universe.

When you start reading this book, or any of the *Strange New Worlds* anthologies, think of each story as a weekly episode of your favorite show. That's what they are—if you were to turn a *Star Trek* show into print, it would only be the length of a short story.

In your hands are nineteen new episodes, nineteen new *Star Trek* adventures. When you put all ten volumes of *Strange New Worlds* together, you have over two hundred episodes. If you miss your weekly new *Star Trek* show, you are holding the cure.

However, before you turn to the first great story, let me take this moment to gaze backward and give you a little history of this project.

*Strange New Worlds* was the brainchild of then Pocket Books editor John Ordover. John had the help of Paula Block, who is one of the people responsible for the approval of anything *Star Trek* that sees print. The two of them pushed the lawyers, cajoled the corporate mavens, and somehow—against all odds—managed to get this contest—and therefore this book—approved. One year before the contest was approved, I joined the project.

As a former magazine editor, I knew how to pick the great stories out of thousands that came through the door. I had written novels in every *Star Trek* series at that time, and knew and liked them all. I had no favorite *Star Trek,* unlike most fans.

I figured the contest would last one year, two tops, and that would be it. I'm just about as good at predicting which stock will go up or down. Somehow the contest went on, and year after year after year, new writers, great stories, original *Star Trek* ideas graced the pages of *Strange New Worlds.* Paula Block and I are still here, working on the contest each year. John moved on, and the editorial work at Pocket Books was taken over by first Elisa Kassin and then shifted to Margaret Clark.

One of the great strengths in the *Star Trek* universe that has helped it survive for over forty years is its ability to go forward. From *Star Trek* to *Star Trek: Enterprise,* the *Star Trek* universe is always expanding, never staying in one place for very long. With *Star Trek,* one crew is never enough, and every idea can be explored.

After ten years, *Star Trek: Strange New Worlds* now comes to an end with this volume. The future will hold something new for the fans, I am sure about that. Because that's what *Star Trek* does.

It moves forward.

I'm going to miss the fall ritual of reading thousands of *Star Trek* stories. But just as *Star Trek* does, I'm moving forward with my writing into original books that are pushing me into my own strange new worlds of fiction.

For those of you picking up *Strange New Worlds* for the first time, you have a wonderful treat waiting for you. I would suggest you find all ten of the books, line them up on a shelf, and sit back for hundreds of fantastic trips into the *Star Trek* universe.

Ten seasons of new voyages, new adventures, all in book form.

All written by fans just like you.

It's been a great ten years. Thanks for the ride.

Now, enjoy the adventures, and don't miss a story.

—Dean Wesley Smith
Editor
*Strange New Worlds I–Strange New Worlds 10*

# STAR TREK®
## STRANGE NEW WORLDS 10

# STAR TREK

# The Smell of Dead Roses

Gerri Leen

GRAND PRIZE

**Gerri Leen** lives in Northern Virginia; she originally hails from Seattle, and spends far too much mental time in the worlds of *Star Trek*. This story is for absent friends and family—some long gone, some lost just recently. Leen humbly thanks: friends Kath, Lisa, and Paula for useful crit and encouragement beyond the call of duty; the Paneranormal Society writers for reviews and kicking ideas around; and editors Dean, Margaret, and Paula for making this all happen. She wishes Dean all the best as he rides off into the non–*Strange New Worlds* sunset and thanks him for the wisdom he's shared with new and not-so-new writers over the years. Her story "Obligations Discharged" was in *Strange New Worlds VII* and "Living on the Edge of Existence" appeared in *Strange New Worlds 9*.

Perrin huddled on the balcony, trying to will herself into invisibility as the fight between her parents raged on. She stared out at the other building, hating that the people across from her might be staring back, might be feeling pity.

"Perrin?" Her sister snuck out through the open door and crawled into her lap.

"It'll be all right."

Nanda was too little to understand what had happened. She'd been bouncing around Perrin all day. Excited to eat Perrin's birthday cake—cake that was now all over the floor.

It had made a strange sound as it hit, knocked off the table by her father. Not a crash—it was too soft for that. But not a gentle sound, either. There had been a sucking noise, as frosting met wood, as cake smashed down, causing the frosting to spread out even more. Nine candles had hit first. Nine candles that were broken now and would never be lit.

"Why do they yell at each other?" Nanda asked, scrunching her eyes closed as if that could make the voices stop.

"Because they can."

"But it's your birthday."

Perrin looked back at what had been her pretty cake. It had come out of the replicator already decorated with roses in pink and yellow, just the way she'd wanted it. There'd been little forget-me-nots in light blue, and a long, trailing vine of dark green ivy rambling over the whole cake.

It had been the most beautiful cake Perrin had ever seen. She'd just known it would taste better than any of her other birthday cakes.

"Is it because I cheated?" Nanda whispered.

"What?"

"When you weren't looking, I took some frosting. From the back, where you wouldn't see. Is that why they're mad?"

Perrin hugged her close. "No, that's not why."

But Nanda was sniffling in the way that meant she might break into tears at any minute.

"What color was the frosting you tasted?"

"Yellow."

The border had been yellow, all scrolled and thick. "Was it good?"

Nanda nodded. She seemed to relax, crying jag averted.

"I thought it would be." Perrin sighed, and went back to studying the other apartments as the yelling inside her family's went on.

The park smelled like summer, even though it was barely spring. London had warmed early, but the bright sun did nothing to warm Perrin as she walked slowly with her mother. She willed her fourteen-year-old heart to slow down—or just to stop.

How could anything hurt this bad?

Her mother touched her arm. "Say something."

"Such as?" Perrin knew her mother hated her taking that tone. She'd slapped her for it at other times, had told her to stop pretending she was something other than what she was. To stop acting as if she was better than the rest of them.

Perrin thought she was better than the rest of them, if only because she didn't scream first and ask questions later.

"Don't you care that I'm leaving?" her mother asked, her voice edging toward the dramatic end of the scale. Before too long, she'd be crying.

Perrin hated tears almost as much as shouting—both were weapons. "Would caring stop you from doing it?"

Her mother swallowed hard.

"You're leaving me with him."

"Things will be better if I'm not there. He won't have anyone to fight with."

She stroked Perrin's hair, and it felt comforting, until Perrin thought about how she wouldn't feel it anymore after today.

"You're so calm, Perrin. You never get mad. You soothe him, the way we don't."

We: her mother and Nanda. Nanda wasn't calm. Nanda was quick to anger, quick to yell, quick to rile their father up. It was why Nanda was going away with their mother. She'd earned herself a ticket out of Hell by being a spoiled brat.

Perrin wished she could yell and scream, but it wasn't her way. She was the good girl. The one who stayed calm.

"I love you, Perrin."

Her mother started to cry, and that was the last straw. Perrin ran from those tears, ran hard and fast, knowing her mother would never be able to keep up. She pelted down the path, heading for the rose garden.

It was already in bloom, and there was a large cluster of people to her right, seemingly on a tour of some kind. Perrin turned the other way to avoid them and ran hard into a robed figure. Stepping back, he caught himself, but she fell to the ground and stayed there, more in defeat than actual pain.

"Are you hurt?" His voice was the calmest thing Perrin had ever heard.

She looked up at him, realized he was Vulcan. "I'm sorry," she said, barely able to get the words out.

"You should be more careful." Those words coming from her father would have been followed by a hard slap. Her mother would have turned them into a wounded monologue, the precursor to more accusing words and finally tears. This man just said them. They were just words.

She took a deep breath. "I didn't mean to."

"I hope not."

She realized there was some warmth in his eyes, and a soothing humor that hurt no one as it lay cradled in his air of dignity.

"Sarek, what have you got there?" The voice was melodious, full of good will. A human woman—petite and smiling—stepped around the Vulcan. She pulled Perrin to her feet, checking her knees and elbows. "Nothing damaged."

"I ran into him, ma'am." Perrin tried to sound older than she was, wanting this woman to think well of her.

"Did you?"

"I didn't mean to, though."

"I'm sure you didn't, dear." The woman studied her. "What's your name?"

"Perrin Landover."

"Well, Perrin Landover, you just ran into Ambassador Sarek from Vulcan. I'm afraid this may have the making of a diplomatic incident."

Panic rose inside Perrin. To her surprise, the man put his hand on her shoulder—the briefest of touches.

"I believe I will recover, my wife. I feel only minimal damage from the collision."

It took Perrin a moment to realize they were teasing her and each other.

The woman laughed softly. "I'm Amanda, my dear. Why were you running so desperately?"

Perrin was about to tell her—even though she never shared her troubles with anyone—when she heard her mother calling her.

"Your mom?" Amanda asked with a knowing smile.

Perrin nodded.

"She appears to be worried," Sarek said.

"Maybe for her pretty new future." Perrin mumbled it so they couldn't hear.

And Amanda didn't seem to, but Sarek cocked his head to one side, an eyebrow rising slowly as he studied her. Perrin suspected those pointy ears made him hear better.

"I think she is worried, dear," Amanda said, turning Perrin to face her mother. "I know that tone. Now, go on."

Perrin's mother came into sight, waving furiously at the sight of her.

"Go," Sarek said. He and Amanda moved off, and for Perrin, the moment was frozen in a sense of calm and the smell of just-opened roses.

"Wait." She did not know why she called out, and when Sarek and Amanda turned to look at her, she wasn't sure what it was she wanted to say.

"Goodbye, my dear." Amanda smiled at her gently.

They walked away.

"Goodbye," Perrin said, trying to hold onto the serenity she felt from them, but failing as her mother came up, her voice harsh and accusing.

Perrin imagined herself as Sarek, tried wrapping herself in dignity the way he did. She looked up at her mother, letting one eyebrow rise the way his had.

Her mother stopped talking, her angry lecture finding no purchase in a face of stone.

The funeral was crowded, not just humans and Vulcans standing around the gravesite, but beings from all sorts of species. Perrin stood off, near a large mausoleum, and watched the service—and Sarek. She'd followed his career, and sometimes, once she'd come to San Francisco for school, she'd even followed him and Amanda around town. She'd noticed over the years, since she'd first run into them at the park, that Amanda had seemed to be getting weaker. And one day, Perrin had only seen Sarek walking, his face unreadable, but sorrow evident in the way he took his steps, in the set of his shoulders. Amanda had never come out with him again.

A few days ago, the newsvids had announced that Amanda had died. That kind, gentle woman was gone, and Perrin felt more grief than she had when her own father died, beaten to death in a barroom brawl on the darker side of London's East End.

Perrin's mother had been wrong. Perrin's ability to soothe her father had been short lived—or perhaps he'd just lost the urge to even try to be decent about things. He'd yelled and slammed things around. And once or twice, in a fit of drunken rage, he'd hit her.

Each time he'd done that, she'd run to the park, trying to call up the calm she'd felt that day with these two strangers. Each time, it had almost worked.

Now Amanda was gone, and it was easy to see that Sarek was in pain, even if he hid it. Grief didn't spill out of him the way her mother's had been wept out at her father's funeral. And for no reason other than her mother's love of drama.

Sarek stood straight, his son on one side, a woman that had to be Saavik on his other, as his wife was laid to rest. Perrin slid farther back behind the building, leaning against marble kept cool by the temperate San Francisco weather. Since she'd met Amanda and Sarek, Perrin had made it her business to discover as much as she could about them. And Spock was famous. She'd known about him earlier, of course, but had never connected him to the man she'd nearly mown down in the park.

People started to wander off in groups of two or three, and Perrin realized the funeral must be over. She clutched the rose she'd brought with her, a rose she'd grown on her little balcony. She'd learned to find solace in flowers long ago, when her mother and sister had left her to face her father's anger alone.

Her mother was remarried—another stormy relationship. She'd come to San Francisco a few weeks ago, looking for a place to stay for a while.

Perrin hadn't handed her the keys to the kingdom.

"You're hard. And unforgiving." Her mother had cried, of course. She always managed to cry without smearing her makeup. It was an art.

"You made me hard when you left me with him."

"I couldn't take you both, Perrin. And you were always his favorite. I thought he'd be kind to you."

"No. You thought he'd be less cruel. And there's a difference."

She'd shut the door in her mother's face, had ignored the knocking that eventually stopped.

But she'd watched her mother through the upstairs window, hating that she'd cared as the woman had walked out of her life again.

Perrin closed her eyes, unwilling to relive those memories. Opening them again slowly, she realized there was no one by the grave. She scanned the area; Sarek, Saavik, and Spock were walking slowly up the path. She waited until they rounded a corner and disappeared, then hurried down to Amanda's grave and knelt by it. The grass was cool and still slightly damp, the turned earth smelling rich but final.

"You were kind to me," she whispered as she set the rose down. "You saved me. You may not know that, but you did." Letting her hand rest on the lovely, rose-streaked marble headstone, she said, "Whenever things got too bad, I'd think of you. And Sarek."

She imagined Amanda smiling at that.

"I wish—"

"Who are you and what do you think you are doing?" Sarek's voice no longer had the perfect calm Perrin remembered.

She pushed herself to her feet, shaking as she did so. "I'm sorry. I meant no harm." Her English accent, which she'd worked hard to erase so she'd stand out less here, came back with a vengeance under his glare.

He studied her, his eyebrow going up. "Do I know you?"

"I nearly ran you down in Regent's Park. Eight years ago."

He seemed to be thinking back. "The young girl—Perrin."

"Yes." She felt a flush of pleasure that he remembered her. "I'm so very sorry about your wife. She was kind to me. You both were."

"We did very little."

She could tell he did not remember the day as something special.

"No, you did a lot. You taught me there's such a thing as control. Even the air around you was serene."

"And that is important to you?"

She laughed, the barest puff of air, to show brittle, angry humor. "My life has not always been that way."

"I see." He looked at the rose. "Is that from you?"

"It's one I grew."

"My wife loved roses."

"I know." It was a terrible admission. He'd understand that she'd been too interested in them.

His eyes grew colder. "Did you come to San Francisco just for this—to be . . . close to us?" There was a note of concern in his voice.

"No, I live here now. I go to Berkeley." A liberal place, full of people determined to make the universe better. "I'm in graduate school, studying xenodiplomacy." Her choice of disciplines was because of him.

He seemed to realize it.

"You influenced me greatly, sir."

"So, I see." He looked away.

"I don't mean to make you uncomfortable, and this all must sound quite mad. But you see, meeting you was a revelation. A way to act that did not involve yelling or crying or anything else overly emotional."

He stared at her, then nodded, his expression more wry than she expected. "It is fitting, I suppose. I could not influence my son, but I have this effect on someone else's daughter." She heard the unsaid: someone else's *human* daughter.

"My life has been much more peaceful since I took an interest in Vulcan." She was attending a meditation class at Berkeley, taught by a visiting Vulcan scholar.

"I speak at your school occasionally. Have you attended my lectures?"

"Oh, only all of them."

"I see." This time the concern seemed less, but it was still there.

"I can explain this better than I have."

"I am sure you can." Suddenly, he looked very tired. "I do not, however, think today is the day, Perrin."

"No. You're right. Of course, it's not." She looked down, feeling guilty that she'd intruded on his private time with his wife. "I'll go."

He did not seem to hear her, did not acknowledge the hand she lifted in goodbye before hurrying away.

She had a sick feeling—how badly had she just embarrassed herself with this man?

"These internships are hard to come by," Perrin's friend Monroe said, as he turned to her while they waited in line. "Five openings and all of us." He gestured ahead and behind them, where students stood patiently, waiting to go in for their fifteen minutes of opportunity. Only a quarter of an hour to sell herself. Perrin wasn't sure she could do it.

"Make that six," the student ahead of them whispered. "I heard that Ambassador Sarek has agreed to take an intern. Can you imagine learning from him?"

"Can you imagine interviewing with him?" Monroe asked with a laugh. "The man's a legend. And he has no sense of humor."

"He doesn't need one," Perrin said, feeling her cheeks color as both men looked at her. "I mean, he's Vulcan. They never have one."

"Well, rumor is he's not interviewing today, anyway," the other man said. "He's just going to pick someone. He can do whatever he wants, I guess."

"Perrin Landover," she suddenly heard the loudspeaker announce. "Please report to registration."

"Oh, you're in for it now. What'd you do"

"Nothing." Perrin glanced at the line. They were almost to the front, and she didn't relish losing her place.

The page repeated, her name seeming to fill the crowded hallway.

"Break a leg," she whispered to Monroe as she walked to registration, passing students who would no doubt clinch the slots before she even had a chance to compete.

The woman manning the desk at registration looked up at her. "Oh, Perrin. This was left for you." She handed Perrin a padd.

The message said only, "Thirteen hundred. The Chalice. I have heard you are looking for an internship. —Sarek."

She handed the padd back to the woman and checked the time. She had thirty minutes to either get back in line and secure her future the normal way, or to hurry across town to the best Vulcan restaurant in the city and see if the man she idolized was serious.

She made it to the Chalice ten minutes early. Sarek still beat her. He seemed to be studying her as the maitre'd led them to a table.

She could feel herself blushing under his appraisal—she thought he could see right through her, could determine what kind of person she was just at a glance.

"I have examined your transcripts. They are most impressive. And your professors speak highly of you."

It was odd to think he was now studying up on her.

"I am a demanding master," he said.

"That's fine. I perform well under pressure. Just ask Professor Kincaide. I was his assistant." The man gave new meaning to the word "demanding."

"I spoke with him. He had nothing but positive things to say about you."

"Indeed." She was not sure where this confidence was coming from, but it felt good.

"He did, however, say your life appeared to center around your studies—to the exclusion of all else."

She could feel her face fall. Kincaide had said that? The man who spent every night and weekend at the University? "Coming from him, sir, that might have been high praise."

Sarek seemed to be amused, even though his eyes barely light-ened and his lips did not curl up. He seemed to find some humor in her statement. Or possibly just in her. Was it a good thing if a Vulcan laughed at you?

"Give me a reason to offer you this internship, Miss Lando-ver. There are many students who have already petitioned for the honor."

She met his eyes, did not flinch from them. "I want it more than those others do."

"Why?"

"Because I can learn from you. Not just diplomacy, although I doubt there could be a better teacher. But I would like to learn more about the serenity I sense in you. The control."

"You seem very controlled for a human."

"For every action there is an equal and opposite reaction." At his look, she smiled tightly. "My parents taught me how not to behave."

"Ah. What you were saying in the cemetery."

She was surprised he remembered; that conversation had been nearly a year ago. "Yes. Exactly."

"It will not be an easy assignment."

"Then I am the perfect candidate. I am unused to ease." She met his eyes, keeping her own calm and assured. But her heart was pounding, and she could feel her palms sweating.

"Very well. You will start tomorrow at the Embassy."

"Thank you, sir." She started to get up.

"I did not invite you to this restaurant to leave before eating."

"Oh." She saw the waiter coming, the plate loaded with tradi-tional Vulcan foods, most of which, she knew from her studies of Sarek and things Vulcan, would be exceedingly hot. "A test?"

"Do you think I would do that?"

"Yes."

"Then, yes. It is a test. Let us see how you fare."

She was sweating and her nose was running a bit when she finished. But she didn't choke or sputter.

"It is possible you will work out."

"Eating is important?"

"In your capacity on my staff, you will attend many functions. Being able to enjoy—or at least tolerate—the local cuisine is a key aspect of the job."

"You're a vegetarian. How do you manage?"

"I did not say I had to do it." There was definitely some humor in his voice. "Although if it is not the flesh of an animal, I will find a way to 'choke it down,' as my wife used to say."

"You must miss her." She thought for a moment it was the wrong thing to say, because he became very still and did not answer. "I'm sorry, it's none of my b—"

"I do."

She feared she might say something gushy and human, but the waiter saved her, bringing the bill, which Sarek paid, then leaving them alone again.

Sarek rose gracefully from his chair. "I will see you at oh-six hundred at the Embassy tomorrow."

She got up, probably with much less grace, but she was too excited to worry about it. "Thank you, sir. You won't regret it."

He did not answer, just left her with a quick nod of his head.

She nearly floated home. Her apartment seemed too confining, so she went out to the balcony, busying herself with her roses as she tried to relax. The bush that she'd cut Amanda's rose from last year seemed to have come alive, the blossoms open and perfect, their aroma beautiful in the still air.

She knew she'd remember this day forever.

Perrin felt a surge of happiness, bit it back so that it would not find a way to her face. Spock would not approve of her if she was overly emotional. He'd barely tolerated her as it was as his father's intern, then as Sarek's assistant. Now—what would he think of her becoming his father's wife?

She could feel her legs shaking and decided to walk, roaming the halls of Sarek's house. This lovely place she'd worked in until all hours of the morning, helping Sarek prepare for a mission, would be her house soon. She'd surrender the comfortable suite of rooms he'd given her and move into his—into theirs.

She walked out to the rose garden Amanda had started. The garden Perrin had found dying when she'd first visited the house some years after she'd started working for Sarek as an intern.

He'd looked at the garden, then had turned away as if in pain.

She'd wandered around the plants, checking them. Someone had watered them, but not enough. And they needed pruning.

"Those were Amanda's," he said softly.

"I can save them. Make them thrive again."

It had been a big claim. They'd been very nearly dead—and in this Vulcan heat, she'd be hard pressed to bring them back. But she'd wanted to do it. For this man she'd come to respect and enjoy so much. For the woman who had been so kind to her on the day she needed it most. And maybe for the son she'd only met a few times. The son who'd stared at her with such disdain, as if he thought she was trouble.

She realized now that Spock had understood how she felt about Sarek long before she had.

She'd gone to work on the garden the next day, when she'd been between duties for Sarek. It had taken a long time to make the roses beautiful again. A great deal of coaxing and tending and fertilizing. And of course, water. A commodity so dear on Vulcan it was almost a crime to waste it on flowers. Except that it would make Sarek happy, and she'd wanted that more than anything else.

"Perrin?" Sarek was coming down the hall. He, too, looked nervous. Was the idea of telling Spock so terrifying? Did he think Spock would disapprove?

She thought so but hoped that her fear was just a case of human nerves. "Sarek, all is ready." Her voice was more resonant since she'd been with him; she thought it was from the breath control she'd learned in her twice-weekly meditation classes. She'd progressed much more rapidly here, where she was surrounded by all things Vulcan.

He looked at the garden. "When you asked me if you could restore it, I did not think it was possible."

"Then why did you let me try?"

His expression lightened, and there was something—something that felt like love—in his eyes. "Because you wanted to."

She smiled. The restrained smile he liked best. She'd learned to do that, to scale back her emotions. It felt good. It felt right. It felt light-years away from what she'd grown up with.

"Saavik is coming today, too."

Perrin worried that she didn't have enough food. But Spock never ate much when he came over. It was as if he lost his appetite the minute he crossed Sarek's threshold.

"Saavik was most pleased to accept," Sarek said.

Perrin read the contrast in Sarek's words: Saavik's reply had been gracious; Spock's must not have been.

"It is not you, my dear." Sarek actually sighed. "You must not think this is about you. Or about his mother. Spock's issues have always been with me."

"What issues could he have with you? You are such a good man."

"Such blind loyalty." Sarek touched her cheek gently. "You love with such ferocity, Perrin."

It always startled her when Sarek spoke of love. But he did, and often. He understood it. He embraced it. Perrin suspected it was why Amanda had seemed so filled with joy—to be loved by a man like this was extraordinary.

The chime rang.

Sarek sighed. Spock could have just come in—to ring the chime established a distance, a sense that this was not his house. Saavik would have just come in, calling out to them in her brusque way that somehow combined Vulcan dignity with warmth and humor.

Perrin hurried to the door, unwilling to let the dark feelings get worse, and opened it, to find Spock standing with his hands behind his back, his face stoic in the extreme.

She stood aside. "Please, enter."

It was not the ritual greeting. One did not use the ritual greeting with family. And to take advantage of that was a moment of rebellion she had not intended to indulge in.

Spock looked at her in surprise, then his face tightened even more. He turned to Sarek. "You have news, I take it?"

"Perrin and I have decided to wed."

Of all the ways he could have put it, that was the most neutral. But it included her in the decision, made her part of the choosing, not just the prospective bride who'd waited to be chosen.

"My congratulations," Spock said, every note perfect. But the temperature in the house seemed to go down several degrees.

"What are we congratulating them for?" Saavik asked, coming up behind him, her expression easy.

"Perrin and my father are to be married."

"That is very good news." She sounded like she meant it. She pushed past Spock, touched Perrin's arm gently. "It is a pleasure to welcome you to the family."

Spock did not look like he shared the sentiment. But he was part of the family by birth. Saavik, like Perrin, had been taken in. She was a member by chance, a member by the desire of those within. In Saavik's case, all of those within. Perrin could see she'd have to settle for two out of three.

"You should see the rose garden, my son." Sarek sounded as if any diversion at this moment would be a good one.

Perrin led them down to it. Spock wandered it in silence, while the other three looked on from the doorway.

"It looks healthier each time I see it," Saavik said. She'd had a hand in the restoration, too. She'd often helped water the plants.

"I am very pleased with it," Sarek said, his gaze warm as he looked at Perrin.

She smiled back at him.

"My mother would be pleased," Spock said, and his tone was more open.

"I hope so." Perrin sensed Sarek drawing Saavik back into the house. "I restored her roses, Spock. I didn't plant new ones. I'm not trying to erase her."

"Yet, you take her place." He stood staring at the ground for a long moment, then looked over at her. "Forgive me. My words were not kind. I do not bear you any ill will."

"No?"

"It is not your fault this happened."

"Fault? Your father is happy. He's been alone for some time. Is it so bad that he has found someone he wants to share his life with?"

Spock started to say something then bit it off, turning away to stare at the sky. He always seemed so alone. Saavik had told Perrin that the death of James Kirk had changed Spock, robbing them of a man who'd understood his human side—who'd made peace with it and embraced his own form of warmth and good humor.

She wished she'd met that Spock.

"Come," she said, "dinner is nearly ready."

He seemed almost to attempt to make small talk as they enjoyed the meal. Saavik worked extra hard to draw him out, glancing over at Perrin as she did so. Sarek seemed pleased at how hard Spock appeared to be trying.

Perrin forced herself to relax. Maybe this would all work out?

Cardassian roses bloomed along the path of the government center, filling the air with a meaty sweetness that Perrin found offensive as she hurried after Sarek. He was angry. Visibly angry.

"How dare he disagree with me in public?"

She was angry, too. Angry at Spock, yes—he could have found a way to do what he had to do in a less public way.

But she was angry at herself, as well, for not seeing what had been right in front of her.

Sarek had been getting more emotional. He'd been having short memory lapses. Had seemed to reminisce more, to express frustration more. And now this: anger. True, raw anger.

She'd known the danger of Bendii's Syndrome. The doctors

at the Institute had told her what to watch for, but she'd only listened with half an ear. Sarek was her touchstone when it came to control. He'd never give in to something like Bendii's. The disease would find him too great an opponent to bother with.

She'd been a fool to think that.

"I will make a statement," Sarek said. "And then I will disown him."

She touched Sarek's hand, trying to calm him, but he whirled on her, slapping her hand off his, his face reminding her of her father's. She shrank back.

And he seemed to understand immediately what he had done, and where she had gone for that moment. "My wife, I beg . . . I beg forgiveness."

He stood, staring down at his hand as if it had betrayed him. "I have never struck you."

"You did not mean to this time."

"I did." There was confusion in his eyes, pain in his voice.

"No, Sarek, you didn't. I just surprised you. You were startled and reacted by instinct." She touched his hand again, and this time he did not flinch, instead put his other hand over hers.

"I would never hurt you, Perrin."

"I know." But she felt suddenly trapped by his hand.

He let go of her, and she knew by his face that she had been transmitting what she felt.

"Sarek, it is forgotten. We must plan how you will counter Spock's argument. I know you did not expect him to oppose you, but he has. And now we must find a way for you to win."

His look was very bitter. "I never win when it comes to him."

"Then forget it is Spock. Think of it only as a puzzle you must solve. I have faith in you, my dearest." She took his arm, urged him to walk more down the path.

He did as she wanted, drawing her with him, his hand coming over hers again, but not trapping. It showed how much he needed her that he would touch her this way in public. She had somehow become his touchstone, too.

She pulled every bit of control she had around her and made him talk, plan, strategize. He would win this one, or if he could not win, he would fight it in the way only Sarek of Vulcan could, with overwhelming logic. With the natural timing of a master swordsman. With the pure power of centuries of Vulcans behind him.

And she—one small, human woman—would help him. Even if she did not feel up to the task. Even if she was nothing compared to him. She would help him.

They walked, and he spoke while she listened and offered a suggestion here, a correction there. All done evenly, calmly. All done to hide the fact that this man she loved so dearly was beginning to lose his mind.

He must never, ever know. Not until it was so bad that she couldn't hide it from him anymore. She began to assess who in their household she could trust, which of her family, how many of Sarek's staff. The number was overwhelmingly small.

Saavik. Saavik could be trusted. And Sakkath.

She would have two allies in this. That was all.

"My wife? Are you listening? Is this not a fitting argument?"

"Very fitting, my love." She patted his arm, realized she'd done it as if he were a child—or an addled old man.

He was neither. He was Sarek of Vulcan. He was the greatest man his planet had ever produced. And she would protect him if it killed her.

They walked on, the overpowering smell of Cardassian roses only adding to her muted despair.

Perrin walked through Amanda's rose garden, trying not to step on the trampled flowers that just that morning had been afire with blossoms. Blood-red blosoms—the color of the blood in her veins, not in Sarek's. Although there were drying green stains on the door from where Sarek had rested his thorn-sliced hands before pulling the door open savagely and striding inside and back to his study. He'd paced for hours.

He hadn't yelled as he'd caused this destruction. He hadn't shouted or hit her. And she hadn't cried. But, during the time it had taken him to destroy the garden she'd been back in London. A frightened child trying to not attract the attention of a raging adult.

Perrin heard the door open again and braced herself in case it was Sarek.

"It is only I," Saavik said, walking gently as if she could do the roses any more damage than Sarek already had. "Oh," she said, taking in the amount of the damage.

"It is the disease." That was Perrin's answer for everything. Sarek laughing uproariously at a joke only he understood: the disease. Sarek calling her by Amanda's name and saying things she knew had nothing to do with her: the disease. Sarek huddling in the corner of their bedroom crying for his sons: the disease. This damned disease that was making Sarek act . . . human.

Saavik walked over to one of the bushes near the back. Sarek had missed it, or perhaps some part of him had overruled the wild man and made him leave something standing.

"These were her roses," Perrin said.

"They're yours, too."

"So I shouldn't assume he's just striking out at her?"

Saavik shot her a look full of compassion. "Yes, that is what I mean."

"I used to come out here when I wanted to feel Amanda's presence. I know he did, too." Perrin sank down in the middle of the garden. The scent of crushed flowers rose around her, and thorns poked into her skin. "Why would he destroy this?"

Saavik sat next to her, her face giving no evidence that she, too, probably had thorns ripping into her flesh. She took Perrin's hand, letting it sit between hers, and said gently, "It is as you said. It is the disease. None of this is Sarek's fault."

Perrin nodded and started to get up, but Saavik didn't let go.

"I'll make tea, Saavik." Tea. The answer to an Englishwoman's woes. Bread refusing to rise? Drink tea. Aphids eating the roses?

Drink tea. Living with a man three times your strength, who was more than a little crazy? Drink lots of tea. It had been Perrin's way of coping with her father—would it now be her way of coping with her husband?

"Tea can wait." Saavik pulled Perrin back down, back to the piercing thorns and the sickly smell of bruised roses. "Has he done this kind of thing before?"

Perrin recognized the tone, the careful wording of the question. It was the way those who came from the Institute to check on Sarek would have asked—with ever so much politeness—if she was all right. Many times, they had offered her the out of this being too much for her. But she'd never taken it.

She loved her husband. And, in his way, he loved her, too.

Even if he never called out her name, anymore. He seemed locked in the past. Stuck with his lost sons and his dead wife.

"You need help here," Saavik finally said.

"We'll be fine."

"I don't want to leave you alone with him."

Perrin laughed, imagining what her life would have been like if her mother had only said that and taken her with her.

"Perrin."

"If my husband has hurt me, I've learned there's very little left of the Sarek we knew to blame."

Saavik's face was full of unending compassion. "This disease rips away everything that matters."

Alcohol had been like that, too. What kind of man would her father have been if he'd never been infected with his taste for drink?

"Do you think Spock will come home?" Perrin asked, knowing Picard would find him. Picard found everything he sought. He'd found out about Sarek when Perrin had tried so hard to protect him and his reputation.

Saavik shook her head, deep sorrow in her expression. "No. Spock has chosen his cause. And we are not it."

We. His family. Saavik had never not included Perrin in that. It was why Perrin loved her so.

She felt tears sting her eyes and tried to blink them back.

"Don't." Saavik's voice was gentle, calling up Amanda's, making Perrin feel like she was fourteen again and back in that rose garden in that suddenly beautiful park. "Let go, Perrin. I won't tell."

"Let go," she thought she heard a ghostly whisper say in Amanda's voice.

She let go, but only so much. She allowed the tears to fall, but refused to give in to the sobs and tangled breaths her mother would have called up. She cried silently, her throat getting tighter and tighter, her vision blurring.

Saavik's hand settled on her shoulder, an easy grip, meant to comfort, not contain.

"He's going to die," Perrin managed to get out with a mouth nearly frozen in pain.

"I know."

"Soon. It will be soon." Perrin tried to stop the tears, but they weren't ready to cease falling. So she stared up at the sky, and squeezed blooms as her fingers found them, causing the scent of roses to grow.

She thought she would probably never want to smell roses again once this was finished.

But what would she have left once this was finished?

She was not Vulcan. She was not anything except Sarek's wife.

"Where will I go?" she said, realizing too late that she'd given voice to the thought.

Saavik looked at her in surprise. "Go? Why would you go anywhere? This is your home."

"This will be Spock's home, soon."

"Spock has no home. Or if he does, it's not here. It's never been here, Perrin." Saavik stood up, holding her hand out to pull Perrin up. "I plan to stay on Vulcan. You should, too. This house is big enough for both of us." She sighed and closed her eyes. "When the time comes."

Perrin let her pull her up. She kicked at the roses. "What should we do with these? I'd like to tear them up. Jasmine would be nice here. Wouldn't jasmine be nice?"

"It would. But it would be wrong." Saavik smiled at her sadly. "Replant the roses, Perrin. They're as much yours as hers."

The door opened, and Perrin recognized the look on the servant's face.

"Call the priestesses," she said to him. The priestesses must come so they could find Sarek's *katra* somewhere in his muddled mind and set it free.

The servant nodded, shutting the door quickly.

"It is time," Perrin whispered.

She imagined her father at this moment, railing at the stars, his voice harsh and loud.

Her mother would have fallen in a lump on the roses, making much noise and fuss.

But Perrin—Perrin would face this thing as she'd learned from Sarek. She'd face this with dignity, hiding the emotion. She wiped her face. There must be no trace of tears.

Then she followed Saavik in, walking slowly down the hall to her husband's rooms, knowing that no matter how many times she walked down this hall in the future, it would not be to a room that held her husband.

Saavik reached back, squeezing Perrin's hand when she grabbed hold. At first, Perrin thought Saavik had done it to comfort her. But as Saavik caught up to her, she could see by her expression that Saavik had been seeking comfort, not giving it.

"It'll be all right," Perrin said softly, and Saavik nodded.

It would be all right. Perrin just had to keep telling herself that. She would find her way—on her own.

The door to Sarek's room stood open and she walked in, head held high, breath slow and easy despite the fear that washed over her. She walked in, ready to face her future—a future without Sarek to guide her.

It would be all right.

# The Doomsday Gambit

Rick Dickson

**Rick Dickson** is a Seattle native who enjoys flying airplanes, scuba diving, snowmobiling and reading books. Rick read Dean's request to submit a story in the introduction to *Strange New Worlds VII* and couldn't think of a single reason not to accept the challenge. Much to his surprise, he has now discovered that he enjoys writing stories, as well. Thanks, Dean!

The planet screamed!

Out of the clear sky, the blue beam streaked in from high orbit and slammed into the ground, biting deeply into the crust and wrenching yet another piece of the planet into space. The beam returned again and again, each time prying off larger slices of the uninhabited world. All too soon the dying planet was reduced to a cloud of rubble and the Doomsday Machine settled down to begin its feast.

The planet's death did not go unnoticed. High in the night sky, thousands of miles above the planet killer, a solitary being studied the carnage from his perch in the middle of empty space. Eyes normally filled with irreverent amusement looked instead upon the destruction with a terrible and profound sense of sadness, soon to be replaced by a stoic resignation to the chain of events that would follow. Necessity was a cruel master.

"What do you think you're doing?" the new arrival shouted. He looked human, but was clearly something far more. Brushing a lock of blond hair from his ageless face, he stomped furiously across space as if marching on solid ground.

The first creature tore his gaze from the planet killer and glanced over to the other. "Oh," he said, boredom dripping from his voice. "Hello, Q. What brings you out of the Continuum and into *this* dreary corner of the Cosmos?"

"I asked you a question!" the taller Q fumed. "Those . . . *things* are a menace. If I recall correctly, and I always do, even you were appalled by their creation! Wasn't it you, Q, who went to such great lengths to make your displeasure known to those responsible for building them in the first place? What could *possibly* have possessed you to resurrect one and bring it here, to *this* universe?"

The dark-haired Q returned to his quiet contemplation of the solitary planet killer as it swept through the debris field, hungrily gobbling up asteroids and other planetary remnants like a ravenous shark in a feeding frenzy. "Oh, they're a menace, all right," he said softly, almost to himself. His eyes lost focus as he remembered another time and another great race, long since extinct. "They were so proud of their mighty creation, so arrogant in their presumption of superiority. So sure they could keep their little fleet of technological terrors under control." He shook his head and sighed. "Such fools."

"I'm waiting, Q," the second growled.

The first Q glared resentfully at his brother. "It so happens, my dear Q, that I didn't resurrect anything. I found this one! Quite by accident, actually."

"Q!" the other warned, touching his own temple. "Remember? All-seeing, all-knowing . . . !"

"Oh, all right," the first one muttered. "I *may* have had a small something to do with it." He sighed and stood up, dusting off his black slacks and picking an imaginary piece of lint from the gold sleeve of his Starfleet commodore's uniform. Ignoring his brother's fury, he said, "As to what I'm doing, I'm teaching these humans a lesson they can't learn soon enough, if you really must know. They seem to think they've been given a divine mandate to explore the universe just because they've learned the rudiments of space travel. They've given *no* thought to the consequences, placing their trust in their handful of pitiful starships—their own fleet of technological terrors—to get them out of any mess they might happen to stumble into. I'm simply showing them that they aren't nearly as ready to meet their neighbors as they'd like to think!"

The Doomsday Machine continued its single-minded task of funneling planetary debris down a maw that could easily swallow a dozen starships. As it reversed its course for another pass through the debris field, the pale light from the distant sun glinted along the nearly endless length of its conical hull. The blonde Q folded his arms across his chest, tucking his hands into the sleeves of his long brown robe and watching its progress as he contemplated his brother's words.

"So, this is simply another of your famous tests," he finally concluded. "Frankly, I'm baffled this time, Q. I'll grant you that there *is* a certain elegance in using an extinct civilization's ultimate weapon of mass destruction to teach a constructive lesson to a younger race, but I just don't see how it can work in this case. These humans aren't strong enough to win, after all, and they can't learn very much if they're all dead."

"Don't be silly!" the first Q scoffed. "I won't let that happen, but I will throw a scare into them that they'll not soon forget. They're going to learn that there are things out here far worse than their precious *Klingons* and *Romulans* and that a handful of *toys* isn't going to do them any good whatsoever!"

He chuckled and added, "They have no idea."

The planet screamed!

This time, fate was kind and its screams were heard by a more compassionate audience than a pair of coldhearted Q. As the Doomsday Machine continued its mindless attack on a solar system so remote it only had a number instead of a name, a shining white speck streaked to the rescue from the darkness of deep space: *U.S.S. Constellation,* NCC-1017.

"The fourth planet is breaking up, Commodore!"

"Can you identify a cause, Number One?" Commodore Matt Decker asked from his command chair in the center of the bridge. Although approaching the end of his career as a starship commander, Decker remained as physically fit as any officer half his age, with only the slightest hint of gray frosting his dark hair. He leaned on his elbow and absently gnawed a knuckle as he watched the main viewer.

"Sensors are picking up a force beam originating from a large spacecraft in orbit around the planet. The beam seems to be composed of pure anti-proton, Commodore."

Decker looked up in surprise. "Anti-proton? Is that even possible? Who has that kind of technology?"

"Unknown," his first officer replied, twisting a dial on the side of the hooded display at his science station. "We have no record of any such scientific advancement, nor do we have any record of that ship's configuration in our database."

Decker leaned back in his chair and exhaled sharply, trying to ignore the sudden throbbing at his temple. First contact scenarios always gave him a headache. This one promised to be no different, especially since the aliens were already snacking on one of his planets.

"Communications, open hailing frequencies. Let's see if we can talk to them," he said over his shoulder.

The red-shirted communications officer shook his head. "Sorry, sir! There's too much interference in the area. We can't punch through."

"Can you get through to Starfleet?"

"No, sir!" he replied. "Subspace is a mess."

"Very well. Keep trying to raise the aliens and prepare a communication to Starfleet Command. Advise them of our situation and send it off when you can."

"Aye, sir," the communications officer acknowledged.

Decker went back to work on his knuckle while he mentally reviewed his first contact protocol. Avoiding miscommunication was critical, but protecting Federation lives was paramount. Unfortunately, he didn't remember very much about this remote corner of space. "Are there any lifeforms in this system, Number One?"

"None on the fourth planet, Commodore, but preliminary surveys indicate the existence of plant and animal life on the third planet. No detailed results are available. It was marked as a planet of sufficient merit to warrant a second expedition, however."

"That complicates things a bit," Decker muttered. "We can't

very well let that thing keep chewing up planets if there's intelligence down there."

The first officer nodded his head. "Agreed, but perhaps it would be prudent to withdraw until we can gather reinforcements. That's one powerful ship over there."

Decker laughed. "In case you haven't noticed, we've got a pretty powerful ship over here, too, Commander. She hasn't let us down yet, has she?"

"No, sir, but . . ." the first officer began.

"No 'buts' this time, Number One. I think we can handle it. Helm, move us closer."

The starship changed course and closed the distance with surprising speed. The planet killer continued to attack the planet, apparently far too intent on its meal to either notice or care about one Federation starship.

"Still no response from the aliens, Commodore," the communications officer said.

"So much for doing things the easy way." He thumbed a button and began speaking into his armrest communicator. "All hands, this is Decker. Red alert!"

An alert siren echoed a shrill warning across the room as the bridge crew scrambled to prepare stations for emergency readiness. Backup power was quickly brought online and redundant systems were double- and triple-checked. Tactical diagrams began springing to life across the small overhead screens surrounding the bridge. From the navigation console, a deadly targeting computer rose ominously from within its hidden compartment at the helm, the low growl from its straining servos offering chivalrous forewarning to the enemy as *Constellation* completed its transformation from peaceful explorer to deadly warship.

"Commodore," the science officer shouted over the din of the battle preparations, "I've managed to punch through the interference. Sensors show no life signs aboard that spaceship. It's some kind of giant, automated . . . probe."

"A probe? You're telling me that thing is nothing more than

an unmanned alien *robot*?" Decker leaned back in his chair and adjusted his tunic. "That's just great!" he said with disgust.

"The probe is firing at the planet again, Commodore," the helmsman advised as he locked its signature into his targeting computer.

"All right, people!" Decker impatiently barked, "Let's pull this thing's plug. We'll sort the rest out later. Helm, fire phasers!"

The starship attacked from extreme range, raking the giant probe with a blistering volley of phaser fire. Ruby red beams that should have easily sliced through the deep blue hull instead bounced harmlessly back into space, barely managing to scratch the surface of the alien ship.

"Phasers had no effect, Commodore," the helmsman reported, studying the display from his hooded targeting screen as the Doomsday Machine slowly emerged from the cloud of space dust that had been blasted from its hull by the phaser barrage.

"Confirmed," the science officer agreed. "Trace analysis indicates the hull to be composed of an extremely dense neutronium alloy. We may not have the power to punch through, Commodore."

"Nonsense! Maintain fire!" Decker ordered.

The alien machine continued to attack the planet as the *Constellation* moved to close the distance, raining fire on it from afar. Once the *Constellation* entered the planet killer's defensive sphere, its proximity finally did what its phasers could not. The alien probe broke off its attack and turned to face its new foe.

"Dear God!" the helmsman exclaimed, looking down the fiery throat of the Doomsday Machine and into the raging atomic inferno burning deep within.

"Belay that!" barked the Commodore. "Arm photon torpedoes. Full spread. Match bearings and fire!"

The bow of the great starship came to bear on the target. Four pairs of blinding energy globes flashed from its tip and shot through space, impacting deep inside the bowels of the Doomsday Machine, but the fury of the exploding photon torpedoes was lost amid the staggering energies already flaring from the sub-atomic conversion of the planetary debris consumed by the probe. To a machine that fed on energy, the explosions from the torpedoes only served to further whet its appetite.

"Helm, veer off and give us some maneuvering room!" Decker shouted.

*Constellation* quickly spun on its axis and sped away, but the alien machine sensed the great power at the heart of its anti-matter core and raced off in pursuit.

"Vessel is closing," the helmsman reported.

"Increase to full impulse!" Decker ordered.

"We *are* at full impulse, Commodore," he replied.

"And it's still closing? That's impossible!" Decker stared in awe at the image of the gaping maw of the alien vessel as it chased them down, promising an undignified end to the magnificent starship's stellar career. "Nothing is that fast!"

A bright beam flashed from the mouth of the probe and the bridge lurched wildly to the side. Another powerful jolt quickly followed, kicking the starship violently from the rear. "We're taking heavy fire from the enemy vessel, Commodore. Aft deflectors are down to sixty percent," reported the First Officer.

"From *two shots*?" Decker demanded. "You've got to be kidding me!" He hadn't seen such a lopsided battle since the *Kobayshi Maru* simulation from his Academy days, and that simulation was designed so the starship couldn't win!

The bridge rocked again, this time throwing crewmen from their seats. "Forty-two percent, Commodore!" the First Officer shouted.

"Prepare to go to warp!" Decker said.

"Negative, Commodore!" the navigator reported, climbing back into his chair. "Warp drive is down!"

The bridge shook again and sparks exploded from the engineering station. "Eighteen percent!" the First Officer cried.

"Helm, reverse course! Attack pattern delta," Decker ordered. The next shot from the Doomsday Machine missed wide to the rear as the fleeing starship did the unexpected and doubled back on its pursuing enemy, corkscrewing in for another attack. The constantly changing vectors from the dizzying spiral confused the alien targeting algorithms, but not the gunners of the starship's crew. Eight more globes of energy leapt from the bow of the *Constellation* and disappeared down the planet killer's throat, while a blistering fusillade of continuous phaser fire ripped through the night, momentarily obscuring the probe in a small cloud of ionized particles and vaporized space dust. *Constellation* burst through the cloud, streaking directly toward the nearby third planet.

"Full speed ahead!" Decker ordered. "Let's get behind that planet while that *thing* can't see us. Move!"

"Engineering to bridge," the intercom whistled to life. "Phasers banks are completely drained, Commodore. We need time to recharge!"

"Acknowledged." Decker pointed to the corner of the view screen. "Over there, helm," he said. "Tuck us in behind the planet over there. That should give us enough cover to make repairs."

The starship sped around the planet, but a tremendous crash from the rear shook the bridge, sending the crew tumbling and announcing the resounding failure of Decker's desperate plan. The Doomsday Machine hadn't been fooled, after all.

The ship continued to rock as the blue force beam repeatedly lashed out and mercilessly pummeled the weakened shields. With a final blast, the deflector screens buckled and the force beam slammed into the port nacelle, instantly draining its remaining power and completely deactivating the anti-matter core.

Decker wrenched the *Constellation* hard to port and the alien machine sailed past, allowing the starship to finally scurry out of sight behind the planet.

The Doomsday Machine turned to follow.

Against the darkness of space, a once-mighty starship drifted on minimal power, now a nearly deserted derelict. Its sole occupant, Commodore Matt Decker, sat deep within the ship, staring blankly at the lifeless view screen from his post in auxiliary control, the pleading calls from his dying crew still echoing in his ears. Behind him, a flash he couldn't see and a ringing he couldn't hear accompanied the arrival of two members of a highly evolved race of beings known simply as the Q.

"Pathetic!" the dark-haired Q spat with contempt.

"Still, it was rather heroic, wouldn't you say?" his tall brother asked. "It takes a lot of courage to stare into the face of doom like that. I haven't seen such a display in ages!"

"Abject stupidity, more like," Q snorted, moving around the console to gaze critically into the vacant eyes of the defeated Commodore. "It never even occurred to him that one starship might not be a match for that *thing*. He should have retreated and called for backup when he had the chance. Now, that *thing* is going to rip right through the heart of his galaxy and nobody will know it's coming until far too late. That one display of 'courage,' as you put it, may very well have doomed his entire civilization."

The other's eyebrows rose in mild surprise. "You almost sound as if you expected them to win," he observed.

"Of course not!" Q replied, "but they should have done much better! I didn't count on sheer pigheadedness getting in the way of sending a warning back to Starfleet. Humans were nothing like this the last time I checked in on them." With a heavy sigh and a sad shake of his head, he folded his arms and quietly added, "perhaps there was nothing special about this race, after all."

"No, I disagree," the other argued. "I'm beginning to see what you find so fascinating about these humans! I'll grant you they could have done much better toward the end, but I think you're being too hard on them. They did quite well until they dismissed its intelligence. Hiding behind the planet was such an *obvious* tactic. Who knows what might have happened without that one blunder?"

"If they were better prepared, they wouldn't have made that mistake in the first place!" Q insisted. Walking to the middle of the room and adopting a tragic stance, he raised his hands and stared imploringly at the ceiling. "And would someone *please* explain that last tactic to me?" he begged.

The other made a face and scratched his head. "Yes, that has me a bit puzzled, too. Why anyone would beam his entire crew down to a planet when there's a known planet-eating machine in the system is a bit beyond me. I can't even begin to imagine what he was thinking." With a mischievous grin, he asked, "What *have* you been teaching these humans, old boy?"

"Very funny! I'm no shepherd and you know it. I'm far too busy for that type of nonsense," Q replied as he began to wander absently around the auxiliary control room, stopping occasionally to examine a particularly ingenious piece of Federation technology. "Still, I do try to stop by every now and again to give humanity a push in the right direction. The Black Plague, the Industrial Revolution, the fossil fuel crisis . . . they've always risen to the challenge. Until now, that is," he added. "Since my latest little gambit seems to have failed so miserably, I would imagine they're in for a rough ride this time."

"Children are like that," the other remarked. "One minute, they're amazing us with their leaps of intuition and the next minute we're baffled by their inability to understand the obvious. Being a parent takes patience, Q."

"I suppose so," Q remarked. "I had such high hopes for this race, but I guess they're only human." With a snap of his fingers, his Starfleet uniform was instantly replaced by a simple brown robe identical to the one worn by his brother.

"So," he said brightly, clapping his hands sharply together and changing the subject. "We seem to have some time on our hands before that *thing* arrives at the heart of their galaxy. I know of a star cluster that's about to explode. It should be quite a sight. Care to come?"

"Not so fast, Q. We might not be done here. Look over there." He pointed through the hull and out to the edge of the solar system. Another Federation starship was cautiously advancing into the sector. *"U.S.S. Enterprise,"* he read aloud. "Perhaps this one will do better."

Q glanced outside. "I don't see how. We've already tested a commodore; this one's only a captain. That star cluster promises to be a much better show. Let's leave these humans to their fate and head over there before all the good seats are taken."

"You go ahead, Q. I think I'll stay here. Unless I miss my guess, things are about to get interesting." With a snap of his fingers, his robes were instantly replaced by the slacks and tunic of a Starfleet captain. Before the other could object, he smiled and asked, "Would you be so kind as to call that *thing* back before you leave?"

No loss was easy, but sacrifice was sometimes necessary in order to win. Nobody knew that better than Captain James T. Kirk. Aboard the crippled *Constellation,* now barely alive and crawling its way slowly toward the Doomsday Machine, Kirk stood defiantly in the middle of auxiliary control, determination on his brow and fire in his eyes as he stared down the throat of a hungry planet killer that was growing larger by the second in the auxiliary viewer. His determined gaze flicked across the instruments and briefly came to rest on the delayed detonator built for him by his chief engineer. Flip the switch too early and the starship would explode before it could be swallowed by the planet killer; too late and he might not get off the ship alive. He was walking a thin line, but walking that line was the duty of every starship commander and Kirk was one of the best.

"Steady as you go," he quietly urged the mortally wounded starship.

When Kirk arrived aboard the *Constellation,* he found Matt Decker alone in auxiliary control, traumatized and incoherent. As Decker began to regain his senses, Kirk learned of both the battle with the Doomsday Machine and its tragic climax. Adrift and without power, Decker beamed the entire crew to the third planet, remaining behind to attempt repairs. When the Doomsday Machine returned to destroy the planet, he could do nothing but watch.

Kirk sent Decker to safety aboard the *Enterprise,* but the man refused to stay out of the battle when the Doomsday Machine inexplicably returned to resume the fight. Decker died alone in a shuttlecraft, one man against an invincible foe; but his death was not in vain, for it revealed the sacrifice that would be necessary in order to win. Now, Kirk was going to help the *Constellation* finish the job.

"It's time," he whispered softly to the starship, rubbing his hand slowly across the command console. Then, with a final triumphant look at the doomed planet killer, Kirk paid his silent respects to Decker and his crew and deliberately flipped the switch.

"Beam me aboard, Mister Spock!" he ordered.

*Time froze.*

"That was magnificent!" the tall alien exclaimed, materializing behind Kirk and affectionately thumping him on the back.

"It wasn't *that* great," Q snorted as he materialized beside his brother. "They very nearly lost again, thanks largely to our esteemed Commodore Decker."

"That's not what I meant," he waved dismissively. "I'm talking about the drive, the determination!" He rounded on Q and grasped him at the shoulders, shaking him to emphasize the point. "These humans are amazing! Kirk *knew* he wasn't going to lose. He didn't know precisely how he was going to win until the end, but he *knew* that he couldn't be defeated as long as he refused to give up. That's always been the hardest lesson for the new races to learn, but these humans understand it instinctively!"

"This one needs a different lesson," Q spat, batting aside the embrace and walking over to Kirk. "Humility!" he said, flinging an accusing arm at Kirk's proud pose—chest out, chin up and jaw thrust forward. "Just look at that! Such arrogance! He hasn't learned a thing. This whole encounter has just been one more battle to him. He's not interested in who built that *thing* or where it came from. He has given no thought to what he would do if he stumbled across another one tomorrow, nor does he care!"

"Well, unless you happen to find another—quite by accident,

of course—he won't," the taller Q remarked, a hint of anger returning to his brow. "I strongly recommend that you not go out of your way to find any more, either."

"I don't need any more," Q told him. "This test has shown me everything I need to know. Decker demonstrated a disappointing lack of insight and Kirk did nothing to change my mind. They're a menace to their universe!"

"Don't be such a sore loser, Q," the other smirked. "You were testing their strength, not their potential. It's not their fault you didn't need to rescue them. They beat you at your own game! Accept it and move on."

"I will not accept it and move on!" Q shouted, inflamed by the other's attitude. "They're barbarians! Their minds are far too small to understand the grand purpose of the universe and their arrogance far too great to let them realize it. I think it would be best if we simply wall them off to make room for the next race."

"I'm not sure why you're getting so worked up, Q."

"This isn't about me," Q told him. "These humans have demonstrated that they have the power to defeat one of the most destructive forces ever to exist, yet they've also just shown that their intelligence hasn't even progressed beyond the first level. We need to decide what to do about them now, before they're allowed to do any real damage."

"As you wish," the tall Q said. Closing his eyes for a moment, he began communing with the Continuum. Moments later, a slight smile tugged at the corner of his lips at the same time that a look of sheer horror crossed the face of his brother!

"That's outrageous!" Q exclaimed.

"Congratulations, Brother. You're elected!"

"I don't have time for this! My work is far too important to set aside while I baby sit an insignificant race in a remote arm of a backwater galaxy!"

"You know the rules," the other Q said. "You called for the Assessment. You're the one who gets to gather the evidence and present it to the Continuum."

"What about the results of this test? Surely that's sufficient!"

The other shook his head. "You heard the Continuum. This test was designed with force as its only answer. It wasn't a fair test of their true character. Personally, I think you're looking at this the wrong way. There's a lot of potential here, Q. Maybe all they need is wise counsel to help them bring it out. Until now, you haven't given them your full attention. Perhaps it's time for a change."

It had all been a trap. Q realized that, now.

Before his brother left, he offered a heartfelt condolence and some final encouraging words of advice. As he winked out of existence, however, the momentary gleam of satisfaction that lit his face revealed the lie. The other Q had been trying to persuade him to take a race under his wing for countless ages. Thanks to a few hasty words, their gambit was a complete success.

Q studied Kirk for a very long time, eyes lost in thought as an idea slowly began to take shape. If the Continuum was truly united, there would be no appeal, but that didn't mean he couldn't find some fun along the way.

"You've caused me quite a bit of trouble, Mister Kirk," he finally mumbled. "Quite likely, more than you could ever possibly understand with that microscopic brain of yours. Have you anything to say for yourself?"

The frozen Kirk ignored Q and continued to stare fiercely at the tiny screen, facing down the terrifying image of the planet killer.

"Hmm? You still worried about this thing?" Q asked, casually jerking his thumb at the view screen. "Don't be. It's as dead as last year's uniform," he smirked, glancing down at the simple green tunic currently favored by Kirk. "Your race, on the other hand, has had a stay of execution—a last-minute appeal from a higher power, as it were."

Q stood up and paced around auxiliary control. "My brethren seem to feel that I haven't given you a fair test. They're wrong, of course, but your pitiful race isn't worth a confrontation with the Continuum. So, I'm going to give you another chance," he offered magnanimously.

"You'll need to be patient, though. What I have in mind is going to take some time," he explained as he walked back to Kirk and sat on the edge of the command console. "You see, I'm going to borrow a page from their own playbook. I won't be the one to design your next test, I'll let you humans do that for me. We'll use your own rules to test whether or not you can live up to the standards and expectations you set for others. That should satisfy even the most difficult of critics, would you not agree?"

He leaned closer to Kirk and whispered, "I'll be watching you humans very closely from now on. I'm sure you'll hand me a golden opportunity before long—I'd give you a hundred years, at the most." With an evil chuckle, Q snapped his fingers and disappeared, but his parting words echoed eerily throughout the quiet room.

"And on that day, *Mon Capitaine,* I'll be back."

# Empty

David DeLee

**David DeLee** lives in central Ohio with his wife Anne, his favorite daughters—they made him say that—Grace and Sarah, and four cats. After appearances in *Strange New Worlds 8* ("Promises Made") and *Strange New Worlds 9* (A Bad Day for Koloth"), "Empty" marks his third entry in *Strange New Worlds.* He wishes to thank his family for their support, his parents John and Barbara for always being there, and a special thanks to Dean, Margaret and Paula for making it all possible. Now severely infected by the writing bug David is hard at work on several new writing projects.

The shipwide intercom whistled. It pierced the silence of the captain's quarters but could not penetrate the somber pallor settled over the room like a shroud. A second whistle blast was followed by Spock's voice. "Bridge to Captain Kirk."

At his desk Kirk reached out from the shadows, thumbed the switch without sitting up. "Kirk here."

"We've received clearance to depart Starbase 2, sir."

"Thank you, Mister Spock. Prepare for departure. I'll be up momentarily."

"Yes, sir. Spock out."

"Time for one more?" McCoy faced him across the desk, held the bottle of blue Andorian ale over Kirk's glass. When he didn't get a response he filled the glass then topped off his own.

Kirk sat and tapped a metal nail file on the desk and stared at the narrow glass of ale. He'd found the grooming implement on his desk a week ago, left behind by Janice Lester while she occupied his body.

Why hadn't he thrown it away?

A reminder? Of what? A keepsake?

"I'll say one thing for the Andorians," McCoy said, taking a sip of his drink, "they sure brew one hell of a batch of hooch."

Kirk tapped the nail file, paying no attention.

"Jim?"

He looked up. "What's going to happen to her?"

McCoy's forehead wrinkled with concern, his blue eyes studying Kirk. "Who? Janet Lester?"

Their reason for being at Starbase 2, to turn Janet Lester and her assistant, Doctor Arthur Coleman, over to Starfleet authorities. The senior staff had spent days debriefing Starfleet security regarding the recent events aboard the *Enterprise* involving Lester and Coleman. Kirk, Spock and McCoy had spent even more time with the SCE and archeological teams assembled to return to Camus II to examine the alien mind transference machine they'd discovered there.

Kirk nodded. "Janet."

"She'll undergo a full battery of tests—medical, psychological, emotional." McCoy sipped his drink. "If she's found free of mental disease or defect, in other words sane, she'll stand trial. Answer for her crimes on Camus II, and for what she did to you."

Kirk listened but didn't really hear. "How'd it happen, Bones? What causes a person to become that . . . obsessed?"

"I could give you the long, drawn out, and ungodly boring clinical theories to explain it. Complete with a lot of psychobabble words thrown in, but that's not what you're asking."

Kirk went on, hardly hearing a word. "She blamed me. Hated me, for what I'd achieved. What I'd become. Could it somehow be my fault?"

"Of course not," McCoy snapped, banging his glass down and leaning over the desk. Kirk started to protest but McCoy cut him off. "Hold it a minute, Jim. Just hold it."

He took a moment to gather his thoughts. "The mind's a complex thing. Even with all our fancy equipment, our diagnostic beds and our scans and optic probes and cortex mapping, there's still a hell of a lot about it we don't know yet. Things get especially fuzzy when you start trying to nail down abstracts like emotions and morality, our sense of right and wrong, our feelings. Just ask Spock." He paused. "What makes a person snap like that? Who the hell knows?"

Kirk stared past his desktop monitor. Past the bulkheads of his quarters, past the vacuum of deep space outside, back to another time, another place. "She was in her second year at the academy when I met her."

"Tell me," McCoy urged.

"Advanced xenobiology." Kirk's lips curled into a smile. "I was in my last year, spending way to much time in the simulators preparing for my practicals. My academic grades were slipping. Professor B'Targi . . ."

"I know him. Tough old bird."

". . . he dressed me down one day about my grades. Told me if I didn't get them up in xenobiology he'd see to it I didn't graduate regardless of whatever else I had going for me."

"Sounds like B'Targi."

Kirk nodded. "His heart was in the right place. He had a promising young cadet who could help me, he said. The next day he assigned Janet Lester to tutor me."

"And you being Jim Kirk around a pretty woman couldn't help but be . . . Jim Kirk."

He gave McCoy a self-effacing smile. "Am I that transparent, Bones?"

McCoy considered. "Let's say predictable."

"There were signs, Bones, even back then. We'd talk for hours about what it would be like to command a starship, to explore galaxies, see things, go places no other human being had ever been before. She was so passionate, so determined to be selected for command. So . . ."

"Obsessed?"

"It was all she talked about. How she would let nothing get in her way. Nothing else mattered to her."

Kirk took a slug of his drink. "I should have seen it, Bones, should have been able to do something to help before it was too late." He put his glass down, slowly turned it, stared as the muted light reflected off its angled sides. "But I was too wrapped up in myself, too blind to see it. Or maybe I just didn't care enough—"

"Don't be so hard on yourself. Jim. You were young, under a lot of pressure. It wasn't your place."

He smashed his fist into the desktop, stood up. "Damn it, Bones. Don't you see? Janet, Ruth Cartwright, Areel Shaw, Carol Marcus. Different names, different people but they're all the same; women who cared about me, who put their trust in me. And I gave them nothing in return. Except pain."

"That's unfair, Jim. To you and to them."

Kirk turned, tapped the back of his fist in the palm of his hand. He paced, felt like a caged animal. His quarters suddenly felt too small, too confining. He wanted to get out, get away, to escape. An entire galaxy out there and he felt boxed in.

McCoy stood. "There are people in our lives, all of us, who we've hurt. Or who have hurt us. You're no different than anyone else, Jim. Those women, every one of them, they knew who you were going in. They knew what you were about and they came along for the ride anyway. If they meant to change you or thought you were something else, that was their problem. You've never deceived anyone, never said you were more than, or less than, who you really are. Don't take on something that's not yours."

Kirk nodded but he wasn't convinced. Maybe what McCoy said was true, maybe it wasn't. All he knew was he felt responsible; responsible for the pain, the tears, the loss.

McCoy continued to scrutinize him. "There's something else, isn't there? Something you're not saying. What is it?"

Without acknowledging McCoy was right, Kirk opened the drawer of his desk. He extracted a file and dropped it on the desk with a slapping noise. Across the cover was marked; STARFLEET CONFIDENTIAL.

"What's this?" McCoy asked.

"Orders. The *Enterprise*'s been called back to Earth, the San Francisco Fleet Yards for a refit."

"A refit! No damned way. Why?"

Kirk looked around his quarters as if the answers were somewhere on the barren off-white bulkheads. He wished they were. "She's old, Bones. Been through a lot."

"Poppycock!"

Kirk raised an eyebrow, and a smile touched his lips. "Twenty-five years of service, she's worn out, Doctor. There's new technology out there. A new, vertical warp core, new warp narcelles, impulse engines, weapons, computer systems, integrating interfaces. She needs a face-lift."

McCoy gave him that sideways glance Kirk hated. It was the one that made him feel like McCoy could see right through him.

"How long?"

"How long what?" Kirk asked, though he knew exactly what McCoy was looking for. He was buying time, time to sort out the answers. Hell, to find the answers.

"You know damn well what. The refit. How long are we going to be hung up in dry dock?"

"Eighteen months."

"Eighteen months! Jesus, Jim, what'll we do in the meantime? Twiddle our thumbs?"

He could've answered with words. Instead Kirk extracted another file from the desk. This one was considerably thicker than the last, and it took two hands to hold it without spilling its contents. He tossed it onto the desk. Several of its four hundred and thirty pages fanned out from between the brown file covers.

"What's this?"

"More orders."

McCoy gave him a quizzical look. "What kind of orders?"

"Transfer orders."

The size of the file was not lost on McCoy. "No God damned way, Jim! There must be—"

Kirk nodded. "Four hundred and thirty."

"That's the whole damned crew."

Kirk nodded again. "It's over, Bones. Our five year mission, when we reach dry dock, reach Earth, it's over."

At a loss for words, McCoy stared at the thick file. Finally, he said, "Transfers to where?"

"Other duty assignments. Some are opting out, retiring. Promotions for most of them. The senior staff. With my recommendations they'll have pretty much their choice of assignments. Ships, command positions. Their choice. They've earned it."

McCoy reached for the chair behind him. He slumped into it, heavy, hard. With a sigh he stared at the dark carpet and shook his head.

The silence in the room had a bereaved quality to it. Like at a funeral with a room full of people, everyone wanting to say something, the exact right thing, but no one knowing what that was. Afraid to say something wrong, they say nothing at all and the silence grows, taking on a life of its own.

Finally McCoy lifted his head, stared at Kirk. "We need to fight this. You need to fight this, Captain."

Kirk shook his head before downing the last of his ale in a single gulp. "No."

McCoy blinked like he'd been slapped. He came to his feet in a shot. "No? What do you mean, no?"

"Exactly what I said, Bones. No." Kirk crossed over to his desk, deposited his glass and moved into the sleeping area of his quarters.

McCoy followed, stopping at the partition between the two areas, respecting the division of privacy.

Kirk activated the wardrobe, stripped off his wraparound tunic, dropped it into the laundry receptacle, and pulled on a gold duty uniform top. Once dressed, he stepped past McCoy and back behind his desk to call up the day's duty roster on his monitor.

Feeling McCoy's continued scrutiny he snapped off the monitor again. "It's a tour of duty, Doctor. And it's over. Done. Move on."

Kirk stepped passed him, headed for the doors.

"Hold it." McCoy practically barked the words out.

Kirk whirled, not yet close enough to activate the doors to his quarters.

"That emotionless, 'let's move on' cock-and-bull might work for Spock but not you, Jim. What's going on?" McCoy's gaze nailed him to the spot with the intensity of a force field. "There's more. What is it?"

Kirk cocked his head toward the desk. "My orders. They're in there too, Bones."

When it was clear Kirk wouldn't tell him, McCoy crossed to the desk, and flipped the file folder open. Kirk's was the first one. Right on top. McCoy read it, looked at Kirk then read it over again, like it might have changed in the interim.

He seemed to have trouble finding his voice. When he finally did, he said, "To any other man in the Fleet I'd say congratulations, shout it out from here to the Neutral Zone and break open the closest case of bubbly."

"And me?"

"Clasp you on the shoulder," which he did, with a smile. "And say well deserved, Captain—which it is—and now let's get back to work."

"Bones."

"Maybe we *should* break out another bottle. You got anything stashed around here, Jim?"

"Bones."

"Chief of Starfleet Operation." He opened a cabinet, then another in his search for a hidden something to drink. "Are they daft? What on Earth would make them think you'd even consider it? Rear Admiral James T. Kirk. Does have a ring to it, though." Abandoning his search, McCoy straightened.

"Bones."

He pulled Kirk by the arm toward the door. It swished open, startling two passing crewmen. McCoy gave them a quick nod as he stepped into the corridor. He turned back. "Come on, we'll go down to Scotty's quarters. He's bound to have something we can drink. Talk to him about this crazy refit nonsense."

"I'm taking it."

That stopped him cold. "Say again?"

"The promotion." Kirk joined him in the corridor. "I've thought about it and I'm taking it."

"Maybe you're the one who's daft."

Kirk shook his head and walked down the corridor to the nearest turbolift.

"Captain," a crewman said, passing him.

McCoy trotted to join up with him again. "Jim. Why?" He swept an arm out in front of them as they walked. "You'd give all this up. Space. Exploration. The *Enterprise*. For what? A corner office at Starfleet Command? Bureaucracy and paperwork? A secretary? That's everything you despise. Why, for God's sake?"

The turbolift doors opened. Kirk stepped in, seized the interface grip and twisted it. "Bridge."

The lift started. Kirk leaned against the wall. He felt as if the weight of the universe was pressing down on his shoulders. It was a weight familiar and constant. "There's a reason these missions are only five years, Bones. I'm tired. Worn out. Beat."

McCoy scrutinized him, a hand on a grip of his own. "So take some shore leave. I'll write you a prescription."

"I can't do it anymore. I saw that with Janet. I can't be responsible for all this anymore. Everyday I go out there. I see it in the eyes of the crew. That kid, Lanier, we just passed in the corridors. All of them. They look up to me. They trust me to hold their fates in my hands. To decide who will live . . . and will die."

"You're their captain, Jim. It's your job."

"How much of that can I take, Bones? How much can anyone take? I see them and I ask myself, which one will make it through their duty shift alive? And if they make it through today, what about tomorrow? Or the next day? Will I have to choose who lives and who dies? I don't want to do that anymore."

McCoy studied the floor. The light in the glass by his head flashed yellow, registering the decks they passed.

McCoy broke the silence. "It was Janet Lester, what happened with her brought this all on?"

"Not really. The camel's last straw maybe, but no. There's a whole list of Janet Lesters, Bones. Gary Mitchell. Ben Finney. Will Decker. Specialist Tomlinson. People who trusted me to be their friend, to be their captain, to protect them, to keep them alive. And I failed."

Before McCoy could respond Kirk went on. "Do you have any idea how many letters of condolence I've written? How many parents or loved ones I've had to tell their son or their daughter, their wife or husband or brother or sister are dead. Died in the line of duty. Died because they put their lives in my hands and I failed them. How many?"

When McCoy didn't answer, Kirk answered for him. "Fifty-eight. Thirteen point five percent of the total ship's crew complement. You want a breakdown of officers to crew? Rank, names—"

"Now hold it a damned minute." McCoy released the interface grip and the lift slid to a stop between decks. He let his words sink in before going on. "And how many people are here, alive and well, because of you? How many civilizations have been saved, how many wars averted, how many galaxies haven't been destroyed because of James Kirk? How many?"

"It doesn't make up for it, Bones."

"Yes, Jim, it does." McCoy stood face to face with him. "This isn't about those who have died. Those few you couldn't save. This is about Jim Kirk. About your doubts, your fears, your nightmares."

His word hit like physical blows. He couldn't close his eyes without seeing the faces—every single one of them—without hearing their accusations; he hadn't done enough; if only he'd tried harder, if he'd worked harder, he could have saved them.

If only.

"Don't look so surprised. I'm your physician, Jim, and your friend. I know how hard these things affect you. I know the depth of your guilt, your regrets, your doubts, the pain you feel over every one of these young men and women.

"And I also know you're the most competent, most courageous man I've ever met. The best chance of survival those men and women ever had was being by the side of James T. Kirk."

"Doesn't change the facts, Bones. I put 'em in harm's way and I got 'em killed."

McCoy shook his head. "That's way too egotistical for me. Circumstances put them there, Jim. Plain and simple. Those men and women were there because of their sense of duty, their sense of honor. It was their commitment to Starfleet, to the Federation that put them there. Not you."

He stepped back, returned his hand to the grip. "But think about this while you're beating yourself up. For every one of those men and women, the ones ripping your heart apart—and they should. It's what makes you Jim Kirk. What makes you the damned fine starship captain you are. For every one of them there's a hundred more examples where you made a difference, where people came out alive because of you, and only because of you. I'm one of them, a dozen times over."

Kirk let that sink in. Intellectually he knew McCoy was right, no argument logically, but emotionally . . . that was a whole different story. He wasn't Spock. He couldn't shut it out, couldn't suppress it. Each one ate at him, like a cancer, destroying him piece by little piece.

"You say a lot of those kids were killed by circumstances beyond their control, perhaps even beyond my control. You might be right too. But maybe, Bones, just maybe, I can change those circumstances. Change them so these kids do have a fighting chance against what they face. Maybe I can make a bigger difference than I can with one little ship, in one little corner of the universe."

McCoy made a noise. "Flying a desk at Starfleet Command? Come on, Jim. Who you trying to kid?"

"Bones. I'm tired."

They faced each other, McCoy clasped his shoulder. "You need a break, Jim. I understand that. Hell, maybe we all do. God knows I've thought about tossing in the towel myself. Retirement does sound damned inviting sometimes."

"See."

"But there's a difference."

Kirk waited.

"You're not a doctor, Jim. You're a starship captain."

McCoy arched his eyebrows and looked around the lift, like he could see all of the *Enterprise,* from that one sweep of his eyes. "Hell, what do I know? Maybe this refit's a good idea after all. Give everybody a break, some time. But think about this. . . ."

Kirk had to prompt him. "Go on. Say it, Bones. Say what's on your mind."

"You take that promotion," he looked around again for emphasis, "you give her up and you've lost her forever. Won't be anything on God's green earth that'll get her back to you. You've thought about that?"

"I need to do this, Bones. I need to."

McCoy nodded, twisted the interface grip. The turbolift ascended the four remaining decks to the bridge. The doors swished open and the familiar sights and sounds of the *Enterprise* bridge greeted them.

As the doors parted, heads turned. Spock, in the captain's chair studying a padd, stood.

"I haven't told anyone else yet," Kirk said under his breath as he strolled onto the bridge.

McCoy nodded, following him to the captain's chair. "Fine, but I still say it's a mistake, Jim. Mark my words."

Spock handed Kirk the data padd as he and McCoy stepped down into the command circle. "A mistake, Doctor?"

McCoy opened his mouth to speak.

Kirk shot him a look.

McCoy's jaw snapped shut.

"A difference of opinion, that's all." Kirk dropped into his chair, pretending to study the padd. Spock took up his customary position to Kirk's right. McCoy stood to his left, his hands clasped behind his back, rocking on his heels.

"Perhaps I can be of assistance?" Spock offered.

McCoy snapped his head around. Kirk silenced him with yet

another glare as he waved a dismissive hand to Spock. "It's nothing, Spock. Forget it."

Unable to resist, McCoy leaned over, whispered in Kirk's ear. "You give her up and you'll never get her back."

Spock raised an eyebrow.

"Enough!" Kirk compressed his lips into a tight line. "I've made my decision, Doctor. It's over." He passed the data padd back to Spock. "Helm."

Sulu twisted in his seat. "Yes, sir."

"Lay in a course."

"Heading, Captain?"

Kirk stared at the infinite starscape on the viewer. He'd been so far, visited undiscovered worlds, encountered dozens of alien species, many of them first contacts, had crossed the galactic barrier . . . and gone beyond. And now it was over. Done. Finished.

"Sector zero-zero-one, Mister Sulu," he said. "It's time for us to go home."

# STAR TREK:
# THE NEXT GENERATION

# Wired

Aimee Ford Foster

**Aimee Ford Foster** fled the cold, gray skies of Ohio eight years ago for sunny Florida where she lives with a husband, a daughter, a demon dog and the required writer's cat. In the previous versions of her life, Aimee was a full-time sports writer, most notably during an eleven-year stint with *The Blade* in Toledo. Nowadays, she freelances when an editor, or an empty bank account, calls. Mostly, though, she plays mom to four-year-old Delaney. This is Aimee's first professional fiction sale. An insufferably proud graduate of Ohio University's journalism school, she would like to thank everyone that makes *Strange New Worlds* possible—with a special shout out to Dean. She would also like to thank her husband, Marvin, whose gentle criticism was essential to the story.

Will Riker inhaled, taking in the fresh air and the scintillating view in one deep breath. Tall, colorful, gleaming buildings glittered in the brilliant orange light of the early afternoon sun.

Courtyard and walkways leading from the plaza he had picked as a beam-in site were immaculate and every piece of greenery was precisely trimmed. The word that came to Riker's mind was marvelous. The only thing missing were the colonists the *Enterprise* was reestablishing contact with. Ursae Majoris Two was settled in the late twenty-first century. Although the colony, known as ePlanet by the group from Earth's North America who settled it, had early contact with Earth and United Earth Space Probe Agency, nothing had been heard from it for almost 150 years.

That had changed when the *Enterprise* picked up a looped transmission a week earlier, audio only.

*"Can anyone hear me?"*

Starfleet sent the *Enterprise* to investigate. Despite evidence of a highly evolved technology, and a large population, the ship had failed to make contact with anyone.

"Pretty, but definitely quiet," Riker said to Troi. Data was busy scanning the area. Worf and two security guards were alert.

"Commander, it may be quiet, but as we found on the ship there are many life-sign readings in these buildings. And we are being scanned," Data said.

"So, they know we're here. Stay alert. Stay close. It's their turn to make a move."

"Aye, sir."

After two tense, quiet minutes, Data's tricorder beeped.

"We are about to have company, Commander. From that door," the android said.

Riker turned to face the double doors set in a shining, blue building that sat at the farthest reaches of the courtyard. Over the doors, now sliding open, was the encryption: 3601 GATES BOULE-VARD.

"Greetings, how may we help you?"

Riker stiffened and let his hand drift toward his phaser. The rest of the away team had a similar response to the creatures in front of them. The team clustered tighter, forming a better protective unit.

No one had pulled their phasers. Yet.

But Riker couldn't keep his eyes off the beings in front of him. The two were human, vaguely anyway, with the required number of limbs on the usual torso.

Their faces were naked to the sun, but the rest of their heads were covered by a silver, metallic casing that glinted in the sun like the buildings. A tear-shaped attachment sat in one ear, with a delicate silver tendril reaching toward their mouths. Another arm reached to one eye. Riker couldn't tell if the opaque shields there were coverings or implants. More tendrils snaked down their necks into their bright, loose tunics.

One was clad in royal blue, right down to his leggings and shoes. The other wore purple. Each wore a small device, about the size of a hand phaser, strapped to one tricep. Each had a large, cylindrical attachment in place of one hand and forearm.

To Riker they looked like a more refined version of the Borg.

"I'm Commander William Riker of the *Starship Enterprise.*"

"Ah, the Federation," said the one in blue. "Come at last. I am Paulus. This is Willus. I am a representative on our ruling Conclave. Willus is my assistant. We are both direct descendents of the founders of City Zero-alpha."

He waved his hand to indicate the surrounding city.

"You, of course, know what planet you're on," Paulus said.

Riker willed his stomach to unclench and took half a step forward. He had to look down to see into Paulus' face. He was half a head shorter than Riker and much slimmer.

"Forgive me for gawking, but you look a lot like a race we've had some troubles with," Riker said.

"You flatter us, Commander," the purple-clad Willus said. "We know of the Borg, of course, but we are not Borg. We're simply descendents of the humans that settled this planet several hundred years ago. I believe you are also human?"

"I am from Earth," Riker hesitated and glanced at Troi. With a slight nod she gave him assurance that the Paulus was being truthful. "You just don't look very human."

Paulus smiled.

"No, I suppose I don't."

Data, who had been quietly scanning the two, stepped toward Riker.

"Commander, they are human," the android said. "There is the typical percentage of genetic drift associated with colony settlers. Also, they are somewhat . . . robotic."

Riker forced his hand to relax.

"I can see that, Data. Thank you."

"We would be more than happy to share the history of our world and ourselves." Willus gestured with what should have been his left hand, but was a sleek, silver appendage instead. "But we do not receive, nor desire, many visitors. Why are you here?"

Troi, at Riker's left, shifted her stance slightly. Riker saw the movement and knew something wasn't right.

"We're here because we received a looped transmission from this planet," Riker said, narrowing his eyes. " 'Can you hear me?' We thought it was a distress call, emanating from this area. This is an Earth colony. We're investigating.

"Now that we're here, though, I am a bit confused. You obviously have the technological means to contact any passing ship. Yet you must have ignored our hail.

"Since we had no luck contacting anyone from orbit, the away team was sent down."

While Riker was talking, activity in the city around them increased noticeably. Doors opened and closed as more brightly dressed ePlanetians assumed their daily activities. From somewhere in the distance, came the sound of children laughing and shouting.

"I know of no one in distress, Commander," Paulus said. "Frankly, I would be surprised if this was anything other than a misunderstanding. We're not interested in interstellar contact with the Federation or anyone else, which is why it was so difficult for you to try and reach anyone here.

"However, you and your comrades are free to explore our city, if only to satisfy your curiosity. I personally would be happy to answer any questions you may have, but Willus must return to Conclave headquarters."

"Worf," Riker said with a jerk of his head. "Take the security team. Explore. Data and Troi, you're with me."

Riker turned to follow Paulus into the blue building.

Willus, he noted, went in the other direction, disappearing into golden doors in a bright fuchsia building.

"Do you think the Captain would let the crew have shore leave here?" Ensign Jakaru said to Lieutenant Worf. "I've never seen anything like this."

"Ensign, stay focused," Worf grunted.

Focus? It wasn't easy, not even for the Klingon.

Worf had led the team to the most populated area he scanned, which turned out to be an entertainment grid filled with shops that used live models in their display windows. Exotic aromas came in waves off food sizzling in outdoor cook spaces. Music filled the space, as did people clad in the same kind of bright clothes Paulus and Willus had worn.

It was fantastic.

It was also fruitless.

Given the isolationist view voiced by Paulus, Worf didn't expect to be greeted like an old friend. The truth was far worse.

Vendors ignored the team when they entered any store. Conversation stopped abruptly when the team neared any cluster of people. When they stopped in a large square to observe the goings on, no one came within twenty-five meters.

"This is not going well," Worf said as he reached for his comm badge. "Worf to Riker."

*"Riker here."*

"Commander, we are a bit . . . conspicuous. Suggestions."

*"Beam back to the* Enterprise. *Inform Captain Picard. He'll take it from there."*

"Aye, sir."

"Data, please join Worf back on the *Enterprise,*" Riker said.

He turned his attention back to Paulus. They were in a museum where a series of mosaics told the history of the planet.

"Sorry. So, your ancestors left Earth because they were unhappy with the way technology was being developed?"

"In essence, yes. They were interested in a more personal experience."

"More personal, how?" Riker said, stopping in front of a mosaic that showed the exodus of six colony ships from Earth orbit. "This is nice."

"Yes, thank you. It's my favorite piece as well."

"I like that one," Troi said. She gestured to the opposite wall, which depicted the first crop of the new planet.

Paulus acknowledged her comment with a nod of the head.

"As I was saying, personal, as in on the person. Since we share a history, to a point, I won't go into all the detail. Early in the twenty-first century though, humanity flirted with small electronics like music players and communication devices designed to be with you at all times. The overriding achievement was the proliferation of the Internet, of course, and how small it made the world.

"My forefathers wanted it to be smaller."

Riker glanced at Troi, who appeared to have lost interest in the conversation. He knew better.

"I've read the history, Paulus. I assume your founders were successful and you're all wired together?"

"Yes. Our version of the Internet is wired inside our brains."

"A hive mind?"

The next piece in the museum made Riker's stomach clench. It showed a dozen figures hard-wired to a large computer.

"No, and yes," Paulus said with a smile. "Much like that old Internet, static information is stored on a series of servers which can be accessed faster than I can say. Ask me when the street outside was constructed and I can find it without delay.

"Yet the individuals who make up our society remain separate entities. We do communicate silently, but it's much like your communications devices. No one can just barge into my mind."

Riker scratched his neck, while he digested Paulus's story.

"But you're all connected?"

"That is simplistic, but accurate," Paulus said with a shrug. "It is how we live. It is why we exist. Our founders felt unwanted on Earth, maybe even a little persecuted. After the Eugenics War, the kind of manipulation they favored seemed to fall outside the lines of acceptable advances."

"Excuse me," Troi said. She was no longer examining the mosaics. Riker wasn't sure she ever had been interested in the art. "I'm not sure I understand the intricacies of how your system works, but you'd know if someone had sent the signal we intercepted?

"You do seem certain no one did."

Paulus bowed his head, just a bit, in Troi's direction.

"No, I do not know if someone sent the signal," Paulus conceded. "We're not mind readers, not even like such touch telepaths as the Vulcans. We have our own kind of internal security devices that maintain our individuality. That is part of our humanity. I'm not eager to lose that."

Troi nodded and smiled.

"I see. You have kept current with the galaxy, haven't you, even if you've been silent."

She paused, for just a split second, and then turned back to the display.

"You know, this really is a remarkable art gallery."

Willus was sitting at a conference table, alone, but not without company.

His mind was racing, sending pulse after pulse into the servers that connected his world. "Find them. Now. Find them. Now."

"I didn't like it," Riker said.

Troi nodded. She was seated at Riker's left in main briefing. The department heads gathered as soon as the entire away team was back on board the *Enterprise.*

"He wasn't lying, exactly," she said. "What I felt was that Paulus had a secret. Willus was unreadable."

Opposite Riker, Captain Picard's face was also unreadable.

"I see," he said.

"Sir," Worf said, his deep voice resonating in the small space. "When my team and I explored the city, the inhabitants avoided us. We tried to shop . . . and no one would serve us. While we were walking, everyone remained at a distance from us."

"You sound frustrated, Mister Worf," Picard said.

"Yes. I believe the ePlanetians were told to not to speak to us," Worf said, grinding his teeth.

Picard leaned back, tracing a thumb against his jaw. The rest of the room was silent.

"Data," Picard said, dropping his hand. "You will lead an away team back to the planet surface at 1700 hours. Take two of Worf's men. Counselor Troi, please join them. Doctor Crusher please see that this team does a better job of blending in with the natives."

"I hope no one asks me to use this thing," Troi whispered to Data, gesturing with her left hand. The metallic casing that matched the ones they'd already seen on the planet was cumbersome, but at least it wasn't heavy.

They were already nearing the entertainment complex that Worf had explored with such promise, but no success, earlier that day.

The security personnel were following the two officers at a discreet distance.

Data and Troi, now indistinguishable from the ePlanetians and unrecognizable even to Riker, were masquerading as a couple on a date. They hoped to overhear something that could dispel the mystery of the distress call.

As they entered a boulevard rife with eateries, Data cupped Troi's elbow and led her to a café and a table near the pedestrian area.

"Shall we?" he said.

Troi smiled and leaned toward the android.

"I wish I could get a better sense of what these people are feeling," she said. "Something about their technological web seems to be interfering with their emotions or my ability to read them."

Data sat down across from Troi and glanced around the plaza.

"I am sure if we are diligent we can ascertain the truth, Counselor," he said, turning his head slightly. "Perhaps I shall overhear something useful."

"Perhaps. I just feel like there must be a better way."

The two spent half an hour at the café and then joined the crowd promenading about the plaza. That included the first children any of the *Enterprise* crew had seen. The smaller ones were, by all appearances, unaltered humans. The older ones sported the beginnings of the cranial attachments. The teens had just one natural hand. One was striding on a set of four artificial legs that reflected randomly in the nighttime lighting.

Troi had stopped to admire a fountain when she was bumped from behind.

"Excuse me, kind lady," a young voice said loudly. She turned to see a man, clad in red, bowing his apologies.

"You are being watched," he said as he straightened. "Please go to the flower shop behind you to find what you seek."

By the time he melted into the crowd, Data was at Troi's side, offering her his arm. She casually slid her hand into the crook of his elbow and briefly rested her head on his shoulder.

"Contact?" he asked.

"Yes," she said, leaning into his shoulder once again. "We're supposed to go the flower shop behind the fountain. We're being watched. I think we should tour the plaza again, and make a few purchases before you declare your undying love with a single, precious flower."

"Captain, we have triple-checked our communications grid and the only message that could possibly be your mystery distress call is actually coded as a classroom experiment at one of our secondary schools," Paulus said.

Picard leaned back in his chair, glancing at the fish tank in his ready room.

"Our records are exhaustive, given the linked nature of our culture."

"Oh yes, I'm sure they are," the captain said. "If you're satisfied that we were mistaken in our interpretation of the message, I see no further reason to continue our investigation."

Paulus smiled.

"I thought that might be your response."

"Yes," Picard said, tapping a finger on his chin. "I see no reason, however, to waste our trip out here. While I understand that you may not be ready for full contact with the Federation, I think this would be a capital opportunity to establish a fledgling relationship. Don't you?"

The smile faded as Paulus listened to Picard. *He wants us gone,* Picard thought. *What are they hiding?*

"Indeed, sir," Paulus said. He wasn't, quite, clenching his jaw. "Our full Conclave meets in . . . thirty-one hours. Would you care to address the meeting?"

"That is just what I was about to suggest," Picard said. "Please send the coordinates for the meeting. Picard out."

He look at Riker, who was sitting on the other side of the desk.

"Can we find out what they're hiding by then?" the first officer said.

"I hope so Number One, I hope so."

"That blue one, please."

"Excellent selection, kind lady," the flower vendor said.

"It smells wonderful," Troi said, smiling. "These are my favorites."

"I doubt that, offworlder," the vendor said, bending over a computerized cash register. "Your disguises are good, but your identities are known. When I nod my head, please step past the curtain behind me."

He handed Data a receipt for the flower and, as their hands made contact, quickly nodded. The duo stepped behind the curtain. The security guards remained behind, lounging near the fountain, vigilant. But no one followed the officers into the back room of the shop.

The room was dark, close, like it hadn't had a fresh breeze blow through in decades. A lone figure emerged from an even darker corner.

"Welcome to my ePlanet," she said.

Troi gasped when she saw the young, unaltered woman standing in front of her. She was taller than Troi, with pale skin and shoulder-length dark blond hair. She had two eyes and two hands. She was about twenty-five years old.

"Alloyed scrambled the local sensors when he touched your friend's hand," the woman said. "You should be safe, for now. I think you were looking for me."

"You sent the distress call," Troi said. It wasn't a question.

"Yes. I request political asylum for myself and my friends," she shrugged. "If it still works like that. The country our founding parents came from was big on that, according to our history lessons."

Troi looked at Data, who was scanning the room.

"There is an energy reading," he gestured toward the corner the woman had stepped from.

"We need to talk to Captain Picard," Troi said.

"There isn't time," the woman said. "You must come with me, now, or the Conclave will find me. If it finds me, all our hope it lost."

Data nodded and tapped his hidden communicator to contact the security guards.

"Lieutenant Dan."

"Yes, Commander" he said into a small communicator set into the collar of his shirt.

"Have we been observed?"

"A small military unit just entered the plaza. Orders?"

"Return to the *Enterprise*. Tell Captain Picard the Counselor and I have made contact. Data out."

The woman stepped back into the corner. Data and Troi followed.

"You have transporter technology," Troi exclaimed as the trio materialized in another dark room.

"Matter-to-energy-to-matter?" the woman said. "Yes. We call it a transfer station. The one we stepped into was temporary and no longer functions. This one is permanent. It's been invaluable in our struggle." She shrugged again and turned away from Troi.

"Wait," Data said, grabbing her wrist. "We are no longer in the main city, but I am unable to determine our location."

The woman glared at Data.

"That would be our jamming device. Your communications won't work either. But come. You are in no danger here, unless you reveal our whereabouts to the robots you met earlier."

Data released his grip. Troi stepped forward, trying to take advantage of the rapport she felt earlier with the woman.

"Who are you?"

"I am Dayna. I live among the free, the persecuted, and the human. I sent the distress call. That a Federation vessel, an Earth ship, would be the one to receive it is something I only prayed for, but never really believed would happen. But I was overjoyed when I heard of the meeting with Paulus and Willus in government square.

"If we leave this room, which you can't do unless I go first, you'll meet the rest of us. At least the ones who live here."

Troi's confidence soared as she soaked in the intense emotions rolling off the woman.

"She's telling the truth, Data," she said. "I'm Troi. This is Data. Lead the way."

Dayna picked her way through the dim light, keyed a security pad and turned back to the duo as a door rolled open.

"Welcome to my world," she said.

Still at the table, Willus sat in silence.

"Find them. We are compromised. Find them."

"Captain, I cannot believe that you inserted an undercover team into our city. This is quite distressing," Paulus said. "We formally protest this action, revoke our invitation to you to attend the full meeting of our Conclave, and ask that you leave our planet."

Picard was alone in his ready room.

"Seems that we have each given the other reason to be distrustful," Picard said.

"I have no idea what you're talking about," Paulus said. "We have been forthcoming to a fault."

"Then why are two members of my away team missing without a trace? The message they sent to the ship was that they had 'made contact.' My assumption is that they contacted the person or group that sent the distress call we intercepted. You maintain that no one on your planet sent such a message. That leaves us at an impasse."

Paulus was quiet. The distance between the ship and the planet seemed to grow ever wider.

"Your protest is noted," Picard said. "However, this is an Earth colony and your citizens have rights."

He leaned forward.

"This ship will not leave orbit until my officers are safe and we have unraveled this mystery. Picard out."

Troi flexed her hand, pleased Data had been able to remove her false implant.

"So this is just one outpost of the resistance?" she said to Dayna.

The village was small, tucked beneath trees and rocky outcroppings of the great, limestone hills that were everywhere. Nearly fifty people called it home, a number that changed almost daily. The power sources were deep inside the hills, where natural mineral veins masked the readings. Rural, but not primitive.

Dayna led Troi and Data to a small area filled with flowers and benches beneath one of the rocky overhangs.

"Not even I know how many of us there are," Dayna said, settling on a bench. "Like this place, most of them are off the main continent, far from City Zero-alpha.

"But they still pursue us. They still want to force their way on us. We don't want to be robots."

"I'm not sure I understand," Troi said. "All citizens of this world are forced to have implants at birth? We saw unaltered children in the entertainment plaza where we met you."

Dayna grimaced, nodding to several villagers who drew near, wanting to hear the Starfleet officers talk.

"No," she said slowly, shaking her head. "Those children were wired in at birth. The chip implant is small, behind the ears. They stay like that until their bone structure is more mature. Then the other changes are gradually made.

"It used to be just the cranial implants, the enhanced eye, the communication devices in the ear canal. But they're starting to butcher themselves in the name of technology."

Troi noticed then that one of the men sitting with them had just one hand. The other arm ended just below the elbow.

She nudged Data.

"The implants are growing more extreme?" he said.

"Yes," Dayna said, voice low and urgent. "They didn't use to wire the babies. That was the first step, I guess about twenty-five years ago. Our parents rebelled.

"For the most part, they were left alone.

"But as the implants became more bizarre, more people started questioning what was going on. We love technology. Harroldus always liked being wired to the system, didn't you?" she said to the man with one hand.

"I did," he said. "But my employer forced me to get an artificial attachment for my arm. I . . . I never liked it. My unhappiness tainted my connection to the system. I got fired. I got unhappier and when I picked up the idea that they were coming to reprogram me, well, I tore my implants out. That's why I'm here."

"What do you mean 'picked up'?" Troi said.

"I heard it through the Net," he said.

"Counselor, if I may" Data said.

She nodded, growing comprehension on her face.

"Paulus was emphatic in describing the limitations of your Internet," Data said. "He told our Captain it was not a hive mind. Yet, it seems like you had less . . . individuality . . . than Paulus would have us believe."

Dayna nodded.

"Yes," she said through clenched teeth. "We used to be individuals, and I'm not sure that's true anymore. Something changed our world. Paulus hasn't been a representative for very long, but his party has ruled for thirty years. For the last twenty, they have been unopposed.

"I can remember my parents talking about some controversial elections. But I was still a little girl when people quit talking about things like that for fear of retribution. There was a lot of fear."

Her voice had dropped to a whisper. She shuddered, took a deep breath and continued.

"Some people vanished. Our thoughts were no longer our own. That's when we knew the Net was changing. That's when my parents went underground. I have never been wired."

She buried her face into her hands, rubbing at tears she couldn't stop.

"But before we went, the Conclave stole and wired my older sisters. I haven't seen them since."

Troi was silent. Data cocked his head to one side, opened his mouth then shut it.

"What do you want?" Troi asked.

"Asylum. I said that."

"Yes, but to what end? To be free to live here without being persecuted, or . . ."

"No!" Harroldus said. "I want off this planet, away from these people. I want to be human. I want to be like you."

"Sir, I am not . . ." Data began.

"Data," Troi interrupted. "Never mind."

Troi quit her seat, moving to sit alongside Dayna.

"What will happen if they find you, or any of your outposts?" she asked in a gentle voice.

"They'll wire us. Take the children. Destroy who we are by invading us with technology we don't want and have never asked for."

"Are you sure?" Troi asked, brushing Dayna's hair back so she could look into her eyes.

The resistance leader drew a shuddering breath.

"Yes, but even if I wasn't, we need help. We are tired of being afraid. Fear is a powerful weapon."

"We have to talk to Captain Picard. We trusted you. Now you trust us."

Willus was slumped forward, forehead resting on the brilliant sheen of the glass table, when Paulus entered the chamber.

Neither needed to say a thing.

"They are from Earth. We wouldn't be violating the Prime Directive if we just take the unaltered groups and relocate them," Riker said.

"None of this makes sense," Worf said. "The main settlements on this planet are limited to one continent. Cannot other parts of the planet be settled by those who do not wish to be joined to the computer system?"

Picard leaned back and adjusted his uniform jacket.

"You're right, Will. And that's a very interesting question, Worf," he said.

"Sir, if I may?" Data interjected.

Picard nodded from his position at the head of the table in the briefing room.

"This culture bears much of the stamp of the Earth they left in the twenty-first century. Politics and power seem to be the overriding concern of the ruling body, as opposed to the prosperity and profligation of their people."

"In other words, Data, the powers that be want all these people controlled because it enhances their own power and prosperity in some way," Picard said.

"Yes, sir."

"Maybe it's a lot simpler than we're trying to make it," Troi said.

"How so, Counselor?" Picard asked.

"Maybe there are just a lot more people than we realize that don't want to be wired into the system. That would promise change on an almost revolutionary scale for this world. That's not just about power, it's about the survival of the people who wholeheartedly embrace the technology and those who lead them."

Troi leaned back in her chair, catching a wan smile from Riker as she did.

"We're talking about civil unrest, or maybe war," Geordi La-Forge said.

Doctor Crusher was nodding. "These people feel like their ancestors, their founding fathers, left Earth because their attempts at integrating these kinds of computer systems into the human body was not widely accepted," she said. "I've read some of the histories."

"That is true, Doctor," Data said. "In fact, there were some accusations that the group was trying to follow Khan Noonien Singh's path to improved humanity."

"Which would explain not only their desire to not have outside contact, but to keep this the closest of close knit worlds," Picard said. "Counselor Troi, do you think you can convince Dayna to visit us?"

"I think so," she said.

Picard smiled, nodded and rose.

"Then let's let the genie out of the bottle."

"I just wanted to let you know we have recovered our missing crew members," Picard said. Paulus was sitting behind a nondescript desk in an equally nondescript room. He appeared to be alone, but Picard knew that was an illusion.

"Ah, that is good news, Captain," Paulus said with a satisfied look. "You'll be taking your leave of ePlanet, then?"

"I think not."

Picard stood, took three strides toward the main view screen, and then reached out with his right hand. His eyes never left Paulus's image. The leader flushed a deep red when Dayna joined Picard.

"Well?" Picard said.

"Well, what, Captain? Consorting with our enemies?"

Picard pursed his lips and expelled a deep breath.

"So, you were well aware of who sent the distress call we intercepted. And it was a distress call." It was not a question.

"We will deal with this situation ourselves," Paulus said. His face was so red, it clashed with his bright tunic.

"You see, I have a problem with that," Picard said, crossing his arms. "Dayna and her colleagues aren't just citizens of ePlanet. They're Earth colonists. They're human. They have rights, including the right to live life as they would, to think as they would, without fear of repression, reprisal or worse. They have the right to not be enhanced with technology. They have the right to be free.

"Is that not humanity's constant quest?"

"You don't understand," Paulus said, nostrils flaring. "We live in harmony. They do not. They have destabilized our system, from within and without. What about the dreams of our founders and our people? The freedom we seek is within and with each other."

Dayna took a step toward the view screen.

"Paulus, it's a big world. Let us go. Let anyone go who doesn't adhere to your so-called harmony. Let us escape the constant fear which is all I have ever known. Free us. Free yourselves," she said, smacking her left fist into the palm of her right hand. "Let us all be free."

"What choice do we have" Willus asked. "Maybe Picard is right. Maybe we're all better off apart."

Paulus snorted, and continued to pace around the table.

"Do not be snide," he said. "I know what you think. I know what the Conclave thinks. I know what everyone thinks, of them, of us, of me. I do not care.

"Do you all hear that? I. Do. Not. Care."

He was shouting. Willus was silent, within and without.

Then he stood.

"It's over Paulus, as least as we know it."

Paulus whirled. He could no longer read Willus through the Net.

"What's going on here? What are you doing?"

"I think I am leaving," Willus said, lifting his chin high. "I think I am tired of all of this and would like to try to something new."

Paulus snarled and rushed his former assistant, unsheathing a cutting tool from his arm accessory as he raced across the room. Willus never flinched as he was pinned against the wall.

"You are a traitor," Paulus spit the words out. "You sicken me."

Willus never blinked as he regarded the leader.

"I am not afraid of you, Paulus," he finally said. "Either cut open my throat or unhand me. The choice is yours, just as this choice is mine."

Paulus closed his one eye and pushed away from Willus. He was sobbing as he collapsed into a chair at the desk. Willus rubbed his throat, staring at his former friend.

"Oh my. Are you still plugged in at all?"

"Of course, I am still plugged in," Willus said, stepping toward the desk. "I simply am limiting access to my thoughts, for now. Where I go from here is anyone's guess, even mine. Perhaps I will unplug for good. Perhaps I will seek a simpler life within the Net.

"As we both can tell, though, it will not be the same community that it was when we all awoke this day."

"No," Paulus whispered. "We will be lucky if this city is still standing when everyone is finished choosing."

Turmoil rippled through the Net. Confrontations between friends, family and lovers were spreading as the people opened up to the newest day on ePlanet. Paulus could hear it all on the server inside his head.

"Just remember Paulus, it was you and not I who turned to violence," Willus said as he neared the door. "Perhaps the unaltered were right to fear for their lives. Perhaps you should blame this on yourself and those most like you."

The thunk of the door as it closed behind him was deafening in the ensuing silence. Paulus, head in hands, could only listen as his world unraveled.

"You wanted to see me, Captain?" Troi said as the doors to Picard's ready room whooshed closed.

"You seem troubled by my solution, Deanna."

She shook her head. "I am concerned about what we left behind on ePlanet."

"Please sit," Picard said as he lowered himself onto the long, low seat.

"Given the fact that the new colony has already voted for full offworld contact with us and with the idea of establishing more normal contacts with the sector, including a trading post, I am not worried the original colony will try to overcome their former residents."

"Then what?"

"This has hurt so many, sir. Families have split. Dayna was reunited with her sisters and neither had any interest in becoming unwired. Others have rejoined, but are struggling because they're strangers now. Some of the unwired have chosen to rejoin the original colony, now that it's a choice and not a demand. Some see that as a betrayal."

Picard sat forward, elbows on knees, fingers steepled together under his chin.

"It'll be a generation, maybe two, before the fallout settles, Counselor."

"I know, sir."

"You can't help them all."

Troi sighed and nodded.

"Perhaps for the first time since the founders of this colony left Earth, these people really are free. Free to live as they would and free from fear that their choices will not be their own," Picard said. "I meant what I said to Paulus. The human condition is never finer than when it's free."

# A Dish Served Cold

Paul C. Tseng

**Paul C. Tseng**'s third story for *Strange New Worlds* scores him a hat trick, or in other dubious circles a "Wardy." He would like to thank Margaret Clark and Paula Block for all their hard work and support. Most of all, he wishes to thank Dean Wesley Smith for all his encouragement and confidence. If it were not for him, Paul would probably not be a professional writer today. Finally, he would like to thank his beautiful wife and children for their unconditional love and support.

W E ARE THE BORG. YOU WILL BE ASSIMILATED. LOWER YOUR SHIELDS AND SURRENDER YOUR SHIP.

Every console on the bridge shuddered, as the green tractor beam locked onto the small wedge-shaped ship. Captain Grebnedlog looked curiously at the distinctly simple design of the Borg cube that held his ship in tow.

"Uh huh," Grebnedlog replied, vacuously. "We are Pakleds. Our ship is the *Mondor.* We look for things. We make things go."

Reginod, the *Mondor*'s engineer, ran from his station to the Grebnedlog's chair. "We cannot go. They are strong."

"They are Borg," Grebnedlog replied, with a wide grin. "They are stronger than the Federation." He had heard that the Borg were the most feared enemy of Starfleet. It pleased him to know that the people of Commander William T. Riker, of the *Starship Enterprise,* were not *smart* enough to stop the Borg. He drooled at the thought of Borg technology, which made them so formidable an enemy of the Federation. "They can help us pay back Riker and the *Enterprise!*"

*"WE WILL ADD YOUR BIOLOGICAL AND TECHNO-LOGICAL DISTINCTIVENESS TO OUR OWN. YOUR CULTURE WILL ADAPT TO SERVICE US. RESISTANCE IS FUTILE."*

A scanning beam bathed the *Mondor* in a blinding light that penetrated its hull.

*"SHIP COMPRISED OF ARCHAIC TECHNOLOGY*

*FROM VARIOUS KNOWN SPECIES: HUMAN, ROMULAN, KLINGON, JARADA, FERENGI. . . ."*

Grebnedlog smiled at Reginod. "They like our things. . . ."

Reginod's apprehension left his face, upon seeing his captain's smile. He nodded and laughed. "They are smart, they look for things too!"

*"SHIP'S COMPLEMENT: TWO INDIVIDUAL BIOLOGI-CAL LIFEFORMS. ASSIGNING SPECIES DESIGNA-TION—95012—PAKLED. INTELLECTUAL LEVEL, MAR-GINAL."*

The Pakled Captain's smile quickly turned upside down. He glared back at the viewscreen. "We *are* smart! We make things go!"

*"ASSESSMENT: ASSIMILATION OF SPECIES 95012 WOULD PROVIDE NO BENEFIT TO THE COLLECTIVE AND REQUIRES AN INEFFICIENT APPROPRIATION OF RESOURCES. PAKLED SHIP, YOU WILL NOT BE ASSIMI-LATED."*

Grebnedlog's mouth gaped open as the Borg ship released the *Mondor* from its tractor beam. It began to pull away from the Pakled ship at full impulse, before warping out of the sector.

"They are going," he said. "We need to go too."

"Why?"

"Because they are smart; we want to be smart."

Reginod smiled and nodded slowly. "And they are strong; we want to be strong."

The *Mondor*'s recently retrofitted warp drive bucked and roared, then finally kicked in to pursue the massive Borg cube. The jolt threw Grebnedlog and Reginod from their chairs flat onto their rotund rumps. They pointed at each other, snorting and chortling.

"Ferengi engines, haw-haw," Reginod chuckled.

"They are fun!"

Despite the laughter, Captain Grebnedlog kept focused on his mission. For the past eight years, he had lived with the humiliation of having been tricked by Commander Riker into releasing Geordi LaForge from capture. That failure had caused him to lose stature with the Pakled Intelligence Group; *Enterprise* had become the *Moby Dick* to his Captain Ahab. He became so obsessed with revenge that he passed up opportunities to command more contemporary ships, despite the fact that all his crew had left him, except for the ever-loyal Reginod, his chief engineer.

The *Mondor* trailed half a light-year behind the Borg Cube, unable to intercept due to the limitations of the Ferengi warp drive not being fully compatible with Pakled technology.

*I am hungry,* Grebnedlog thought. *I want to eat.* "Reginod, we need food."

"There is food in the box we stole from the Klingon trading post."

Grebnedlog winced. "Klingons are angry. They want to hurt us."

The Pakled engineer dragged over a large cargo container and struggled to pry it open. "Uhhhn!" Reginod banged on the lid with his fist but to no avail. Grebnedlog offered his assistance as well, but even with their combined efforts, they were not able to open the box. Little did they know that container was upside down and the unlocked latch was on the bottom.

Grebnedlog stood up and kicked the container with all his might. "Ow! That hurt! And I am still hungry!" So he took out the phaser he had replicated when he had abducted Geordi LaForge, and pointed it at the box. Reginod scrambled to his feet, just barely escaping the blast of glowing duranium shards flying in all directions. As soon as the smoke cleared the two Pakleds stood over the open container and looked down in disgust.

"Worms!" they cried, staring down into the writhing and very much alive Klingon delicacy, *gagh.* The odor that wafted from the container was so pungent that Grebnedlog's eyes began to water. He couldn't believe that anyone actually ate those smelly, slimy things, alive!

He put his hands on his formidable belly, rubbing it delicately. "I am not hungry now."

Just then, the viewscreen showed a fleet of Federation starships speeding past the *Mondor*. Grebnedlog got back to his seat and examined his monitor. He turned to Reginod and the corners of his large mouth crept upwards. "Federation ships."

"But they are smart," Reginod answered, anxiety creasing his brow. "And they are strong."

"We are smart too!" Grebnedlog replied. "Send a message to them!"

Reginod opened hailing frequencies and put out their typical distress signal. He looked back to his captain who was rubbing his fleshy hands together and grinning broadly.

One of the ships slowed and stayed behind. It turned back and matched speeds with the *Mondor*. The viewscreen then displayed a bearded starfleet captain with a slightly receding hairline.

"This is Captain Morgan Bateson of the *Starship Bozeman*. How may we be of assistance?"

The *Mondor*'s captain blinked his eyes a few times, to make sure he was seeing correctly. "You are not Riker."

"I most certainly am not," Bateson replied. "Are you in need of assistance?"

"Uh-huh."

The bearded captain's chest rose and fell, letting out an impatient sigh. "Well? What is the matter, then?"

"We are . . . far from home." In his twenty-five years in the P.I.G., Grebnedlog had never failed to use his standard tactic of luring well-intentioned victims into lowering their guard by "playing dumb."

But he heard a voice over the com on the *Bozeman*'s bridge.

"U.S.S. Bozeman, *this is Lieutenant Commander Worf, commanding the* Defiant. *You have dropped out of formation with the* Thunderchild *and battle group Psi. What is your status—are you under attack?*"

Bateson sat back down in his chair and hit a button on his armrest. "This is Captain Bateson. We are answering a distress call, but are having some challenges in communication."

*"We are en route and will rendezvous at your coordinates in two minutes.* Defiant *out."*

This was quickly becoming more complicated than Grebnedlog would have preferred. But his encounter with the Borg had emboldened him. He had a plan and felt that with another Federation starship on its way, he would be able to try these new tactics he had just developed on both of them. In no time, he would be able to hunt down Riker and the cursed ship that had caused him disgrace and shame for nearly a decade. For now, he resorted to tactic number Two-Five-One: answer all interrogations with *"uh-huh,"* and stare blankly.

It surprised him how quickly the second ship, called *Defiant,* arrived.

Captain Bateson was now livid with frustration from trying to communicate with Grebnedlog; he was gritting his teeth. *"Defiant,* I have had no luck establishing communication with the captain of this ship; can you see if you are more successful?"

*"Worf here. We will attempt to ascertain whether this is high enough a priority to delay our arrival with the rest of the fleet."*

"Be my guest," Bateson answered, rolling his eyes.

On the *Mondor,* when the viewscreen image switched from the bridge of the Bozeman to the *Defiant*'s, Grebnedlog and Reginod gasped so hard they began to choke on their spit.

"You!" Worf snarled. "I remember you, Pakleds!"

Grebnedlog cowered and sputtered. "Uh . . . uh . . . We . . . we will return your worms! We didn't eat them!" The very thought of the worms caused his stomach to churn. He feared he might be sick all over the bridge.

Worf's eyes flashed. "I am not interested in *gagh!*"

The pair of fumbling Pakleds let out a simultaneous sigh of relief.

Worf lowered an intimidating gaze on them. "If you are attempting to steal equipment or abduct Starfleet personnel, you are wasting your time."

*Time for my plan.* The corpulent captain of the *Mondor* rose from his chair and attempted to stick his chest out as a symbol of boldness, but his imposing stomach detracted from the dramatic effect of it all. Nonetheless he made his best effort to sound menacing.

"WE ARE ARE . . . THE BORED. YOU WILL BE A-SIMULATED. . . ."

To Grebnedlog's chagrin, Worf threw his head back and laughed heartily. But Grebnedlog continued, certain that if he could convince the Federation ships that they had joined forces with the Bored or Borg, whatever it was they called themselves, that they would surrender their technology in fear.

*"LOWER YOUR SHELLS AND SURROUND-ER YOUR SHIP . . ."*

Worf shook his head and laughed heartily.

This further incensed Grebnedlog. "Don't laugh! I want to go on!"

"Go right ahead, my friend!" Worf said. He then opened a channel to the *Bozeman*. "Worf to *Bozeman*. Proceed to Sector 001. We will meet the battlegroup there in twenty minutes."

*Acknowledged. Bateson out.*

Grebnedlog began to panic. *I just need to finish my speech; then they will be afraid and give me their weapons so I can attack the* Enterprise *. . . wherever they are.* He continued his recitation as best he could recall.

*"WE WILL EGG YOUR BI-ILLOGICAL AND TACK-NO-LOGICAL DESTRUCTIVENSS TO OUR OWN. YOUR CULT-ORE WILL ADEPT TO RESURFACE US. RESISTANCE IS FERTILE."*

The next thing he saw on the viewscreen was the brilliant starburst of the two Federation ships warping out.

"They are going," said Reginod, blankly.

Though deception had always worked for the Pakleds, and though this plan of impersonating the Borg should have surely frightened even the mightiest of Federation captains into accepting their demands, Grebnedlog once again found himself sitting on the bridge of his ship, the laughing stock of the P.I.G., and the entire Federation. His lust for revenge on the man who had destroyed his reputation and career grew more and more insatiable.

"Find the Borg!" Grebnedlog shouted. "They can make us strong."

It was to Grebnedlog's delight that the Borg cube had stopped to regenerate. He brought the *Mondor* alongside the massive ship and tried to contact them.

"Borg ship, we are Pakleds . . ."

There was no answer.

"We want to be a-stimulated!"

The only sounds that broke the utter silence on the bridge were the clicking and whirring of old instrument panels, and the snort-like breathing through the nostrils and open mouths of two slack-jawed Pakleds.

"They do not think we are smart," said Reginod. "We should leave them alone."

Grebnedlog scratched the sides of his portly belly with both hands. "But we want to be nothing, if not persistent. We will go to their ship and they will make us strong."

"And smart?" Reginod asked.

"And smart."

The *Mondor* docked within the Borg cube and remained tucked away, undisturbed. Grebnedlog beamed over with Reginod to the Borg vessel arriving with a sense of anticipation. They walked around with mouths wide open and stared at the thousands of drones in their regenerative cycles. The smell of burnt flesh and circuitry wafted through the dark and cold corridors of the Borg cube's interior. Terrible as it was, it didn't compare to the horrid scent of the *gagh*.

Grebnedlog naively lifted the arm-appendage of one of the

drones, admiring the integrated disruptor and cutting device. A whirring sound from the Borg's arm startled him so much that he dropped it and ran. Then, as quickly as it had awoken, the drone returned to sleep mode. Continuing down the corridors, the pudgy pair of Pakleds went in search of someone in charge—someone who could help them get a-stimulated.

"Hello? Anybody home?" Grebnedlog called out. "Yoo-hoo!" He heard his own voice echo for what seemed like an eternity. As he turned the corner, Grebnedlog got a view clear to the other end of the ship. It seemed to stretch endlessly.

As they walked down the long corridor, the entire ship rocked and a klaxon began to sound. Hundreds of drones emerged from their alcoves and were being beamed off the Borg vessel.

A VESSEL HAS BEEN DETECTED. FEDERATION VESSEL, *NORWAY*-CLASS, DESIGNATION: *ENDEAVOR*. UNIMATRIX 3-5-2, GRID 5-3-4, BOARD VESSEL AND ASSIMILATE.

Grebnedlog's ear's perked up at the utterance of the word "assimilate." He began to follow the drones to the transport site. One by one, they beamed out as he tried in vain to talk to them.

"We want to be a-simulated."

But they ignored him and continued to beam away. The explosions outside the hull of the Borg cube subsided, and in a matter of minutes, green transporter beams brought scores of zombie-eyed Starfleet personnel onto the Borg transporter pad. A handful of drones began herding them toward a large room.

PREPARE HUMANOID BIOLOGICAL LIFEFORMS FOR ASSIMILATION INTO BORG COLLECTIVE.

Two drones organized the pre-assimilated Starfleet officers into queues of nine. One by one they entered the assimilation chamber and eventually emerged, fully "borgified."

Pulling Reginod along by the arm, Grebnedlog slinked over and set himself at the end of one queue. Reginod stood adjacent to him in the next queue. Immensely pleased with the situation, Grebnedlog looked over to Reginod and wagged his thick, conjoined eyebrows up and down. He giggled in delight. "We will be a-stimulated."

Reginod didn't seem to share his enthusiasm and just faced forward. "A-stimulated."

By the time they had reached the end of the queue, where the two Pakleds stood, Grebnedlog could barely contain his excitement. He was bouncing up and down like an excited little child in a pastry shop, looking forward to a treat.

But the drones grabbed them by the shoulders, forcefully, turned them around and shoved them away.

SPECIES 95012, UNACCEPTABLE FOR ASSIMILATION.

Hitting the ground with a heavy thud, Grebnedlog looked up at the drones with a pathetic smile. "But . . . I want to be a-stimulated."

DESIRE IS IRRELEVANT, YOU WILL NOT BE ASSIMILATED. And with that, the drones walked back to the transporter pad and vanished.

Reginod rubbed his portly rump as he stood up. He tapped his captain on the shoulder and said, "They do not like us. Let's go back to our ship."

"But we *are* smart," Grebnedlog answered. "I have a plan, just wait!"

"Uh-oh," Reginod groaned.

In a matter of moments, more Starfleet personnel appeared on the transporter pad. Like the previous batch, they were being lined up in groups of nine, for assimilation.

Grebnedlog walked towards the queues of assimilation candidates. He grabbed two of them by the arms and pulled them towards an open door. As he walked off, he whispered back to Reginod, "If they get near the end of the line, just yell."

Reginod's eyes glazed over. "Yell."

After the Pakled captain vanished behind the doorway with his captives, the sounds of struggling and grunting could be heard. Then it was quiet. Grebnedlog stuck his head out from behind the wall and hissed at Reginod. "Psst! Reginod, Reginod!"

"What?"

"Take off your clothes!"

Reginod squinted incredulously. "Off?"

"OFF!" The captain disappeared behind the doorway again.

The lines grew shorter and shorter as Reginod proceeded to remove his uniform and gear. He noticed that there were only two people left on each line.

"Arrrrrggghhhhh!"

A loud clank came from behind the doorway, followed by a startled Grebnedlog, rubbing his forehead. "What?"

"You said to yell," Reginod responded, now wearing nothing but his underpants and a bashful grin.

Grebnedlog emerged from the access doorway, half-dressed in a Starfleet uniform that was much too small for him. His large belly prevented him from zipping closed the front of the grey and black uniform and the blue shirt underneath was so short that it revealed his fuzzy midsection. He arrived at the back of the line and handed another uniform to Reginod.

"Here, put this on. Now, they will a-stimulate us into the Board Corrective."

"But . . ."

"It will work. Try to look like the others!" Grebnedlog said, as he faced forward trying to look as he too was being prepped for assimilation. Staring blankly in front of him and plodding along as the line advanced, he suppressed a chuckle as Reginod nearly tumbled over while trying to squeeze into the female Starfleet ensign's uniform.

Once again, they had reached the end of the line. This time, Grebnedlog was certain he and his sidekick would be taken into the assimilation chamber.

SPECIES 95012, UNACCEPTABLE FOR ASSIMILATION.

And just as they did previously, the guard drones grabbed the Pakled duo by the shoulders and shoved them away. But this time Grebnedlog refused to be snubbed. He stood tall and walked back towards the Borg drones. "We WILL be asimmilugated!" But the first drone lifted his arm with a glowing cybernetic appendage.

"Uh-oh," Grebnedlog gulped and backed away with both hands lifted in the air. "Don't shoot! We just want to be strong, like you!" But his pleading didn't seem to move the Borg in the least, so he tucked tail and ran.

A green bolt of energy shot out of the drone's integrated hand-weapon and crackled smack on the heavy hindquarters of the Pak-led captain. He let out a loud yelp, grabbing his burnt backside.

"Ow!"

Everything went black . . . or was it green?

A VESSEL HAS BEEN DETECTED: SECTOR 001. FEDERA-TION *AKIRA*-CLASS, DESIGNATION: *U.S.S. THUNDER-CHILD*.

The words rang in Grebnedlog's ears and caused his head to ache. He awoke from the stun beam to find that the stream of incoming humanoid assimilate-ees had stopped.

FEDERATION SHIPS SHIELDS MODULATING, UN-ABLE TO BOARD AND AQUIRE ADDITIONAL LIFE-FORMS FOR ASSIMILATION.

The ship shook with a thunderous explosion somewhere on the far end of the cube. Grebnedlog realized that they were in the midst of a fierce battle.

A VESSEL HAS BEEN DETECTED: FEDERATION *DEFIANT*-CLASS, DESIGNATION: *U.S.S. DEFIANT.*

More terrifying explosions sounded and got closer to their location. He got to his feet and woke Reginod.

"They are running out of people to a-stimulate!"

"We should go back to our ship and leave," Reginod said.

A maddened rage flashed in Grebnedlog's eyes. "No! We are very close. They can make us strong and smart. Then we can fight the *Enterprise* and that . . . that . . . Riker!"

A VESSEL HAS BEEN DETECTED: SECTOR 001. FED-ERATION *SOVEREIGN*-CLASS, DESIGNATION: *U.S.S. ENTERPRISE.*

*"Enterprise? Enterprise!"* Grebnedlog shouted. He then ran up to

the Borg drone that had stunned him earlier. It was preoccupied with the dwindling numbers of humanoids for assimilation.

"A-singulate us, Mister Borg!" Grebnedlog shouted. "We want to help destroy the *Enterprise!*"

The drone shut his eyes momentarily, as if to consider the request. Then the collective voice spoke over the intercom again.

RESOURCES LIMITED. REPLACEMENT DRONES REQUIRED. INTELLECTUAL STANDARDS SHALL BE LOWERED TO ADMIT SPECIES 95012 FOR ASSIMILATION.

The Pakled twosome held each other and jumped up and down in excitement, cheering wildly, as the Borg drone directed them into the assimilation chamber.

The ship shuddered again. Hissing sounds could be heard all over. A klaxon began to blare.

Grebnedlog shook an angry fist into the air. "We'll get you, *Enterprise!*"

"You too, Riker!" shouted Reginod.

The drones in the assimilation chamber were unperturbed by the crumbling bulkheads and fires burning around them. They simply stuck tubules into the necks of the Pakleds, and the assimilation began.

At first, the sound of thousands of voices in his head frightened Grebnedlog. But gradually, they began to harmonize, like a well-tuned choir.

*SPECIES 95021, PAKLED LIFEFORM, GREBNEDLOG. REDESIGNATE: AUXILIARY ADJUCT 9 OF 9.*

Order . . . efficiency . . . unified purpose . . . he began to smile as he realized he was being made "smart" and "strong." Riker and the *Enterprise* would soon pay for what they had done to him, years ago.

Grebnedlog's thoughts as an individual began to ebb. He accessed the cultural database of the Borg collective and instantly came upon a set of Klingon Proverbs. He found one that fit his situation perfectly. Just before the assimilation procedure was complete, he began to laugh out loud as he recited to himself: *REVENGE IS A DISH BEST SERVED COLD.*

FEDERATION VESSEL *ENTERPRISE* HAS BREACHED GRID 3-2-1-0. HULL BREACHES IN CRITICAL ANTIMATTER CONTAINMENT SECTIONS. WARP CORE BREACH IN TEN SECONDS. BORG QUEEN WILL EVACUATE IN SPHERE 0-0-2-0-1.

He thought his last individual thought, as the transformation from Grebnedlog, the Pakled into Auxiliary Adjunct 9 of 9 completed.

*UH-OH.*

# The Very Model

Muri McCage

**Muri McCage** has just realized that this is all Leonard McCoy's fault. He was the first *Star Trek* character to make her desperately want to write fiction, period. Now, with her third *Strange New Worlds* appearance, she is very grateful for the nudge. She continues to write original fiction, scripts, and poetry for the sheer joy of it, though she strives toward publication for the sheer joy of that as well. She would like to thank Dean Wesley Smith, whose gentle guidance has taught her things she hadn't known she'd needed to learn. Thanks also to Margaret Clark, Paula M. Block, and Elisa J. Kassin, and a special thank you to John Ordover for the unforgettable first phone call for *Strange New Worlds VII*. And to Lisa, for the friendship and encouragement—"Gopher it" indeed!

The holodeck doors opened with a dramatic swoosh. Unfortunately, the drama ended there. Or at least any dramatic appearance. Instead of some bold scenario of derring do, or a romantic getaway, the large open space was empty black. A yellow grid-pattern added a dash of color, as did the two figures occupying the center, one seated on a simple stool, while the other bent forward slightly, as if silently urging some much-desired action.

Captain Jean-Luc Picard stood just outside the doors for a moment, then sighed, and stepped forward. Two heads swiveled in his direction, yet only one face showed recognition.

"Captain."

Picard nodded, grimly. "Any change, Geordi?"

The engineer shook his head, though the answer wasn't entirely in the negative. "Occasionally."

"Still the sporadic outbursts?"

"Yes, sir. Though I can't say for sure, I think I'm starting to see at least the beginning of a pattern."

"What kind of pattern? One we can build on?"

"I think it's more that we need to let him do whatever it is he's doing, without interference." Geordi LaForge shrugged eloquently. "As for the pattern itself, you know the way some people are auditory learners? They have to repeat information out loud over and over, to get it to lodge in their, for lack of a better term, organic data banks?"

"Yes, of course."

"Well, I think that's what we're dealing with here. I mean, it's all in there already. But it's as if he's having to learn to access the information we uploaded, as well as to utilize it. My best guess is that the silent periods are when he runs a search subroutine, and the outbursts are when he's trying to learn how to use what he gets hold of." LaForge used one foot to brace himself against a rung on the stool. He rubbed his eyes exhaustedly, only then reminding Picard that not so very long ago his VISOR would have prevented such an instinctive action.

So much technology was contained at the moment in this one space, yet so little they could do to control the situation. Really, when one thought of it fully, there was little they could do to control anything at all, beyond the simple choices such as when to pause for a cup of Earl Grey or how often to comb one's hair. Assuming one had hair to comb. Finding himself face to face with a clone he hadn't known existed had turned Picard to philosophical musings, when he wasn't occupied with the effort to avert disaster, but he had no time at the moment to indulge himself.

He realized then that it was possible they . . . he . . . had become too dependent on their android crewmember. Data was indispensable. He was Picard's first officer, and his friend. Of course that was the other Data. The one that was lost to them, in a climax to his lifelong quest to attain humanity that would have astounded even his positronic brain. Instead they were faced with a shell. A mirror image of their own Data on the outside, yet inside was a chaotic morass. Chaos that at some point they just might be able to tame and soothe and amend, until it was as if Data himself had been given a second chance.

For now . . . for now, they had a problem. It walked like Data, it talked like Data, it looked like Data, but, at the moment, it was most definitely not Data.

"Isolating him in here was wise, Geordi. Seeing such a vivid reminder is very difficult for the crew right now."

"Not to mention hearing him!"

"Yes. He does ha—" Picard laughed a little self-consciously. "I was about to say he has quite a set of lungs on him."

"Well, he does. Or a reasonable facsimile thereof."

Picard sighed. "It's so very easy to forget entirely that he's not really human at all. Not this version so much, but our own Data . . ."

"Our own Data, the hero. Life can be strange, can't it, sir?"

"Very. He wanted so to be as much like us as possible. I think it wouldn't be out of line to say he surpassed us every one—"

"Three little maids—

"from—

"from school—

"from school—

"are we—

"we!"

The android's outburst ended as abruptly as it had begun.

As one the two humans removed themselves several paces from the vicinity of the stool. Organic eyes met ocular implants, and they chuckled together at the incongruity of the three occupants of the holodeck juxtaposed with the high decibel lyrics.

"Yes, Geordi." Picard barely stifled the impulse to rub at his ringing ears. "Bringing him here was very wise indeed. The soundproofing alone . . ."

"We can keep him here indefinitely. Take shifts with him, maybe. It might not come to that, but there's no way to tell how long this whole process will take. I'll admit that I'm just a tiny bit worried that it could be years."

"Surely not!"

"I just don't know, sir." The brilliant engineer gave the reluctant impression of exploring uncharted territory. "He's made differently enough that I'm having trouble anticipating how this learning process is going to work with him. I'm hoping it'll hit a stage where his memory buffers will acquire enough information, even if it seems random to us, to trigger a critical mass protocol and initiate some kind of cascade effect. If that happens, it will all fall into place, and he'll be a whole—"

"Am I a real boy, yet?"

LaForge didn't miss a beat. "No, Data. But you're getting there."

That seemed to satisfy the childlike android, and he fell back into silence.

"As you can see, Captain, he sometimes responds to external stimuli." Laughing in spite of himself, LaForge made an unconscious gesture toward the entry. "When Will and Deanna stopped in to say good-by, he heard Will's voice and started playing Dixieland Jazz."

Taking a moment to dart a glance around the almost-empty holodeck, Picard wondered if he were missing something. "Why did you delete the instruments?"

"I didn't! There weren't any. He synthesized the sounds—trombones, a piano, and even a grand finish with cymbals. It was pretty impressive."

"I see. What happened next?"

"Not much. He got real quiet. Then launched into that awful Klingon opera Worf likes so much. I think he made the connection to Worf, from Deanna's presence. It's a complex process he's engaged in. That's why I said I think it's best to leave him to it as much as possible."

"Agreed. Make it—"

Before Picard could finish indicating that they should make Data's recovery a top priority, the android's head tilted inquisitively. Golden eyes revealed a slight glimmer of intelligence. "Captain?"

Two sharply indrawn breaths from the humans, and one mimicking hiss from the android filled the empty space. A sense of ludicrous pantomime, mixed with deadly serious, hope permeated the very air. Picard took a few cautious steps closer to his questioner.

"Yes, Data. Do you recognize me?"

"Certainly, sir. You are Jean-Luc Picard, captain of the *Constellation*-class *Starship Stargazer*, registry number NCC-2893. Commissioned on Starda—

"*Frère Jacques* . . .

"*Frère Jacques* . . .

"*Dor—*"

Silence fell once more. This time it was a silence heavy-laden with renewed hope.

"What just happened, Geordi?"

"I'm not sure. But if we're lucky, he just made some kind of leap. You're the first person he's come anywhere near really recognizing."

"I'm not due back on the bridge for some time. Should I remain with him? Take the first shift, perhaps? If we're going to let this thing run its course, perhaps my presence will trigger another moment of, at least near, lucidity."

Another of the engineer's all-inclusive shrugs. "Makes sense to me. It sure couldn't hurt."

"I'm certain you could use some rest, at any rate."

"Yes, sir."

"When's the last time you slept, Geordi?"

The ensuing hesitation spoke volumes. "I—"

"I understand. Too long, will suffice." Picard made shooing motions with both hands. "Off with you now. We'll be fine."

As if to emphasize the captain's words, the android became animated once again. "Captain Picard?"

"Yes, Data?"

"Why am I on *Stargazer*?"

Picard turned to the closest thing he had to a New Data expert. "Will it do any harm to answer his questions?"

"I don't think so, sir. It's possible some of the verbal input will act as a sort of catalyst. Get things stirred up. In a good way." LaForge started moving toward the exit, then turned to impart a final bit of instruction. "Just don't volunteer anything. Answer his questions, almost as you would deal with a child asking about the facts of life. Give him what he can handle at any given moment, and bump up the level of input as he seems to get more coherent."

"I'll do my best."

"That's all any of us can do. Good night, sir."

"Good night, Geordi. Pleasant dreams."

Picard watched his chief engineer disappear through the briefly parted doors, then turned his attention back to his companion. "Data?"

Golden gaze swung his way. "Yes, sir?"

"Do you remember asking why you're on *Stargazer*?"

"Of course. I do not remember coming aboard."

"You didn't. We're not on the *Stargazer*, Data. This is the *Enterprise*."

"I see. Aye." The familiar voice launched into a thick Scottish burr. "Tell me, laddie, is this *Enterprise* the bloody *A, B, C,* or *D*?"

Taken aback, Picard sought frantically for the correct response. Apparently Data was processing a memory of time spent with the legendary Captain Montgomery Scott. If Picard said the wrong thing, it might throw the android's data access process back to another *Enterprise* in another era. Worse yet, he might thrust him too fully into his own present. Still, he couldn't very well lie. So he quietly, simply stated fact.

"This is the *Enterprise*-E, Data."

Silence.

The empty room seemed to expand on the stillness, stretch it out to the breaking point. Picard wished suddenly that he had not been so hasty in sending LaForge off to his bunk. He was in over his head, and there was so very much at stake.

Without warning, Data leaped off the stool and confronted Picard urgently. "The ship, Captain! *Enterprise* is in danger!"

Careful. Lucidity did not necessarily last. Particularly in a recently simple-minded android, trying to assimilate an entire lifetime lived by someone else. Cautiously, gently, Picard laid a hand on the lifelike forearm.

"It's all right, Mister Data. *Enterprise* is safe. She was saved by a very heroic crewmember."

More silence.

Data returned to his stool.

Then another lucid moment. "I am glad to hear that, Captain."

When the next silence fell, it lasted a very long time. Picard grew weary of standing, and settled himself as comfortably as possible on the hard, shiny floor. He could have instructed the computer to provide any manner of holographic comfort for his use, but dared not take the chance. A suddenly appearing bed, perhaps a book or two, would be most welcome, but such unexpected distraction could wreak havoc on the considerable progress that had already been made.

Eventually, Data began humming. He went through most of *The Mikado,* then seemingly tiring of Gilbert and Sullivan, progressed to an exceptionally accomplished recitation of several most difficult passages, taken at random from *The Complete Works of Shakespeare.*

Picard quite enjoyed the performance, and felt pleased that Data's delivery seemed to become more coherent with the passage of time and effort.

So pleased was he by the progress they were making that he was not overly alarmed when the steady flow of artistic endeavor drifted to a halt. Another very long pause segued into an even more lengthy silence. He knew having his friend and trusted colleague returned to him whole, as if conjured by Prospero himself, was too much to expect.

Picard was encouraged enough by the way their long night together played out. Moments of chaotic outburst, interspersed with brief and beautiful conversations reminiscent of times spent with this android's own brother . . . that was the night Picard spent in the almost empty holodeck. As the hours passed, he became more and more optimistic, so that the occasional non sequitur caused him less and less disappointment.

When he grew weary enough, he stretched out on the floor at the foot of the stool, Data once again perched there, engaged in the fascinating process of merging almost man and flawed machine into a unique and amazing being. When he was finished, the android Picard watched over would not be the Data he remembered. He would be his own person, his own individual being, and with luck and skill and patience, perhaps he would once more become Jean-Luc Picard's dear friend . . . his new Number One.

For now, all was silence.

Until the next outburst.

The next outburst made Picard smile.

"I am . . .

"I am . . .

"I am the . . .

"I am the very . . .

"I am the very, very . . .

"Model of, of, of . . .

"A modern major gen—gen—general."

There followed what Picard could only think of as a very pregnant pause. He could almost hear the positronic brain regrouping itself, adjusting, settling, until it appeared ready to make an announcement of utmost import.

"I am the . . .

"very model . . .

"of a modern . . .

"major general!"

Perfect pitch, strong clear baritone. Emphatic in its assurance, the familiar voice sang straight into Picard's smile.

Then again it came, a sense of accomplishment, almost a tactile feeling in the gently recirculated air.

"I am the . . .

". . . very model!"

"Not yet, my friend. Not quite yet. But, perhaps, very soon."

"Captain?"

Picard came awake immediately, and looked up at the strung tight figure of his chief engineer. "What is it, Geordi? Is my shift of Data-watching over?"

"Not exactly."

He yawned as discretely as possible, and rubbed a fist into either eye. They felt like sandpaper. From the looks of LaForge, he must be in an even more sleep-deprived state.

"Did you get any rest at all?"

"Not much. I nodded off a little, but then I had an idea."

That brought Picard scrambling to his feet. "Tell me."

"Well . . . I think it'll be better if I just show you." LaForge darted a considering glance to the place where what might again become their android friend stood, muttering to himself. He drew a deep breath, and spoke into the air. "Computer, run program LaForge 172-D."

For a moment Picard thought nothing at all was happening. The holodeck remained the same yellow-on-black grid . . . and then . . . she appeared.

The viscerally real, slender young woman stood facing Data.

Still, except for a questioning tilt of the head, she watched him watch her for several long seconds. Then, matter-of-factly, she spoke to him.

"Father?"

A long moment of silence. Picard could almost hear the positronic brain whir, as it searched and searched for the correct information. He understood then what Geordie was doing. That one word could very well be the catalyst Data needed to finish what they'd started what seemed a lifetime ago with B4.

He suddenly realized he was holding his breath, and a glance at the engineer by his side showed the same rapt attention.

Feeling a need to go over and physically nudge Data, Picard made himself stand perfectly still and wait.

When it came, though quietly spoken, the single word was an unconscious jubilation.

"Lal."

"Yes, Father."

"Why are you here?"

"I have questions."

Picard stopped breathing again. If Data said he had questions too, they'd be sunk. A dialogue was what they needed, what he longed to initiate himself, but it had to start with Data. And it did.

"I will answer what I can."

"Why are we here?"

A pause.

"Because my father, Doctor Noonien Soong, made me. And . . ."

"And . . ."

Another pause.

"And, I made you, Lal."

"Why?"

The pause came again, but of shorter duration this time.

"Because . . ." A Data-like tilt of the head. "Because I wanted a child. You are my child. I created you. You far surpassed my expectations." The flow of words came faster, more assured. "Your programming grew, advanced, you became everything I wished for you and more. And then . . . you . . . died."

A sudden silence signaled a dramatic change. Picard tore his gaze away from Data and Lal to search LaForge's features. The engineer was nodding, smiling, believing. Picard started to believe as well. Really believe that they were getting Data back with each passing moment.

Data held himself still, wearing his silence like a cloak of rippling knowledge. Apparently, he had progressed beyond the earlier stage of auditory learning. The hoped-for cascade effect seemed to be happening spontaneously, information falling into place in one long, rapid data stream.

It stopped as quickly as it began.

Data blinked his yellow eyes, and for the first time he looked around, taking in his surroundings lucidly. He met Picard's gaze briefly, moved on to study his engineer friend, and then turned back to the holographic image of his daughter.

He touched her cheek, and she smiled.

"Thank you, Lal."

Then he stepped back. He spoke, decisively, firmly:

"Computer, end program."

Lal disappeared, and it was as if she had never graced their presence. Picard suffered a momentary pang, over the loss of Data's remarkable child, then turned his attention back to Data himself.

With his familiar odd mix of slight android stiffness and military bearing, Data approached his friends. Picard marveled at the difference such a seemingly simple interaction had wrought.

"Data?"

"Yes, Geordi." Data nodded formally. "Thank you."

"You can't imagine how welcome you are."

Picard laughed delightedly. "We missed you, Mister Data."

"It is good to be . . . home."

"Are you . . . you?"

"Yes, Captain. The data stream is still falling into place, but the majority of the information has been stored properly. I am . . . intact."

Picard hesitated, needing to know, yet afraid of any misstep that might cause some new setback. "How much do you remember?"

A pause. A tilt of the head.

*Merde! What if he'd—*

"I retain all of my own memories, up until the download into B4's memory banks." Those innocent, yet all knowing, artificial eyes met Picard's worried gaze. "It is all right, Captain. All but some small segment of information, any minor thing that may have happened between the downloading of my memories and now, are readily accessible."

"I see. And what of B4?"

"B4's memory files have been compartmentalized, for future access. I could have overwritten them, once I gained control of his neural pathways, but . . ."

"But it would seem like killing him, if you'd overwritten him entirely?"

"Exactly, Captain. Though I am not certain why that should matter. For all intents and purposes, he is already dead."

"It matters because he was your brother, Data."

"My brother. You are right, Geordi. That is very important. No matter how underdeveloped a prototype he may have been, he was still my brother." Data blinked at his friends. "If my father named this prototype B4 there may have been more. If he used an alpha numerical naming system, and was not merely being whimsical, it is quite possible that there was an A, and then an unknown number of A models, before he even began on the letter B."

The childlike sense of wonder that was so much a part of the Data they remembered enveloped the android. "There could be a number of prototypes out there. It is a real possibility that I may find more of my family someday."

Picard smiled, simply enjoying the moment. Then he sobered, and grasped the palpable strength of the android's forearm. He gripped the simulated muscle and bone in a fierce gesture that spoke even more deeply than his words.

"Someday, Data. Perhaps. But regardless of that you must remember that we are your family. We on the *Enterprise.*"

"I remember, Captain. I am very fortunate."

Picard gave the arm a final squeeze. "It goes beyond good fortune, Data. You've earned it."

# STAR TREK:
# DEEP SPACE NINE

# So a Horse Walks into a Bar . . .

Brian Seidman

**Brian Seidman** has been at times a bookseller, a newspaper reporter, and an English teacher. He currently works as an editor in Montgomery, Alabama. Born in Marietta, Georgia, he received his BA in Journalism from New York University and his MA in Creative Writing from Miami University in Oxford, Ohio. Visit him online at www.brianseidman.com.

Lewis Zimmerman waved his hand at the faint smell of cigar smoke that filtered through Deep Space Nine's holographic lounge, shaking his head to focus. He slowly slipped a hypospray from his right pocket and looked around. Vic Fontaine and the Ferengi bartender from downstairs stood engrossed in conversation a few feet away at the end of the bar. Zimmerman pressed the cold metal to his own neck and then hid the hypospray away. Immediately, he could feel clarity returning, the exhaustive symptoms briefly at bay.

"Geez, Quark," Vic was saying, "I'm trying to give my patrons a good time, not scare the bejesus out of them." Between them, a wire cage sat atop a cart, the cage partially covered by a crimson sheet. Vic peered inside with a dubious frown.

Zimmerman shifted on the leather barstool, stretching his arthritic knee joints grown stiff from waiting until he and Vic were alone. He watched as the silver-haired hologram, dressed in a black suit with a matching bowtie, listened to Quark with pursed lips. There was no lag time, no hint of the hologram accessing its programming; the holomatrix's smoothness rivaled that of Zimmerman's Emergency Medical Hologram. He began to feel dizzy again; where had such a sophisticated program come from?

Quark jostled Vic out of the way, smoothing down the sheet. "It's called a lounge lizard," he said, gesturing with one brightly-colored sleeve. "All the old time bars had them. Just think, people will pay you to look at it. We'll split the profits thirty-seventy, what do you say? Consider the possibilities."

"I don't know, Quark." Vic took a step back. "If you'll excuse me, I have customers." He started toward Zimmerman, wiping his brow in mock relief. Quark sighed dramatically, giving Zimmerman a glance as he wheeled the cart from the room. Zimmerman saw momentary surprise on Quark's face, or maybe the scientist just felt self-conscious; the severe bend in Zimmerman's back, the rasp in his voice, how his thin hair had gone from brown to bleach white. *I'm a fool,* Zimmerman thought, *for thinking no one would notice. How did the motto go? The Department of Holographic Imagery and Programming. Illusion is our reality.*

"So a horse walks into a bar," Vic said, by way of greeting. "The bartender asks the horse, 'Hey, buddy, why the long face?' " He waited for a reaction, but none came. He looked at Zimmerman curiously. "Say, aren't you the guy who created all those docs-in-a-box?"

"If by that you mean the Emergency Medical Holographic Systems, then yes."

"Yeah, my friend Fritz used to talk about you all the time." Zimmerman's hand gave a slight twitch. The bartender took a triangular glass from a washbin behind the bar and slid it into a slotted rack above his head. "Fritz is the one they say gave me my sparkling personality. Force fields and light bulbs and such, you know."

"Yes, your friend Fritz is making quite a name for himself." Zimmerman rubbed at a water spot on the bar in frustration, but it didn't fade. *A holographic spot as it were,* he thought, *on a holographic bar.* "There's talk of offering him a position on Jupiter Station."

"Oh, yeah? Well if you see him, tell him I said congratulations. Couldn't have happened to a nicer Joe."

"And you know Fritz well?"

"Oh, yeah, Fritz and I?" Vic chuckled. "We go way back, sure." He moved farther down the bar, wiping the counter studiously with a rag.

"Tell me," Zimmerman called, "how is it that you understand who made you, and where you come from?"

Vic stopped wiping, his eyebrows arched in confusion. "Look,

Doc, I know plenty of guys who aren't exactly sure how to draw their family tree, you know what I'm saying? So my background's a little unusual." He winked. "Hey, at least I can sing."

Zimmerman walked down to Vic, and leaned over the bar. "It took years to program the EMHs with a functioning understanding of their own holomatricies." He rolled his eyes. "You should have heard the philosophical moaning of the Mark NX-O-Two when he learned he wasn't 'real.' How could you have gained such self-awareness so easily?"

"Look, pal," Vic said. "You want to know how I know that I know what I know? I don't know. I'm just trying to run a restaurant here. You want philosophy? Go ask Mister Worf. I've heard he's got some interesting ideas about what heaven is like."

"And I've heard you can appear in other holoprograms at will. Interesting." Zimmerman tapped his lip with one finger as if in deep thought, his tone full of sarcasm. "Because theoretically, it would be near-impossible for one single component of a ready-made holographic program to remove itself from its program and integrate itself into the program of another, especially while that program is locked and running."

Vic offered a shrug. "Hey, what can I say? I'm a bartender, not a scientist."

"Ah, but you see," said Zimmerman, darting forward, "neither is your friend Fritz."

"Eh?"

"With all the hoopla surrounding this Fritz, I thought I'd go see for myself. Everyone says he could revolutionize the holographics industry. 'He could be the next Lewis Zimmerman,' they say. But I sat down and questioned him, and the truth is," Zimmerman leaned close, speaking in a whisper, "he can't really explain some of the things you do any better than you can."

"Is that so?" Vic said, laughing. At the same time, Zimmerman saw that Vic couldn't help but wipe a holographic bead of sweat from his forehead. Vic's eyes scanned the room, as if to make sure no one had come in while the two had been talking. "Well, that's all very fascinating, but I'm sorry, I've got to close up now." As Vic spoke, the lights of the bar slowly went out on their own, until only a bit of dim illumination came from the stage. One by one, the chairs flipped themselves onto the polished wooden tables. "You want to talk more shop, you're going to have to come back tomorrow."

"On the contrary." Zimmerman reached into his pocket and withdrew a small padd, laying it on the bar with a slap. "This is Starfleet directive 731.9, authorizing me to remove the Vic Fontaine holomatrix to Jupiter Station for further study."

Vic picked up the padd, stepping around the bar as he read it. His face glowed in the shine from the screen as he mouthed the words to himself in astonishment.

"Hey now, pallie," he said, "wait just a minute." He slipped his arm around Zimmerman's shoulders. "I was too abrupt before. Let's talk a while, see if we can't work something out."

"I think not," Zimmerman said, shaking him off. "First Starfleet retires the EMH Mark 1, saying they're 'too abrasive.' I spent years working on the Mark 2, and now Starfleet says they're 'too skittish.' Everyone wants to know, 'Why can't they be more like that Vic Fontaine program on Deep Space Nine?' Well, I tell you, I will not be made a fool of!"

"But Doc," Vic said, "who's going to tend my bar if you take me back to Jupiter Station with you? You think Captain Sisko's going to let you deprive the station of Vic's?"

"I've thought of that." In a raised voice, Zimmerman said, "Computer, initiate Emergency Culinary Holographic System."

The air between Zimmerman and Vic rippled, and there appeared a perfect replica of Vic Fontaine, from hair to spats. "Hey!" Vic said.

The second hologram stared straight ahead, nonplussed. "Please state the nature of the culinary emergency."

Vic walked over to stare at his duplicate nose-to-nose. "Knock me over with a feather," Vic said. "He looks like me, but he sounds like you."

"I get that a lot," Zimmerman replied.

Vic walked a circle around the ECH. "Yeah, but Doc, even you admit I'm not your everyday lightshow." The duplicate Vic stood at attention, blinking occasionally. "You think anyone's going to settle for this look-alike when they could have the real deal?"

"I assure you, the ECH is fully functional. Observe." Zimmerman raised two fingers to catch the hologram's attention. "I say, bartender, could you recommend a drink?"

The ECH blinked once more. "Hey pallie," it said stiffly, "how about a martini? Will that be vodka or gin? Shaken or stirred? Marinated olives or cocktail onions? Anchovies? Dirty or—"

"All right already," Vic interrupted. "Doc, you got to be kidding me with this. Even if I had any interest in going to be poked and prodded by the likes of you, do you think I'd leave my bar in the hands of Robby the Robot over here?" He addressed the hologram again. "Tell me, big shot, what would you do if a Changeling came in here with a broken heart?"

"Well, pallie, I was talking to Dino and Sammy the other day, and they said—"

"Enough, enough!" Vic waved a dismissive hand at the hologram. "Sorry, Doc, but you can go find somebody else to play mad scientist with. No way am I leaving, so you can take your 'pallie' there and scram."

As Vic retreated behind the bar, Zimmerman said, "I'm afraid you don't have a choice." The doctor took a thin cylindrical data rod from his pocket and waved it toward the bartender. "When I said I had authorization from Starfleet, I meant full authorization. Either I find out what I want to know, or in twelve hours I'll be on the next shuttle back to Jupiter Station with you riding along in this data chip. I'm the foremost expert on holography across the universe; I can download you with or without your assistance." He laid the cylinder down on the bar; it rumbled across the wooden surface and stopped with a bump at Vic's open hand. "Those are your only options."

Vic rolled the data rod in his palm. He considered it closely, as if actually picturing himself inside it. Suddenly Vic appeared very serious, and Zimmerman realized just how far Vic's ever-present smile went toward making the hologram seem years younger than his character actually was. Vic looked old. For an instant, Zimmerman thought he saw the unusually clear hologram lose cohesion, as if he might blink out of existence altogether.

"You know, Doc," Vic said finally, "what if I . . . had some insights that might clear up your confusion? Do you think that might be enough, that you might lay off the kidnapping?"

Zimmerman regarded Vic carefully. "Possibly. It depends on what you have to say."

Vic contemplated the data rod. Between he and Zimmerman, the ECH waited, barely breathing holographic breaths. The bartender snapped his fingers, and his doppelganger disappeared. Zimmerman stared at the empty space in surprise.

"Tell me, Doc," Vic said, "can you keep a secret?"

Even Lewis Zimmerman, the universe's foremost expert on holography, felt momentarily jarred when the room changed, no longer Vic's sparkling lounge. Instead, Vic and Zimmerman suddenly stood in a dark, panel-walled room, small lights blinking on every surface. It was Engineering, certainly, but remote, even rougher than the Cardassian-built Ops center of the space station.

They were not nearly alone. The engineer, O'Brien, sat at a makeshift computer console; standing behind him were Captain Sisko and the Bajoran officer, Kira. Zimmerman recognized them all from the interviews he had conducted about Julian Bashir, but their uniforms were different—both men wore Starfleet uniforms from a few years back, with bright shoulders and gray collars. As was Vic, Zimmerman saw—whereas Zimmerman noticed with surprise that he himself wore a drab uniform with a Bajoran emblem. Most of the time, holoprogram users donned period costumes before they entered the holosuite—that Vic could feign others' wardrobes using holograms required skills that even Zimmerman wasn't sure he could code. He felt his right leg tremor.

O'Brien peered over his shoulder at Sisko. "Ready, Commander."

Sisko glanced side-to-side, as if concerned the walls might begin moving around him. "How long do you expect it to take?"

"If it works, we ought to be able to get all the probe's files manually transferred to the six isolinear rods in less than sixty seconds."

Vic watched every movement, an entranced smile on his face. He mouthed the words as Sisko said, "Let's do it."

O'Brien hesitated only momentarily. "Computer," he said, "run a level five diagnostic of all power systems on board."

"Requested function will require forty-three minutes," the computer's female voice replied. "Stand by."

Zimmerman tapped his foot. "What's going on?"

"Oh, just a regular day at the mill." Vic pulled at the bottom of his uniform-shirt, straightening it. He looked at Zimmerman with feigned boredom. "They're about three minutes away from a reactor breach."

Though Zimmerman knew he was still safely in a holosuite, he couldn't help but feel slightly ill at the thought of the station exploding around him. O'Brien's voice startled him. "Crewman," the engineer said impatiently. "You have your orders."

Zimmerman turned to Vic. "Me?"

Vic gave Zimmerman a little push toward a compartment to O'Brien's right. "They want you to begin removing the core memory while they distract an errant sentience in the computer," Vic said. That the level of Vic's technical vernacular had risen was not lost on Zimmerman. He felt torn between his curiosity and the pain he would experience bending down. Bracing himself against the side of the console, Zimmerman gingerly lowered himself to his knees, and eased open the compartment, slowly beginning to pull out the clear isolinear rods.

126 Strange New Worlds 10

"Computer," Sisko said, "give me an analysis of all Cardassian traffic along the border."

"Processing long range sensors. Stand by."

The Trill woman, Jadzia Dax—now deceased, if Zimmerman understood correctly—spoke up from an operations station behind him. As the computer acknowledged her complicated request—purposefully so, Zimmerman surmised—the usually unflappable computer voice began to pause and hiccup, slowly at first, and then with increasing fractures.

Zimmerman had four of the six isolinear rods in his hands. To his right, Vic spoke, presumably filling Zimmerman's own role in the holodrama: "Computer, access musical files in the Bajoran master database and create a concert program of Bajoran serenas."

Zimmerman dipped forward, watching the slow rise of the isolinear rods. The fifth moved stiffly from the slot, reminding Zimmerman of his own joints when he woke in the morning. He stared at the metallic shine, momentarily hypnotized by the glow. Had time slowed down? He heard the computer hoarsely begin, "Stand—"

Then the console in front of O'Brien exploded.

Zimmerman felt the heat sear past him, shutting his eyes instinctively against the blast. He recovered almost immediately, startled more by the sudden silence than anything else. He opened his eyes.

They stood in an expanse of foggy cloud-white, completely absent of any form or landmark. Vic was back in his tuxedo, Zimmerman in his traveling clothes.

"Is this the inside of a reactor breach?" Zimmerman's voice still shook from the surprise of the explosion; he tried to mask it with a note of testiness.

"Nah." Vic paced through the mists, his hands in his pockets. There was a slight echo, even as the space was empty. "Just a little place I heard about, conducive to thinking about the past."

"And what, pray tell, was the point of that little jaunt, other than blowing up a computer in my face?"

Zimmerman took a few steps away, and Vic hurried after, stopping just short of putting his arm around the doctor's shoulders. "Aw, Doc. I was just having a little fun with you there." Vic walked around the doctor to face him. "That moment's always had a tender little place in my heart, see?"

"A tender place?" Zimmerman scoffed. "Your heart?"

"This probe came through the wormhole; the Chief downloaded its memory core, trying to find out what it was. Except it turned out the thing was alive, and it started playing racquetball with the station's systems. The Chief and company had to pull the con you just saw in order to get the thing to let go."

Zimmerman squinted at Vic. He opened his mouth to ask a question, but faltered. He felt cold, suddenly. Zimmerman started, "What does that—" and paused, staring at Vic with a look of concern. "Go on."

"The Chief ended up creating a little bachelor's pad in the computers for the alien to live in. Only more like a library, because even though it couldn't go anywhere, it could still access all the data on the station. The Chief would visit it every once in a while, move some files around and such, but eventually with the war and his family, you know how these things go, right? So for a long time it just sat there, watching the world pass by in front of it."

"What happened?" Zimmerman's voice had a flat affect that momentarily startled Vic. "What happened?" Zimmerman repeated.

"You've got to understand," Vic said. "I mean, all that time, just sitting there, learning about the crew, and then with the war and all . . . when Julian installed the Vic program, I mean, the matrices were compatible. I'd joined myself to it before I'd even really known what I'd done, honest!"

"You're an alien."

"Well, an alien-holographic hybrid, I guess you'd say. Formerly a non-biological lifeform. Never simple, is it?"

"And that's why you have all these abilities," Zimmerman said, almost to himself. "You're an alien. All this time you've been an alien, and no one ever suspected."

"Well," Vic smiled, "I ain't saying it was a flawless switcheroo."

He snapped his fingers, and the mists parted, slowly fading as they were replaced, once again, by Vic's lounge. Now, however, the bar was crowded with people, from tuxedoed men and well-dressed women at all the tables, to a second Vic and his full band up on stage, to a nearly full contingent of Deep Space Nine senior officers standing in the back, where Zimmerman and the current Vic stood off to one side.

On stage, the band raised their instruments in a loud finish, and the second Vic thanked the audience for attending. Zimmerman looked to his Vic, who nodded his head toward the scene.

The second Vic shuffled through the restaurant toward the gathering of Deep Space Nine officers, pausing at various tables for a handshake. The hologram had a suave, fluid walk, but from Zimmerman's outside vantage point, he imagined he detected a slight uncertainty to Vic's smile—a hint of nervousness.

"Vic," Julian Bashir gushed, "You're terrific." The others chimed in with similar compliments.

"I know what you're thinking," said the past Vic. "He has pretty smooth pipes for a lightbulb."

Next to Zimmerman, the "real" Vic leaned in close. "First time I met 'em all as Vic. Way I figured it, best to go for the direct approach. Let them know something was up, but then give them an easy answer for it."

"He knows he's a hologram?" O'Brien was asking.

Bashir smiled knowingly. "Felix designed him that way. Thought it would give him the right attitude for the era."

"If you're going to work Vegas in the sixties," laughed the past Vic, "you better know the score. Otherwise you're going to look like a Clyde."

Just as a discussion began on the definition, exactly, of a

"Clyde," the scene froze. "See?" said the present Vic. "It's the old bait-and-switch. Offer up a little information, then toss in a confusing Earth-term to change the subject. Trick's older than my Aunt Sally."

"And that was it?" Zimmerman asked. "The so-called greatest minds of Starfleet, fooled by holographic doublespeak?"

Vic examined the frozen scene for a moment. "You know, the day after, Odo came to see me, and for a minute, I was absolutely sure the jig was up."

The crowd faded away, and behind Zimmerman, another Vic faded in, sitting at the bar. Odo stood next to him in a dark brown uniform. This Vic had taken off his jacket, and he had a half-full glass of whiskey in front of him. The room had darkened, and Zimmerman shivered against a sudden chill in the air.

"Yesterday," Odo said, his voice raspy, "when my friends and I were here, you seemed to know things."

"I've been around the block a couple times," the jacketless Vic replied.

The exchange seemed casual, but Zimmerman sensed a hint of desperation, like an interrogation. "You were trying to distract him again," Zimmerman said. Next to him, Vic winked.

"You seemed to know specific things," Odo insisted. "For instance, Dax and Worf are married, the Chief misses his wife."

"Do you see that?" said the present Vic, whispering excitedly. "The way Odo pushed like that? That's why he's the best. Man, I thought he had me."

The past Vic lifted his drink, swallowing a healthy gulp. "You don't have to be an Einstein to clue into any of that."

Zimmerman held his breath, caught up in the anxiety of the scene. Vic stood motionless beside him. Each waited for Odo to spring.

For the lie to come suddenly into the light.

Odo looked down and said, "At one point, you were going to make an observation about Major Kira and myself."

Zimmerman exhaled, and next to him, Vic did the same. "Gets

me every time," Vic said. "But at that point, I knew I had the cat fooled, and I could get on with what was really important—getting those two lovebirds together. And they've been happily ever after ever since, well, more or less."

"That's quite a tale." Zimmerman leaned against a bar stool, the joints in his knees burning. Odo and the second Vic faded from view and the lights in the restaurant brightened.

"Hey, Doc," Vic said, "I sure am sorry about having given you the run-around before. And sorry I muddled your experiments and whatnot for a while." The bartender raised his shoulders to his ears and then lowered them, relaxing. If he recognized Zimmerman's distraught pose, he didn't acknowledge it. "Man, it feels good to finally get that off my chest. You know, Doc, you're the only one who knows that. You and me, we're simpatico now. Next time you come in here, your drinks are on the house, I mean that. Least I can do for you, keeping my secret."

Zimmerman's head was down, reviewing information on his padd. He tapped a few more keys.

"Doc?" Vic said.

Zimmerman only gave him a passing glance before looking back to the padd. "I'm afraid there won't be much time for making drinks," he said. "Our transport leaves in eleven hours."

"Leaves?" Vic stared at Zimmerman, his eyes large. "But didn't you hear me? I'm not fully a hologram. You've got no competition from Fritz. Everything's fine, right?"

"Fine?" Zimmerman scoffed. "There's nothing 'fine' about it! You and I may know your story, but the rest of the world still considers Fritz a genius. Do you know they're considering him a candidate for the Daystrom Prize for Holography? They created that prize for me! No, no. No, I think not. You'll be coming back to Jupiter Station with me so I can verify your claims."

"But Doc, you said if I came clean, you'd leave me alone. We had a deal."

Zimmerman ignored the pain in Vic's voice. "I said I'd think about it, Mister Fontaine, and I have." He felt his tremor returning. "I'll give you some time to put your affairs in order, and then I'll be back. We have quite an endeavor ahead of us." With that, Zimmerman turned and walked from the bar as quickly as he could manage.

Holographic pain, from a holographic . . . alien? He shook his head as he went. If anyone understood, it was Zimmerman, that we don't always get a say in the choices life makes for us.

Zimmerman paused on the stairs as a searing twinge went through his leg. Below, he spotted Leeta near the bar, loading drinks onto her tray. Still every movement held the fluidity of a dancer. The noise of the full room grew louder as he gingerly made his way down, flexing stiff muscles. He reached out to tap her exqui-site shoulder—and nearly collided with her tray of drinks as she turned around, liquids sloshing over the edges of glasses and onto the floor. "Oh, Lewis!" Leeta said. "I'm so sorry! I heard you were on the station, and I've been meaning to—"

He put his hand on her arm. "Not to worry," he said in his most lilting tone. "It's nothing a cup of Amielian tea won't fix, and the pleasure of your company." His wet shirt-front dripped onto his shoes.

Leeta looked from Zimmerman to Quark, busy trying to pawn off the red-draped "lounge lizard" cage to a portly Lurian sitting at the bar. "Well, I guess I could take a break. Being part of the family has its privileges." She glanced over her shoulder at the bar and whispered, "As long as you don't tell the proprietor."

Leeta guided them past a replicator for the tea, and then up the stairs to a table on the second floor. Zimmerman felt warm gratitude when Leeta slowed on the staircase, silently allowing him to catch up. At the table, Zimmerman wrapped tight fingers around the teacup, soothing his hands. Leeta's flowery perfume enveloped them both. "So," he said, "you're a married woman now."

"Over a year," Leeta said. The diamond and platinum ring shone on her finger as she held it forward. "Rom is such a sweet man. And you should meet his son Nog. He's so smart! He's going to be a Starfleet officer, you know."

"You're a stepmother, too. That's . . . fantastic." He looked away from her. "You know, we never did find an adequate restaurateur on Jupiter Station."

"Oh, Lewis." Leeta gave a soft laugh. "I really am sorry." She regarded him seriously. "But truly, how are you?"

"I'm fine. The long-term medical holographic system is still in the planning stages, but it's no matter. I've been spending a lot of time in the lab perfecting the EMH Mark Two."

"No." Leeta stared at him until his eyes met hers. "That's how work is going. I asked about you."

Zimmerman readied a glib reply, but with Leeta watching him, he felt suddenly abashed. Visions of giggling, bright-eyed children with his intellect and her hairline played through his mind. He saw he and Leeta growing old together in front of a holographic fire. "Acute subcellular degredation," he said, scratching one finger against the table. "It began with the loss of pigmentation in my hair. My bones have become brittle. As it worsens, my joints will begin to atrophy and break down. In a matter of years, I'll no longer be able to walk or feed myself. Already I'm finding it hard to focus; I have to use a hypospray just to get through the day."

Leeta gasped softly. She wiped at her eyes swiftly with her knuckles. "You should have called. Let me know sooner."

"You have a life here now. A family." Zimmerman peered away, over the railing. "I didn't want to worry you."

"Lewis," she said. She reached over and placed her hand on top of his. "Even if things didn't work out between us, who can you turn to, if not your friends?"

He leaned over and put his other hand on top of hers, resting on the table. "You're very sweet—"

"I knew it!" came Rom's voice, startling Zimmerman. He and Leeta each looked around; she was the first to spot her husband, pointing to where Rom glared up at them from the ground floor below. "Sitting there together!" Rom yelled. "Drinking tea!" He stopped, noticing abruptly that every customer at every table in Quark's stared at him. "Table-sitting!" he spat, still caught up in his anger. "Tea!" He sputtered once, and then stalked off.

Leeta looked at Zimmerman apologetically. "He's been so high-strung about your visit. I should go after him." Zimmerman nodded. Leeta stood and squeezed his hand once. She cupped his chin in her palm, looking at him fondly, and hurried away.

Zimmerman took another sip of his tea, shook his head, and shrugged.

As he crossed the Promenade, Zimmerman felt fatigue pulling at his every step, as if the station's artificial gravity had been enhanced. He stumbled and had to grab a bulkhead for support, breathlessly waving away an officer who tried to help. What Zimmerman hated most was the not knowing—was he simply tired, or was his tiredness a symptom of his condition? Was he more exhausted because he constantly worried about the significance of his exhaustion? At least with holography, you knew where you stood: everything was fake.

Quark had dimmed the bar lights, casting vague square shadows from the tables to the floor. The bartender spoke urgently to a viewscreen on one side of his bar, vehemently trying to convince someone to help him "get rid of this damn lizard." Zimmerman shuffled past, grasping the staircase railing as he took the steps up to Vic's.

At the landing, Rom hurried out from Vic's curtained entrance. Zimmerman tensed, half-expecting an attack. Instead, Rom greeted him with a toothy grin. "Well, hello, Doctor."

"Rom. You're looking somewhat more chipper than this afternoon."

"Oh, that." Rom waved a hand at the doctor as if to dismiss an unpleasant memory. His face burned dusky in the Ferengi equivalent of a blush. "I think I overreacted a little."

Zimmerman let himself relax. "So you're no longer upset?"

"No, no," Rom said. "I talked to Vic for a while, and he helped me see. Leeta loves me."

"That she does." Zimmerman extended a hand, and Rom shook it heartily. "Take care of her."

Inside, Vic's was as dark as Quark's, the only illumination spotlighting the proprietor behind the bar. Vic stood cleaning glasses again, much the same as when Zimmerman had left.

"I tell you," Vic said, "I haven't had a doc in here so much since that night the Klingon chef served a bad case of *gagh.*"

Zimmerman stared at Vic, nonplussed. "I'm a scientist, not a physician."

"I meant—ah, never mind. Coffee?"

Zimmerman took a stool at the bar and Vic set a mug in front of him. The steaming liquid was already cooled with a drop of milk and, when Zimmerman took a sip, a hint of sugar. "Just the way I like it," he said. "A lucky guess, or do you read personal logs as well as station databanks?"

Vic shrugged. "So much for peacemaking." He pushed back his sleeve to check the gold wristwatch on his arm. "Almost time for that transport, eh?"

Zimmerman drank deeper from the mug, feeling the heat pervade his muscles. "You really had an effect on Rom."

"Yeah, well, that Rom's a good guy. A family man, got to respect that." Vic leaned his elbows on the bar. "He's got brains, a wife that loves him, a son to be proud of. His life is good. But give him a reason, and the guy's more jealous than Bogie watching Frank and Betty from his deathbed. Thing is, Rom doesn't believe himself worth the ground he's standing on. Never has. I've just got to remind him he's an okay guy every once in a while, and everything shakes out fine." Vic shook his head, chuckling to himself. "You know, most of the time, with Rom and the rest, when they come in with problems, they already know what the answer is. They just need me to give them a push in the right direction."

"And as for me," Zimmerman's voice sounded skeptical, "do I already know the right answer to my problems?"

"Ah, see, but that's the thing," Vic said, teasing. "It's not the ones who don't know the answer. It's the ones that don't know the question that're the doozies."

"Touching." Zimmerman took another sip of his coffee, then pushed it away, resenting the warmth.

"People here, they work hard," Vic continued. "It's good for them to be able to go someplace where they can get a little R&R once in a while. And why not here? I'm light bulbs and force fields, you know? I'm air. The rent on this joint is paid, the casino brings in a good take every night; why shouldn't I help out? What better thing could a cat like me do with his life?"

Zimmerman looked up, giving Vic a hard glare. "Besides letting people open up to you while pretending to be something you're not? Did you ever once think that your little subterfuge might have an effect on somebody else?"

"I'm sorry I hurt your rep," Vic said, but then he shook his head, feeling a surge of anger himself. "Cut me to the quick, why don't you? You know, you're a real Mack the Knife there, Doc."

"I'm sure I've been called worse." Zimmerman stood up from the stool. "It must be nice, being the benevolent alien probe, dispensing your wisdom day and night from your cushy holosuite without a concern in the universe."

Zimmerman had begun to yell, and Vic matched him in volume. "Least I don't make it my business uprooting people's lives every time I come around. And here, I was just starting to warm to the idea of taking off to Jupiter Station. Pay you back for the mess I made of things. Thought it might be fun; maybe you and I could come to an understanding."

Zimmerman scoffed. "Thank you, Mister Fontaine, but I don't need your 'understanding.' What do you think you can tell me that I don't already know? That I'm here on a wayward space station in the middle of a war chasing down any errant hologram that even hints at threatening me or the legacy of my life's work? That my crowning scientific achievements are used for waste disposal? That they've become the laughing stock of the galaxy? That

I'm dying and I'm afraid I'm going to be forgotten?" Zimmerman looked Vic in the eye and spoke sharply. "Trust me, Mister Fontaine, I already know."

"Yeah, Doc, you only think you're going to be forgotten," Vic shouted back. "Truth is, you ain't scared of how you're going to be forgotten, you're scared of the way you're going to be remembered—a bitter old man who blamed everyone else in the galaxy for his own misfortunes, except himself."

Both men stopped, out of breath—Vic holographically, if not in fact. Softly, Vic spat, "And I didn't need your personal log for that one, either. I could tell that much just by looking at you."

They stared at each other, the rage that they felt slowly fading, replaced with the silence of the restaurant. Zimmerman turned his face in embarrassment, and took one step away from the bar. Vic looked down at his hands, sheepish. "Well, enough of my jabbering on," he said. "Time to hit the road, right?"

"Yes," Zimmerman said quietly. "My shuttle leaves in ten minutes. I just came in to say goodbye."

"Goodbye?" Vic paused. "You mean . . . ?" A hesitant grin spread across his face. "Wait a minute, Doc. Wait a minute. Are you saying I've got a stay of execution?"

Zimmerman averted his eyes again, trying to downplay Vic's excitement. He sighed impatiently. "Something like that."

"Hey, Doc, thanks." Vic came swiftly around the bar. "Look, you know, I'm sorry for what I said. Really I am. I didn't mean it." He took up Zimmerman's hand in a hearty handshake, which Zimmerman barely returned. "So what was it that changed your mind, huh? What did it? When you came in here, was it all that stuff about helping out Rom?"

"No. But you make Leeta's life easier," Zimmerman said. "I . . . may not be around much longer. If I can't be here to look after her, someone has to be." And so much, he thought, for bright-eyed children.

"So the tin man's got a heart after all," Vic said. Zimmerman, nodding vaguely, turned to go. All of the sudden he felt too tired even to try to piece together the hologram's—the alien's—strange allusions. "Hey, Doc," Vic called after him, "that offer of a drink still stands, next time you drop by."

Zimmerman barely looked back. "Sure."

"Look, hey." Vic hurried to follow, sounding concerned. "So the docs-in-a-box didn't work. Smart guy like you, you've got to have more ideas. What about a holographic zoo, huh? Kids'll love it. Or holographic spy cameras? Join the war effort, no?"

"I appreciate your help." Zimmerman held on to the wall for support. "But maybe it's time to let a new generation take over."

"You know," Vic said, "I had this friend, Leonard. Guy tried for years to learn to play the harmonica, never could get it. But man, he blew that thing night and day. You could hear him all the way down the alley! It's like a wise man once said, if you can't sing it well, at least sing it loud." Vic put his arm around Zimmerman's bony shoulders. "So your holograms are being used for waste extraction. I bet, with a little tweaking, you could have your face on the best darn garbagemen in the whole galaxy."

Zimmerman stepped away, rubbing at his scalp through his whitening hair. "That's just the problem," he said. "I look less and less like them every day." And he walked out, leaving Vic alone behind him.

"Holographic zoo," Zimmerman muttered as he stepped carefully down the stairs. He snorted bitterly.

At the bar, Quark rested his head in his palms, looking bored. The wire cage he'd brought to Vic's sat uncovered next to him. Inside, Zimmerman saw a long green lizard with a glossy horn-rimmed neck. As Zimmerman walked past, it looked up at him with plaintive eyes.

"What is that?" Zimmerman asked.

Quark kept staring straight ahead. "It's an old Earth-lizard," he said. "Iguana."

"Curious." The scaly animal tilted its head to peer at Zimmerman again, bored and wry at the same time. Despite himself, despite it all, Zimmerman couldn't help but smile. As he exited through Quark's wide doors, he tried the word between his lips: "Iguana." He said it again: "Iguana."

From the curtained doorway of Vic's, despite the lack of holo-projectors, Vic Fontaine peered out into the hall and over the railing, watching Zimmerman slip away. Did he see the man standing just a little straighter?

"Crazy, baby," Vic grinned. Whistling to himself, he went back inside to prepare for late-night customers.

A guy's got to make a living, after all.

# Signal to Noise

Jim Johnson

**Jim Johnson** makes his third appearance in the pages of *Strange New Worlds*. He's still in northern Virginia with his lovely wife Andi, four cats, and a chestnut mare. By the time you read this, he'll have two original novels making the rounds and will be working on his third. Huge thanks to the Paneranormal Society and all the fine members of the Yahoo! *SNW* Writers group (http://groups.yahoo.com/group/SNW_Writers). All my thanks and appreciation to Paula Block, Margaret Clark, Elisa Kassin, John Ordover, and especially, Dean Wesley Smith, for making *Strange New Worlds* live and breathe lo these ten years.

Biting at his thumbnail, Jack stared at the data displayed on his computer screen. "Damn, damn, damn! I'm out of time. Time, time, there's no more time!"

*Roughly Sixty Trillion Years Later*

The universe, for eons condensing unchecked, finally collapsed upon itself and exploded in a conflagration of light and energy, near-simultaneously annihilating and recreating everything in the entire universe.

*Stardate 53425.6*

Jack stared at his computer screen, running his thumbnail between his two upper central incisors. His calculations just were not adding up. Something was missing.

The sudden scent of wood laced with graphite wafted past his nose. Jack frowned, inhaling the familiar scent and looking around. His small ward at the Institute hadn't changed. Same small bed, same small door leading to his small necessary, same small dresser containing his few personal effects. He didn't have any pencils—not any more.

The smell faded, and Jack looked around in confusion. His peripheral vision caught his reflection in the computer screen—wait, no, not *his* reflection. He stared into the computer screen, looking beyond the data displayed there. His own puzzled visage stared back. For just a moment, though, he could have sworn he had seen someone else—someone he'd heard had died well over a year ago. Captain Benjamin Sisko, his fellow mutant friend Julian's old commanding officer.

*Roughly Sixty Trillion Years Later*

The universe, for eons condensing unchecked, finally collapsed upon itself and exploded in a conflagration of light and energy, near-simultaneously annihilating and recreating everything in the entire universe.

*Stardate 53434.3*

Jack stared at the data displayed on his computer screen, picking at his moustache. Several variables shifted toward the negative. He closed his eyes and cradled his head in his hands. They were all doomed. No one could see that but him. No one listened to him; they just said "Yes, Jack," or "All right, Jack," or "Why don't you take this and go back to your room, Jack? You'll feel ever so much better."

After a long sigh, he opened his eyes to get back to work, but discovered that he was floating—standing?—in a thick white nothingness. All around him pulsed a sound which he quickly connected to his own heartbeat. He was no idiot; of course it was his own heartbeat—his own genetically enhanced heartbeat, beating in a genetically-perfect rhythm.

He raised his hand to his mouth so that he could nibble on his thumbnail. He looked around at the blank white expanse. "Hello? Is there anyone there?"

His own question reflected back in the white otherness, but no response came to him. Frustrated, he wandered around, or at least thought he did. He could feel the commands electrically sent to his muscles, could feel his muscles contracting and expanding, but his environment didn't move, didn't change.

He tried again. "Hello, is there anyone out there? Patrick? Lauren? Anyone?"

No answer to these questions either. Annoyed, Jack gnawed anew at his thumb.

An odd voice filtered in through the white. "Doctor Wykoff, please come to isolation ward four. Doctor Wykoff to isolation ward four."

Jack looked around in alarm. Who had said that? He couldn't see anything, didn't hear anything else other than his heartbeat pulsing around him, inside him.

"Hello?" Still no answer. Then, just as suddenly as he had appeared in the white nothingness, he found himself seated again at his computer in his little ward room, seeing the same grim results displayed on the screen as before. He slapped the monitor. "Damn! I'm wasting too much time."

*Roughly Sixty Trillion Years Later*

The universe, for eons condensing unchecked, finally collapsed upon itself and exploded in a conflagration of light and energy, near-simultaneously annihilating and recreating everything in the entire universe.

*Stardate 53442.8*

Jack paced back and forth in front of his little computer desk. He stopped, considering a new variable. He leaned over and entered an adjustment into his computer. He frowned at the results. "No, no, no. That's no good, that's no good." He worried at the cuticle around his thumb. "Do that and you lose another hundred million years. Too soon, too soon."

He stared at the computer screen again, entered more commands. As he sat down to review his work, he smelled graphite and then found himself surrounded by that white nothingness again. This time, however, a large door, off-white and in desperate need of a fresh coat of paint, loomed in front of him. He didn't see anything around it or behind it, nothing other than that same strange impenetrable mist.

Jack crossed his arms and gnawed on his cuticle again, taking in this new variable. Should he knock, should he open it, should he leave it? If he left it, where would he go? He turned away from the door and looked around. All around him was the whiteness.

There was nowhere else to go. He had no idea how long he had been here before, no idea how long he'd been there this time. His internal clock, enhanced by the genetic manipulation forced on him when he was a child, didn't seem to wind quite right here.

He turned back to the door, considering it. That same strange voice filtered out of the nothingness. "Doctor Wykoff, please come to isolation ward four. Doctor Wykoff to isolation ward four."

This time it sounded like the voice came from beyond the other side of the door. Jack reached out to the door, drew his hand back, but then reached out to knock on it, forcefully and repeatedly.

There was no response to his knocking, so he tried the doorknob. It opened at his touch. Curious, he looked in through the doorframe.

The room beyond was full of couches and chairs and tables, all of which were occupied by men and women—humans—wearing what looked to be pajamas of varying hues and styles. Some of them sat quietly at their seats, some rocked themselves, and still others thrashed about or beat themselves. From time to time a man or woman dressed in white would walk here and there, their white shoes squeaking on the dull blue tile floor. They would pause to talk to a person—patient—Jack corrected himself, and sometimes they would lead one of them away, through one of the many other doors connected to the room. No one seemed to pay Jack any mind. Confused, he stepped forward into the room.

*Roughly Sixty Trillion Years Later*

The universe, for eons condensing unchecked, finally collapsed upon itself and exploded in a conflagration of light and energy, near-simultaneously annihilating and recreating everything in the entire universe.

*Stardate 53445.1*

Jack stared at his computer screen, nibbling a new furrow into his thumb cuticle. He stopped, blinking at the screen. Something had happened. Where had he just been? What the hell was going on?

He stood up to head for the door, but found himself back in that white nothingness, staring at an off-white door, different than the one he'd seen before. He could tell from the areas of flaking paint that it was a different door. The familiar scent of pencil lead caught Jack's senses.

He tried the doorknob. It was unlocked. He twisted it and pushed the door open. What, or more specifically, who he saw inside the room stunned him.

Captain Benjamin Sisko stood in front of one of the room's walls, wearing eyeglasses and a simple white tunic and pants. He had a short pencil in his hand and he was writing on the wall. Sisko turned to glance at Jack, his pencil half-raised.

"Hello, Jack. I've been waiting for you."

Confused, Jack walked into the room, his arms crossed. "Captain Sisko?"

Sisko stifled a giggle. "Sisko? No, no. He's just one of the characters in my stories." He gestured at the walls, which were just over half-filled with tightly-packed writing from ceiling to floor.

Jack stared at him. This wasn't Captain Sisko. He cleared his throat. "If you're not Captain Sisko, then who are you? And why am I here?"

The man grinned and gestured with his pencil at the wall. "I'm Benny Russell. I'm a writer."

Jack nodded at the walls. "Clearly." He leaned closer to the wall to read a section of the tightly-packed text. It concerned Deep Space Nine and the war with the Dominion.

"Why . . . why are you writing on the walls, um, Benny?"

Benny flourished his pencil stub. "Because I'm a writer. Because I might be a threat to myself, or to other people." He shrugged and giggled again.

Jack grimaced. He'd heard words like that before. Then, one of Benny's earlier comments struck home. "Wait a minute! You said that Sisko was just one of your characters. What's that supposed to mean?"

Benny smiled. "I told you. I write stories. Captain Sisko is one of the stars of my stories, or at least he was until he fell into the Fire Caves on Bajor." Benny gestured toward one of the writing-covered walls. "Now that he's there, I have other stories to write, other tales to tell."

Jack nibbled on his thumb. This didn't make any sense. More to himself than to Benny, he asked, "What am I doing here?"

Benny shrugged and turned back to the section of wall he'd been writing on. Over his shoulder, he said, "You'll have to wait until the end of your story to figure that out."

Jack stared at Benny as he resumed writing on the wall. The door behind Jack made a strange noise, and he turned to examine it . . .

. . . and found himself standing just outside one of Deep Space Nine's large round airlock doors as it cycled open.

"That's a stupid question!" yelled a voice Jack recognized as belonging to his friend and fellow Institute inmate, Patrick. Jack glanced just ahead and saw Patrick in his stolen Starfleet admiral's uniform, his usually wild thinning hair combed back in an orderly fashion. Two security guards stood in front of Patrick, trading confused looks.

Thinking fast, Jack moved quickly to get in front of Patrick. He said, "Ah, the admiral is here to see Doctor Bashir." Quickly, he added, "You don't want to keep the admiral waiting, do you?"

The two security guards traded glances. The senior of the two nodded at Jack and Patrick. "Sorry, Lieutenant, Admiral. Welcome to Deep Space Nine."

Jack glanced down at himself and saw that he was wearing a Starfleet lieutenant's uniform. He nodded at the two security officers and led Patrick onto the Promenade and toward the station's Infirmary. He glanced at Patrick as they walked.

"What are we doing here?"

"That's a stupid question!"

Jack squeezed Patrick's arm, hard.

Patrick winced. "Ow! What'd you do that for?"

"Don't play the Starfleet admiral with me! What are we doing here?"

Patrick looked downcast. "You wanted to come here to see Julian. You asked me and Lauren to come with you." He sniffed. Jack could see tears welling up in his friend's eyes.

Jack glanced around the Promenade. "Lauren's here?"

Patrick nodded. "Yes. She's securing the shuttle we, ah, borrowed from the Institute." He rubbed his arm where Jack had squeezed it. "Why are you so mean?"

Jack crossed his arms. "I'm sorry. I didn't take your arm off, you know." He grabbed a *jumja* stick off a nearby kiosk. The proprietor of the stand objected, but Jack ignored her.

"Here, take this." He handed the *jumja* stick to Patrick, who accepted it with a large grin. "I'm sorry. All better now?"

Patrick stuck the confection in his mouth and nodded.

Jack said, "Now let's go find that doctor." He led the way to the Infirmary, where he expected to find his old friend, Julian Bashir, fellow mutant freak and quite possibly the only person who could help Jack figure out what was happening to him.

Jack leaned his head into the Infirmary, noting that there was just one nurse on duty and no Doctor Bashir at his desk. The nurse noticed Jack.

"Can I help you, sir?"

Jack giggled at the reference and crossed his arms. "Why, yes, yes, you can help us. Me. Us. We're looking for your commander-in-chief, the head doctor."

Lauren, Jack's lovely friend and also a guest of the Institute, slid in next to Jack and gave the nurse a winning smile. She was wearing a lieutenant's uniform as well. She said, "We're such dear friends of Julian's and we'd just love to see him."

The nurse glanced at Lauren, then turned back to Patrick. "I'm sorry, sir. Doctor Bashir isn't on duty at the moment. If this is an emergency, I can contact him for you, of course."

Jack shrugged and crossed his arms. "Thank you, but I think we can find him on our own."

Lauren leaned in. "It's a surprise for Julian, you see. He'll be so thrilled to see us."

The nurse moved toward the Infirmary's comm system. "Here, let me call him for you. . . ."

Jack blocked her path. "No, no, don't bother." He gave her a quick once-over. "Thanks for your help anyway. We'll find him ourselves."

Jack led Patrick and Lauren out of the Infirmary, leaving the nurse behind. As they moved toward one of the station's lifts, Patrick said, "We could have let her contact Doctor Bashir. She was only trying to help."

Jack crossed his arms as they entered the lift. "She wasn't moving fast enough. We don't have time to waste." He glanced at the ceiling. "Habitat ring, section D-47."

As the lift moved toward their destination, Lauren draped herself on the handrail. "You're in such a rush, Jack. You should really step back and enjoy the moment. That nurse liked you."

Jack chewed on his thumb. "I know, I know that! I don't have time for attractions, for dilly-dallies. I have the universe to save, and I need Doctor Bashir's help." He paused as the lift slowed to a stop. He glanced at his two companions. "But don't tell him I told you that."

He turned around and stepped off the turbolift . . .

. . . and through the off-white door into the large white room with blue tile and dozens of patients in pajamas. Jack stopped in his tracks and looked behind him. The door he had walked through was behind him, closed. He tried the handle, but it was locked. There was no sign of Patrick or Lauren, or DS9 for that matter.

He glanced at the patients in the room. As before, some of them busied themselves with games, books, or jigsaw puzzles, while others sat quietly or mumbled to themselves. A couple of them hit themselves, but the ever-present orderlies were quick to move over and stop them from the self-flagellations.

Jack stepped over to one of the orderlies who had a stethoscope draped over her neck. "Excuse me."

The woman turned her attention on Jack. "Hello, what are you doing up and about?"

Jack blinked. "What?" He glanced at her nametag. "Why shouldn't I be up and about, Doctor Wilson? Hmm?"

She gave him a small smile. "You know this is your rest time, Jack. Didn't you take your medicine?"

Jack crossed his arms. "My medicine? I don't have to take any medicine."

She placed her hand on one of his arms and led him toward one of the side doors. "Now, Jack, you know you need your medicine or you're never going to get better. Why don't you come with me." Jack noted that the last statement was an order, not a question or a request. He pulled his arm out of her grasp.

"No, I don't need to go with you, and I don't need any medicine. I'm here . . ." He paused. Why was he here? He wasn't sick, he wasn't losing his mind. He was here to find . . . Benny?

A voice filtered over the loudspeaker set in one corner of the room. "Doctor Wykoff to isolation ward four. Doctor Wykoff to isolation ward four."

Jack nodded. He'd heard that before—every time he was here or in that white fog, he'd heard that same voice.

He looked at Doctor Wilson. "Take me to isolation ward four. I want to see Benny. Benny Russell."

Wilson gave him a smile that Jack suspected was utterly insincere. "I can't do that, Jack, but I can get you close. You're staying in isolation ward five. We'll go right by four. Okay?"

The tone of her voice suggested to Jack that she'd brook no argument, so he nodded and allowed her to lead him through the door and out of the main room.

They walked down a wide off-white corridor lined with several additional doors. As Wilson led him deeper into the labyrinthine building, Jack said, "Can we hurry it up a bit? I don't have time to waste."

Wilson kept moving him forward. "We're almost there, Jack."

She pointed at one door as they passed it. "That's isolation ward four."

Jack craned his neck to keep it in sight as they passed by. It looked like any of the other doors in the corridor. Wilson stopped in front of the next door down the hall. "This is your home. Isolation ward five."

Jack glanced at her, then at the door. He nibbled at his thumb nail. "What if I don't want to go home?"

She shook her head and unlocked the door, swung it open. "This is your home, Jack."

Jack crossed his arms again. He leaned into the small room. The walls were covered in some white fabric, and there was a small window set high in the far wall, casting a little filtered sunlight into the room. The room was otherwise featureless.

Jack shook his head. "I don't want to go in. I want to see Benny!"

Wilson sighed. "Jack, don't do this again." She gestured into the room. "Go on in and I'll bring you something to drink."

A gruff voice behind them asked, "Is there a problem here, Doctor Wilson?"

Jack and Wilson turned to look at the newcomer. A dour man about Jack's height stood in the hallway, wearing a frown and a white lab coat.

Wilson said, "Actually, yes, Doctor Wykoff." She indicated Jack. "Jack doesn't want to go into his ward room."

Wykoff stared at Jack. "Why not, Jack? You know you're much more comfortable in your room."

Jack shook his head. "No, I want to see Benny. I need his help."

Wykoff shook his head. "I'm sorry, Jack. You know you can't see the other patients in the other wards. Benny has enough problems of his own—he can't help you until he helps himself." He paused, staring at Jack. "The same can be said for you, actually."

Jack blinked, then in a flash, grabbed Doctor Wilson and clamped his hand around her throat from behind. "Let me see Benny!"

Wykoff raised his hands in alarm. "Jack! Don't do this! Let Doctor Wilson go and we'll talk about this."

Wilson struggled in Jack's grasp, but he managed to keep hold of her. He yelled at Wykoff, "Open Benny's door! I want to see Benny!" He tightened his grip on Wilson's throat. She fought with him, tried to drag his hand from her throat.

Around Jack's grip, she croaked, "Open the damn door!"

Wykoff stared hard at Jack, then backed up to the door to isolation ward four. He pulled a ring of keys from his pocket. He glanced at Jack as his hands sorted through the keys. "Okay, Jack. I'm going to open the door. Don't hurt Doctor Wilson."

Jack watched Wykoff from behind Wilson. "Just open the door."

Wykoff found the right key and unlocked Benny's door. Jack pushed Wilson into Wykoff and dove for the door. It swung open, and Jack fell into Benny's room.

*Roughly Sixty Trillion Years Later*

The universe, for eons condensing unchecked, finally collapsed upon itself and exploded in a conflagration of light and energy, near-simultaneously annihilating and recreating everything in the entire universe.

*Stardate 53445.6*

Jack stared at Bashir's computer screen, biting at his thumb. Bashir keyed information into the computer at a high rate of speed, his nimble fingers hammering away at the keypads. Jack closed his eyes for a few moments, reorienting himself. One moment he was in that place, wherever it was, and the next, he was here. If he didn't know any better, he would have thought he was getting used to the jumps back and forth. Maybe he was finally losing his mind, and wouldn't *that* make the people at the Institute happy?

Jack opened his eyes and looked at the computer screen again. He pointed at a series of variables. "See, see? The gravimetric coefficient is all wrong."

Bashir nodded as he worked. "I noticed. Trying to compensate." He entered a few more commands, then ran the test program. Jack and Bashir watched a computer simulation of the galaxy expand, contract, and implode.

Jack stared at Bashir. "It didn't work."

Lauren, lounging on Bashir's couch, said, "You two are so boring to watch when you work." She slithered around to leer at Bashir. "Isn't there something better you could be doing with your time?"

Bashir nodded. "Actually, yes, there's plenty I can be doing. But," he glanced at Jack, "I thought I'd give Jack a hand."

Patrick, still dressed in his admiral's uniform, glanced up from his seat on the carpeted floor. A small pile of multi-colored building blocks lay scattered in front of him. He said, "It's not nice to humor Jack, you know."

Bashir stared at Patrick. "I'm not humoring him. . . ."

Jack crossed his arms. "Yes you are, but I was being polite and not mentioning it."

Bashir rolled his eyes at him. "What did you really expect, Jack? You come here in the middle of the night and drag me out of bed, and tell me a story about how you're trying to stop the galaxy from imploding." He paused, pointed at his computer screen. "Which, according to your calculations, isn't supposed to happen for several million years!"

"Trillion." Jack turned away, defensive. "I thought you Starfleet types were supposed to be protecting the galaxy."

Bashir sighed. "We can't protect the galaxy from itself!" He indicated the computer simulation again. "We're all going to be well long gone before that occurs, Jack. I expect the whole galaxy will be very different once that finally occurs. I certainly won't be around to see it."

Jack brushed him off. "Technicalities. We need to do this, Doctor Wykoff. And I need your help."

Bashir stared at him. "Doctor who?"

Jack bit at his thumb. "What?"

"Who is Doctor Wykoff?"

Jack glanced at Lauren and Patrick, saw no help there. "Doctor Wykoff?"

Bashir frowned. "Jack, I don't have time for your little games. You just called me Doctor Wykoff."

Jack mirrored Bashir's frown. "I did?"

Bashir nodded, emphatic. "Yes, just now." He turned a critical eye on Jack. "Are you feeling all right? You look pale."

Jack turned away from Bashir. "I'm fine." Then, that familiar pencil lead smell struck Jack, and he smiled.

*Roughly Sixty Trillion Years Later*

The universe, for eons condensing unchecked, finally collapsed upon itself and exploded in a conflagration of light and energy, near-simultaneously annihilating and recreating everything in the entire universe.

Jack turned around and looked at Benny, again standing by his writing-covered wall in isolation ward four. He had a new pencil in hand, but he was looking at Jack with an expectant look.

Jack smiled. "Here I am again."

Benny nodded. "Any closer to the end of the story?"

Jack shook his head. "It took a turn I wasn't expecting." He considered it, finally nodded in defeat. "I don't think I can save the universe."

Benny shrugged and giggled. "That's all right. No one expects you to do the impossible."

Jack sighed. "So what am I expected to do?" He tapped the side of his head. "I've been genetically altered to be smarter, stronger, and faster that most other people. If I can't save the universe, what can I do?"

Benny grinned as he rolled the pencil between his long fingers. "You just said it. You're smarter, stronger, and faster than most other people. I'm sure there's something you can find to do, something to contribute."

Jack sat on the floor and picked at his cuticle. "I'm open to suggestions. I've spent most of my time recently trying to save the universe."

Benny tapped his pencil against his lips then pointed it at Jack. "You should go to Bajor. To the Celestial Temple. I bet you'll find an answer there."

Jack stood up. "You think so?"

Benny grinned and gestured at a section of his writing. "I think so." He smiled at Jack, a strange twinkle in his eyes.

Jack stared back, and grinned.

*Stardate 53558.9*

Jack stared at his computer screen, nibbling at his thumb. The simulation displayed on the screen showed the universe expand, contract, then explode in glorious multicolored violence. He couldn't stop it, he knew that now, but the knowledge didn't bother him. There were other things he could do; other ways he could contribute his genetically enhanced intellect to the universe at large, and to a small corner of it in specific.

He keyed in some new commands. The screen switched to a schematic of Deep Space Nine and its nearby wormhole. According to the calculations he had made while visiting DS9 with his friends Bashir, Lauren, and Patrick, he was sure, absolutely sure, that the wormhole the Prophets lived in was going to collapse in fifty million years, give or take.

Jack grinned as he started a new program and began entering data. He had to find a way to prevent that from happening. The Bajorans and the Prophets needed to be protected. He wanted to do it for them and for Captain Sisko, wherever he was. He also wanted to do it for his new friend Benny, and, to be honest, for himself. If he couldn't save the universe, maybe he could save a part of it. Maybe.

Jack shrugged, grinned, and then got back to work. He just had to find out how his own story was going to come out.

# STAR TREK: VOYAGER

# The Fate
# of Captain Ransom

Rob Vagle

**Rob Vagle** is a writer living in Eugene, Oregon, who likes to work on both short stories and novels. His short stories have appeared in *Realms of Fantasy* and *Polyphony 5.*

It had come to this: imminent warp core breach.

Captain Rudolph Ransom sat in the *Equinox*'s engineering room as the warp core groaned and shuddered, sending plumes of gray smoke across the floor. His feet dangled in the haze and he braced himself on the console in front of him.

Burke's life sign faded. He had been killed by the attacking nucleogenic lifeforms, the ones the *Equinox* had used for fuel. *Damn it, Max,* Ransom thought. *You shouldn't have mutinied.*

The console chimed. On screen showed Captain Janeway on *Voyager*'s bridge. *"Captain?"* she said.

"Things didn't work out exactly as I planned but you have everyone worth getting," he said. *Voyager* had the last of his crew, five of them in all.

*"We're beaming you out of there,"* she said.

Heat radiated against his face. His back was slick with sweat. "This ship is about to explode. I've got to put some distance between us. I've accessed helm control."

Everyone worth getting didn't include him and he wanted *Voyager* to reach Earth. Janeway would get *Voyager* home without killing lifeforms for selfish means.

Janeway stood up from her chair. *"You can set auto-navigation and then transport to* Voyager.*"*

"There's no time!"

Another explosion ruptured from the core, sending up larger plumes of smoke. The ship rumbled from the stress and the vibrations shook through him.

"You've got a fine crew, Captain. Promise me you'll get them home."

*"I promise,"* she replied.

Ransom nodded in her direction, cut the communication, and powered the *Equinox* away from *Voyager.*

He picked up his synaptic stimulator and applied it behind his ear as the ship groaned from stress. He had used the stimulator to run away from responsibility and his conscience, but now he felt he had set right what he had done wrong. The stimulator would make death easier and much more peaceful.

Falling bulkheads and the billowing smoke of engineering faded away.

And he stood alone on an alien coast, a place he had never physically been. The odd spice smell hung in the air. Mist from the jade colored waves crashing into the rocks dampened his face.

He still had the physical sensations of his body back on the *Equinox.* His back was pressed against the chair, his uniform wet with sweat. Heavy vibrations no longer rippled through him. With some focus, he listened to the engineering room. No explosions, no sounds of falling bulkheads—only a drawn out drone, like the sound of a metal rod tracing the inside of a metal barrel.

The *Equinox* still hadn't exploded.

He raised his hand to remove the synaptic stimulator and the hand in his mind's eye rose to his neck. His body back on the *Equinox,* however, didn't move. He was paralyzed.

"Even at the moment of death, you still hide," she said.

He found Seven standing next him as if she'd been there all along. Her face was smooth and unblemished, the Borg implants gone from her forehead and cheekbones. Her long blond hair tossed in the breeze like the foam from the crashing waves below them. Her expression was cold and clinical. Her eyes scrutinized him.

Things hadn't been right with the synaptic stimulator ever since they encountered *Voyager.* His conscience manifested in the form of Seven from the *Voyager* crew—at least that's what he told himself. She appeared every time he used the damn alien device. He could no longer hide. He could no longer find peace on this alien coast.

"I earned this," he said. "I saved *Voyager* and I stopped Max from killing more of the lifeforms."

She looked to the sea and wind ruffled the flower-pattern dress she wore.

"Why are you here?" he asked. "Is there some kind of Borg technology you're using?"

"I am not here by technical apparatus. I am here only as a product of your imagination."

"If I don't want you here, you'll leave?"

"Immediately."

"Don't," he said and grabbed her arm. She looked down at his hand on her arm and then turned her attention back to him. "At least don't leave yet," he said.

He released her arm and she gazed back at the sea. "You wish to know why your body on the *Equinox* is paralyzed."

"Yes."

"You also wish to know why the ship hasn't been destroyed and why you're still alive."

"Correct," he said.

She looked at him, her eyes shimmering green like the alien sea. "Since you're paralyzed, the only direction is inward."

"Explain."

"You cannot move your body at will," she said. "Therefore you can't physically seek answers to your predicament. Use your mind to comprehend. Use your intellect. Use your imagination."

"Well, that's certainly logical," he said. "Is it practical?"

"You have no choice," she said, echoing the words he had used when he claimed using the lifeforms as fuel was his only option.

"Imagine," she said, "a rock wall on this coast and instead of caves exposed in the face of the rock wall, there are doors. Imagine as many doors as you wish. These doors are from your life."

She looked the same as when he had used the stimulator in the past. That Seven had talked like her and acted like her. The Seven before him now wasn't talking like Seven at all.

"Who are you?" he asked her.

She ignored the question. "Picture that rock wall and turn around."

When she turned, he turned as if he were her mirrored image. He faced a rock wall that had not been there a moment before. Dark, wet brown sand stretched several yards between him and the base of the wall. The wall vaulted approximately fifty feet meters and stretched along the coast for a hundred meters. The rock was black and porous and dotted among its face were doors, all doors that were familiar to him.

There was the red door to his dorm room at the academy. High up on the wall there was the door to his quarters on the *Equinox*. At the base of the wall there was a door where the rock met sand. No footprints, the sand was unmarked leading to the door of Brianna's apartment in the historic district of San Francisco. The number in brass was 772. The door was white, with blue trim. The door even had a doorknob.

He hadn't focused on the doors when Seven suggested it, yet here they were, all in a rock wall, doors pulled from his mind.

Their shadows stretched across the sand, Seven's dress billowing in the wind around her knees.

"Go through a door," she said.

He waited, feeling the chair in engineering warm against his back. If he listened carefully, he could hear the odd droning sound.

He staggered forward, his feet sinking in sand. Brianna was behind that door. A woman and partner, someone he had made up his mind a long time ago that he'd never see again. The Caretaker and the Delta Quadrant drove the final nail in that coffin.

Even as he worked his way through the thick, heavy sand, he knew this couldn't be real, that this was all in his head. However, his senses were alive as if this place was made of tangible mass, and not intangible, ethereal memories and dreams.

He ran his hand across the identity plate and the door opened inward. Then he looked over his shoulder and found Seven back there watching him. She nodded at him and Ransom went through the door.

The first thing he noticed was the wet dog smell. Brianna had a Great Pyrenees, Moby, a great white dog as big as a small horse. Moby had a thick, wooly coat and whenever Brianna took him out for walks in the cool, fall, evening air, Moby's coat would become damp, sometimes soaked if it rained. He found the smell pleasant in the moment, if only for the nostalgia of his days with Brianna in her apartment.

Moby ambled down the hallway, his thick, bushy tail waving. His dark, almond-shaped eyes sparkled and the dog gave Ransom a firm, soft, "woof." His lips parted and his tongue lolled out, giving Ransom the goofy Moby smile.

"Hello, Moby," Ransom said.

He didn't have to bend to pet the dog. Moby's head came up to his sternum and he stroked his head, letting his fingers catch the tangles of wooly hair down the back of his neck. The dog pressed his muzzle into his belly and made sniffing sounds.

The droning sound from the *Equinox* was remarkably hidden behind the sounds in Brianna's apartment: Moby's heavy-pawed steps, jazz music playing softly in the other room, footsteps on the hardwood floor.

"Rudy, I didn't hear you come in."

Brianna walked down the hall with a brilliant smile on her face. She had her black hair tied up in the back. She wore a white, waffle-weave robe with a plunging neckline that exposed her elegant neck and coffee-and-cream skin.

Ransom didn't know when the *Equinox* might explode, but hoped death would wait a few more moments.

Her smile remained, but she gave him a questioning look. "Well, aren't you coming in? Moby, let Rudy in."

She came forward and slapped Moby playfully on his back end. Ransom wondered about the date, the day, the year, of this memory of a moment now very much alive.

"I have a nice glass of shiraz waiting for you," she said.

Shiraz. He hadn't tasted any Earth wine for six years. Brianna preferred merlot, but she liked to treat him with his favorite wine.

"Computer, music off," she said.

In the living room, the lights were dim with a real fire burning in the hearth. She had been sitting on the floor, an Oriental rug covered with data files and slides. She was in research mode again—she was an exo-biologist just like he was. Her apartment had always been a flurry of data files, strewn clothes, dog hair. Brianna reached for the lone glass of wine on the marble coffee table and handed it to him.

"Thanks, Bri," he said.

In an instant she was narrowing in on an item on the data strewn floor like a bloodhound. She touched a finger to her lips and bent at the waist.

"Take a look at this, Rudy," she said and grabbed a padd in the far corner of the rug and returned to him.

"What's this?" he said even as he started to read it.

It was a report on the *Taurus* incident, an early crash site just after the discovery of warp drive.

"Go ahead, read it," she said and picked up her own glass of wine from the floor.

The ship *Taurus* had crashed on Vega I. The planet had lifeforms, intelligent, yet low-tech. The vagabond species called Sleaks used wheeled carts to pull their families around. The humans were secluded on a mountain with heavy snowfall. Without food and with increasing desperation, Derek Birkeson, the ship's captain, made the decision to eat a small band of Sleaks that seemed as desperate as they were. However, the Sleaks were worse off. Two had died already from starvation and the rest of them were weak with hunger. Instead of helping them, Birkeson had elected to kill them and use their flesh to feed his colony. He never told anyone but his first officer where the food had come from.

As he read the words on the padd, Ransom remembered reading this report in Brianna's apartment the first time. He felt a loss of vertigo as déjà vu pressed upon him. No longer did this seem like his imagination dreaming up a safe place. No. This was a memory, but so much more powerful because it was immediate and filled the moment as if it were happening now, in real time.

Sadly, he had to humor Brianna and read the padd. When he had finished reading it the first time, he had told Brianna that there was no excuse for that kind of desperation, that it was unethical to kill other intelligent, indigenous lifeforms. He had also said he'd never do something like that because he was incapable of it.

A lump formed in his throat and his chest grew heavy. He remembered the choice he had made—to kill nucleogenic lifeforms just to get *Equinox* home.

Brianna didn't know the man who stood before her in this relived moment and all he had gone through.

He handed data padd back to her. "No excuse for what they've done, no matter how desperate the situation."

She took the data pad and considered him. "You'd never do something like that, Rudy."

When he tried to smile, it came out painful and hollow. It must have showed for Brianna's face fell.

"Who knows what I might do in that situation," he said. He didn't want to have this discussion with her. What had they talked about this night he lived once before?

He sipped the wine and glanced at the fire dancing on piled wood. On the mantel there was a picture of him and Brianna standing together in Golden Gate Park, the miniature grandfather clock that had belonged to Brianna's great great grandfather, and the lucite gem from his contact with the Yridians that he had given to Brianna. Everything familiar. Everything the same. Only he had changed and he could not get over it.

"Rudy, is something wrong?"

The wine was heavy and immediately went to work, loosening the tightness of his regret and guilt. This time when he turned to her, his smile came gently, easily.

"No," he said, and to steer the conversation even farther away, he added, "What are you researching?"

She ignored his question and set her glass down on the coffee table. Then she did the same with his glass. When she slipped her arms around him, he wrapped his arms around her. She considered him again, looking him in the eyes, searching. He felt like he was under a microscope, but it was a warm, pleasant feeling.

"Now, what is wrong with you tonight?" she asked.

"Tired," he tried.

"You're acting odd."

"I'm fine, Bri," he said.

"When will you be back from mission?" she asked.

Judging from the digital calendar on the mantel, he'd be lost in the Delta Quadrant in mere days. He felt regret that he couldn't change the past here.

He kissed Bri's forehead and said, "Not soon enough."

Hours later, with Brianna sound asleep next to him, he found that when one's visual cortex was engaged, sleep was impossible. He felt no fatigue and he wasn't tired. He couldn't close his eyes. In fact, he realized, he hadn't blinked since putting on the stimulator.

He listened to Brianna's calm, rhythmic breathing, and felt envious. Instead of lying in bed and staring at a ceiling he hadn't thought about in six years, he got up.

He knew where he was going—out the front door and onto the beach again if he could. And if he was lucky, he'd find Seven there again. He wanted to know what all of this meant. He should have been dead by now, engulfed within the explosion of the *Equinox*.

A light came on in the foyer, above the front door, as he approached. The light shined on Moby, the huge mass of wooly hair sleeping on the floor, blocking the door. He raised his head when he heard Ransom coming. The dog opened his mouth and said, "The problem isn't with the synaptic stimulator."

He stopped and grabbed the wall, staring at the dog. Things definitely weren't right.

Moby's tail began to wag, the thick tail pounding loudly against the door. He stared at Moby, wondering if he had heard the dog correctly. Moby didn't say another thing and Ransom wasn't in the mood to ask him to repeat it.

"Excuse me, Moby," he said as he moved for the door.

Moby gathered his legs up under him, a slow, cumbersome set of moves for such a large dog, and sauntered into the living room.

Ransom whispered, "The problem isn't with the synaptic stimulator."

Then he felt it was true, as if his subconscious had sent him a message through Moby. There hadn't been a problem with the synaptic stimulator before encountering *Voyager,* so there was some truth to the notion. And he couldn't eliminate the stimulator yet as the source of the problem until he gathered more information.

Information he'd get outside Brianna's front door.

The door opened and revealed the alien beach and Seven stood with her back to the rolling, tumbling waves as if she had never left.

He took long strides, stepping through the thick sand, his arms swinging widely back and forth. The ocean wind blew in his face, smelling like spice, and the wind howled as it whipped over his ears.

Seven, or not-Seven, looked at him impassively.

"Who are you?" he asked when he reached her. "You're not Seven."

"You are correct," she said.

"Again: who are you?"

"I will show you," she said and touched him behind the ear.

Seven and the ocean and sky behind her flickered, and he found himself aboard the *Equinox* again, the droning sound now loud in his ears. Columns of thick smoke that had been rolling across the ceiling and floor in engineering were frozen. The smoke looked like cotton or snow, something he could just brush away. A bulkhead with other tumbling debris and dust hung in midair between the ceiling and the floor.

He was paralyzed and couldn't remove his hands from the armrests of the chair. He could only move his eyes around inside their sockets. His heart didn't seem to beat and he felt trapped and claustrophobic. He wanted to scream. He wanted to run. He was suffocating.

Seven flickered, her image vanishing, and in her place floated a specter-like species with no legs and at least four arms. Its face had two large black eyes and a bulbous head, and looking into its eyes, Ransom thought they held compassion. Its body was covered in a blue-gray skin that looked delicate.

He looked back at the frozen-falling bulkhead. One corner had ticked closer to the engineering floor and the surrounding falling debris turned to reflect light from the blowing warp core.

Then he was back on the beach again with the droning sound hidden behind the sounds of crashing waves and the wind blowing across his ears. Not-Seven removed her hand from behind his ear and he staggered back. His heart hammered inside his chest and he felt the urge to fall to his knees to get his bearings back.

"The human mind doesn't process fast enough for you to see us," she said. "However, when you are in a perilous situation or in the moment before your death, your mind speeds up and the perception of passing time slows. This is the only way you can see and interact with us."

He looked up at not-Seven and said, "I was paralyzed."

"Yes," she said. "To study your mind at an increased rate of speed, we isolated the mind by injecting a paralytic. The synaptic stimulator added an interactive interface."

"Why the disguise?"

"We only became the person your mind came up with and we

initiated contact after you attached the stimulator on your way to certain death."

Being a test subject infuriated him, but when he thought about those nucleogenic lifeforms and what he had done to them he became chagrined—how fitting at the moment of his death he had become a test subject for another species' purpose.

"I had planned to die in peace," he said.

"We have no plans to save your life."

He smiled at the species' pure and blunt truth. He was also struck with the continual use of the plural pronoun as if the species shared a hive mind. "May I be left alone?"

"Yes, we can obey your wishes. Understand that we are offering you something close to immortality. We can increase the speed of your working mind and slow time even further. Then you can explore all areas of your life behind other doors."

Seven suddenly focused on something behind him.

He heard Brianna say, "Rudy?"

When he turned he found Brianna walking though the sand. Her door stood open with Moby at the threshold.

She looked distressed. "What are you doing out here, Rudy?"

For no logical reason at all, he'd expected it was impossible for Brianna to walk out of her apartment and onto this alien beach. In fact, she didn't seem surprised. As she walked toward him, her concern was with him, never taking her eyes off of him. The beach didn't matter to her. The missing San Francisco night didn't matter to her—it was all perfectly normal for her.

"Rudy," she grabbed his hand and pulled, "what are you doing in the middle of the street during the middle of the night?"

He staggered and let her walk him back to the apartment. She hung onto his arm as if he might get lost otherwise.

"I'm in the middle of the street," he repeated to her.

"Yes," she said impatiently. She gave him a sideways glance.

"I'm not doing well, Bri," he said.

"Let's get you inside," she said.

They waited as Moby turned his bulk around and ambled

further into the apartment. Brianna walked Ransom to the couch where he knocked his shin against the corner of the marble coffee table. Ransom grimaced and groaned, and collapsed on the couch.

"Sorry," she said.

The pain was real. It amazed him how strong the mind was to create this illusion.

Did he want this illusion?

All he had wanted was a peaceful death.

"You're not fit for the mission," she said as she removed his boots. "You weren't walking in your sleep. Unless you put your boots on in your sleep."

"I wasn't sleepwalking," he said.

She looked at him suspisciously.

"You want to tell me what's going on?" she said.

"You think I'm leaving on the *Equinox* tomorrow," he said.

"Not the way you're acting, you're not."

He sighed. "Yes. But if it wasn't for my condition, you'd fully expect me to leave tomorrow."

"That's right."

"In a matter of days the *Equinox* is going to be lost in the Delta Quadrant and there's nothing I can do because this isn't time travel."

She touched his arm. "Rudy."

"This is all in my head, Bri."

"You're not making sense."

She was right and he knew it. The conversation suddenly seemed pointless and he felt fractured, pieces of him scattered throughout the universe and untethered from time and space.

Yet he had no doubts about his past, crimes and all. The Delta Quadrant had been a dark and horrible place. It had brought out the worse in him.

She sat close to him, her knee touching his thigh. He grabbed her hand and said, "Listen to me, Bri."

The part of him that longed to get home back in the Alpha

Quadrant raised its head and screamed. That's what this was all about. It would be easy to pretend his body didn't sit in a chair on board the *Equinox* heading for certain death. It would also be easy to live here with Brianna and never leave. Of course it would be all in his imagination, living days or months or years—who knew?—but there was a romantic, carefree joy to the idea.

All he had wanted was a peaceful death.

She squeezed his hand. "Go on, Rudy."

Another part of him, in an equally loud voice, raised its head and claimed he didn't deserve this last shot at paradise, a last look at a life lived, and perhaps to linger there.

When Bri squeezed his hand again, he said, "I have a confession to make."

Her face clouded as if all the blood had drained from her face. "You're scaring me."

"I have killed aliens, using them as fuel in an attempt to get the *Equinox* home," he said.

Her brow furrowed and with much tension in her face she said, "When? In your sleep?"

She released his hand and pushed it away. "This is just ridiculous, Rudy."

"I need to go back out, Bri." He said.

"In the street?"

He thought about it and nodded. From her point of view it was the street.

"I need for you to know this. I didn't think I was capable of it until I lost over half of my crew trying to get them home. We were hungry. We were alone. Like Birkeson I made an unethical choice. I used lifeforms for fuel to get us home."

She threw her hands in the air and looked at the ceiling. "Oh, why are you telling me this?" Then she gave him a mournful look. "You're here now."

He stood and her eyes followed him. "The *Equinox* never made it back. Warp core overload."

She gave him a hurtful smile and grabbed his hand. "I still love you, Rudy. Don't go back out there."

She forgave him. Of course she would. His mind would be comfortable with that and he could just stay in her apartment. Around the room he saw the photograph of the two of them on the mantel, the empty bottle of wine, and Moby sitting in the corner observing all of this. This had been his life and it had been lost long ago. He couldn't go home again, not even in his imagination.

He looked down at Brianna and she pulled lightly on his arm.

"I have to go," he said.

His arm slipped from her grip and her face became pinched in frustration. "Rudy!"

He walked to the door with Moby at his side. The dog looked up at him and said, "Perhaps someday she'll learn what you had done."

Then Moby let out a deep "Woof."

Well, he was confident *Voyager* would get back to Earth. When he reached the door, it opened to the beach again. He ran to the lone figure on the beach.

"Rudy!" Brianna called.

Not-Seven with her relentless cold stare watched him approach.

"I wish to be alone," he said. "There's nothing I want to relive in my past, not behind any door."

"Come back inside!" Brianna called.

Not-Seven nodded. "Very well."

"Rudy! Talk to me!"

He refused to turn around and look at Brianna. Her voice was so real to his mind, as well as her pain. His heart broke to hear it.

Not-Seven stared at him.

"Go away," he said. "Leave me alone."

Then she was gone, vanishing like the sky had sucked her up.

Brianna's voice picked up, louder, and she said, "Come back. . . ."

Suddenly she was cut off.

When he turned, the doors were gone and the rock wall loomed before him. The silence was deafening. His heart broke again, sharper and deeper.

"Goodbye, Bri," he said.

He sat down on a rock and stared at the sea. Something crashed in engineering, but he ignored it, focusing on the horizon.

The *Equinox* shuddered toward certain destruction.

And Captain Rudolph Ransom waited for, and welcomed, oblivion.

# A Taste of Spam

L. E. Doggett

**L. E. Doggett** lives in the Central San Joaquin Valley of California, the small city of Clovis to be exact. He lives with his wife of twenty-eight years and a daughter of seventeen years, along with a little dynamo of a dog they adopted and a cat that adopted them. The family attends a dynamic, hopeful church. Louis is a blue collar worker with a collage education. He got interested in *Star Trek* when he and his dad watched the original *Star Trek* when it first aired. The series inspired daydreams that had him acting like a crew member with the same duties as Chekov. At times he thought he was born two hundred years too early. Now he is an aspiring prowriter (he has been a non-pro writer for quite a while), hoping this story is the first of a lifelong series of sells. He also thanks his wife, Dean for his advice to writers, and Margaret Clark, and Paula Block.

"Need a face-lift? Wrinkles removed, or need your natural wrinkles redone? Come to the Beautiful Being Institute. We do beautifying surgery for multi-species. Whatever your species considers young-looking, we can do . . ."

"Get that, that . . . advertisement off of the view screen!"

Captain Janeway of the Federation *Starship Voyager* did not raise her voice, but everyone on the bridge knew they had better do their best to carry out her order, or they were in big trouble.

Ensign Harry Kim standing behind her and to her right, glanced at the view screen that made up the wall of the front of the bridge.

Few of the bridge crew heard his uncharacteristic, "Damn," under his breath, as his hands flew across the control board he was standing behind. He pressed keys like a squirrel on uppers, but nothing he did would delete the ad. It was the latest in a series of such ads that had been plaguing them for the last few days. It was like the computer didn't know that there anything there to delete.

A second later the image of the alien building disappeared, along with the announcer's voice. The stars that had been showing before the ad started were again showing.

"Good work, Ensign."

"That wasn't my doing, Captain. I think it just finished the message."

"That means it will be back."

"Most likely, Captain, along with new messages," stated Commander Tuvok.

Kim continued, "I have tried to block the signal that keeps adding new messages, but so far I have had little success."

"I want you two to work full time, to find out how those messages keep popping up, and where we picked up this intrusion into our computer. Most important, stop them."

A few hours and four more messages later, the bridge crew met in a conference room.

Captain Janeway spoke. "Any success in stopping those ads?"

Both Harry Kim and Tuvok said no. Neither could find any way to stop the ads.

Tom Paris asked, "Where did this spam come from?"

Neelix asked, "Spam? My translator stated that was Special Pressed American Meat."

"It's a computer term from the late twenty-first century, meaning unwanted E-mail usually made up of product advertisements."

Neelix nodded his head to indicate he understood.

"Where did we pick up this . . . spam?" the Captain asked.

Kim answered, "I believe we picked up a virus in that sector we went through three weeks ago."

Paris said, "I think it was a 'trojan horse' rather than a virus."

"It infected our computer, so it was a virus."

Paris opened his mouth, but then Janeway spoke up. "I really don't care what it is called, we need to put a stop to it. It is a danger to the ship. If one of those ads were to run while we are in a battle, trying to communicate with a warrior group, or someone we need supplies from, or when the ship is maneuvering through an asteroid belt, the ship would be put in danger."

"We would still have sensors, Captain, and they are more accurate than visual images."

"That may be true, Tuvok, but I like to see what is going on. It would handicap our responses, possibly slowing down our response to dangerous levels. Do it. This . . . spam is so blasted frustrating."

"Yes, Captain. I will concentrate on solving this problem."

"Good."

Two days later Janeway had the ship stop for a few hours to study a star that looked like two stuck together. Tom said it reminded him of a double-yoked egg. A minute into watching the sun, an ad for a multi-species dentist appeared.

With a whispered "Damn," Kim ran his fingers over his controls, pressing various touch points. He touched certain points twice and even three times, but his attempts had no effect on the ad. He frowned as he concentrated on his board. Another ad started and he tried to ignore it.

An hour later in sickbay, Tom Paris was arriving for his shift. The place was empty so he sat down to await the appearance of the doctor. A second later the Doctor came into being behind him.

Tom's first indication that he was not alone anymore came as he heard the Doctor's voice.

"Are you ashamed of the size of your sexual organ?"

His head spun around and his mouth fell open, and he stared at the Doctor as the holobeing continued, "Most females of many species are attracted to larger male sexual organs. If you are of a race that this description fits, and if your organ is smaller than you feel comfortable with, comm us, or come by our offices in the palatial Sinton Space Wheel. We can fix any sexual organ of any species. We are long-term experts. You may need surgery, or need to order chemical XY. It comes in pill form, a spray form, or a lotion you can rub on."

Paris said, "You too, Doctor?"

The Doctor looked puzzled, then thoughtful, then finally a look of incredulousness came over his face. "That wasn't me."

His image blinked out for a second and when it came back he continued, "I purged my matrix of that ad and two others I found, but I don't know how those files got there. I don't know if I can stop any others from infecting my matrix. . . . You need to do something."

"The ship's computer has been infected by some type of spam virus, or trojan horse. Somehow it got past your filters. Kim and Tuvok are working overtime to purge *Voyager*'s system."

"Tell them to hurry. This is embarrassing, and I can't work with my usual genius if I have to stop to clear my matrix of these things every few minutes."

On his way out the door Tom promised that they would be doing their best.

The next day as Tom arrived on the bridge, he noted that Harry was there already. His friend looked frustrated and tired, as if he had been up all night working on something he hadn't been able to finish.

*Which he probably had been,* Tom thought. He glanced at the Vulcan officer, but Tuvok looked as rested as usual. Working twenty-four-hour shifts didn't bother him as much as it did humans.

Looking closer though, Paris saw a tightening around the Vulcan's lips. So he was just as frustrated as Kim.

Just then Captain Janeway walked in and sat in her chair.

Tom said, "Good morning, Captain."

She nodded to him as she turned to Tuvok, saying, "Were you able to get rid of the spam program?"

As if in answer her question, music started playing and colors flashed on the view screen. As they all turn to look at the forward screen, pictures started flashing across it. They started on the right side, sliding across the screen and disappearing on the left. It was one picture right after the other.

The images slid by rather quickly, but the bridge crew could make out that the pictures were of females of various species. Or at least they thought they were all female, it was hard to tell with some of them. Some of the females were gyrating, while wearing skimpy outfits.

As the parade of females continued, some seemed to be just standing or sitting, while exposing various secondary sexual parts of their bodies.

*Breasts,* thought Tom, all those woman are showing their breasts.

*Or what passes for such,* he added as an image appeared of nonhumanoid pulling off a tunic and showing something that looked like an indentation in her side. It had what looked like a nipple on the bottom of it, but the picture went by too fast to be sure.

A few seconds later as the women were pulling off their pants or slipping off what looked like half robes, a voice started.

It said in perfect English, "Lonely tonight? Far away from the females of your species? Just feeling like having some fun by yourself? Then tune into our channel. We have terabytes of images of each of these females. Our images include visual, 3-D, and holographic with interactive programs so the girls will do whatever you want them to do."

"Turn that off!" Janeway practically shouted as Kim shook himself out of his reverie and started working on his console.

Neither her command nor his actions stopped the show.

The voice continued, this time in a husky female voice. "If we don't have the type of female you are looking for, we would sure to have something close. As you know you males can be aroused by the opposite sex of many species. So come on by and check us out. We can send you the images over your comm, or you can stop at one of our places of business located throughout the Windu sector of space."

By that time the females in the streams of images were showing more than just their nude tops. Both Harry and another human male were trying to take quick covert glances at the images while still working. Tom was staring open mouthed.

Janeway said, "I want that off now and no repeats."

Tom said, "But Captain, this one isn't bad, it can raise morale."

"Tom Paris," she said in a dangerous tone.

"Opps, sorry, Captain. You're right, that one needs to be purged right away."

"We have enough trouble with these . . . ads, on board this ship without a comment like that."

"Hey, that looked like a picture of a set of twins I knew back on Earth," Tom said.

Tuvok said, "I believe it was of two females of a species that are co-joined. We had business dealings with members of that race six months ago."

"Yeah, I remember them all right, but are you sure these two were of that race?"

"Yes, I am. And it would be physically impossible for images of the twins, you know, to get here before we arrived."

"With these two girls I wouldn't be too sure about that. They probably would appreciate having their images where many types of men could look at them."

Before Tuvok could respond, Captain Janeway said, "As fascinating as this conversation is we need to clear *Voyager*'s computer of this . . . and all the other, um, spam."

"I have been trying, Captain, but it is very resistant to normal procedures," Kim said.

"This is not a normal program, Captain, it is very resistant to standard methods of cleansing the computer."

"You are going to have to find something that isn't normal, in that case. Especially since this is getting worse. Two weeks ago, when it started, it just affected our communications. That was bad when it kept interfering with my comm signals and interrupted my log entries. Now it's affecting ship operations. I have already explained why that is serious. Every time we think we got rid of it, it comes back, and now it's putting that," here she pointed to the screen with the fading music and images, "on our viewscreen."

She clenched her hand and said, "I want it gone! Do you understand, gentlemen? I don't care how, or if you have to shut down the computer and reboot it, I want it gone."

With an audible swallow Kim said, "Yes, ma'am."

Tuvok said, "We will do our best, Captain," in his normal unflappable tone.

Later that day the senior staff were in the conference room discussing the problem.

Paris was saying, "I'd like to know where we picked it up."

Tuvok said, "I believe we picked it up three weeks ago, as we were transversing the business district, when we stopped to trade for supplies."

"I remember that. There seemed to be a lot of businesses set up in that area, more than we have ever come across, even in the Alpha Quadrant."

"Just the type of place to pick up a spam virus," Kim said.

Tom said, "Trojan horse—they had a different purpose than viruses."

Just then the doors slid open, and Janeway walked in.

"As I said gentlemen, I don't care what it is, as long as we get rid of it."

Tuvok said, "It's a very sophisticated program, Captain. I would like to meet the being who designed it. The way it infiltrated our filters, penetrated our firewall, then learned our language, is remarkable."

"It might be remarkable, Tuvok, but we are still going to purge it, every bit of it, from our systems."

"Yes, Captain, we were just discussing how to do that."

"Have you come up with any solutions?"

"No, Captain, but we are still working it."

Kim added, "We do think its main program is hiding from us, We have been able to delete certain aspects of it, and copies, but we can't find its main file, which is why it keeps coming back."

Tom said thoughtfully, "I wonder if it's hiding in the holodeck matrix."

"Why would you think that?"

"The Doctor was infected a few days ago, by three ads, right after he spent some time on the holodeck."

"I've run a through check on the holodeck, and the Doctor's matrixes."

"Run another one then, and dig even deeper this time, Tuvok."

"Yes, Captain."

Captain Janeway stood, and started to walk toward the door, but as both parts of the door slid sideways, she paused.

She turned and said, "Do you think that whoever designed this infernal spam virus would be able to undo it?"

"Without talking to him directly, I think it's probable."

"In that case I want to find that individual and have him remove it."

"I believe Kim and I will be able to find it and delete it."

"You might be able to, but I want to make sure we get rid of it. We will turn around and head back to the place were we traded for the supplies."

Just then an image appeared on the monitor on the table. Something that sounded like it could be music sounded, followed by a voice saying, "Need legal help? call us at Bong, Bong and Biennium." The last name was pronounced a deep stretched out B sound. "If you have been hurt in some type of industrial accident or by a careless ship pilot, comm us and we can help you. We know the laws of a hundred different societies. Comm us right now, we have assistants standing by."

Janeway stared at the ad then said, "And I want you to pilot us at full warp, Tom."

"Full warp, Captain? We haven't done that for months."

"I know, but I want this fixed. Full warp and don't spare the engines, Tom."

As she turned back around and went through the door, she finished with, "I want this problem fixed, yesterday."

The next day Captain Janeway entered the mess hall, sniffing as she did.

She said, "Trying something different, Neelix?"

"Yes indeed, Captain. I had to dig deep in your computer files, but I finally found something that explained what everyone was talking about these last two weeks."

After a look of puzzlement appeared on her face he continued, "I realize you were talking about E-mails and comm signals, but as I mentioned before, every time you said the name of that virus, my translator translated it as processed meat. Since one of my duties is cook, I decided to find out all I could about this processed meat. I found a program for the replicators. I replicated twenty of those little loafs of Spam. I read that one of the favorite ways to serve it, was with eggs."

She said. "You mean you're frying some spam?!"

He said, "Yes, ma'am," while missing the incredulous look on her face, "I replicated some omelets and some bread since people also like, um, sandwiches made with fried Spam, there is also a recipe for something called teriyaki Spam with fried rice I'm thinking of trying, and for those adventurous eaters there is jalapeños and Spam. Those jalapeños sound interesting, I might try them with other dishes."

Neelix paused in his oration, asking, "Captain, are you still here?"

He looked around the corner of his work station, seeing no one he shrugged his shoulders.

He mumbled to himself, "She must have been called to the bridge for something, I need to save some of this Spam for her."

A week later *Voyager* was docked in front of one of many stations. Her bow was pointed directly at one of the many sets of windows in the middle widest bulge of three that made up this particular station.

Janeway said, "Are you sure this is the business the original signal came from?"

"I'm ninety-seven point eight percent positive, Captain. I was able to back-trace the comm signal to here. As you know, Lieutenant Paris was correct, the program was hiding in the holodeck matrix, and even though I wasn't able to delete it, I was able to dig into it. Once I found the basic section, I was able to find the designers' signature. This company's logo was part of the signature. They evidently wanted everyone to know who was responsible for it."

"Could it be a fake to throw us off the track?"

"I would speculate not. The comm signal validates what I found, but the possibility does exist, which is why I am only ninety-seven point eight percent positive."

"That's good enough for me."

The captain paused, then said, "Hail them, Ensign."

"With pleasure, Captain."

A few seconds later the image of the station morphed into an image of a being sitting behind a desk. He was humanoid, with what looked like blue feathers slicked back against the top of his head. He wearing a thin blue jacket over a light blue vest.

He smiled and said, "Captain Janeway, I am Suddon Blyth Conction Ulllma. What can I do for you this fine hour?"

"You can start by sending for one of your employees, a Rando Setten Curlu. We have something of his we would like to return," Janeway said in a pleasant voice.

"I'm not sure if we can get him at the moment. He is busy working on a new project for us."

"I can understand how someone of his talent would be busy, but if you don't get him right now, I'm going to blow a hole all the way through your establishment," she answered, still using the pleasant tone.

While was still sounding pleasant, she made a small movement with her hand, above her head. Tuvok, who had been watching her, ran his hands over his weapons control.

Suddon Blyth Conction Ulllma continued to smile until she finished the threat, and then he looked puzzled and said, "Could you repeat the last? There must be something wrong with our translator."

"I believe you heard me correctly."

Janeway leaned forward and her tone changed to one of cold steel. "If you don't get Rando Setten Curlu up here immediately, I will unleash a barrage of phaser fire, powerful enough to blow your whole business establishment away."

It looked like he swallowed, then pressed a button on his desk, saying something too low for the comm pickup. A few minutes later another being, obviously of the same race, rushed into the room.

This new being's clothes looked disheveled. His was missing the jacket and vest, but was dressed much the same as the others. He, however, had red and bright yellow feathers on top of his head, some of which were sticking straight up.

He said, "I am Rando Setten Curlu. What can I do for you?"

"You can undo the spam program your company downloaded into our computer."

His eyes narrowed and he said, "Spam? I don't understand."

"Sorry, I meant the program you designed to display all those ads with."

"Oh, yes. That was one of my better works, my personal favorite."

"Yes, I've been told how ingenious it is, but we want it gone and we can't seem to be able to get rid of it. We want you to take it back."

"Urr, I'm . . ."

"I really don't care if you are busy. If you don't take it back we are going to wreck your employer's business."

Suddon Blyth Conction Ulllma said something to him in a language the translator didn't translate. His eyes widened.

He said, "I need access to your computer."

"That can be arranged."

"I need to get a piece of equipment. I'll be right back."

Janeway waved her hand at him, and he rushed out the door.

While they waited, Suddon Blyth Conction Ulllma said, "What you are doing is against the law. You can get into tremendous legal trouble."

"Where we come from, so is infecting our computer with a program we don't want. Besides, we have consulted with Bong, Bong and Biennium."

She pronounced the last with a deep stretched-out B sound.

Suddon Blyth Conction Ulllma's eyebrows went up as he heard the name.

Janeway continued, "And according to them we are within our legal rights to return something we did not order."

Before he could answer Rando Setten Curlu was back. He was now carrying a small electronic device.

"I am now ready."

Janeway turned her head slightly and nodded in Kim's direction. He pressed two spots on his console and Rando Setten Curlu disappeared in a cascade of twinkling lights.

A second later he reappeared on the *Voyager*'s bridge standing in front of Captain Janeway. He looked around in surprise, then looked back at Janeway.

She said, "We are in a hurry. Your little program interrupted a journey we are on."

He stared at her and she said, "You can access our computer over there," pointing toward Tuvok's work station.

He swallowed again and said, "Yes, of course. I'll get right on it."

"And make sure you do just that. My security officer, who is a computer expert, will be watching you."

He looked up at the Vulcan, who stood a quarter of a meter higher than Rando Setten Curlu, then got to work.

Twenty-six minutes later, after tapping two buttons on his device, then two more on the console, he straightened and said, "I'm done. The program is completely purged from all of your systems, and there will be no residual effects."

"Good. After a check by my men, we will be on our way."

Tuvok and Ensign Kim ran a complete diagnostic followed by some basic commands.

When they were done Tuvok said, "Everything checks out, Captain."

"Good."

She waved her hand again and Kim sent Rando Setten Curlu back to where he belonged.

She said, "Let's get back on target for the Alpha quadrant. Full warp until we are out of this sector."

"Yes, Captain," Kim said with a smile.

Once they were on their way Tom asked, "Would you have really blown a hole all the way through their business?"

"No, not really, there would be too much collateral damage. Starfleet frowns on that type of thing."

Tom said, "Nice touch using the name of the law company they advertise for."

"Thank you. I figured that, even though we didn't contact them in reality, their name would confuse Suddon Blyth Conction Ullma. And I figured that law would be one most societies, especially one based on commerce, would have."

After a pause she said, "Tuvok, did he take along the surprise we left for him?"

Tuvok responded, "I watched him the whole time, and as expected, he didn't take the time to look over the program fully. I believe the virus I placed in his program's matrix is still intact. It will be copied and will infect every copy of this program it comes in contact with. After an unspecified amount of time his personal favorite program will cease functioning."

Janeway smiled, as she relaxed back into her chair.

# Adjustments

Laura Ware

**Laura Ware** lives in Central Florida and considers sanity to be an overrated state of mind. She writes a weekly column that appears in the *Highlands County News Sun* and has been known to mention *Star Trek* on occasion. She also is a contributing writer for *The International Book of Days*. Her first fiction sale is "Adjustments," but she hopes it won't be her last! She would like to thank God for giving her her writing ability, her husband and sons for their support and patience, the *Strange New Worlds* Yahoo! Group, and the Oregon Writer's Network, for all their instruction, encouragement, and the occasional smacks upside the head. You can read her ramblings at lauraslook.blogspot.com.

"I hate you!" Naomi screamed at her father. "I wish we'd never come back from the Delta Quadrant!"

"Naomi!" her mother said, but the girl wasn't interested in hearing anything her parents had to say. She whirled around and stomped to her room, locking the door behind her.

"Let her be, Samantha," Naomi heard her father say. "She needs to absorb the news."

"Gresk, this isn't like her," Naomi's mother said. "She's usually so mature . . ."

Naomi flung herself on her bed and grabbed a pillow. She put it over her head, covering her ears so she wouldn't have to hear her parents talk about her.

She knew she wasn't being mature. She didn't care. Everything had seemed to go wrong ever since *Voyager* had returned to Earth.

Everyone else was so happy to be here. All of Naomi's friends had scattered to different places, busy with their lives. Too busy to keep in touch with her.

Even Seven, who had never been to Earth, was spending time with her Aunt Irene on her farm in Kansas. Naomi had gotten one message from the former Borg so far. There had been no mention in it if or when Seven would return to San Francisco.

Then there was the matter of her father. Though they had talked some while *Voyager* had still been in the Delta Quadrant, she still felt as if he were a stranger.

Her mother, on the other hand, was delighted to be reunited with him. She started spending a lot of time with him, and

Naomi, who was used to having a large portion of her mother's attention, felt abandoned.

And tonight, after dinner, her parents had sprung the worst news possible. They had decided to accept assignments on Ktaria VII, and not return to space.

Naomi had been appalled. "Why?"

"Sweetheart, you both have been gone for so long," her father said, an arm around her mother. "I thought it would be great if you had a chance to spend time on my homeworld, get to know that part of you."

"But not be in space?" Naomi felt tears start. "Mom, you don't want to do this, do you?"

"Naomi, all you've known is life on a spaceship. We both think this would be good for you."

"But it's not what I want!" Naomi shouted.

The argument had continued until Naomi's declaration of hate. Now, alone in her dark room, a pillow over her head, she shed hot tears on the unfairness of life.

Naomi slipped out of the quarters Starfleet had assigned her family. Her parents were asleep.

Naomi got outside. The sky was clear, stars liberally sprinkled against a black background. The moon was not in the sky.

Naomi felt her throat close as she looked up at the stars. How could she not be among them? How could she stay on one planet, when there were so many to explore?

She bit her lip. There had to be a way. If her parents were going to insist on living on Ktaria VII, then Naomi would have to figure a way to go into space without them.

She walked without any clear idea of where she was going. The cool air made her shiver. She had not thought to bring a sweater. The temperature on *Voyager* had always been controlled.

Naomi rubbed her arms and shuffled her feet through the grass. She heard some music drifting on a breeze and raised her head.

A small building had light spilling out of its windows. Someone had opened a door, which had let out the sound of music. Naomi frowned as she tried to recall the genre. She thought it might be something called "jazz."

Naomi found her feet taking her to the place. She opened the door and felt warmth, music, and noise wash over her.

It was a bar, she realized. A band was set up on a small stage in a corner. Four-legged wooden tables were scattered around the room. A long bar with a huge mirror behind it was to her left.

"In or out," a voice said behind her. Naomi jumped and turned to see a tall human in a Starfleet uniform frowning down at her. His bearded face looked familiar, but she couldn't place him.

She noted the pips on his collar. "Sorry, Commander," she said, taking a few steps inside the bar. The man, frowning slightly, moved past her to sit at the bar.

Naomi didn't see any familiar faces. She wondered if she should leave. But it felt so comfortable here.

"Hey!"

The commander was looking at her. Naomi walked over to him. He cocked his head. "You're a little young for this place, aren't you? What's your name?"

"Naomi Wildman," she said. "And I'm old enough."

A grin split the man's face, and Naomi relaxed. "I bet you are." He stuck out his hand. "Will Riker."

She shook his hand, awed. "From the *Enterprise*?"

"The one and only," Riker said. "And you were on *Voyager*, weren't you?"

"How did you know?"

"Your name," Riker said. "Captain Janeway speaks highly of you."

"She does?" Naomi felt herself blushing.

"Absolutely," Riker assured her. "Captain Picard and I have been part of the group debriefing Captain Janeway, and I've had a lot of chances to hear about you. Not just from the captain—Seven of Nine also has had some complimentary things to say."

"Seven? She's here?" Naomi asked.

"She returned from Kansas a couple of days ago. Captain Janeway had wanted to give her some more time to acclimate, but there's just too much we need to know." He looked closely at Naomi. "You look pretty chilly. Have you ever had hot chocolate?"

Naomi shook her head.

"Well, belly up to the bar, as they say," Riker said, slapping the red-covered stool next to him. "Barkeep! A hot chocolate with whipped cream for my young friend here."

Naomi slid onto the bar stool, a mixture of feelings colliding within her. Seven was back, but hadn't come to see Naomi. And it didn't address her main problem of getting into space.

"It's been hard, hasn't it?" Riker asked.

"Sir?"

"Coming home."

Naomi sighed. "This isn't home."

"Ah," Riker said. The bartender brought a crystal mug filled with a dark liquid and topped with a white creamy froth. "Here, try this."

Naomi took a cautious sip. Her eyes widened. "This is quite good."

Riker grinned. "I have a friend who is an expert on chocolate. Maybe you should meet her."

Naomi smiled, but couldn't hold the expression.

"So," Riker said, sipping his own drink, "What's a nice girl like you doing in a place like this?"

Naomi sighed. "I had to get out of my quarters."

"Trouble at home?" Riker said with a knowing look.

Naomi took another sip of her hot chocolate. "My parents want to stay on a planet and not go back into space!"

"I see. And you don't agree."

"Space is my home!" Naomi burst out. "And my father wants to take all that away!"

"Hm," Riker said. "Father problems. He wasn't with you on *Voyager,* was he?"

Naomi shook her head. "I wish some of my friends on *Voyager* could talk to him and my mom—I'm sure they could talk them out of this." Tears filled her eyes. "I wish my friends on *Voyager* would talk to me—but everyone is too busy."

"Wow," Riker said. "Sounds like you've got some big issues." He handed her a napkin.

Naomi wiped her eyes. "I want to go back to space. If my parents don't want to, I'll go anyway."

"How will you do that?" Riker asked.

"I'll find a way," Naomi said. "I'm going to be a captain someday, and captains can always find a way."

"I see," Riker said. He looked down at his empty glass and then checked down the bar where the bartender was chatting with a Ferengi. "I'm going to go get a refill on my drink here. Be right back."

Naomi nodded and took another swallow of her hot chocolate. It warmed her, as did Commander Riker's sympathetic ear.

A few minutes later, Riker came back to her. His glass was already half-empty. "Miss Wildman, would you be willing to accompany me someplace?"

Naomi narrowed her eyes. "May I ask where, Commander Riker?"

"You may ask," Riker said, draining his glass. "Let's just say I contacted someone who wants to address your desire to go into space personally. They're waiting for us."

Naomi perked up. "Really? Who?"

"That's all I'm permitted to say," Riker said. He took off his uniform jacket and draped it around Naomi's shoulders. "Are you ready to go?"

Naomi gulped down the last of her hot chocolate and nodded.

Commander Riker took her to Starfleet Headquarters. Even in the middle of the night, it was busy, with people of various races in Starfleet uniforms scurrying here and there. Several of them recognized Commander Riker and stopped to say hello. Riker returned the greetings but said he was hurrying to an "important meeting."

Naomi tried to keep her curiosity in check. They finally stopped at a door labeled BRIEFING ROOM 3." Riker pressed a button on a panel next to the door.

A familiar voice called out, "Enter." Naomi felt her heart start to pound. When the door opened, she was greeted with not one, but two surprises.

She had recognized Captain Janeway's voice. Sitting next to the captain was Seven of Nine. Both women looked tired but smiled to see the young girl.

"Captain! Seven!" She looked from one to the other, delight filling her.

"Come in, Naomi," Janeway said. "Have a seat."

Naomi picked a seat on the other side of Janeway and facing Seven. Riker chose to lean on the wall near the door.

"Seven, it's good to see you!" Naomi said. "How was Kansas?"

"Kansas was agreeable," Seven said. She glanced at Janeway, who nodded slightly. The former Borg drone continued, "Commander Riker says you've been experiencing some difficulties adapting to your life away from *Voyager.*"

"More than that," Janeway said, her smile gone. Folding her hands on the table and leaning forward, she said, "the Commander tells us you are considering violating your orders."

"Orders?" Naomi looked at Riker, who appeared to be studying Seven of Nine. "I don't know what you mean. What orders?"

"Your parents' orders, of course," Janeway said.

"Oh," Naomi's face fell. "You're just going to tell me I have to do what my parents say."

"Your parents are superior to you in the chain of command," Seven said. "It follows that you would have to obey them."

"But they want to go live on Ktaria VII!" Naomi said. "They won't let me go back to space! That's where I want to be!"

"It is understandable that you would wish to return to your

familiar surroundings," Seven said. "However, it is unrealistic."

Naomi blinked back tears. She didn't want to cry in front of Seven and she especially didn't want to cry in front of the captain. "But does that mean I have to never see anyone from *Voyager* again?"

"Why would you think that, Naomi?" Janeway asked, tilting her head.

"Because I don't see anyone now," Naomi said sadly. "Everyone's too busy when we're all here. If I go to Ktaria VII, maybe I'll never get to the stars or hear from any of my old friends."

"Oh," Janeway said. She and Seven exchanged a look. Then she reached out and took Naomi's hand. "Naomi, I'm sorry. We have been busy—catching up with our old lives, being debriefed by Starfleet Command. We didn't mean to neglect you."

"I understand, Captain," Naomi said, trying to keep her voice level.

"You have also had to catch up with someone," Seven said. "Your father."

Naomi looked down at her and Janeway's intertwined fingers. "Mom spends all her time with him. I think it's his idea to go to Ktaria VII."

"It seems to me," Riker said as he straightened up and approached the table, "that all of you are having to adjust to a certain extent. Including your father, Miss Wildman."

"My father has to adjust?" Naomi said, surprised.

"Your father did not have a daughter when *Voyager* was trapped in the Delta Quadrant," Seven said.

"Not only that, but for a time we all thought that *Voyager* was lost," Riker said. He put his hands on the black table and leaned forward. "It's one thing to think you've lost someone you love and then have them turn up again. Add a new member of the family and that's a lot to take in."

"I'm sure your father is having to learn about you just as you are having to learn about him," Janeway said, squeezing her hand.

Naomi thought about that for a minute. Now that the adults had spoken of her father having to adjust, it made sense. But . . . "But I still want to be in space. I don't want to go to Ktaria VII."

"Starfleet officers don't always get to pick their assignments," Riker said with a rueful grin. "Sometimes you have to just suck it up."

" 'Suck it up . . . ?' " Naomi asked.

"A human saying," Janeway smiled. "It means to put up with a situation. Besides, you're not seeing all the opportunities you'll have to learn things that will help you should you still want to join Starfleet."

"Captain Janeway is correct," Seven said. "There is much you still have to learn."

Naomi sighed. "I know. But I thought you both would be the ones to teach me."

"Who says we can't?" Janeway said.

"Last time I checked, subspace communications can reach Ktaria VII," Riker observed.

"I would be happy to continue communicating with you," Seven said with a smile. Naomi couldn't get used to Seven smiling, but she liked it.

"You know," Riker said, "It's late, and I think we'd better get a young lady back to her quarters before her parents start to worry."

"I will accompany Naomi back to her quarters," Seven said, standing.

Janeway nodded. She gave the girl's hand a final squeeze before releasing it. "I expect to hear great things about you, Naomi. And I promise you'll hear from me again soon."

"Thank you, Captain," Naomi said. She shrugged off the uniform jacket she'd been wearing and handed it to Riker. "Thank you, also, Commander."

He took it with a grin. "Always glad to assist a young lady and future starship captain."

"Come, Naomi," Seven said.

It was still chilly outside, so both Seven and Naomi hurried to get to the building where the Wildman quarters were located. Once they got to the door, Naomi took Seven's hand. "Will you contact me soon?"

"I shall," Seven said. "I still have much to tell you about Kansas. Perhaps we can share a meal together soon."

Naomi smiled. "I'd like that." She hesitated, then threw her arms around Seven and hugged her. "Thank you, Seven."

Seven gently returned the embrace. "You will be a fine starship captain someday. You will learn much in time to come."

Naomi slipped into the dark quarters. Things were still quiet. She yawned, realizing how tired she was.

She went into her parent's room. "Mom? Dad?"

Her mother's tousled head lifted up from the pillow. "Naomi?"

"Half lights," her father said. The room went from complete darkness to a dim light. "Is everything all right?"

She didn't see anger in his eyes, just genuine worry. "I wanted to say I was sorry for how I acted before."

Her mother looked at the chronometer by the bed. "Sweetheart, haven't you been to bed yet?"

Naomi shook her head. "I was—I was at a meeting."

"At this hour?" her father's eyebrows shot up. "With who?"

"Commander Riker, Captain Janeway, and Seven of Nine."

Her parents exchanged a long glance. "Naomi, you left here to meet with the captain without telling us?" her mother asked in a tone that warned Naomi that she was in trouble.

"I'm sorry, Mom, but I had to."

"Well," her father said, getting out of bed, "what was this middle of the night meeting about?"

Naomi looked from one parent to the other. "Adjusting."

"Adjusting?" her mother looked confused.

"Yes," Naomi said. She took her father's hand. "We are all having to adjust. I am sure I will learn a lot about adapting on Ktaria VII. And," here her voice faltered, "I hope . . . I didn't mean it when I said I hated you."

Her father looked at her, then suddenly pulled her close in a hug. "I love you, Naomi," he said in a chokey voice.

"I love you too," Naomi said. She caught herself yawning again.

Her mother got out of bed and hugged them both. "Well, I think we'll deal with the rest of this tomorrow, after we've gotten some sleep."

"Yeah," her father said. "You'd better get to bed. We'll talk about you going off in the middle of the night later."

Naomi kissed both her parents and went to her room. She was so tired she dropped her clothes on the floor instead of putting them away.

Crawling into bed, she let her eyes fall on the holographic model of Ktaria VII she'd created while on *Voyager.* She smiled. It's someplace new to explore, she thought.

She was still looking at the hologram when she fell asleep.

# The Day the Borg Came

M. C. DeMarco

**M. C. DeMarco** lives in Brookline, Massachusetts, with one ailing house plant and a wall of books. This is her second appearance in *Strange New Worlds,* and she regrets that writing about the Borg full-time is not a viable career path. In the Collective spirit, she acknowledges those fellow alumni of the Odyssey Fantasy Writing Workshop who critiqued an earlier, imperfect version of her story.

The day the Borg woke up, we didn't even know what they were. The wind was howling outside the module, and the cybernetic corpses lay on metal slabs as dead and remote, I thought, as King Tut in his wrappings. We had dug two alien, well-preserved bodies, out of the arctic ice, never expecting the mummy's curse.

At least, not until one mummy's drill-bit hand started spinning. The hair rose on the back of my neck when I saw that. I worked fast on the standard lab tests, believing that decay would set in soon. But the chilly air in the small prefab shelter remained fresh, tainted only by the acrid scent of the bodies' cybernetic parts. Maybe there wasn't enough organic material in them to rot.

I hunched over my microscope; in my samples, tiny nanotech machines were repairing both the organic and inorganic material. I thought I tasted metal—paranoia, I told myself, but fearing infection, I set aside everything else to test the microscopic machines. My instruments were crude and clunky compared to the corpses' technology, but they sufficed to prove that the nano-machines could not survive in the air. I would not be infected by *that* route.

How the pharaohs would have loved such advanced embalming technology! The nanotech had kept these dead aliens intact for a hundred years or more. Yet I doubted these ugly creatures had cared about preserving their bodies for the afterlife. Something else was going on. I felt a chill that was more than polar air leaking in the door seals.

So I asked Drake to put them both into cold freeze in module 3. I think he might have done it if Starfleet hadn't been so curious about our cyborg Tut and Nefertiti. Military interference in scientific research rubbed me the wrong way, though I was as pro-space as any other Terran. I was no soldier—then.

My armed backup went over to module 3. Not being a soldier either, he had other demands on his time. I said I'd be fine watching over the mummies, but I jumped at any sound and knocked my coffee into the drysink. When heard a blip on one of the monitors, I went to look—without my gun.

Still gray, still dead, and the monitors were silent. Yet the hair rose on my arms, and then suddenly Nefertiti's pulse started beeping and she drew a breath.

Her EEG and all her vitals shot up, and I leaned over her, fascinated. I didn't even see what hit me, but I screamed at the pain in my jugular, stumbled, ran, and fell. My neck burned in the cold; the burning spread out along my veins and the last thought of my own I had was of those nanomachines that could not survive in the air.

The first thought we had as a subcollective of isolated drones was to transmit our location to the Collective, so far away in both space and time.

The day I come for the Borg, they aren't ready. Do they think they're the only ones who can use time-travel against their enemies? It gave me a headache, but I've figured out the paradoxes—Borg fleeing into Earth's past and Captain Picard pursuing, the tactical sphere wrecked in the Arctic at the dawn of warp flight to be found by scientists a hundred years later, defrosted drones escaping from Earth pursued by Jonathan Archer, sending one last subspace message to Borg Space in the far reaches of the Delta Quadrant.

Now, inside the Collective myself for a last, brief assimilation, I can access the assimilated memories of those unfortunate early scientists to verify my theories. To his credit, Captain Archer figured it out, too, because of something Zephram Cochrane let slip, and he logged it all. I have read the old records, those long-discounted fables of the early space age.

Later, Picard thought Q had brought the Borg upon us—and in his way he did. Bringing the first cube led inevitably to the tactical sphere that Picard chased into the past. Dug up a hundred years later, frozen drones were assimilated the archaeologists and sent their message to the Delta Quadrant, *et cetera, et cetera*.

I hate time paradoxes. I touch the memories of a child I never knew, though I deeply mourn the woman she became. . . .

The day the Borg came aboard our ship, I was seven years old. Daddy had been looking for them for as long as I could remember. Since he'd found them, we had followed their cube and hidden behind special shields. Mommy said the shields allowed Daddy to observe the Borg without interfering in their behavior—like the Prime Directive. He had been so happy then, but the day the Borg came he was upset. He tried to hide it, but I knew.

The ship still smelled like the lightning that had come out of the console during the storm. Mommy said the shields went down. I knew that meant we weren't hidden anymore, so I crawled under the sheets where the Borg wouldn't see me. *We'd been spying on the Borg,* I thought, *and now they were mad at us.* I would be, too, if I was them.

Daddy came in and said the Borg were just curious about us, like we were about them. I hoped they had a Prime Directive, too. He went away, and I listened to him and Mommy arguing in the other room. I put my fingers in my ears but I could still hear them.

After a long silence, they started talking again. Daddy said something about a planet. The ship shook, and I smelled lightning again. I tiptoed to the door—the gravity felt strange, like the time it was broken and it took Mommy a week to repair it. That was fun, but this wasn't.

I saw the drones materialize on the bridge. They grabbed Mommy; she told me to run, but I couldn't move.

"Annika!" Daddy said, struggling in the drone's hands. A drone came at me, and I cried to Daddy for help. "Hide, Annika!" was all he said.

I hid under a console in the engine access corridor. I saw the legs coming for me—metal legs. I wondered if I would have metal legs when I was a drone. I shrank back, but the drone leaned down and found me, and pulled me out.

Then the *Raven* went away and we were in a green place—the biggest place I'd ever seen. The corridors went on forever and ever. I was too surprised to be afraid. The Borg were bigger than my toy cubes, bigger than the images on the *Raven*'s screen, bigger than my father—bigger than all of us.

They put me into a little box on the big cube—a maturation chamber, the voices told me—and slowly, irresistibly, I became Borg.

I first come to the Borg in their own backyard. I force them to elect a representative to speak for the Collective. They choose Seven of Nine, Tertiary Adjunct to Unimatrix Zero One—Annika Hansen, assimilated as a child while her parents were studying the Collective.

Her memories are too painful for me to linger over for long. In my timeline the woman I freed from the Collective died decades ago because I stranded *Voyager* in the Delta Quadrant for twenty-three years. If I succeed in creating a new timeline she will be saved. This very day she will see Earth for the first time.

But Seven was not the first human to speak for the Borg. . . .

The day the Borg came humanity was unprepared. *I* was unprepared. They had annihilated New Providence, leaving only a crater behind them. I thought they might destroy the *Enterprise;* in my worst nightmares they wiped out the Federation. I never imagined, as I sat on my bridge staring at a cube, that the Collective could want only me.

The cube bristled with machinery. The gray-black framework of struts and bracing appalled me—a ship bearing humanoids yet open to space seemed more alien than the strangest lifeforms I had ever encountered.

And they wanted me. I could not consent, not even to save the *Enterprise*. Some forces must be resisted, no matter how irresistible.

With a show of overwhelming force the Borg attacked the *Enterprise*. She was breaking up, pieces of her being sliced off like limbs from my body—all too apt a metaphor with the Borg. Only Data was fast enough to save us by firing back at superhuman speeds. Clearly it was Data whom they should want; Data represented the height of Federation technology. I was just a man like any other.

Shelby had a plan—a burst of energy that might disable the cube—but Geordi needed more time to adjust the deflector. We did not have that much time left. How could we delay this implacable foe? How could I reason with a hive mind, a Collective callously indifferent to individuals and quite possibly unstoppable? Human, Klingon, Betazoid—to them we were all fodder for a vast, parasitic machine.

So why did they want *me* in particular?

My ship rocked when they drove us out of the nebula with magnetic charges. They hit Deck 9 and took out the shields. Drones—the color of corpses—appeared on my bridge. Worf shot two, but the third adapted, tossing Riker aside and defeating Worf as easily. I thought the assimilation of my ship was beginning then, but as they'd promised—or threatened—they took only me.

The cube where I rematerialized was as horrifying inside as out. A vast, open chamber surrounded me, all out of proportion to the thousands of humanoid cyborgs who staffed it. The cube set course for Earth, and the Collective spoke.

My captors explained themselves at last; the Borg wanted a human collaborator to guide Species 5618 into the Collective. I told them that humanity would never submit—that freedom and self-determination were paramount for us. To the Borg, however, our values meant nothing. Freedom and self-determination, they said, were irrelevant.

Despite the horror of my situation, I was as awed as I was afraid. Standing on their ship, with their technology extruding from the walls, stretching in straight lines so long they met at infinity, I felt more than ever as if I were caught in the works of an amoral, unstoppable machine. It could not feel my anger; anger and fear would be assimilated, declawed, recycled into something else.

I cursed Q for attracting the Borg's attention to us. I prayed that he would appear, wave his hand, and make the Borg disappear—but I knew Q would not save me. I was on my own, facing death and worse, knowing that I was not the last but the first of an endless number the Borg would consume using my knowledge, my face, my defeat. Knowing that soon I would not care whether I was the instrument of genocide.

They held me fast so I could not struggle. I could resist in my mind, as I'd promised humanity would do, but I did not doubt that resistance would be futile. I feared they were also correct when they said that death was irrelevant—or would soon be to me.

The drone to my right twitched; I steeled myself to join the ranks of the living dead. The drone plunged its tubules into my neck, and I heard the voices—first a trickle, then a flood, then an ocean in which I drowned.

And then I, Locutus, spoke for the Borg.

When I come to destroy the Borg I have Picard's words in mind: "The Borg are utterly without mercy—beyond redemption, beyond reason." The disintegrating Collective mind shows me similar fragments of his thoughts before assimilation.

It once gave me hope that they chose Locutus to communicate with humanity. The Collective is coming to realize that they must meet us on our own terms, that we are not just another isolated victim species of the Delta Quadrant. We resist.

There is something in us that cannot be assimilated. If they want it, they must negotiate for it, speak our language, *adapt*. In return I helped them against what I once believed was a more dangerous foe.

For a while then there seemed to be a chance the Collective would change—influenced by drones like Hugh and those who could access Unimatrix Zero in their dreams. But not everyone was willing to wait for that change to come. . . .

The day the Borg came I was alone. I woke up on a ship—a small transport with peeling enamel and the smell of fried circuitry. I searched the old hulk from stem to stern, but my parents were not aboard.

I didn't understand. I thought perhaps the Borg had returned to Brunali, but then how had I escaped alone? I did not recall launching the transport. I examined the controls. The computer informed me that I was locked out of navigational access—no surprise that an adolescent would be. So I could not have escaped on my own, and yet I was alone.

The puzzle fascinated me. We had so few ships left after the Borg's previous visits—legendary attacks I was too young to remember clearly. I imagined all manner of exotic explanations: a final Borg assault on Brunali of which I was the lone survivor, kidnapping by rogue traders, time loops, wormholes and tears in the fabric of space.

My fantasies were interrupted by a voice—a billion voices all speaking as one: "We are the Borg. You will be assimilated. Resistance is futile."

I believed them. To me the Borg meant vast gaping chasms in the crust of my world where Leucon said cities had once stood; they meant a hush and a trembling whenever adults looked up at the sky. I was afraid, though I didn't know of what. I searched desperately for weapons, but the ship had no defenses and no hand weapons in storage.

Before I could cower in a corner or make my last, brave stand, gray men were *there,* all around me, filling the ship. Some stood by the controls and seemed disappointed in them somehow. Others appeared behind me, where I did not see them until something cold and sharp plunged into my neck. Then I could see them all, looking at each other, looking at Icheb, and yet I was still looking at them through Icheb's eyes.

We sensed the wrongness of the situation; the ship was not what it had appeared to be on our sensors. A class-one transport of no technological value to the Borg had been designed to project a false warp signature into subspace for unknown purposes. The child, alone, was anomalous as well. Species 2461 protected their offspring during an unnecessarily protracted period of adolescence.

We considered several theories, but the new drone provided little data and no conclusion was reached. We took the drone and left the transport behind. We did not associate our later malfunctions with the new drone.

The day I come to destroy the Borg, I come like Icheb, bearing a pathogen. His destroyed a cube; mine is destroying the Queen and her entire unimatrix. So I'm watching the Borg fall apart, literally and figuratively. The neurolytic pathogen is spreading to other unimatrices already, but I will not live to see the end result.

From Icheb I learned that assimilation could transmit infection, if you came under cover with a new vector they would not recognize. The Borg believed his ship's false readings, like they believed my cover story of traveling into to the past to help my younger self.

No one knows the Borg like I know them. I've negotiated with them, infiltrated them, and infected them before. I have traveled through their space, freeing drones and stealing transwarp coils. I have seen humanity's hopes disappointed; the Collective has become a nearer and more dangerous menace over the years.

Suffice it to say that I have learned the lessons of history. When the Unimatrix blows, as it will soon, I and my temporal paradoxes will die with the Collective. Maybe a databank will survive somewhere to record that *I*, Admiral Kathryn Janeway, am the one who brought chaos to order.

# STAR TREK: ENTERPRISE

# The Dream

Robyn Sullivent Gries

**Robyn Sullivent Gries** has loved *Star Trek* since she discovered *The Original Series* in reruns when she was a kid. *Trek* introduced her to science fiction, which led to Robert Heinlein and Isaac Asimov, *Forbidden Planet* and *Outer Limits,* Forry's *Ackermansion* and a hefty collection of sci-fi books, DVDs, and film scores, not to mention her soulmate and husband, who is also nuts about the genre. In her spare time (ha!), Robyn indulges in her other love, needleworking. She is positively giddy that her first professional short story sale is for a *Trek* story. Becoming part of *Strange New Worlds* has been a grand adventure, and an experience that she will treasure. Heartfelt thanks to Dean, Margaret, and Paula.

Trip didn't want to wake up. His head hurt too much.

He could hear voices. He couldn't make out what they were saying, but they were upset. And there were alarms buzzing somewhere, insistently demanding attention. He heard the hiss of a hypospray, thunderingly loud.

*Would somebody just shut the damn noise off and let me sleep?*

"Wait a minute," came a new voice. "Not so fast."

Trip cracked an eye open. Through the glare, he could see someone standing over him. "No more time for sleep," the man said.

Weirdly, the fellow looked and sounded just like Trip, except he was wearing a gray jumpsuit instead of Starfleet blue. "Who the hell are you supposed to be?" Trip asked.

"You," the man in gray replied.

"Yeah, right." Trip squeezed his eye shut again. "Never mind. Leave me alone—I need more sleep."

He felt a poke in the ribs. He was up and glaring hotly at the guy in an instant. "What's your problem?"

"You are." The fellow didn't seem at all intimidated.

Trip massaged his sore side. "If you're supposed to be me, you're doing a lousy job. I'm not as annoying as you."

The man in gray smiled faintly. "You are when you're right about something."

Trip rubbed the back of his head; it was pounding something fierce. "And what are you so right about?"

"You don't belong here." The fellow pointed straight down. "You belong *there*."

Trip looked down—and sucked in a breath of shock. The two of them were hovering in mid-air, near the ceiling of Sickbay. Below them, Trip could see Phlox, swathed in surgical gray, feverishly working on a patient. Captain Archer was on the other side of the biobed, looking drawn and haggard, holding something over the patient's face—giving him oxygen. Trip could still make out the patient's features, though. He reminded Trip of—

*Holy hell.*

"That's me," he said in a stunned whisper.

"Right now, it's not much of anything," the man in gray said. "Not with you up here, messin' around."

*What does that make me, then? Some kind of spirit?* Trip couldn't take his eyes off the ghastly scene below. "What happened?"

The other man shrugged. "An engineering test went bad. You were performing one of your Tucker miracles to head off a reactor breach when you ran smack into a complication." He glanced down at Phlox, who was attaching a cardio-stimulator to his patient. "The doc's term for it was, 'Blunt-force trauma to the posterior cranial fossa, resulting in cerebellar herniation and damage to the midbrain.' You've been in a coma for ten days."

Phlox activated the cardio-stimulator, and the patient on the biobed lurched sharply. Archer, hovering close by with the oxygen mask, flinched as he watched, his face agonized. As the doctor administered another hypospray, Trip asked softly, "Am I going to die?"

His double studied the bioscan monitors. "According to those numbers, you already have."

A wave of dizziness washed over Trip. *I'm dead? No, this has to be some surreal, Alice-through-the-looking-glass dream. . . .*

"And you're gonna stay dead unless you get back in that body." The man in gray was regarding him expectantly now.

Trip felt groggy and confused. How the hell did this guy expect him to get back? Trip didn't even know how he'd gotten out in the first place! "Who died and made you my keeper?" he said irritably.

"I did, I guess." The man with his face gave him a familiar, lopsided smile. "And if you think I'm gonna let it all go to waste, you don't know you very well."

Trip rubbed his temples, trying to quell their throbbing. The word games were making his head hurt worse. "Who *are* you, anyway? My guardian angel? My conscience?"

"Technically, I'm the guy who saved your life," his counterpart replied. "You might say I have an investment in you."

"Come again?"

The fellow smiled as he tapped Trip's head. "You owe me one."

Below them, Phlox was shaking his head at the flatlining bio-monitor gauges, stepping away from the patient. Archer, his face filled with desperation, seized the doctor by the shoulder. "Keep trying!"

"There's nothing more to try, Captain!" The doc was more upset than Trip had ever seen him. "The body either responds to stimulation, or it doesn't. Commander Tucker is not responding."

The man in gray was staring at Trip, uncomprehending. "What the hell are you waiting for?"

Trip's head felt as if it were about to explode. "Pipe down, will ya? It's hard to think with you yelling at me."

The other man gestured to the motionless body on the biobed below. "There's nothing to think about! Get back in there!"

"I don't know *how*!" Trip shot back. He wanted to scream, *Didn't you hear? Don't you get it?* "It's *not* too late anyway. If I'm dead—"

"It's *not* too late, dammit!" his double said in frustration.

Trip glared at him. "Okay, Mister Know-It-All. Show me how to get back."

"It doesn't work like that."

"Then how does it work?" Trip demanded.

Suddenly he and his twin weren't up above Sickbay any longer, but down on the floor. Trip was staring at the body—*his* body—

on the biobed, pale and unmoving. "Try just a little longer," Archer was asking Phlox, his voice drained by despair. Trip could see now, by the dark circles under the captain's eyes, that he had hardly slept for days. But there was something more in those eyes than worry for a dying friend . . . something haunting him, eating away at his soul.

"Cap'n's a mess," the man in gray observed from behind Trip. "He's had a hell of a week, and I expect it'll get even worse for him. He's going to need his best friend."

There was another disorienting change of scenery, and Trip found himself in engineering, looking down from the upper catwalk to the warp core. He gaped at the ragged hole torn in the outer housing, with a big chunk of the EPS and coolant conduit systems blown away. The engineering crew swarmed around the open wound like ants, tending to it with blowtorches, replacement parts, and scanners.

"Who the hell did this to my engines?" he said in outrage.

His look-alike, leaning on the catwalk rail beside him, looked almost apologetic. "You did."

"Me?"

"During your warp test, the ship entered a nucleonic particle field. Particles flooded the manifold, triggered an injector flare . . . and led to this." The man nodded toward the wrecked warp core housing. "At least you got the reactor shut down before the system overloaded. It could've been worse."

*Not much,* Trip thought miserably. It looked from here as though every system in engineering was in the process of being rebuilt or replaced. "How are the repairs coming?"

"Slowly," the fellow said. "Nobody knows these systems better than you do. Add to that all the modifications you've made on the fly to compensate for being in the Expanse. . . ." He eyed Trip. "Makes things all the harder, without you down there."

Trip ran a hand through his hair. This was bad, very bad. Every hour the ship remained crippled, the entire mission was put at greater risk. *Earth* was at greater risk.

He was hit by another sensory shift—damn, it was even more unsettling than being inside a transporter beam—and the deep thrum of engineering faded away, replaced by the quiet beeps and blips of the bridge. Nothing seemed amiss here, but Trip sensed an edgy expectancy in the air.

He looked more closely. Malcolm was pacing from the tactical station to the situation room and back, checking and rechecking the various diagnostics on the walls, but mostly just looking uncharacteristically nervous. At the helm, Travis fiddled with different readouts, as if he didn't know what to do with his hands. Hoshi was scanning Xindi text on one of her comm screens, but her eyes kept wandering down to her board, which remained dark: no incoming calls.

In the center chair, T'Pol looked cool and collected in her ice-blue jumpsuit as she calmly perused a padd in her hand.

The man in gray looked from Trip to T'Pol. "Honestly, I don't know how you could be all right about leaving *her*."

"T'Pol?" Trip didn't know what the guy meant. "She doesn't need me." He approached her . . . and realized she wasn't reading the padd at all, but looking right through it, without seeing it.

To the rest of the bridge crew, she undoubtedly appeared composed, but Trip had learned to recognize tiny nuances of her expression and body language, after weeks of neuropressure sessions and the familiarity that had grown between the two of them. He saw the tense set of her shoulders, the too-tight grip of her hand on the padd. And her face . . . to Trip, it was an open book of concern, a breath held and waiting for an outcome yet unknown.

*She worries . . . for me?* The discovery was so amazing, so unexpected, that it left Trip shaken. He hadn't even thought it possible.

Suddenly, he saw with stunning clarity what he hadn't seen before . . . or hadn't let himself see. His feelings for T'Pol, which had begun three years ago as antagonism, and painstakingly evolved into respect, then friendship, had become something far deeper and heartfelt over the past several weeks. There was a connection building between them, fragile and unique, that Trip yearned to explore further, especially now.

"Take me back to Sickbay," he told the man in gray.

Nothing happened. Trip turned to the guy—and stopped short. He was looking at T'Pol too, with a wistfulness that sent a chill through Trip from head to toe, and made him surprisingly angry at the same time.

"Now," Trip told him bluntly. "Right now."

"Why?" the man asked, without looking away from T'Pol.

"Because I'm through sightseeing!" Trip declared.

He saw the ghost of a smile on the fellow's face—and then, in another jarring lurch, T'Pol and the bridge were gone. Trip half-expected to wake up inside his own body again, with Phlox looking down at him, one of those impossibly wide Denobulan smiles splitting his face, while Captain Archer beamed beside him.

But as sickbay materialized around the two men, Trip saw that it had all gone terribly wrong.

Phlox stood over the lifeless patient on the biobed, shoulders slumped in defeat. His chin trembled as he pulled off his gloves and threw them on the surgical tray beside him, amid the litter of hyposprays, empty ampules, discarded cardio-stimulator and scanner. Archer had backed away from the biobed, putting a hand to the wall for support. His expression was a mixture of disbelief and horror, and tears glittered in his eyes. Beside him, the bio-monitor gauges all lay deathly still at zero.

Trip's head felt as though it were going to split open. *They gave up on me. They think I'm gone—*

"No!" he shouted in a panic. "I'm here! *I'm right here!*"

There was no reaction from either the doctor or the captain. Phlox reached for a sheet and slowly drew it over his lost patient, as Archer turned away from the finality of the sight, looking sick.

Trip didn't know if he was more terrified or furious. *"No! Don't you give up on me. I won't let you, dammit."* He strode to the biobed, looking from Archer to Phlox, as the man in gray watched silently behind him. "I have to go back. I *need* to. For you, Cap'n—for the ship, and the mission—and for T'Pol! I am *not* leaving you behind!"

The biomonitor gauges sprang abruptly to life, startling Archer and Phlox. At the same moment, sound and movement, very faint, came from under the sheet.

Phlox tore the cloth away. His patient was still pale as ashes, unconscious, but most definitely alive and struggling for a breath.

Archer was beside the doctor now, hope shining through the tears in his eyes. "Doc?"

Phlox scanned the steadily rising bioreadings, the disbelief on his face giving way to cautious optimism. "Oxygen," he said, as he administered a stimulant. Archer grabbed the mask and secured it over the patient's face.

Trip felt lightheaded, even euphoric. His head wasn't hurting any longer. The fuzziness that had jumbled his thoughts and senses was gone, too. And he felt a subtle force tugging at him, pulling him toward his body on the biobed.

The man in gray gave him a lopsided grin. "Looks like you figured out the 'how' part."

Phlox ran a hand scanner over his patient, then prepared another hypospray. "Vital signs are stabilizing," he said briskly.

Archer hovered close beside the biobed, looking so nervous that he was practically shaking. "What happened?"

Phlox allowed himself a small smile as he answered, without looking up. "He responded, Captain. To what, I'm not sure."

"What else can I do?"

The doctor injected his patient. "Hope for the best."

With each passing second, Trip felt better, stronger, more— more *alive*. But he resisted the pull; he had a few things to get straight with his mysterious companion. "You told me you saved my life . . . and you died. Who are you?"

"Think of me as a casualty of war," the fellow answered simply.

Trip studied this mirror-image of himself, whose face and voice and mannerisms were eerily similar to his own. "I know you're me . . . and not me. But I don't understand it."

His counterpart shook his head. "It doesn't matter."

"It matters to me," Trip said. "My life isn't worth dying for."

The other man had a look of peace about him. "Now you've met somebody who thinks differently."

Trip felt his throat tightening, and his eyes tearing up—or maybe it was just the light getting brighter behind the guy, making it hard to look at him.

Trip was being pulled insistently toward his body now; he couldn't stop the process any longer. The man in gray watched with satisfaction. "Have a good life," he said. "Do me a favor—make it a long one."

He wasn't making any move to follow. Trip felt an unexpected pang of concern. "You're not stickin' with me?"

The fellow shook his head. "I did what I came to do."

"What's gonna happen to you?"

"Don't worry about me. I'll be fine." There was somebody else with the fellow now . . . a woman. It was hard for Trip to make her out, with all that light behind them. She moved closer to the man with Trip's face, slipping her arm through his, and gave him a kiss on the cheek. As she nestled her head comfortably on the man's shoulder, Trip was able to make out her long, golden-blond hair and sunny smile.

Of course. It was Elizabeth.

It felt right, seeing them together, though Trip couldn't exactly figure out why. For a moment, he thought he saw the sparkle of tears in the fellow's eyes. . . . Perhaps it was a trick of the light.

As Elizabeth and the man in gray receded rapidly into the distance, he gave Trip a final smile. "Take care of T'Pol for me."

Trip smiled back. "And you look after Lizzie for me."

From the foot of the biobed, Jonathan Archer watched Trip open his eyes . . . and for the first time in ten days, the captain began to breathe easily again.

Archer watched his friend blink carefully, as if learning the skill for the first time. Trip looked fuzzily around, then finally fixed his gaze on the first face he found: that of Phlox, standing beside him. He worked his mouth for a while before forming a word, barely more than a whisper. "Doc."

Phlox smiled warmly at his patient. "Welcome back, Commander. How do you feel?"

Trip seemed to consider the question for a long moment. Faintly, he smiled. "Alive."

Archer felt giddy. Trip was processing images and information, using memory recall, speaking lucidly. Phlox had cautioned the captain that it might be days before the transplanted neural tissue had properly integrated. Leave it to Trip Tucker to work another miracle.

Trip's eyes were wandering again. They found Archer, and carefully looked him up and down. A frown creased his brow. "Cap'n . . . you *are* mess."

Archer laughed, realizing he must look like hell—unshaven, exhausted. Suddenly, he was blinking back tears of relief. "I wouldn't talk, if I were you," he replied.

"I didn't say it," Trip remarked mildly. "He did."

Archer traded a puzzled glance with Phlox, who shrugged. "Who?" the captain asked Trip.

"The guy." Trip looked around foggily. "The man who looked like me. He was right here in sickbay. . . ."

Phlox raised an eyebrow as he exchanged another look with Archer. "Strange dream to have," he commented quietly.

Trip fixed his gaze on the ceiling above them for a long moment, his brows knitting thoughtfully. Finally he relaxed, settling back into his pillow. "Huh. He musta left with her."

The captain and the doctor looked curiously at each other again. "Her?" Phlox echoed.

"Elizabeth."

Archer knew that Trip had dreamed often of his sister, but they had been horrific nightmares of the Xindi attack, the cause of his insomnia. This time, he didn't seem disturbed at all. But why would he dream of himself with her?

"She'll take good care of him," Trip murmured, his eyes slipping shut.

"A mythical 'visit to death', do you think?" Phlox asked the captain.

Archer shrugged. "Maybe it's as simple as . . . he misses her."

Trip chuckled softly. "Lizzie always liked me in gray. . . ."

Archer and Phlox stared at him, as his breathing slowed and deepened, signaling that he had fallen asleep.

When Trip awoke hours later, he had no memory of the dream, or Elizabeth, or the man in gray who looked like him. In fact, his last memory was of a neuropressure session with T'Pol the night before the accident in engineering. Of course, he had no knowledge of Sim, who had lived and died while Trip was in a coma.

Archer and Phlox were left to wonder. But they took comfort in the intriguing possibility that the dream might have been something more.

# Universal Chord

Carolyn Winifred

## THIRD PRIZE

**Carolyn Winifred** lives in Vermont and has been a *Star Trek* fan since the seventies reruns. Her various employers contributed time and computers to forward her writing, and her family has always been encouraging. This will be the first work they actually get to read! She would like to thank Paula and Margaret and Mother Nature, without whose actions the vote might have been very different.

She hadn't thought this through. Of course the rest of the audience would be human. The inadequacy of the ventilation system was becoming noticeable. Having arrived promptly, she had taken a seat close to the stage. Behind her now all the small tables and chairs were occupied. To make her way out would be very disruptive. Her first time among humans and she already wished to leave.

"It's packed. I love this intimate setting thing." The woman at the very front table voiced her opinion unasked.

T'Pol did not have a chance to respond. The lighting had been barely adequate when she entered; now the lights went down completely. Various colored lights illuminated the stage. The audience exploded in applause and yells as figures emerged from the back curtain.

T'Pol had to chasten herself a third time. Quite a bit of time had gone by since she had first heard the music. She had not recalled humans aged faster than Vulcans. Their lifespan was less then half the Vulcan average. Taking center stage was an elderly man with a trim white beard. Another man, of equal age, as swarthy as the other was pale, bounded across the stage. He picked up a stringed instrument from a stand. At the far side a man had taken a seat behind a long, flat box on thin legs. The deep lines of his face were accentuated by a spotlight. The percussionist was obscured behind a large set-up.

Then, out of a hushed silence, suddenly came music.

T'Pol was relieved to find age had not affected the deep, rich voice she remembered. She was familiar only with the one song, but composers usually chose to work on a theme or elaborate on one that had proven to have resonance with an audience.

When she had first been introduced to their music she had been unfamiliar with the language. Now she found she still could not make much sense of the lyrics. Disappointment was illogical, but, somehow, as something to experience, the song spoke of strength gained. It was the sigh before each chorus. "Ah, disappointment." He seemed to put a long life into each expression of regret. Surely there was knowledge to be gained by the experience.

At the end of the piece all the cheers and applause were acknowledged with a simple, "Thank you, *grazie,*" from the singer.

Immediately they launched into the next selection. T'Pol kept anticipating the singer would begin singing, but the song was completely instrumental. She missed the voice, initially, but the darkness of the venue became the vastness of space. The small white lights on the ceiling were stars. The beams of colored lights were nebulae and interstellar gas. They made the background noise, the radio emissions of stars. The musician closest to her produced rapid popping sounds on his twelve-stringed instrument. The man at the box manipulated it with his fingers, creating the long distorted sound waves of solar wind. And they made music. The box released sounds sometimes like a stringed instrument, sometimes a wind or percussive instrument, its almost Vulcan-like master calm and seemingly unaffected. The other player roamed the stage, almost distracting in his wanderings, but musically, a superb technician. The singer's six-string instrument played the lower notes. Either the percussionist was not human, but was of some species whose eyes were protruding and black, or he was human and wearing small dark goggles. He was not simply marking the beat, but adding tonal color with rattles and cymbals.

If there was sound in space, it would be this.

The audience was very still and focused on listening. They erupted in applause as soon as the band stopped playing.

"I love you," the woman at the front table called out.

"Like the song says, love the planet you're with."

In the brief pauses between songs the audience called out various titles. Some asked for the piece she knew. T'Pol did not join in the calls. It seemed a crude way to conduct a concert. And which piece the band chose to perform next did not seem to relate in any way to what was called for.

"You can't have the old ones until you've had the new ones."

"Newer," the drummer quipped.

"Newest, available for purchase at the back of the hall. Please indulge yourselves."

They managed to create many sound and vocal layers live in front of her as she watched. There was no reliance on machines to create the complexity, other than the instruments in their hands. The singer and the sitting man were blending their voices, smooth and smoothest.

Stars were not like that at all, as if they were an actual item one could touch. Nonetheless, she was shivering. Was there some trick involved in this?

If there was a voice of eternity, it would be his, like honey and wine. She was back in zero gravity training. The sense of inner self one was encouraged to concentrate on when left out in space in only a spacesuit. Time faded in such scenarios. His voice was her inner voice talking to her, explaining it all to her. She knew she wouldn't be able to convey the understanding later. It was just this moment, alone in the cosmos, and everything fit together perfectly.

They were carrying on a conversation via their instruments, across the stage, each bent studiously over their instruments. They were not very visually engaging. How Vulcan, really. She admired their skill. Every Vulcan child learned an instrument—the physics and mathematics of music were interesting subjects. Joy in playing music, beyond the satisfaction of perfect performance, was not encouraged.

Listening, she forgot to watch. Colors and stars swirled before her. They played piece after piece, sometimes with lyrics, sometimes instrumental. She traveled all over the universe with them.

"It's not a gig in America until somebody yells out 'Hey, Marco,' " the vocalist intoned.

A big grin lit up the wandering musician's face and he bowed to a swell of applause.

With a gracious nod the singer stepped back beside the drums and gave center stage to Marco.

Marco sang of chromium needles and basket cases. Though, as T'Pol understood it, a basket and a case were essentially the same thing. His voice was rough and slightly off-key, but he sang with the passion of a Klingon Basai master. His topknot was rapidly disintegrating. Long hair, much of it gray, whipped around as he moved his head. He curled over his instrument, alternately playing it with his fingers and with a plectrum. He put the plectrum in his teeth when not using it, but often simply dropped it. Obscured behind a box a slim hand was reaching out from the side of the stage, always there with another plectrum as needed. He ended the song almost bent double. His hand on the strings was a blur.

The response was ecstatic. If her hands were beginning to hurt, from clapping politely, the rest of the audience must have bleeding hands.

There were more calls for the song she knew.

"This is not a greatest hits tour."

"Greatest hit," Marco spoke as he wandered behind the singer.

"*Ode to Joy,*" someone in the crowd yelled out.

"Really?" the singer laughed.

"Not my anthem," the drummer spoke up.

"You know, we're not really a Euro band. Piqué and I were born in countries that don't exist anymore."

"Ex-grunts of ex-countries of an ex-Hegemony," the keyboardist Piqué spoke quite despairingly.

"Aren't we all supposed to be part of one big happy family now?"

Laughter, some of it uneasy, came from the audience.

"I'll take you in and we'll be a big happy family," the drummer said.

"Thank you, your enthusiasm supports me. We try to keep it under wraps, but Tyg is Australian." The three others turned with suspicious looks to the drummer, who gave a somewhat sinister impression to T'Pol, with the goggles and trim dark beard and sharp grin.

"And of course Marco, our American."

*"No comprendre Ingles,"* was Marco's response.

T'Pol noted the outmoded allegiances lingering in the general populace. Earth was united under one government, had been for some time, but had suffered severe provincialism, and still clung to some regional differences. The High Command reported often having to deal with delays caused by internal dissension.

"War hero." T'Pol thought it was the same voice calling out.

Marco's movements stopped abruptly.

"Guitar hero, now, and we thank him very much." The singer's soothing voice relaxed Marco.

"Old soldiers never die."

"We smell that way." Piqué's response to the audience member echoed T'Pol's thought.

"I've had death. Give me individuality. The Honorable Eskey Inglesei, member for Bohemia." With that the singer led into another song featuring stately vocal delivery from Inglesei and Marco together. The rough and the smooth.

"This is a great going away song, and we're going away now." The way Inglesei stepped back indicated that the piece would be instrumental. He stood, half turned to the drummer, eyes closed, face calm. T'Pol was not aware humans could look so calm. The keyboards were supplying the melody, the bass and drums a steady pulse. The guitarist was picking at her brain as he picked at his guitar, reaching out and tapping her on the forehead. The music threatened to invade her thoughts. Sometimes the sound came from the left, sometimes from the right. She tried to maintain focus on determining the exact location, but ended up floating away.

Inglesei said quickly, "You've been a great audience. *Grazie.* Good night." Piqué shook hands with people near his corner of the stage. The woman in front of T'Pol shouted, "I love you," again. Marco shouted "We love you." He put his guitar back on its stand and left the stage.

The concert was over, and they had not even played the one piece T'Pol had come to hear. She had checked the Earth database, and it was the only piece they were known for. The other pieces they had played had been excellent, but she was surprised they had left out their best known work.

She clapped politely for a moment then stood up to leave. She confronted a wall of humans. Everyone else had left their seats and crowded closer to the stage. They were beginning to rhythmically clap and yell. She turned back, the lights were still low, but the stage was empty. Perhaps they were disappointed and this was the Earth way of demanding performance of the piece. She did not yell or scream, and did not understand the sound wave dynamics that putting fingers in her mouth would produce such a shrill whistle.

After only a minute or two the band members trooped back on stage. They took up their instruments again to a swell of cheers. T'Pol didn't understand what the false ending had been for.

"Loyal fiends. You've been a swell audience and now, right before your very ears . . ."

It was still not the song. Perhaps its time had expired.

"We were almost famous, once, long ago."

The crowd started to get restless.

"Perhaps in some universe, alternate reality, you know." He was paraphrasing the lyrics. T'Pol recognized the opening notes. As Inglesei began to sing, the audience joined in, raggedly. The song would have been much better without their off-key participation. She had waited through all the others just to have the piece she particularly liked ruined by this interference.

Inglesei walked away from the center spot. The human was struggling with his composure.

Sitting behind Eskey, Piqué nonetheless seemed aware of his plight, for he began an extension of the song's theme on the keyboard. As Piqué and Marco joined up on a variation of the melody the audience continued to try and sing the song. Some sang the lyrics, some the chorus. Tyg responded to and with them, marking the rhythm.

Inglesei stepped forward again. T'Pol was embarrassed to be witness to such a loss of control by the elderly man. He rejoined the music with a subtle, simple but solid bass line, index finger on his instrument. Eyes closed, cheeks damp, with a beatific smile he formed his ragged choir into shape.

*"Univerrsal chord."*

He turned the chorus into a call and response with the audience. It wasn't the way the song went at all.

*"Universal chord."* His voice, made even deeper with emotion, gathered them all up.

Piqué began the main movement of the song again, looking totally serene. How many times was she going to think that? Marco was almost still, head down, swaying slightly, just taking small steps forward and back.

With guitar and drums in sync and a solid strong base they ventured farther into the darkness. The audience could not keep up with them. It became one great wave of sound moving through space, surrounding T'Pol while she moved through the dark abyss of space.

Marco stood dangerously close to the edge of the stage. Inglesei moved steadily back, until he and his instrument slipped out. Marco's hand was a blur again. He controlled crashing waves of noise, however he positioned his guitar. Piqué was pounding the keyboard with his elbows and forearms. The instrument rocked precariously on its thin legs. With a final flourish up and down the keys he stood up. He caught hold of Marco and pulled him to the back of the stage and off.

The drummer continued, if anything, becoming more frenzied. Splinters flew off the wooden drumsticks. Working his entire assemblage he hit the cymbals with the gourd rattle, he slapped the drums with his hands. It was not a cacophony of sound, though. The strong rhythm matched her rapid heartbeat, caught it, and accelerated it. When she thought she might burst, Tyg concluded, releasing them all. He staggered out from behind his drums, made a deep bow to the audience, hands clasp reverently before him, then limped off the stage.

The house lights came on abruptly. It was a sharp jolt back to reality. T'Pol had not realized how mesmerized she had been. She was surrounded by others equally surprised to find themselves in a small room on Earth again. She clapped as long as the rest of the audience clapped. People stood for quite some time though the lights were brighter than they had been when she entered. There seemed little chance of the band returning. It was a way of thanking them, totally ineffective and impractical. The humans expressed their disappointment with sighs, quiet comments to their companions. A few wiped tears from their eyes.

The crowd began to slowly make their way out. T'Pol sat down again. There was little point standing, waiting for the crowd to thin out. And she needed a moment.

"Need a moment to collect yourself?" The other woman at the front, blocked by the crowd, was still at her table.

Collect herself. *Yes,* T'Pol thought. *That was very apt.* She had just traveled the cosmos. She had quite forgotten herself in music.

"Aren't they the greatest band ever?" the woman continued.

*It was doubtful,* T'Pol thought, *that they were the greatest musical group of all time, on Earth, or in the Universe.*

"They are very accomplished musicians," she did admit.

Instead of making their way out some people were approaching the stage, leaving green bottles of liqueur, small parcels tied with ribbon. A thin woman wearing a light summer dress and highly impractical high-heeled sandals stepped out on the stage to collect the gifts. T'Pol suspected she had been the arm handling the plectrums.

The woman at the front rail had tried to take images through-out the performance. As they made their way out through the thinning crowd she was looking through the images she had tak-en during the concert.

"That's a good one of Eskey." Close up, the image showed a white-haired, bearded, sweat-soaked, man. His age seemed to have fallen away. With his eyes closed he could have been in a meditative trance.

"I must have five-thousand pictures, but never a clear one of Marco.

"Piqué is Piqué is Piqué." Every image of the keyboardist re-minded T'Pol of a Vulcan Kolinhar Master.

The audience had been urged to buy merchandise repeatedly. T'Pol was not sure what this entailed, but it was impossible to exit without passing a table displaying various items.

"Everyone's into just datafiles, but hard copy is always good."

The fact sheet from the Consulate had indicated humans were given to conversation, and if one did not respond they were likely to stop talking. T'Pol had not spoken for a while, but the woman was not deterred.

"Hi," she said to the young woman behind the table.

"Oh, hi."

The young woman had dark skin, similar to Vulcans of the Southern continent, and humans of the Earth's African conti-nent. But there was something different, fundamentally different about her. T'Pol had never looked into such ancient eyes. Deep, solid black in a young, ageless face. They stared up at her.

T'Pol naturally had her identity card with her, which was also a credit chip. She had first used it on Earth to pay the venue's admission. "I believe this will work," T'Pol said as she handed it to the young woman.

A quick swipe across the reader produced a beep and a green light. "What would you like?"

"What do you suggest?" T'Pol asked her talkative companion.

"What? Besides everything? Two of everything?" The woman

pointed to one of the displayed data fiche covers. "The comp, *Hindsight and Foresight.* It has the best from, like the past six albums, and, what, sixteen new tracks? All great."

The merchandise girl picked one from a crate behind her and waited for T'Pol's nod before swiping it across the reader. "Anything else?"

"T-shirt?"

"Excuse me?"

They both pointed to the back wall, where various articles of clothing were pinned up. Each displayed a different vibrant design and the logo of the band.

"No. I do not believe so." T'Pol could not think of any occasion she would have to wear such things.

"Anything for you, Kittie?" the young woman asked.

"Already have it all, Pet."

The overwhelming odor almost made T'Pol's eyes water before the man arrived.

"Time, Pet."

"Give me a minute or two."

"Hi, Marco," Kittie said.

"Hey Kittie," the man said over his shoulder as he was weaving his way back through the tables to the stage. The kinetic guitarist had been standing right next to T'Pol. He had changed his attire, but not bathed. His hair was severely confined again, pulled into another topknot.

"Great show," Kittie called after him.

"Positivity!" he yelled back.

It was a relief to step out into the warm San Francisco evening.

"Coming backstage?" Kittie was still walking beside her.

The road back to the Consulate ran beside the club. There was already a small crowd at the rear of the building.

It was common on Vulcan to speak to the artist, to express one's appreciation for the well-crafted piece, to ask for explanation of artistic choices. Expound on theory. She would like to commend them for their musicality.

"Has Eskey left already?" Kittie asked.

"Haven't seen him."

"Must be pretty pooped after that show."

"Great, wasn't it?"

"I can't believe they played *Floating on Ardana*."

"They were on fire."

"Their vans are still here." Kittie indicated a black hovervan pulled up to the building, and a smaller red one parked in the parking lot behind the venue.

"Could have gone with someone else."

The black hovervan was dirty. Along the sides and across the back doors words had been written in the dust. T'Pol could make out "Shine on crazy diamonds," "Get the jazz on," "Wash me," "Cytherea or bust."

Behind the van came a tinkling water sound. A man apparently was relieving himself.

She should return to the Consulate. T'Pol spun around to leave as the drummer came out the stage door.

"Close encounter of the musical kind," he said. She had almost bumped into him. "You're a bit of a rarity. Come a long way?"

"The Vulcan Consulate is just up the road."

A line of dark stubble along the edge of his face and chin accented his sharp smile. His eyes were pale blue. There was a small cut on his forehead, most likely from his own flying debris. He appeared, though T'Pol cautioned herself that she was still an inexperienced judge, to be quite a bit younger than the other band members.

"Saw you in the lobby before the show. Setting up Pet's table. Figured you were here for The Hit."

"It is an amazing song. I was on a ship," T'Pol began. "In space. Deep space. The moment when I heard you." She was having difficulty explaining it.

Tyg's smile told her she didn't need to explain it.

"The song is always the same, always different, it depends on the moment. Travel by thought will take you strange places. You get to go, we get to dream. We go in our music. Someday humans will really be out in space. Someday soon."

T'Pol did not know what to say. They had captured space, yet they had never been.

Tyg guided her to the parking lot guard rail. It was unclean, but they rested against it slightly.

"They were in danger of being filed away with just that. Well, actually that had already happened. And a Spinal Tap of drummers didn't help. But I had to say, 'No, not yet. Listen to this, and there's still more.' We honestly suck at doing anything else."

"Eskey programmed his targeting computer to rhyme words for lyrics," Kittie put in.

"Already categorized," Marco walked by with a box of equipment, "already filed."

Others who had gathered at the stage door approached Tyg with their fiche covers, visual hardcopy, T-shirts and other items. He marked them up, with a pleasant word for every person.

Trapped against the building Piqué was also surrounded by people offering up items to sign.

"Want me to sign that?" Tyg indicated the fiche she held.

Tyg defaced the fiche cover. What he had written, or scrawled, did not resemble any Earth writing symbols. From her own name, T'Pol thought a "T" should be recognizable.

"Thank you," she said, to be polite.

"There's a nice roof pool where we're staying. Killah has to have his swim. I'd really like to chat some more. Want to come back to the hotel?" Turned toward her, his knee pressed against her thigh.

"I should be going." She stood up.

Piqué intercepted her. He was amazingly tall, the tallest human T'Pol had yet encountered. His thin frame accentuated the height. How had he folded himself behind the keyboard? His craggy face was well-lined with age, curly hair streaked with gray. He wore dark clothing with a familiar Vulcan cut.

He raised his hand in the Vulcan greeting. *"Dif-tor heh smusma."*

He was the first human whose Vulcan she could understand. He held one of the gift packages. "Cookie? Totally vegan."

The Consulate Information Packet had indicated that vegan foods were acceptable for a Vulcan to eat. But T'Pol declined, not having the proper utensils to eat with.

The woman with impractical footwear helped Marco guide the long keyboard case to the black van. Marco returned inside.

"Tiara," Tyg called to the woman and mimed drinking. She frowned and shook her head.

She smiled pleasantly at T'Pol."You've come a long way."

"The Vulcan Consulate is just up the road."

"Oh."

Here was another human T'Pol found unclassifiable. There was an overall Oriental look, an Earth race T'Pol could already recognize from the large demographic in the San Francisco area, but with Caucasian features, too. T'Pol was not aware of any race or species capable of and engaged in so much cross-breeding as humans. Almost every other species she had encountered disliked the differences they had to deal with in others.

"I'm gonna be jonesing for jazz with you guys gone," Kittie said.

"To the moon, Kittie. To the moon!" Tyg replied.

"I can't afford it."

"Apply for a grant. With the generous support of the Lunatic governing council."

"Luna," Tiara corrected quietly.

"Lunatics love us," Tyg said.

Kittie laughed.

Crates of merchandise went into van. The dark girl, Pet, wandered outside. Humans certainly did come in all colors and sizes.

"Tell him to hurry his ass up." Tyg's sharp comment sent the girl back inside.

"My daughter," Tyg turned back to T'Pol. "Or close enough to call me Dad."

"She calls you Da," Marco corrected on his way past yet again.

"We were the only two who crawled out of the bomb shelter. She was about nine months old. She did most of the crawling." Tyg rapped on his knee, which produced a hollow plastic sound. It took T'Pol a moment to realize Earth still repaired injuries with artificial limbs. Possibly Tyg was insensitive to its location at times.

"I read Vulcans were looking for a second counselor location," Piqué said.

Tyg broke in. "Can I put in a vote for Canberra? Vulcans would love it there. Not love love, I mean, emotionally, but they would find it very suitable."

"I will mention it to the attaché," T'Pol said.

"Fifty light years ahead of our time," Marco sang as he deposited another box. "Marco does not have Killah's sexy voice and cannot do the sexy voice."

"Please have this," Tiara held out a bottle. "You haven't eaten all day."

"Marco is very hungry," he agreed. "Marco must finish loading the van first."

Tiara sighed.

"Not only do we drive VA administrators mad, we go through tour managers like water," Tyg said.

"It has all kinds of long words in it, like potassium and magnesium." Marco returned to the building.

"There is a method to his madness. He has a system. The van has to be loaded up a certain way. Just don't get in his way."

T'Pol was suddenly aware of a stillness in the crowd. Conversations had faded out and people were turning toward the stage door. There was a man standing just beyond the spill of light from the door. He was dressed all in black, and his shape seemed to merge with the case strapped over his shoulder.

"Hey, Eskey," someone said.

He was quite small for a human, not much taller than herself. He was slight, as well. The instrument case seemed almost too much for him. What sophisticated equipment had they used to make him appear so much larger and more impressive on stage?

"Take the axe, man." Marco had barreled past T'Pol, but halted, hovering over Eskey Inglesei.

Inglesei seemed reluctant to let the case go. Marco took it firmly in his large hands, carried it with some reverence to the hovervan. The crowd parted to let him pass, then closed up again. Inglesei was surrounded, at a respectful distance, by the people who had waited at the stage door. T'Pol thought the elderly man looked frightened. The crowd was between him and the van.

Kittie spoke effusively, "You were great. As usual."

Everyone seemed to be expecting something from him. T'Pol did not think this frail person should be so strained.

Inglesei's hand was extended towards her. He had defaced all the fiche covers of the semi-circle of people around him, and T'Pol was next. As it already had Tyg and Piqué's markings on it she gave it to him. He added his squiggle.

"Thank you," she said.

He let her take it from his hand, not meeting her eyes.

"Did you like the show?" He didn't really want to know. He did not seem interested in her reply.

"We have to get the oldies to bed," Tyg stepped in. "Butter the cat," he pointed Pet to the van. "And drive like you're as old as them combined."

"*Kol-Ut-Shan,*" Piqué said.

"Your accent is very good," T'Pol commended him. He smiled, and all the creases of his face form into a smile with a smile in his eyes.

Of the infinite possibilities infinite combinations afforded, these four had come together. The universe was an amazing place, full of wonders.

Pet escorted Inglesei to the red van. Piqué had folded himself into the front passenger seat. Once he was settled in the back seat, the interior light illuminated Eskey's wispy hair, his instrument case strapped in beside him. Piqué offered up the box of cookies, but Eskey declined.

T'Pol felt caught when Eskey looked back at her looking after him. She realized she was staring. Neither seemed able to look away. After a moment the light inside the vehicle went out. She had been caught off guard, again.

Tyg stood beside her. "Your arrival meant a lot to those in the trenches at the time."

At first T'Pol did not understand him. Then she was going to say that she had not been part of the original scout party.

"New generations on Earth are born and raised to believe all things are possible. Which is nice and I'm not knocking the kids. But to live at the bottom, and then be given hope, that makes the future special. Every day. Nothing like being down, to know you're going up."

Vulcan High Command had made new contact with a space faring species. It took some time to determine that the species merited continued contact. General intercourse, trade, diplomatic, cultural exchanges, began. The humans, as the species were called, from planet Earth, put together a package showcasing their scientific and cultural achievements. T'Pol, as an agent of Vulcan High Command, had received the package. She hadn't had time until in transit aboard a Betazed star cruiser to review it. The humans' achievements were moderately impressive. Their advances periodically suffered setbacks due to emotional illogical reasoning.

The cultural package contained examples of art, sculpture, dance, and music selections. *The Best of 2088* began playing. A voice that was described in the accompanying report as a mordant tenor sang a song of space and time and beauty. She had been caught off-guard. Never had any alien aesthetic affected her so.

"Thank you for coming. To our little planet, and our show."

Marco was sitting on the rail, beside Tiara. He was finally drinking the beverage she had been holding for him.

"Anti-oxidants."

"You should take a picture of Marco now," T'Pol said to Kittie.

"Why?" Marco and Kittie asked at the same time.

"Because he is not moving," she answered.

Kittie got a clear image of Marco, sitting still, but laughing.

Marco surged up and came rapidly at T'Pol. Dropping the beverage container, he reached for her fiche. She allowed him to take it. He signed it, going diagonally across the cover, over the signatures of the others. Tiara positioned herself by his side and caught the stylus and cover when he lost his grip.

"Time for bed for you," she said.

"Difficult to get Marco to sleep."

"Can we give you a lift?" Tyg asked.

"I do not need one. The . . ."

". . . Consulate is just up the road." The three spoke in unison. The humans laughed. T'Pol didn't understand what was humorous, exactly.

"Very nice meeting you," Tiara said, getting into the driver's seat. T'Pol was mildly alarmed that she would drive in such unstable footwear.

"Ta," Tyg said. He guided Marco into the van.

"Marco is not allowed to drive."

The dark van vroomed off.

T'Pol was glad that she had come. To the performance and Earth.

# You Are Not in Space

Edgar Governo

**Edgar Governo** is an aspiring writer living in Winnipeg, Manitoba, Canada. By showing him a future he could believe in, the *Star Trek* universe has had a profound impact on him from a very early age, and he is grateful for the opportunity to finally contribute something to it. When not writing or researching, he enjoys engaging in witty repartée, spending copious amounts of time online, and thinking more about popular culture and fictional history than he usually cares to admit. This is his first professional fiction sale.

Hoshi Sato slammed her hands against her console and swore to herself in Russian, a language known for its curses—but more importantly, one she knew none of the bridge crew could speak. The crew turned to her and stared, and it occurred to her as she took in all of their startled expressions that her outburst probably needed no translation.

A verdant planet, much like Earth, filled most of the bridge's viewscreen, and Hoshi had started out thinking of it as a beautiful sight—one of many they had encountered in their travels. At this point, however, that planet only seemed to taunt her with its constant presence, and her sense of the crew's expectations combined with that silent challenge only served to heighten her frustrations.

Captain Archer stood up from his chair and walked over to her. His face held a note of compassion as he leaned in towards her and said, "My ready room, please, Hoshi."

Once they were in the ready room and the door had closed, Archer looked at her and asked, "What was that?"

Hoshi looked at the various sketches on the wall before turning back to him and answering, "I think you know, sir."

Archer sighed a bit at that before sitting down at his desk. "Hoshi . . . everyone knows this is going to take a while."

"It shouldn't, Captain," she replied. "I feel like I'm wasting everyone's time."

"Five days is not too much time to spend trying to contact an entirely new civilization, especially one that is already trying to contact us."

To her rational mind, Hoshi knew this made perfect sense. With no frame of reference at all to draw upon, it was no surprise that there would come a time when a new world's communications would not be immediately decipherable to her. Still, there was normally some sort of breakthrough within the first day or so, and this world's words were gibberish to her after nearly a week of effort.

Hoshi tried to change the subject. "How are the other scans of the system going?"

Archer glanced at a screen and called up a summary of *Enterprise*'s science reports. "They're fine. T'Pol tells me our sensors have gathered up a treasure trove of information. We've already looked at all eight planets in the system, along with the three moons around the planet where . . . *these* people are located." Hoshi winced at the moment of awkwardness—the captain couldn't even refer to this planet's inhabitants by name, for she had no name to offer him. "They're still communicating the same short message directly to us, along with all of the other transmissions we've been able to pick up."

Hoshi winced at that, too. She needed no reminder of their communications, as the sounds of that message were still echoing in her head. The key to understanding it seemed just beyond her reach, but she had to find a way to let Archer know that the wait would pay off.

"It won't be much longer," said Hoshi, endeavouring to bolster the captain's confidence in her. "I've never heard a language I couldn't learn." She neglected to add that it had never taken her this long to get at least the basics of a language figured out.

Archer looked at her once again, and Hoshi was reassured by her sense that he was conveying patience as best he could. "Everyone on *Enterprise* knows you'll be able to figure this out eventually. We've been sending out the same message since we got here, too, and they obviously haven't been able to figure it out, either." He smiled. "It's Tuesday. Why don't you give Movie Night a try? I think there's a comedy on, so it should be packed."

Hoshi considered this for a moment. Her first instinct was to turn the captain down and tell him she needed to get back to work on the translation—but if enlightenment wasn't coming to her now, she didn't see what was going to happen in the next few hours to change that. Captain Archer had also known her longer than anyone else on the ship, so in her eyes, an offer of a little escapism coming from him made more sense than it would from anyone else.

She nodded slowly. "All right," she said. "I'm going to the movies."

"I don't get it."

Travis leaned in his seat toward Hoshi and answered, "He's getting everyone in the city to enjoy life the way he's enjoying it."

"So . . . he's just allowed to interrupt the parade and take over?"

"That's the whole point—they put the rules aside and just have fun."

Hoshi was still confused, but the people around them in the mess hall were beginning to look annoyed at their conversation, so she dropped the matter. She had taken the captain's advice in earnest and was honestly trying to take her mind off the language problem, but she couldn't quite let go and enjoy the movie on its own merits.

Movie Night was usually a fun diversion for her in the course of their normal exploration, even if she found that the movies tended to blend together after a while, and it was sometimes hard to relate to how popular culture worked almost two hundred years ago. She could break down the use of colloquial language easily enough, as the slang in this particular movie hadn't thrown her off, except for a song earlier on which had featured an odd combination of English and German.

Hoshi cut off her own train of thought at that point, rolling her eyes at the realization that her mind had never left that linguistic mode at all.

While everyone else around her seemed to be enjoying the dance sequence which had erupted onscreen, all she could think about in that moment was that the main characters were supposed to be from Chicago, but sounded to her like they were from New York. In one case, an argument could also be made for Ohio—

She stopped herself again. This was ridiculous.

Absorbed in her analysis of their accents, Hoshi had completely lost track of what was going on in the movie itself. She knew there was someone going after the three main characters, and he was the focus of the scene before her now, but she couldn't even remember his name. She glanced over at Travis, who was clearly more engrossed in what was going on than she was, and considered asking him to fill her in on what had happened, but it would probably only serve to further annoy the rest of the audience around her. She might as well be working back in her quarters.

"I'm too distracted," she finally whispered to him. "I'm just going to go."

Travis looked a little disappointed at that, but he nodded quietly. Hoshi got up and shuffled past the other crewmembers in her row as quietly as she could before heading out of the mess hall into the corridor.

Her thoughts were back on the translation problem before the door had even closed behind her, so she failed to register T'Pol's presence as the science officer headed towards her from down the hallway.

"Ensign Sato."

Hoshi stopped in her tracks, having been brought back into the moment by the sound of her own name. "Good evening, Subcommander. If you're heading for the movie, you're pretty late."

T'Pol shook her head. "That is not my destination, Ensign." Quickly changing the subject, she asked, "Has there been any further progress on the alien transmission?"

It was Hoshi's turn to shake her head. "I'm at the same point I was the last time you saw me." Hoshi understood why she'd been asked about this so often lately, but she was rapidly running out of different ways to give the same answer every time the question came up.

"I'm sorry to hear that, Ensign. Your outburst on the bridge seemed to indicate you were frustrated."

Hoshi took that to be T'Pol's version of offering her sympathies and gave her a brief smile in response. "Thank you, Subcommander. If you'll excuse me, I'd like to get back to work on that tonight."

"Of course."

With that, Hoshi continued on her way back to her quarters. As she approached the turbolift doors, however, a comm panel nearby interrupted her thoughts once again. *"Archer to Ensign Sato."*

Hoshi made her way over to the panel. "Ensign Sato here. Go ahead."

*"I need you on the bridge, Hoshi. I'm afraid we have a new problem."*

"What is it?"

*"The transmission has stopped."*

Captain Archer stood in the situation room along with T'Pol, Hoshi, and Lieutenant Reed. The main console screen in front of them featured a readout of the various scans taken since they'd entered this system, and the smaller screen in front of Hoshi showed a series of phonetic symbols representing the "text" of the transmission that had previously been directed at *Enterprise.*

"The transmission ceased approximately one hour ago," T'Pol explained, indicating its origin point on the main readout. "Since we do not know why this urban center served as the source of the transmission, it is even less clear why they would choose to stop now."

"We haven't been offering them much in return," said Archer. Turning to Reed, he asked, "Have they made any other moves toward us?"

Reed shook his head. "They've taken no hostile action since first detecting *Enterprise* as it entered this system, and that hasn't changed. We know they have spacecraft in orbit around their planet, but we're not even sure they're capable of ending something out this far. It's impossible to find that out without moving closer to the planet."

"We can't take that chance right now," said Archer. He gave Hoshi a hopeful look as he asked, "Any further progress on the transmissions we already had?"

Hoshi was almost heartbroken at having to reply in the negative, and there was a note of defeat in her voice as she said, "I'm still working on it." She tried to put a positive spin on events. "The fact that they've stopped transmitting doesn't affect things much right now—we still have the recordings, and they've just been repeating the same short message all along." Glancing at Reed, she added, "Since we can't move closer, we haven't been able to pick up most of the specific transmissions they've been sending amongst themselves. We know they're talking, but as it is, this is a very small linguistic sample to work from."

Archer seemed to take a moment to consider that information before continuing. "We all want to make first contact with this species, but the way things are going, that might not be possible. I'd hate to leave them behind, but they've apparently stopped trying, and we can't wait here forever hoping for something to change."

Hoshi felt stung by that last comment, even if Archer hadn't meant for it to be directed at her personally. "I'm sure I'll have something soon," she said.

"I hope so," said Archer. "I'll give you another twenty-four hours to work on it. If you can't find a way to break the language barrier for us to talk to these people before then, I'm going to order *Enterprise* to move on."

With that, everyone returned to their bridge stations, leaving Hoshi alone with her phonetic symbols—and her growing sense of guilt.

Hoshi sat in her quarters, staring at the screen in front of her—a list of greetings in a variety of Terran and alien languages. Standard Latin and Cyrillic letters sat alongside the more cursive alphabets of Arabic and Hindi, Chinese ideograms and Japanese syllabaries, and the almost melodic writing style used on Vulcan. All of these varied forms of communication were familiar and comfortable to Hoshi, and she'd hoped that having reminders of them at her disposal would jog her memory, triggering whatever crucial step her mind had not yet taken.

When she'd taught exolinguistics, learning to say "hello" had been an obvious starting point, but having dozens of examples in front of her now did nothing to lead her any closer to the answers she sought. The padds and textbooks all around her had also proven virtually worthless, serving only to demonstrate how futile Hoshi's "gift" was in the face of this newest challenge.

She could still see Professor Turner talking to her about her facility with new languages, back when she had been a student taking her first exolinguistics courses. Hoshi could remember Turner telling her how important it was that she could decipher the way people communicate so easily, as the miracle of language had allowed even species as fundamentally different as humans and Vulcans to find common ground in the face of adversity over the past century. She wondered what Turner would have to say now, given that it really would take a miracle to bridge the gap between herself and this nameless species which had finally managed to truly stump her.

Hoshi had been stumped once before in the course of their mission—but on Risa, it hadn't gotten in the way of communication. There had been no consequences to encountering that one particularly difficult language, and attempting to learn it in just a couple of days had had certain . . . side benefits. The clock was ticking in a much more serious way this time, however, and Hoshi was all too aware of how much was at stake.

She just knew that she was *close,* somehow, which was perhaps the most frustrating part of all.

The key to translating the alien transmission felt like it was at the very edges of Hoshi's mind, continuing to elude her at every turn and taunting her for not having the answers. As far as she could tell, this should be more or less the same as any of the standard greetings they'd received from other worlds, but something about this message was just *different*. Not a lot, but just enough to keep her guessing.

Everyone on the ship had been understanding with her, but she knew all they wanted now was to get on with this first contact, and she was the only thing standing in their way. Deciphering this language—*her* deciphering this language—would be the difference between really learning about an unknown culture, and possibly making a new friend in this stretch of space, or simply leaving the system with nothing more than dry, lifeless data filling up *Enterprise*'s computer banks.

If that were to happen, she didn't know how she would able to justify staying on the ship.

Hoshi looked past her screen at a deck of cards sitting on the table, then grabbed it and absentmindedly started shuffling, reminding herself that it stood for all the reasons why she shouldn't even be on this mission. Being on *Enterprise* now was a fluke—the Starfleet equivalent of being dealt winning cards on her second hand. She had been on the ship, along with everyone else, for barely a year, and as far as she knew, she was still on probation—she was just lucky enough that her ace in the hole was that she was considered a prodigy. Without that. . . .

She had started to deal an imaginary poker hand, but was now simply laying cards down one by one. Eight, six, nine, four, each of a different suit . . . random numbers that could form patterns if you only knew the rules—full house, straight, flush. This civilization had given her cards without a guidebook, and she was about to lose all her chips because of it.

Hoshi drew another card and put it on the table. The Queen of Hearts.

*Off with my head.*

Early the next morning, Hoshi sat alone at a table in the mess hall, looking down at her padd, containing an array of notes from the linguistic database which she was using for reference; her breakfast, the fuel her mind and body so desperately needed after staying up most of the night; and the Universal Translator—which was quickly becoming her archnemesis.

Feeling battle-weary, she picked up the UT once again and spoke into it. "Planet," she said. It beeped and chirped, but provided no alien word back to her.

"Greetings," she said to it, being careful to slowly enunciate the word. The UT offered the same ineffectual response as it had before.

"Hello," she said, almost plaintively.

"Hello."

Hoshi blinked at the device, but then looked up to see that it was Lieutenant Reed who had responded to her. He and Trip were standing in front of her table, trays in their hands.

"Mind if we join you?" asked Trip.

"Go ahead," said Hoshi, "but I'm not sure I'm going to be very good company right now."

"Don't worry about it," said Trip, as the two of them sat down. "In fact, Malcolm and I were just talking about what a tough time you must be having."

Hoshi allowed herself a brief smile. "Thanks," she said. "It's not easy having a deadline like this hanging over your head." She quickly took note of the time—less than twelve hours before the captain's self-imposed hour of departure.

Reed indicated the Universal Translator, which was still in her hand. "How is everything coming along?"

"It's not," she said. "I keep tweaking the phonetic processor, but none of my ideas seem to make any difference. The UT just doesn't want to figure this one out."

Neither of them had much to offer in response to that, but Reed endeavoured to make a relevant comment. "It's hard when you don't have a . . . Rosetta Stone to help you along."

"One of those would be great right now," said Hoshi, letting out a light, sardonic laugh. "The trouble is, nothing I've been able to gather about this language says that it *should* be difficult. It sounds pretty straightforward, in fact, but it's like they're not saying anything we'd expect them to say."

"Shouldn't they be saying something simple like . . . 'Hi there?' " asked Trip.

"Exactly," said Hoshi, nodding. "Or, 'Who are you?' or even, 'Get out of here.' When you get an initial piece of communication from a group of people, you rely on the idea that they're not going to stray too far from your expectations. I'm out of luck if this transmission says something like, 'Where's my sandwich?' "

"I suppose there are a lot of potential variables to consider," said Reed.

Hoshi took the opening to vent her linguistic frustrations. "Almost too many to count. For one thing, I have no idea what any of the inflections in their speech might mean. Even within a single language, there are so many cultural implications—like knowing that you're from England, Malcolm, and you're from Florida, Trip. We can all understand each other, but that's not going to be so obvious from an alien perspective. Just think of it in reverse, and that's the problem with pronunciation in a nutshell."

There was an awkward moment of silence as Reed and Trip each struggled to find something to say. Finally, Trip began, "Well, I guess when you only have one speaker of a brand new language—"

"See, that's the thing about a new language, especially an alien language," said Hoshi, now fully engaged in lecture mode. "You don't have the proper background to understand where its syntax comes from, how it fits into a family of languages to form its present structure. Even with the Romulans, I was reminded of Vulcan protolanguages, so I had those language trees to draw upon, but with something like this, it's a blank slate. You don't necessarily need that sort of context to figure out semantics on a basic level, but I've always thought that a healthy grounding in taxonomy will save you a lot of time down the road in defining the right grammatical typology."

Reed blinked.

Trip blinked.

Hoshi sighed. She wasn't getting anywhere.

The two men were now staring at Hoshi blankly, forks held in their hands over their respective breakfasts, while Hoshi's own food was all but ignored in front of her. Reed and Trip had that glazed look in their eyes that she recognized immediately, as she had seen it in some of her students back at the university—the look of utter cluelessness.

"Umm, never mind," she said, feeling more defeated than ever.

Trip took a couple of quick bites from his breakfast before getting up. Reed followed suit. "Listen," said Trip, "you clearly have a handle on what you're talking about, but I'm lost when it comes to linguistics. It's just not my strong suit."

Reed's expression seemed to indicate that he felt the same way, but he still tried to be encouraging. "I'm sure you'll figure this out in time."

Having admitted defeat in their attempt to understand what Hoshi was going through, Reed and Trip retreated as subtly as they could from the mess hall, passing Phlox on their way out. Hoshi put her head in her hands.

Phlox went up to Hoshi's table and began to greet her in Denobulan, but Hoshi held up one hand without looking up. "Please, Doctor. I'm not sure I can take another alien language right now."

"All right," he said. "May I at least sit down?"

At this, Hoshi looked up. "If you're willing to take the chance."

Phlox smiled and sat down immediately, but his expression quickly turned to one of concern. "This linguistic conundrum seems to be causing you a great deal of stress."

Hoshi glanced at the door where Reed and Trip had exited moments ago. "I doubt you're interested in hearing the details."

"I'd be delighted, actually," said Phlox. "Besides, a new perspective on the problem might be helpful for you."

"I'm not sure there are any more perspectives on the problem," said Hoshi, thinking of the lecture she'd just given. "I've already tried everything I can think of. I've used transformational models, Geissler variations, generative grammar, and every kind of phrase structure theory I'm familiar with. It's just not working."

The fact that Phlox, like Reed and Trip before him, probably had no idea what Hoshi was referring to no longer seemed to bother her—or Phlox himself, from all appearances, as he seemed no more perturbed than before. "Why hasn't the Universal Translator been more helpful to you?" he asked, sincerely. Hoshi was still a little skeptical that Phlox actually wanted her to elaborate, but she answered his question anyway.

"That's just it," she said. "The Universal Translator is just a set of assumptions provided by *us* about how languages are supposed to work. It doesn't make any determinations of its own when it encounters a new language, it just knows what speech should look and sound like. *This* is bound to be a pronoun, *this* is probably a response token, that sort of thing." Phlox kept looking at her attentively, so she continued. "It's just a summary of the way sentient beings tend to communicate, based on everything we've learned on Earth and elsewhere through centuries of linguistics." She sat back and sighed again, throwing the Universal Translator on the table in front of her. "But these people seem to make every one of those assumptions meaningless."

Phlox looked down at the discarded UT, then looked back up at her and said, "In that case, perhaps you simply need to ignore the rules for a while."

Hoshi considered that for a moment, then got up, grabbing her equipment from the table. "Thank you, Doctor. I'll try." It was time to head somewhere else where she could be left to concentrate on her work—the bridge, her quarters, anywhere—for the few remaining hours she had left before *Enterprise* went looking for a species that was easier to talk to.

As she headed for the door, however, Travis walked through it and smiled. "Great, just who I was looking for," he said, taking her hand and turning back to lead her through the corridor.

"Travis, what are you doing?" said Hoshi, struggling to keep the Universal Translator from dropping to the floor.

"I'm taking you someplace where you can look at things a different way."

"I don't think this is helping, Travis."

Hoshi was sitting cross-legged next to Travis on the sweet spot, looking down at the floor, and the Universal Translator she'd left there, from their inverted vantage point. She'd been to the sweet spot before, marvelling at the oddity of artificial gravity that allowed them to flip in midair and sit on the ceiling in this one part of the ship. This particular conversation with Travis, however, was doing nothing to improve her mood, or even offer a different perspective on her central problem.

Travis seemed to give out a bit of a sigh, but his perpetually positive mood did not seem dampened. "Stop thinking about the translation and just enjoy the moment."

Hoshi was touched that Travis was trying to be such a good friend to her right now, but she couldn't take her mind off the minutes that were rapidly slipping away. "I should be working right now. Everyone's counting on me, and we're running out of time."

"Sometimes, you just have to put the rules aside," said Travis. He grinned at her and added, "Haven't the movies taught you anything?"

Hoshi furrowed her brow, remembering that Phlox had just told her much the same thing. It seemed to be coming up a lot, and it niggled at the edges of her mind, somehow dovetailing back to the transmission. She wanted to believe there was something to that, though the pressure was mounting.

"When it comes to new languages, I'm the one who has to come up with the rules," she said. "I've already lost track of how many alien languages I've had to translate during our mission. If I can get the job done when there's a telepathic creature on the ship, or when we're in the heat of battle with moments to spare, why can't I do it with a simple planetary transmission?"

Travis nodded thoughtfully, no doubt noting the tone of resignation that had crept into her voice. After a few moments, he asked, "Why do you feel like you're the only one who could possibly solve this? You're talking as if this language can't be translated at all unless you're the one to do it."

"I *am* one to do it," she answered. "I'm the only linguist on the ship. It's my job, and if I can't do it—"

"It can't be done?" asked Travis. Hoshi had no response for that pointed question. "See, you do it so automatically, you don't even realize it's not necessary."

"What's not necessary?"

"Taking this whole weight upon yourself all the time." Before Hoshi could argue the point, Travis went on. "Sometimes, a mystery is going to stay a mystery—and that includes languages, Hoshi. If you don't figure this one out, someone else will. You can't have the answer every single time."

"I should, though," said Hoshi. "I should." Her voice carried a note of sorrow as she began to consider the idea that she wouldn't—not this time. She briefly wondered if she could get back her teaching position in Brazil.

Travis turned to face her directly, offering a supportive smile and allowing his empathy for her situation to come through in the tone of his voice. "If the captain says we need to move on, Hoshi, we'll move on, but it's not like you'll stop being a part of the crew because you had trouble with one problem along the way. *Enterprise* will still need you and your skills as much as ever."

Hoshi tried to offer up a smile in return, as Travis seemed to know what she'd been thinking, but it was hard enough in that moment for her to potentially admit defeat in this area, of all things.

After a few moments of silence, Travis spoke again. "Once you stepped onto this ship and became a part of the crew, you were accepted as part of the team, no matter what happens." He paused again, seemingly lost in a memory. "There's this town I remember on Vega Colony. Once you're in the city limits, you're not on the road anymore, you're considered a part of the town, and until you choose to leave—"

*Not.*

Hoshi held up a hand to stop him. "What did you just say?"

"Well, you're a part of the town until you choose to leave. . . ."

It was now Hoshi who was lost in thought, running new linguistic models in her head and comparing them to everything she had tried before. Could it be that simple?

*Not on the road . . . in the town . . .*

"What is it?" asked Travis.

"I can't believe it," said Hoshi. "Of course, that must be how it works. Not!"

Travis was thoroughly confused by that last outburst, but no explanation seemed to be forthcoming on Hoshi's part. She quickly flipped down to the actual floor and picked up her Universal Translator.

"I need to head back to my quarters. It was right there in front of me all along. I just needed to . . . forget the rules about what people are supposed to say." She looked up at the ceiling. "You're a genius, Travis!"

As Hoshi headed back into the corridor, Travis was left alone on the sweet spot, not quite sure how he had just helped, if at all. He flipped down and began to follow after Hoshi, offering only a hesitant, "You're welcome."

Less than an hour later, Hoshi was racing down the corridor from her quarters, and she managed to run into the turbolift just before it closed. Crewman Cutler and Crewman Dickison were in there with her, but she hardly noticed them as she furiously programmed new linguistic algorithms into the Universal Translator—and hummed to herself.

Crewman Cutler made a valiant attempt at conversation by saying, "That was a close one, Ensign. On your way to the bridge?" Hoshi didn't respond, or even acknowledge the question. "Crewman Dickison and I are just heading to the mess, but it looks like you're . . . hard at . . . work. . . ." Seeing that her efforts were fruitless, Cutler gave up, and an awkward silence ensued until the turbolift came to a halt.

The doors opened to let the two crewmen out. Crewman Dickison turned back and said, "Ensign," at that, Hoshi actually looked up, "were you just humming . . . 'Danke Schoen'?"

The turbolift doors closed again before Hoshi could give her an answer.

The same visage of that distant inhabited planet graced the viewscreen as the turbolift doors opened onto the bridge for Hoshi, but she barely glanced at it as she rushed to her station, nearly knocking over T'Pol in the process.

"Is everything all right, Ensign Sato?" she asked.

"Yes, yes, it's fine," Hoshi replied, in the most perfunctory way possible. She sat down and transferred all of the data from her Universal Translator to the console, watching as the newly created algorithm played itself out. After all this time of staring at her screens and listening to this transmission in vain, these last few seconds seemed more interminable than the last week had been.

Before she could further contemplate her own impatience, a result appeared on the screen directly in front of her, and Hoshi needed to sit back and look at that screen a few more times to be sure of what she saw. Where phonetic symbols had taunted her for days, laying out a riddle as frustrating as it was unintentional, the key she now offered took those seemingly meaningless sounds and unlocked their secrets, providing her with words—English words.

The bridge crew picked up on the fact that something was different this time, and were already turning their attention to the communications console when Hoshi laughed softly to herself and rested her head on the console. After a few moments, Captain Archer stood up from his chair and said, "It sounds like you have something, Ensign."

She looked up again at the faces of the bridge crew. Quiet resignation had given way to excited expectation, and she needed no sudden breakthrough to know what they were trying to tell her. Travis, in particular, was smiling at her with that toothy grin she had come to appreciate so much in the year they'd been working together on *Enterprise.*

Knowing that this was the culmination of the crew's built-up expectations, Hoshi cleared her throat dramatically.

"You are not in space," she began, reading directly from her console screen. "You are in the home of the Shisali, as surely as if your feet touched our soil. May our hands and our voices welcome you to all we have to offer."

Everyone on the bridge seemed pleased with the greeting—even T'Pol, though it was unlikely she would show much evidence of her reaction. The bridge crew were no doubt relieved, Hoshi thought, that their mission to this system was not a waste of time after all, and that she could confirm the friendliness of this species.

"Do you think you can put something through the new translation matrix so it will make sense to these . . . to the Shisali?" asked Archer.

Hoshi looked at her screen again and nodded slowly, with a renewed confidence. "I think so."

"Good," he said. "Open hailing frequencies."

Hoshi knew that Archer felt much more in his element now—now that he had more to do than simply *wait,* or consider the possibility of leaving. She pressed the appropriate controls on her console and nodded to the captain once more, letting him know that he could go ahead.

It was time to start communicating.

"This is Captain Jonathan Archer of the *Starship Enterprise.* I'm glad we could leave space for a while to enter your home, and I hope we have a chance to touch your soil soon."

# SPECULATIONS

# Time Line

Jerry M. Wolfe

**Jerry M. Wolfe,** a retired mathematics professor and longtime *Star Trek* fan, lives and writes at the beach in Lincoln City, Oregon, with his wife, Sawat. In addition to writing science fiction and fantasy, he makes frequent contributions to the local economy by attempting to play tournament poker at the local Indian casino. "Time Line" is his third story to appear in *Strange New Worlds*.

Gary Seven frowned in concentration as he rubbed his fingers over the face of a newspaper clipping, pressing it against a page of an album, waiting for the glue to take. Behind his desk, a window air conditioner struggled against the oppressive August heat of New York City while Isis dozed happily on the couch. His shape-shifting companion seemed to enjoy the black cat form she had taken for their time on Earth, so much so that he sometimes wondered if she wasn't really turning into a cat.

The aroma of grilled-cheese sandwiches wafted in from the kitchen and set his stomach to growling. Too much fat in the things, but add a good pickle and a few potato chips, and he couldn't resist them. He had first suggested to Robbie that they send out for Chinese, but she had been adamant.

"Just because I'm an official secret agent, or whatever we are, doesn't mean I can't grill cheese. Besides, I enjoy cooking for you."

When he had given her his best skeptical arch of his eyebrows, she laughed. "Well, sometimes I do. And this is one of those times."

Seven smiled as he pulled his hand away from the page, listening to the spirited if slightly off key humming coming from the kitchen. *Roberta Lincoln Seven.* He still had trouble believing that it was all true. It seemed an eon ago that he had come to Earth, his long-range transporter beam accidentally intercepted by a time-traveling *Enterprise.* Yet it had been only three years since he had met Kirk and Spock. Three years since he helped stop the suicidal orbiting of nuclear weapons. Now he was married, living on Manhattan's Lower East Side and happier than he had a right to be.

And he was still trying to stop humanity from destroying itself.

He read the clipping again. *Famed Biologist Missing*. The piece, over six years old, detailed how Doctor Charles Grayson, one of the world's leading geneticists, had disappeared while sightseeing in northern India. No trace of the man was ever found, and he was now presumed long dead. Seven had glued the clipping next to a copy of a grainy photograph taken only days before by a CIA agent operating out of Tashkent in Uzbekistan in the Soviet Union. Tapping into intelligence sources posed few problems when Seven had his own transport chamber that could take him anywhere in the world in a blink. Every spying device that he set had an automatic recall in case it was discovered. The trick was knowing where to put them, but after three years on the job, he had all the major sources covered.

Gary tapped his index finger at the base of the photo. One of the men in the picture was a high-ranking KGB official, Ivan Kotov, the target of the photographer, no doubt. The picture had seemed routine and relatively unimportant until the Beta 5 computer identified two of the other three men, at least to a certainty of eighty-eight point four seven percent. One was Boris Pachenko, a well-known Russian biochemist who had been reported dead in a plane crash in 1969. The other was Charles Grayson. The fourth, clearly the oldest of the group, was unknown.

Seven had known for some time that a secret project was located about ninety kilometers from Tashkent, but until now, it had been just one of a dozen that he monitored in the Soviet Union and worth only a small portion of his album; until the photo arrived.

Up to that point, he had assumed the Uzbekistan installation delved into biological or chemical warfare. Nasty and repugnant, but not yet a threat to mankind and hence not worthy of intervention on his part. The world was simply too large and complex for him to delve into every piece of Cold War insanity. Besides, his mission was to not intervene unless absolutely necessary for humanity's survival. But now he couldn't see how a geneticist fit into the picture and that made him nervous.

"You want mayo?" Robbie called from the kitchen.

Seven looked up and turned toward the open door. His mind warned *more fat*. His mouth said, "Yes, thanks." He sighed and returned his attention to the album. Filled with pages of heavy, cream-colored paper, it was an absurdly archaic and inefficient method for storing information, even for 1971 Earth. Yet, there was something about the process—the trimming, the gluing, the arranging of reports, clippings, and photos, the feel and even the smell of the paper itself—that he found curiously satisfying and useful. It calmed and distracted his conscious mind, allowing his subconscious to operate unhindered while staying focused on his task.

It was just one of a thousand small things, uniquely human things, that this crazy, primitive home world offered him. Things that even the advanced, nonhuman civilization that had nurtured him and sent him here could not. And working with Robbie, "Miss Lincoln" as he had first called her until something mysterious and wonderful had changed between them, had driven home an important lesson—advanced did not mean superior. The Earth that had shocked and disgusted him when he first arrived now felt as comfortable as an old chair, if one a bit soiled and worn around the edges. The place had grown incredibly dear to him. He'd truly come home.

Gary was still looking at the photo and worrying when a tray containing two grilled-cheese sandwiches, a mountain of potato chips, two pickles, and a glass of orange juice was suddenly plopped down on top of the album face. Then Robbie had her arms around him, kissing his cheek. Several blond strands of her hair fell across his face, and he felt the warmth of her body against his side. Seven laughed and pretended to struggle until she let him go.

"If I'd been an evil alien intent on a quick meal, then you'd be dead meat right now, Mister Seven."

"And where was my trusty protector while you were sneaking up on me?" he said, giving Isis a withering glance which she ignored by going back to sleep. Whatever rivalry might have once existed between Robbie and Isis had vanished after the marriage. Now they were pals. "I think it's a conspiracy," he said as he wrapped an arm around her waist, then kissed her full on the lips. "If you keep spoiling me like this, I won't ever leave the apartment."

"That's my plan. You'll cook and clean while I lie in bed and do my nails," she said, tilting her head back and holding her hands out in front of her as if they were objects of extreme delicacy. Seven laughed and gave her a playful swat on the behind. Robbie moved the album out from under the tray and saw what he had been working on.

"It's Grayson and that business in Uzbekistan isn't it?" she asked, her tone turning serious.

Seven nodded as he dug into the sandwich. He spoke between bites. "I have a bad feeling about it. It looks like the Soviets are going to absurd lengths—even by their standards—to keep this project secret. I don't see where Grayson fits into biological or chemical warfare, or why the Beta 5 has no photo record of this other man," he said, pointing to the fourth man. "He's standing with Grayson and Pachenko, and I'll bet this wonderful sandwich that he's a member of the project."

Robbie's arm tightened around him at the sandwich remark, and he paused long enough to claim another kiss before continuing. "That means he's a scientist, a bureaucrat, or maybe even security, though he looks too old for that. He's in his seventies at least. In all those cases, he should be in someone's photographic records."

Robbie leaned forward and examined the photo more closely. "His suit looks expensive. He's no janitor, that's for sure. You'd think an important man would be mentioned somewhere in all those reports you've copied."

Gary Seven looked into his wife's clear blue eyes, kissed her again and stood up so abruptly that he nearly toppled his glass of orange juice. As often happened, Robbie saw things that he missed. That was one reason they made such a good team. "Your husband can be a fool sometimes. I only asked the Beta 5 to correlate the photo with its files. I didn't think of names." Seven pushed a button hidden under the edge of his desk and a panel rolled back on a wall, revealing the Beta 5's screen. Moving the computer and the transport chamber to their apartment from his Manhattan office had been one of the first orders of business after their marriage.

"Computer, analyze all files pertaining to the project in Uzbekistan. List any names referenced for which no photo exists. Display corresponding reports."

"Processing," the computer said in its hollow, vaguely female voice. Isis lifted her head and watched the screen. In a matter of four or five seconds the Beta 5 spoke. "One name found. Jetter. Report displayed."

The report contained only one phrase with the man's name: "Jetter wants more generators." Seven turned to Robbie. "Jetter is a German name isn't it?"

The computer said, "Many Soviet citizens of German descent live—"

"I was asking my wife, Beta 5," he snapped.

"Please direct future inquiries more precisely," the Beta 5 said.

Gary grimaced and glared at the screen, but Robbie smiled. His struggles with the uppity computer always seemed to amuse her. Or maybe it was just the idea that a computer could be uppity.

"I think Jetter's German," Robbie said. "I had a friend in grade school with that last name, and he said his grandparents had immigrated from Germany."

Seven nodded and turned back to the screen. A hunch had formed which he wanted to check. "Computer, scan historical archives for the last thirty-five years for scientists with the family name 'Jetter.' "

The lights on the computer screen danced silently for a few seconds before the Beta 5 spoke. "Eight matches found. Professor Jacob Jetter, theoretical physicist, currently employed at University of British Columbia, Canada; Gerald Jetter, president of Jetter Pharmaceuticals, Oxnard, California, USA. . . ."

Seven went through the list, but none were old enough except one person, and that scientist was a woman. He frowned.

Robbie must have read his mind. "You think he might be one of those German scientists who worked for the Nazis, like Von Braun?"

He nodded. "The thought had occurred to me, but it looks like I'm wrong. Or maybe, they changed his name. That would be in keeping with the other secrecy measures. Either way, it's a dead end."

Robbie tapped a finger thoughtfully against her lips. "My aunt had a cousin whose last name was Hinkeldorff. She hated the name so much that she changed it."

Seven turned and said, "There is a point in this story, I hope." Robbie pursed her lips and scrunched up her nose in that way he loved and punched him lightly on the shoulder. "She changed it to her mother's last name."

Gary smiled and bowed. "A good point and worth a try. Computer, repeat last request, but this time search for scientists who are not named Jetter, but have any immediate relatives with family name Jetter."

It made sense. If a person were forced to choose a new last name, they might pick their mother's or some other close relative's. Still, it seemed like a long shot. This time the search took longer, and there were twenty-three names on the list, but one stuck out like a subspace beacon—Hans Kommer, Director Eugenics Project, Third Reich, Nazi Germany. Reported deceased, August 1945 by Soviet Commander, Berlin. His mother had been named Jetter.

"I love you," he said and held Robbie in his arms. But a cold knot had formed in his gut. The pieces now made an ugly picture.

Direct tampering with the human genome represented a potential for disaster that few if any on the planet would yet comprehend. He knew of two humanoid civilizations that had suffered destruction by just such a route. One race had vanished altogether, while the other slipped into barbarism and had yet to find its way back.

"You're going over to investigate, aren't you?" she said quietly.

"I have to, Robbie. If they're using genetic manipulation to accomplish what the Nazis tried by selective breeding, the Earth could be in real trouble." *Our children to come could be in real trouble.*

Robbie squeezed him tighter. "Be careful, Gary, and take Isis."

Before Seven could reassure Robbie, the Beta 5 blurted out a warning.

"I have detected anomalous graviton readings, source unknown. Pattern is consistent with entry of interstellar vehicle into normal space-time."

"What does it mean?" Robbie asked.

Seven frowned. "I'm not sure. Visitors maybe. Any further readings Beta 5?"

The machine was silent for several seconds before responding. "No further readings. Long range scans negative."

"Continue scanning for anomalous readings or energy outputs," he said. "In my absence, alert agent Roberta Seven of any new findings." Then he turned to Robbie. "It looks like a false alarm. Lots of things besides a starship can cause a graviton pulse."

Robbie grabbed his hand and squeezed it hard. "I hope so. Dealing with this Uzbekistan stuff is bad enough without little green men butting in."

Seven held Isis in his arms as Robbie inspected his KGB uniform one last time. Behind him, the heavy chromium door to the "bank vault," as Robbie called the transport chamber, was already open. Of course, the chamber looked that way by design, just as the Beta 5 would be mistaken for a television by any 1971 human.

"Colonel Vorsokov, you look good enough to take home," Robbie said with a smile, but he heard the tension beneath her light tone.

"Don't worry. This is just reconnaissance. You can monitor everything from here, and I've got the panic button if I get into trouble."

"Oh, I hate this part," she said and gave him a quick kiss.

Seven stepped into the chamber. There was a flash of light and a familiar instant of disorientation when he felt reality twist and dissolve away. Then he and Isis stepped from what looked like a fog bank onto the crest of a small hill. It was night and a chill wind whipped across the terrain, strongly enough that he had to pull the brim of his hat down. Below them lay a broad cluster of low, flat-roofed buildings surrounded by a tall, barbed-wire fence whose top was split into two strips, one leaning outward and one leaning inward. At each of the four corners of the fence stood a guard tower, replete with search lights. There would be dog patrols around the perimeter as well. Standard security measures. Isis gave a low growl, and her thoughts simultaneously registered in his head.

"Yes, Isis. It does look more like a prison than a research facility. We'll know more once we're inside."

He scanned the compound with a compact device that looked like an ordinary pen, then opened a channel to the Beta 5 and sent the transporter coordinates for a spot in the main complex, one that looked empty.

Soon he stood on a polished floor in a shadowy side corridor. The place smelled of floor wax and chemicals. He set Isis down and got his bearings.

He'd try to avoid contact with personnel, but if it happened, he was on a surprise security inspection. And if that didn't work, he had a special setting on his pen that would put a man to sleep and let him wake with no memory of what had happened. And finally there was the small indentation on his belt. The panic button, as Robbie had named it. Push that and the Beta 5 would transport him and Isis back to New York in an instant, no questions asked.

Seven stepped out into the main hallway and walked at an unhurried pace with Isis running ahead to scout out any trouble. The key was to look bored and confident and hope he outranked anyone he'd meet. His Russian was quite good though he wasn't up on the latest idioms, so he'd have to keep it basic.

Twenty minutes later and two floors lower, he finally stood before Charles Grayson's windowless office. Along the way, he had met several night workers, but they had seemed as uninterested in him as he had pretended to be in them. A pair of security guards had politely stopped him to check his credentials, but when they saw the KGB identification card, they blanched and couldn't let him go through quickly enough.

Seven transported himself and Isis inside and began to search Grayson's files. After several minutes, Seven found what he wanted when he spotted the edge of a black book poking up at the back of a filing drawer. It was Grayson's diary. He scanned through the pages while Isis paced before the door, keeping watch. He found an entry from over six years before: *September 10, 1965: Success! The first batch of viable embryos were produced today. We should know in nine months whether my techniques will work. Pachenko and Jetter are confident, but I am worried. It's all happening so fast. But if we succeed, the next step in human evolution will be at hand.*

Gary cursed. Just what he had feared. He moved ahead in the diary: *June 15, 1966: Eighty percent of the fetuses aborted, but we have one-hundred and twenty-eight healthy specimens. Now the testing begins.*

"They're not specimens, damn you! They're babies!" he muttered. Angrily, Seven flipped pages, reading entries rapidly: *November 5, 1967: The children are magnificent! Smarter, quicker, stronger, healthier than even I had hoped. Superhumans. Pachenko and I will get drunk tonight.*

Seven kept on reading though Isis growled from the doorway. "It's all right Isis. Just a few minutes more."

*July 29, 1970: What have we done? Today, I watched a child calmly choke a kitten to death with one hand, simply because the animal had scratched him. Later, we discovered a boy methodically beating another with a table leg, all over who controlled a sandbox. The child would have died if not for the guard. They have turned into deadly little beasts, selfish and ruthless. We pleaded with Jetter, but he doesn't want to see. He still thinks they can be controlled. For God's sake, he's planning to produce more of these monsters. Pachenko and I will get drunk tonight.*

That was enough. Gary put the diary back and set the room as it had been. He could not have imagined anything worse. This business had to be stopped. A signal came through from the Beta 5.

"Seven, here."

*"Multiple transporter beams detected in your vicinity. Type unknown. Origin unknown. Vector trace shows they originated from outside Earth's atmosphere."*

"Thank you, Beta 5. I'll scan locally and see what I can find out."

Isis leaped onto a desk and gave a throaty growl. "I don't know who's dropping in, Isis, but I think we'd better find out." He brought out his versatile pen and set it for wide scan. Then he slowly rotated one full turn. "Four separate beams came down, but they terminate about ten meters below the bottom level of the complex. No lifeforms. So, it's not *who,* but *what.* And whatever it is, is shielded in some way." Isis complained as he continued to manipulate the instrument, changing the sensory harmonics to try and penetrate the shielding. "I don't like the smell of this, either, but if I can just get a partial reading . . . uh-oh! There's anti-matter down there!"

He probed further into the buried device, but the readings were intermittent and probably unreliable. But the main facts were all too clear. "It's a bomb. Four bombs. This place will be a molten crater in less than six minutes." Gary hated violence, but whoever had set the bombs was certainly solving his problem of what to do about the project.

The Beta 5 could transport the devices one by one into space if he could get precise coordinates, but with the trouble he was having with the readings, that would be too slow and risky. It looked like the project would be obliterated no matter what he did, but there might be time to save lives. Seven quickly phoned security, told them about the bombs and ordered them to signal an immediate evacuation. That took less than thirty seconds, but the fools were wasting precious time to contact the base commander first.

"Let's find an alarm," he said, and scooped Isis into his arms. He left Grayson's office and sprinted down the narrow corridor to where it joined a larger one. He turned left at the joining and almost collided with three young boys who skidded to a halt just in time. With a start, Seven realized he must be looking at three of the "specimens."

They were large and strong looking for five-year-olds with bright eyes and looks of disdain. Not a hint of fear. Still, they were children, and he could not help thinking about Robbie and the family they might have someday. The middle of the three, a tall lad with shiny black hair and eyes that reminded Gary of a hawk, stepped forward and inspected Seven. A fierce intelligence burned behind the boy's imperious stare. And a hint of curiosity. Now it was Seven who felt like the specimen.

"Not the usual sort is he? A colonel with a black cat. Must be KGB. He'll try to put us back, but we've already gotten further than Sanjo and his toads."

Suddenly, the boy bolted past Seven. Or tried to. The child was incredibly quick, but Gary's trained reflexes took over, and he snatched the squirming boy by the back of his shirt and lifted him by one hand into the air. The astonished child stopped kicking and glared at Seven, their eyes locking. Isis dropped to the floor, snarled, and morphed to panther size, blocking the path of the other two. They froze in place.

Seven glanced at his watch. Three and a half minutes! Despite what Grayson had written about them, he knew that he could not just abandon these children to be vaporized. Whatever they might become, they were innocents thrust into a situation they did not create. They did not deserve to be slaughtered. He set the boy down on his feet and knelt down to eye level. He laid his hand on the boy's shoulder, but it was pushed away with surprising force. Meanwhile, Isis returned to her normal size and returned to Seven's side. The hawk-eyed boy had not seen her transformation, but both his companions continued to watch Isis with bulging eyes and mouths agape.

"What's your name, son?"

The child looked insulted. "You must be new here. My name is Khan. Khan Noonien Singh."

"Khan. Listen carefully. There's a bomb in this building. We've got to get the children out of here immediately."

The boy studied Seven's face intently as if searching for a lie or trick. Then he said, "Follow us!" and turned and ran along with his two companions. Sirens began to wail across the complex but probably too late to save anyone. Gary snatched up Isis and ran after the three boys, wondering if it was too late for them as well. His watch gave them less than three minutes.

Khan and his friends took an ingenious route through storerooms and access tunnels that was surely not the straightest way, but avoided all guards. By the time Seven entered the "nursery," less than a minute remained. When he stepped into the room filled with bunks, he found the children alone. A security guard, stationed behind a wall of thick glass, lay slumped over his table near an empty bottle of vodka. Seven wondered if Khan had something to do with that. The children stopped moving and speaking as soon as they saw Seven's uniform. Glancing around, he saw all the colors of humanity. At least the insane Nazi ideas about racial purity had been cast aside in the project.

"Children. There's a bomb, and we're going to evacuate. Everyone come close to me. Crowd in as close as you can. Hurry!" The commands, given in harsh, rapid Russian, had little effect until Khan and his three companions moved forward. Then the rest crowded in quickly but with no sign of panic. Seven took out his pen and spoke to the Beta 5. "Transport everyone within six meters of my present coordinates. How far can you safely move us?"

*"Approximately 1500 kilometers."*

Seven thought for a moment then gave orders to the Beta 5. There were five seconds left when the world disappeared. Then they were all stepping out of a fog and onto sandy soil near a large city glowing in the darkness. Tehran, though the children would not know. No one was nearby. The children burst into animated conversation, and Khan tugged at his leg. "How did you do that? I demand to know how!"

Seven took out the pen and said, "It's simple. You just point this and pull." Khan collapsed to the ground, a peaceful look on his face, as did his two companions, and the five children surrounding them. Soon, Seven had all the children lying senseless, smiles on their faces. When they woke, they would remember nothing that had happened to them during the past hour. The desert air was cold, but he had no intention of stranding them there. Instead, he called the Beta 5 with a new command.

"Beam them all into the courtyard of the Swiss Embassy."

Seven moved away with Isis and watched the children disappear into the night. There would be a big story in the papers, but it would soon blow over. Another unsolved mystery. The explosion in Uzbekistan would probably be passed off as an accident or some nuclear test. It was impossible to predict what would become of the children, but at least now they had a chance to find real mothers and fathers who could teach them something of compassion and responsibility. Maybe. Isis growled in his arms.

"I'm not sure I did the right thing, either. Maybe I stopped someone else from doing the right thing," Seven said, though he had serious doubts about anyone willing to casually slaughter hundreds of people. "I'm not sure. But I couldn't just leave them there. I just couldn't." He stopped and watched the distant lights of the city for a few seconds, then pulled Isis to his chest. "Let's go home."

Gary Seven leaned against the back of the couch and sipped from a cup of hot tea that he held in his left hand. His right arm was draped over Robbie's shoulders and she snuggled into the crook of his arm. Isis slept at the other end of the couch. The Beta 5's screen was exposed on the wall. He was waiting for headquarters to respond to the report he had sent back. Doubt still gnawed at him.

"What's done is done, Gary. You did what you thought best. You chose life over death, and I can't believe that's wrong."

He snuggled his head against hers. "I love you. But what if I've unleashed something terrible on the world? That's what I was sent here to stop."

Before Robbie could respond, the grizzled but kindly face of Zagor, the one who had trained Seven, appeared on the screen of the Beta 5. Zagor was not human, but he took on the countenance of an old man when he dealt with Seven or any other human. That way, no operative could ever reveal who had sent them. This used to bother Gary, but he had finally come to think of Zagor as the man he appeared to be.

Zagor nodded in greeting. "Gary. Roberta. How nice to see you again. We have analyzed your report at great length. Frankly, our social dynamicists are quite concerned. They estimate that the likelihood of human civilization destroying itself will rise to 78.2 percent if these genetically enhanced children survive to adulthood unfettered."

Seven sagged back. "Then I've made a mess of it."

"Perhaps not. There is the matter of the bombs and who set them."

"Do we know who did it?" Seven asked.

Zagor shrugged. "We do not, I am sorry to say."

"But why would they come to Earth to kill a few children?" Robbie asked.

Zagor shook his head and said, "We are not certain. However, the whole business smacks of an attempt to manipulate the time line. Foolish and dangerous, especially since this era is so fragile and unstable for humanity. Even tiny changes could lead to unpredictable results."

"Oh," she said, her face locked into a frown. Suddenly Robbie brightened. "But doesn't this mean that Gary did the right thing?"

Gary squeezed her hand but shook his head. "By making the odds better than three to one that humanity will destroy itself? Hardly a triumph."

"Now wait a minute," Robbie said. "If these time travelers wanted the children dead, then that might be a pretty good reason to keep them alive."

Zagor laughed. "Roberta, I quite agree. My people do not time travel by choice, and we peek into the time line as little as possible. Interpretation is perilous, cause and effect often obscure. We do not know the ultimate consequence of the actions taken by Gary. Who knows what advances may come more quickly as a result of these children?" Then his face grew sad. "Or what grief. Every coin has two faces. You both have much work ahead to reduce the odds of destruction for humanity, but take heart.

"For our part, we will inform an organization in the far future of Earth, one that polices the time continuum to prevent such disruptions." Zagor folded his hands and smiled. "Agent Seven, your report is accepted, and we recommend no further action regarding the children at this time. However, you are instructed to monitor their progress and set up means to detect any further attempts to interfere with the time line."

"We will, Zagor," Seven said. Zagor nodded and his image faded leaving only the blank screen of the Beta 5. Gary pulled Robbie close to him. "You won't be hearing any more doubts from me about my decision. You're right. It's done, and we've got work to do."

"Not for the rest of the day we don't," she said and kissed him long and hard. Then they sat quietly, sipping tea.

"You never finished the story of your aunt's cousin," he said at last.

"What?"

"You said she changed her name from Hinkeldorff."

"What about it?"

"What did she change it to?"

"Oh. Crampot."

It was the first time Seven had used the pen to help remove tea from a carpet.

# Echoes

Randy Tatano

SECOND PRIZE

**Randy Tatano** is a former television reporter making his second appearance in *Strange New Worlds*. His first story, "Remembering the Future," appeared in *Strange New Worlds 9*. The Stamford, Connecticut, native has just completed a novel he hopes to publish. He'd like to thank Margaret Clark, Paula Block, and especially Dean Wesley Smith for his encouragement over the years and for creating a supportive environment for writers on his website. And of course, nothing would be possible without wife Myra, his soulmate and muse for the past nineteen years.

"This is *completely* different," said Doctor Solomon, finishing his third cup of coffee and banging his mug on the table. "Shinzon was a clone. He was evil. It was also two hundred years ago."

"David, you know how the Federation feels about genetic engineering, even to fight the Borg," said Commander Jillian Rush, keeping her voice just above a whisper. The topic was taboo and the Starbase dining room was peppered with Federation officials, though she doubted anyone could hear their discussion above the loud conversation that filled the place. "They'll never go for it." She took another bite of her salad.

The door whooshed open and Solomon smiled. "They already have," he said, pointing to the entrance.

A handsome thirty-something man in a Starfleet uniform entered, moved to the food replicator and placed his order in a British staccato. "Chicken sandwich. Tea. Earl Grey. Hot."

Jillian looked back at Solomon. Eyes the color of pale topaz grew wide as she gestured to the man. "Him?" she asked, talking through the spinach leaves.

Solomon nodded, his smile growing out of his weathered face.

Jillian couldn't believe it, but it was there right in front of her. The broad shoulders, the piercing eyes, the unmistakable swagger were James T. Kirk's. He shot her a smile right out of a Starfleet history book as he picked up his tray and passed their table. His musky cologne remained in his wake. But the accent and deep vocals belonged to Jean-Luc Picard. The voice definitely didn't match the face. "How? When?" she asked.

Solomon leaned forward a bit, his chocolate brown eyes gleaming like a child's on Christmas morning. "I got the approval a few years ago. Acquiring the DNA of Starfleet's greatest captains was a little tricky without raising suspicion, as you can imagine."

Jillian washed the spinach leaves down her throat with sweet iced tea, her lone non-healthy addiction, the sugar giving her a shot of adrenaline she didn't need. "What did you do, employ grave robbers?"

"Time travelers." Solomon ran his hands back through his salt-and-pepper crew cut. "I don't know exactly how it was done. I told them what I needed, and they provided it."

*"They?"*

"The less you know the better. This is *beyond* top secret. Only two high-ranking members of the Federation even know about it. Along with a few covert operatives."

Jillian watched as the Kirk-Picard hybrid began to eat his lunch, and seemed to be quite formal in doing so, wiping the corners of his mouth after each bite. The chicken sandwich may as well have been Beef Wellington. "So," said Jillian, "you're telling me that he's half James Kirk and half Jean-Luc Picard?"

"Uh, well . . . not exactly," said Solomon.

Jillian tossed her fork into the salad bowl. "What do you mean, *not exactly?*" She pulled her dark brown hair back behind her ears, placed her hands on the cool table and leaned forward, looking at him like an angry parent even though she was ten years younger. "What other ingredients are in this recipe, David?"

Solomon looked at the hybrid to avoid her eyes. "Only two others. Kathryn Janeway is one. She dealt with the Borg on a personal level. She had a long, close relationship with Seven of Nine. She knew every Borg still has a soul buried deep inside. And she had other qualities I needed. Or rather, *he* needed." He looked back at her again. "Also, the Picard part isn't totally Picard."

"Huh?"

"His DNA was acquired when he was Locutus. So in effect, his genetic code contains what might best be referred to as *echoes* of the Borg."

"Wow, this just keeps getting better and better. So did you get Kirk's DNA when he was split into the good Kirk and the evil Kirk?"

"No, Kirk is plain old James T. Kirk. From just after the Khitomer Accords near the end of his Starfleet career."

Suddenly Jillian realized there was even more. "You said there were *two* others. Janeway and who?"

He shook his head. "I cannot tell you. Even those behind this project do not know. I'm not sure they would approve. I know you wouldn't."

"Wow, that makes me feel comfortable."

"But it was necessary if this mission is to succeed."

"And this mission is?"

"The end of the Borg. Forever."

"So does *he* have a name?" asked Jillian, cocking her head in the direction of the hybrid.

"He does," said Solomon. He called to the hybrid across the room. "Sam, come join us."

The hybrid looked in their direction, ran a napkin across his mouth, picked up his tray, and walked to their table. He put down his lunch and extended his hand. "I didn't see you over here, Doctor Solomon," said Sam.

Solomon shook his hand. "Sam, I'd like you to meet the best science officer in the fleet, Commander Jillian Rush. Jillian, this is Captain Sam Farragut."

Sam turned to Jillian and extended his hand. "Pleasure to meet you, Commander Rush," he said, Picard's voice coming out of Kirk's mouth.

"Likewise Captain," she said, jaw dropping in amazement like a star-struck teenager as she experienced a warm, firm grip and got a closer look. Solomon's work was incredible. The captains in question were long dead, but every Starfleet officer knew Kirk, Picard and Janeway's mannerisms from holodeck simulations required at the Academy. Sam Farragut could be James

Kirk's brother. The walk with a purpose, the strong jaw, the *look*. The voice was definitely Picard, refined and proper with a little whiskey scratch to it that screamed Kathryn Janeway. The captain pulled out a chair and sat down.

"I've been meaning to stop by, Doctor Solomon," said Farragut. "But my schedule has been rather full. I know we have a lot to do before . . ." He stopped and nodded toward Jillian.

"You can speak freely in front of Commander Rush," said Solomon. "She'll be joining us on the mission."

*I'll what?* Jillian stared enough cutlery to host a dinner party through Solomon, who then gave her his famous *Oh-sorry-Jillian-I-forgot-to-tell-you-about-that-part-of-the-experiment* look.

"Excellent," said Farragut. He turned toward Jillian. "Then you must be as excited as I am."

"Blown away," said Jillian, turning toward Solomon with a faux smile. "You have no idea."

"Jillian and I have worked together on various projects for more than fifteen years," said Solomon.

*And it might not make it to sixteen when I get through with you . . .*

He continued. "She was instrumental in coming up with the plan."

*I was?*

"I'm honored to be chosen to command the mission," said a smiling Captain Farragut. "A once in a lifetime opportunity to rid the universe of the Borg." Suddenly he turned serious. *"Let them die."*

"We're certainly in agreement on that, Captain," said Solomon.

Farragut's combadge beeped. "Farragut here . . ."

*"Priority message for you, Captain."*

"I'll take it in my office," he said. He got up to leave. "Guess I'll have to take a rain check."

"We'll talk soon," said Solomon.

"Make it so. Tomorrow," said Farragut. "Very nice meeting you, Commander Rush," he said, nodding at Jillian as he walked away.

"You too," she said. Jillian waited for him to get out of earshot before she let her voice jump across the table at Solomon. "You wanna tell me the rest of the story, David?"

"I would love to," he said. But then he stopped talking.

"Well?"

"Unfortunately I cannot. You will have to wait till we are under way."

"Under way? To where?"

The turbolift doors opened and Jillian stepped out onto the bridge. The crew was making last minute preparations to get under way. She could feel the excitement in the air, as everyone knew this mission was quite different.

She ran her fingers across the raised letters of the brass dedication plaque adorning the wall. Jillian liked the *U.S.S. McAuliffe,* though the air temperature was a bit chilly for her taste. Commissioned just six months ago, the ship still had a new antiseptic smell to it, yet the corps of engineers had worked out all the bugs. The science station featured the best equipment Starfleet had to offer. Designed for a crew of thirty, she was only carrying seven on this mission. Jillian would like having the ship almost to herself, as she and Solomon were the only people not assigned to the bridge full-time. She straightened her new uniform, which fit her tall, well-toned body perfectly. Jillian slid her hand across the smooth steel railing that ran around the perimeter of the bridge as she walked toward David Solomon, who was standing behind the Captain's chair. Farragut was busy giving orders.

"*Now* are you going to tell me where we're going?" she asked.

"Soon as we get under way," said Solomon.

"Never a straight answer," said Jillian. "No wonder you never got married."

"Guess the invitation to *your* wedding got lost in the mail," he countered.

"Touché."

Farragut heard her voice and turned around. "Commander

Rush, I trust you found the equipment on our little ship suitable?"

"Very nice, Captain."

"Everything check out?"

"All systems working perfectly, Captain. You have some really nice toys. I'm like a kid in a candy store."

"Good." He turned to Solomon. "Are we ready, then, Doctor Solomon?"

"Everything is in place," said David, casually leaning his slender two-meter frame against the back railing.

Farragut turned back and faced the helm. "Take us out, Mister Kaylon," he said, sliding to the edge of the captain's chair.

Lieutenant Frank Kaylon engaged the thrusters of the *McAuliffe* and nudged the ship out of spacedock. This was Jillian's fourth ship, but she always liked being on the bridge as a mission got under way.

The ship moved out into open space. "We're clear, sir," said Kaylon, a thirtyish officer whose square jaw belonged in a Starfleet recruiting poster. "Course heading, Captain?"

*Wow, even the helmsman doesn't know where we're going.*

"Lay in a course for the Borg home planet," said the Captain.

Kaylon turned around and looked at Farragut as though he were crazy. "Sir?"

"You heard me, mister," snapped Farragut.

Jillian's mouth went dry in an instant. She turned on a dime, grabbed Solomon's forearm and pulled him to the back of the bridge. "David, what the *hell* are you doing?"

Solomon took her hand in his own. "I couldn't tell you, Jillian. In fact, the Captain and I are the only people on this ship who knew our destination. We had to maintain the utmost secrecy."

She moved to within a few inches of his face and lowered her voice. "You had *no right* to drag me on a suicide mission without telling me first."

"It's not a suicide mission, Jillian. You have to trust me."

"No, we're just going to drop in on the Borg for a visit. I didn't volunteer for this, David. Stop this ship, right now!"

Sam Farragut overheard and swung his chair around to face her. "I'm sorry, Commander Rush, but that is not possible. Once the mission began there was no turning back. We cannot risk having any information regarding our plan leave this vessel until we complete our mission."

"Why am I even here?" she asked.

"That will become clear very soon," said Solomon.

"I'm sorry if you were misled, Commander," said Farragut, sitting down with Jillian in the otherwise empty dining room. He placed a plate filled with chicken parmigiana and garlic bread on the table. "I simply assumed . . ."

"Well, you assumed wrong," she snapped. She exhaled and realized she was arguing with the wrong man. "I'm sorry, Captain, that was out of line."

"I can understand your feelings," said Farragut. "Traveling to the Borg homeworld isn't exactly in your job description as a scientist. But since the plan was your inspiration I thought you were on board."

*Well, obviously everyone knows the plan but me. Since David is keeping me in the dark, maybe I can pry it out of this guy.* "So what do you think of our chances, Captain?"

"If I knew the entire plan, I could answer accurately."

"Excuse me?"

"For security reasons, Doctor Solomon has only informed me of my part in this mission. I honestly have no idea what the two of you will be doing."

"You're the captain and you don't know?"

"I trust my superiors and Doctor Solomon. They have assured me that everything will become clear at the proper time."

Jillian couldn't even begin to process this giant riddle of which she had become a part. She sat there, fuming, wanting to strangle David Solomon. She ate a few spoonfuls of her minestrone, but it tasted liked ketchup with rubber vegetables. She could smell the garlic from Farragut's plate and wished it was in her soup. She shook her head and looked off into space, trying to find a reason to calm her nerves as she grabbed the side of the bowl to warm her hands.

"Jillian. You know, I've heard that name before, but I can't place it," said Sam Farragut, obviously wanting to change the subject.

"It's not terribly common," said Jillian, still wanting to maintain her anger but being polite. "Kind of old fashioned. My mother named me after a marine biologist of some note. I looked her up once. Turned out she spelled it with a G."

"Regardless of the spelling, it suits you," said Farragut with a flash of Kirk's charm.

"Thank you."

"Doctor Solomon tells me I was named after a distant relative."

"Doctor Solomon told you?"

"I have no memory of my life before I was twenty-seven years old. I was captured by an alien race that wiped my memory clean. But I don't even remember that. I was rescued by Doctor Solomon on one of his science missions."

*So that's how he did it. . . .*

Farragut continued. "Sometimes I think I remember things. When I first heard your name, it seemed familiar. It happens to me a lot. I think I've been places before, met certain people, things of that nature. But that's as far as it goes. I can't ever make the connection. The doctor says there are echoes of the past kicking around in my head."

"Maybe someday you'll remember it all," said Jillian. *Then again, maybe it is best if you don't.*

"Approaching Borg solar system barrier," said Kaylon, as the entire crew gathered on the bridge. "Contact in twenty minutes."

Jillian felt like she had itching powder in her clothes. She'd studied a few captive Borg in her lifetime, but the thought of being this close . . .

"Slow to impulse, but maintain our cloak," said Farragut. He got out of the captain's chair and turned to face David Solomon. "It is time," he said.

Solomon nodded.

"Time for what?" asked Jillian. "Have you two figured out a way to get around that barrier?"

"We don't have to," said Solomon.

"They're going to lower it for us," said Farragut. The Captain turned to his communications officer. "Open a channel to the Borg homeworld."

Jaws dropped all over the bridge as no one could believe the order.

Jillian jumped from nervous to downright scared at warp speed. "David?"

Farragut repeated the order. "Open a channel . . ."

"Yes, sir," said the communications officer. "Hailing frequencies open."

"David, what's he doing?" Jillian asked. Solomon didn't answer.

Farragut moved to the front of the bridge and looked directly into the view screen. His face suddenly went blank.

"I am Locutus of Borg," he said, without emotion.

Jillian pulled David Solomon into the dimly lit ready room just off the bridge. "You just told the Borg we're here." She crossed her arms and stretched to her full five feet ten inches. "Explain."

"We had to," said Solomon. "It is the only way for us to get inside the barrier."

"And what are we going to do when we get there?"

"Destroy one of their suns. We have trilithium missiles on board."

"*Trilithium?* How did you get that aboard a Federation starship?" Solomon started to answer but she stopped him by putting up her hand. "Don't say it. Let me guess . . . I don't want to know."

"You're right. You don't."

"Wait a minute, David. How is destroying one of their suns going to kill them?"

"We're not going to kill the Borg," said Solomon.

Jillian felt beads of sweat blossom on her forehead as her heart jumped into overdrive. She was now convinced that David Solomon, quite possibly the smartest man in Starfleet, had gone terribly mad. She moved to within inches of the scientist, close enough to smell the coffee habit on his breath. "You said this mission would bring the end of the Borg. Forever. I remember your words like you said them five minutes ago."

"The Borg will be gone, Jillian, but no one is going to die."

"Please stop speaking in riddles," she said.

"Remember you asked me about the fourth person to contribute DNA to Sam Farragut?"

"You gonna tell me now?"

"Yes. The fourth person is Tolian Soran."

Her jaw dropped. "You gave Farragut the DNA of a madman? The guy who killed James Kirk? Are you insane?"

"It was the only way, Jillian. Soran's obsession is crucial to the mission."

"How?"

Solomon moved to a computer screen, punched up the view from the bridge camera and swung the screen around so that it was facing Jillian. "Extreme magnification," he said. The computer complied.

What she saw made it all come together.

A giant electric white ribbon weaving its way through space. Toward the Borg solar system.

"The doorway to the Nexus."

"My operatives in the Federation have been steering it toward the Borg homeworld for two years, changing the effects of gravity on the ribbon by destroying five insignificant uninhabited worlds along the way. The destruction of the Borg sun is the final step. It will turn the ribbon directly toward the Borg homeworld."

"You mean everyone on the Borg planet . . ."

"Will be in the Nexus."

"You're going to turn these monsters loose in paradise?"

"They won't be monsters when they get there, Jillian. That's why we needed Janeway in the equation. She reached Seven of Nine. She knew that under all that hardware there was still a little girl who never got a chance to grow up. In the same way Farragut will reach the Borg Collective in the Nexus. All the echoes of all those souls will be heard. They will finally be at peace. Nothing else is possible in the Nexus."

She paced around the room as she tried to process the whole scenario. "You said Farragut will reach them *in* the Nexus. So he's . . ."

"Not coming back. He's known all along. He is obsessed with getting there."

"But Farragut told me he doesn't know the whole plan."

"He doesn't know we're going to destroy the sun. If he did, the Borg would know instantly when he contacts them. He believes the Nexus is simply going to pass over the Borg homeworld. He probably thinks we're simply here to study and dismantle anything scientific left behind to prevent them from starting up again. He wants to go, Jillian."

Jillian shook her head. "Because you made him that way. Because of Soran's DNA."

Solomon nodded. "Soran provided two things. His homeworld was destroyed by the Borg. And he was obsessed with the Nexus. Farragut needed personal revenge to sign on for this mission and an intense desire to get to the Nexus. With Janeway's influence, he knows he hates the Borg, not the beings that were assimilated by them. We needed Picard's echoes of Locutus to get us through the barrier and to communicate with the Borg. And we needed Kirk's ability to pull off the greatest bluff in the history of Starfleet . . . along with someone who doesn't mind bending the rules for the right reasons."

"But even with all the things those four people have endured, how do their memories translate to DNA?"

"Echoes," said Solomon. "It was so simple. If it weren't for you I never would have figured it out."

"*What* are you talking about?"

"Remember the time you injured your hand?" He reached for her left hand, and touched it briefly. She jerked it back.

The memory brought a chill. The lab accident, the horrible burn. The rehab had taken months. "How could I forget it?"

"You still flinch whenever anything comes near your left hand, even though the hand is perfectly normal now. Since the accident you do everything with your right hand, even though you were born left-handed. Your left hand doesn't have brain cells, but it has a memory. It is actually scared of being hurt again. In the same way DNA can be given an echo, when manipulated with certain aspects of the donor's memory engrams. In other words, Farragut knows he wants to liberate the Borg, he just doesn't know or remember why."

Her interest was definitely piqued. "You told me about this hypothesis years ago. It's actually true?"

"I proved it just before I started this project. It was the missing piece of the puzzle. We always knew we'd get a great leader combining the DNA of all these captains. But this mission demanded more. It needed the echoes of their past experiences. Farragut gets his feelings from the engrams, but not the specific memories."

She had to admit, it made sense. "You're a brilliant man, David. Still, I don't understand why you couldn't have confided in me earlier. Especially since this was supposedly *my idea*. Mind explaining that one?"

"Remember that dinner party at Starfleet headquarters a few years ago when the discussion arose about who was the best captain of the *Enterprise*?"

"Vaguely."

"Half the table favored Kirk since he fired phasers first and asked questions later. The others liked Picard's diplomatic ability. Remember what you said?"

"I do now," said Jillian, the memory suddenly vivid in her mind. *"If you could combine those two, you'd really have something."*

Solomon nodded. "I just took your advice."

\*     \*     \*

*"Bridge to Captain."*

Sam Farragut tapped his combadge as he moved behind the transporter room control panel. "Farragut here."

*"Kaylon here, sir. The Borg have lowered the force field. We are through the barrier and have entered their solar system. Looks like they bought your act as Locutus, Captain."*

Sam Farragut double-checked the transporter controls, turned, and shook David Solomon's hand for the last time. "Goodbye, Doctor. Thank you for everything."

"Goodbye, Sam. An eternity of peace is waiting for you."

Farragut moved to Jillian and gave her a firm handshake. "Wish I'd had time to get to know you better," he said.

"You too," she said. "Good luck, Captain."

Farragut tapped his combadge as he moved to the transporter pad. "Farragut to bridge."

*"Bridge here,"* said Kaylon.

"Transferring command to Commander Rush," said Farragut. "Follow her orders to the letter," said Farragut.

*"Aye, sir,"* said Kaylon.

"Energize," said Farragut.

Jillian hit the transporter controls. He was gone in a second.

"We need to get to the bridge right away," said Solomon, leading the way out of the transporter room.

"So is this the part where I come in?" asked Jillian.

"You have command rank," said Solomon, maintaining a brisk pace. "You're a science officer. And you're the only person with those two qualifications I could trust."

"I'm flattered," said Jillian, "I think. I'll let you know if we make it out of this alive."

They reached the turbolift and moved inside. "Bridge," said Solomon.

"So you just need me to fire the torpedo and get us out of here."

"Exactly. Farragut is going to buy us the time we need. But the launch must be precise, within a two minute window."

"Cutting it awfully close, aren't we?"

"I knew Farragut wouldn't be able to buy us much time." He handed her an isolinear chip. "Here is the information you need."

The turbolift door swooshed open, letting in air that somehow smelled different, like a long abandoned trunk in an attic. David Solomon stepped out first.

He turned abruptly and Jillian saw pure fear in his face, just before the Borg drone grabbed him and injected him in the neck with nanoprobes.

"Deck five!" she yelled, and the turbolift door closed just as she caught a glimpse of the entire bridge crew being assimilated.

She was alone on the ship.

Farragut must have failed.

David was gone.

She was the last hope.

She began to shiver, and not from the cold temperature.

*Think, Jillian. You have command rank. Act like it.*

She had one option. The auxiliary control room. If she could get there she could fire the torpedo.

*If* she could get there. The Borg would know she was headed that way.

She took a deep breath and exhaled as much tension as possible. "Stop turbolift. Deck three," she said. The turbolift slowed, then started to move back the way it came.

*Breathe, Jillian. One way or another it will all be over in minutes. When the hell is that launch window anyway? What two minutes are we talking about?*

Her heart was hung up on her tonsils. The computer voice announced her arrival. "Deck three."

She reached for her side, but she had forgotten her weapon. Of course.

She was a science officer, not a soldier.

The turbolift door slid open and revealed an empty corridor. One hundred feet were all that stood between her and the end of the Borg. She ran, long legs eating up huge chunks of hallway till she reached the auxiliary control room door. She paused a moment, listening.

It was quiet.

The door whooshed open and she quickly moved to the computer station. She popped the chip Solomon had given her into the computer. "C'mon, c'mon!" she said, though it only took a second for the information to be displayed. The targeting coordinates were there, along with the timeframe. The helm would automatically turn the ship toward the nearest starbase at maximum warp the second the torpedo cleared the bay.

The computer displayed the two-minute window.

It didn't begin for forty seconds. She'd made it.

Less than a minute and she'd be home free. She drummed her fingernails on the desk. *C'mon clock, move!* As long as . . .

The Borg drone materialized behind her, grabbed her head and injected the nanoprobes into her neck before she even had a chance to put up a fight.

"Resistance is futile," said the Borg. *Or am I hearing that in my head?*

*I hear them.* A thousand voices, no, a million, no, so many more than anyone could comprehend. . . .

*"You are part of the Collective now. . . ."*

*"Your designation is Six of Six. . . ."*

The nanoprobes raced through her body and she began to lose muscle control. Her arms were starting to feel like jelly. She saw the clock ticking down on the computer as she grew light-headed. The voices were pulling the memories from her . . . ripping her private thoughts from the deep recesses of her soul.

*Daddy, I'm going to name my kitten Pandora . . .*

*I just got accepted to Starfleet, Mom . . .*

*I love you, but my life is out there . . .*

*David, are you out of your mind?*

*Let them die . . .*

Twenty-nine seconds . . .

She heard them, voices crying in desperation as they were being assimilated all over the galaxy.

*Help me!*

*No, please don't . . .*

She felt a familiar presence cry out from the consciousness and touch her mind. *"Jillian!"*

*"David?"*

*"Jillian! I'm losing . . . so sorry . . . please forgive . . ."*

She fought to maintain her identity but it was so hard . . .

*Resistance is futile . . .*

Eighteen seconds . . .

She felt her mind moving toward the Collective consciousness now, as if drawn to an irresistible magnet, her strength seemingly draining out of her body. But she continued to fight. She had to. She felt David's identity disappear into the hive, his voice now a lifeless monotone. *"I am Five of Six . . ."*

He was gone.

She was right behind him. It would be over soon. The oxygen in the room began to smell stale.

Seven seconds.

She was almost physically spent. She fought with her last ounce of identity to pull herself up toward the computer.

The Borg who had injected her noticed. He moved toward her as she stretched for the firing button.

Two seconds. One.

"Launch window is now open," said the computer. "You have two minutes to deploy."

The Borg grabbed her right hand just inches from the button. His strength was almost too much . . .

But not enough.

With her last breath as a human being she summoned her remaining life force, reached out with her left arm and smashed the launch button with her fist.

Her last memory as Jillian Rush was that of a torpedo headed toward the Borg sun. She smiled as much as her fading muscles would allow and blacked out.

"Jillian! Wake up!"

*Bad dream. Borg. Six of Six . . .*

*I forgive you, David. . . .*

*Poor Farragut. He never had a chance to . . .*

"Jillian! It's David! Can you hear me?"

She felt a hand patting her face and opened her eyes. Her vision slowly cleared as she realized she was on the floor of the auxiliary control room. "David? But you were . . ."

"It's over, Jillian. You did it. The Borg are gone."

"What?"

"They're gone. In the Nexus. And the ones not in the Nexus are being set free."

"So the torpedo . . ."

"Dead on target. Now you know why you were essential to this mission."

She started to sit up but her head was pounding. "Oh, my. I think I've got a Borg hangover. This is like Romulan ale to the tenth power."

"Just relax," said Solomon. "It will pass in a minute. Your human physiology is reasserting itself."

Within hours the messages began to pour in. Entire worlds that had been taken over by the Borg were contacting the Federation. The souls were being freed of their Borg hardware. Billions of intelligent beings were getting their lives back.

"How do they all know what to do?" asked Jillian.

"After the Borg in the Nexus became free, many left to return to their real life homes. They were still able to communicate with the Borg outside the Nexus, much like Farragut used the echoes of Locutus to reach the Collective."

"What kind of communication?"

"All received the same message. One word. *Peace.* Didn't you hear it?"

"I don't remember anything after launching the torpedo. I guess I wasn't totally assimilated."

"Trust me, you didn't miss anything. I'm going to have nightmares for years." He hung his head. "I'm sorry you had to go through that, Jillian. I really thought we had enough time."

"It was worth it." Jillian sipped her iced tea, appreciating the sugary sweetness like never before. Everything was going to be all right. Still, she couldn't help but wonder. . . .

"David, when you were assimilated, were you aware of Farragut being in the Collective?"

"He wasn't *in* the Collective, he was simply communicating with it. I could hear his messages, but could not access him as I could the other members of the Collective. The echoes from Picard's DNA were enough to convince the Borg that he was already part of their consciousness. He pulled it off. Don't worry, Jillian, he's at peace now."

She knew he was right. "This is incredible, David. How in the world did you ever know this would work?"

"When it comes to pure joy and total peace, you can only be sure of one thing. Resistance is futile. Even for the Borg."

Sam Farragut walked through the forest. It was a crisp, clear fall day, and the leaves were at their peak. He figured he was somewhere in the western part of the United States, but it didn't matter. The mountains looked like a rainbow caught in a light breeze, the reds and oranges and golds flowing like waves.

He heard a sound in the distance and decided to follow it, crunching his way through the woods. Without fear.

He was in the Nexus. Nothing could hurt him. Or would want to.

He'd completed his final mission for Starfleet. The Borg Collective had been easy to reach once it had experienced the pure joy of the Nexus. The souls were being reborn to an existence without barriers of any kind.

He continued walking, the chilly air seeming to flow through his veins, invigorating him even more. The intense smell of pine brought back the few memories he had of the holidays. He could enjoy Christmas every day in the Nexus if he wanted to.

Farragut hopped over a ridge and saw a middle-aged man chopping wood in front of a cabin. The man looked up at him and smiled. "Beautiful day," he said, stating the obvious.

"Yes, it is," said Sam Farragut. The man looked very familiar. "Do I know you?"

"Jim Kirk," said the man, dropping the axe and sticking out his hand.

Farragut nodded and shook it. "Of course. Yes, I studied your missions at the Academy. Captain of the *Enterprise*."

"That's right."

"And if I remember correctly, you left the Nexus. To help Captain Picard."

"Correct again. You get an 'A' in history."

"I'm Sam Farragut, by the way."

"I know."

Farragut walked around and studied Kirk. "So . . . if you left the Nexus, how can you be here? I mean, aren't you . . ."

"Consider me as an echo of the person who was once here," said Kirk. "While I am here with you I am also . . . somewhere else."

"Is there a reason you're here?"

"Thought you'd never ask," said Kirk. "You're the kid with the blank memory."

"Yes."

"The Nexus lets you relive your favorite memories, but since you're a little short in that department, I thought I'd share some of mine. You might say you and I have a lot in common."

# Brigadoon

Rigel Ailur

**Rigel Ailur** began writing stories—including a "novel" *seven* pages long!—in first grade and hasn't stopped since. A fan of *Star Trek* her whole life, she enjoys all five incarnations of the show and all the literature associated with it. Rigel is thrilled and honored to have her work included in *Strange New Worlds*. The proud and doting mother of four felines, Rigel loves cinema and theater and has worked backstage doing lights and sound, and as stage manager. She's bilingual, having lived in Germany, and is an avid reader of all genres but especially of science fiction and fantasy. Rigel is currently working on original fiction.

Jonathan Archer's chair dropped out from under him. After hanging in air for a split second, he crashed down into it, feeling like his stomach had stayed on the ceiling. *Enterprise* lurched sideways, but now that he was prepared he stayed in the captain's seat.

"What happened?" he shouted to be heard above the blaring alarms.

He wasn't likely to get a fast reply. Lieutenant Malcolm Reed no longer stood at tactical; Archer spotted his prone body behind the console.

As Archer moved to the tactical station, he yelled, "Hoshi, help T'Pol!" His Vulcan first officer was pulling herself up off the deck. Green blood poured from a gash at her temple.

Ensigns Travis Mayweather and Hoshi Sato had managed to stay at their positions, aided by the fact that they were seated at their consoles. Malcolm Reed, in contrast, lay crumbled against the wall.

A glance told Archer that Reed was still breathing, and he didn't see any blood, but that didn't preclude internal injuries. Still, Archer's first concern was to keep the ship safe for the sake of the entire crew.

As he studied sensor readings, he muted the alarm on the bridge. His nerves felt an instant improvement when the blaring siren fell silent. The ship had quit pitching, and according to the readings, there was nothing out there except the frigid vacuum of space and an unremarkable star approximately eight light minutes away. . . .

. . . And an Earth-sized planet that had not been there five minutes ago.

"Travis! All stop!" Archer nearly choked on his shock, but even as he spoke, the helmsman echoed his order back to him.

"All stop, Captain. We're at five-hundred thousand and holding," Travis added.

"It is a Minshara-class planet, Captain." T'Pol's voice sounded weak, but steady nonetheless. She continued reporting, "Abundant life-signs, including approximately two billion humanoids."

"Ship's status?"

"Damage and casualty reports coming in from all decks," T'Pol studied the display. "No hull or other structural damage. Engines are intact. Dozens of injuries. Those who are able are reporting to sickbay. Medical teams are transporting those who are critical. I've told Doctor Phlox we need a stretcher up here immediately for Lieutenant Reed. He said to tell you Porthos is fine."

As she spoke, the lift door opened and two medics emerged, and an officer from security to take Reed's post. The slim brunette woman replaced Archer at tactical as the medics tended to the fallen crewmate.

"T'Pol, what the hell happened? Were we attacked?"

"If so, it was a weapon I am unfamiliar with. Residual radiation is consistent with that of an ion storm, Captain. Levels are elevated, indicating that the intensity of the storm was unprecedented."

"Captain, ship incoming from the planet. No shields or weapons, sir," the woman at tactical said.

"We're being hailed," Ensign Sato added.

The man who appeared looked basically like a human in his thirties. He had a pleasant, open face although his forehead was now creased by a frown of concern. Except for pale azure skin and navy hair, and the unintelligible language, he could have passed as someone from Earth.

"I'm sorry, but I can't understand what you're saying," Archer replied, although he didn't expect the other man to understand him any better. He said over his shoulder, "Hoshi, are you having any luck translating?" Out of the corner of his eye, he saw her give a little shake of her head. With a mental shrug, he continued anyway, "I'm Jonathan Archer, captain of *Enterprise*. We're peaceful explorers from a planet called Earth."

The man smiled and said a few more words, and made a rolling gesture with one hand. To Archer, it looked like he wanted him to continue speaking. He only hoped he was interpreting correctly.

Sato said softly behind him, "Captain, we need him to keep talking. The more I have to work with, the better."

"Yes, well, I'm not sure what we're supposed to be saying to each other at this point. I'd love to ask him how his planet appeared literally out of nowhere, but that seems a bit beyond our abilities at the moment." He redirected his remarks to the stranger. "Can you tell me who you are? What you're doing here?" Archer paused, hoping the man would realize it was his turn. Just as Archer was about to mimic the hand motion, the man gave a quick look at something off to his side.

Then he stunned Archer by saying, "Greetings, Jonathan Archer. I'm Gaemes. I apologize for the delay. Our translation device was unfamiliar with your language. Your ship appears to be in distress. Do you require assistance?"

"No, thank you. We're managing. However, if you can tell us what happened . . ." Archer hesitated. He felt silly asking them where an entire planet had come from.

Understanding Archer's confusion, no doubt thanks to Archer's aside to communications officer Sato, Gaemes gave a rueful smile. "Basically it's a fluke of nature. I'd be happy to explain in detail at your convenience. Would you like to come aboard? Or, if you prefer, you're more than welcome to visit our world. We don't get many visitors on this side of the Curtain."

"Curtain?" Archer asked.

"It's what we call the dimensional rift. Every sixth day, we're on this side of it, for just one day. Then we spend five days on the other side. We've been going back and forth for all our recorded history.

"But I can explain all that when you're done tending to your repairs. I'll await your signal."

The building appeared to be made entirely of glass, or another similarly transparent but much stronger material. Although he knew, thanks to T'Pol's scan of the location, that where he stood was merely the top floor of a skyscraper that towered two hundred stories. Archer looked up and saw that the apex of the transparent pyramid soared high overhead. He, Ensign Sato, and Commander Charles Tucker found themselves standing in an indoor park.

Gaemes had assured them they could beam down; their transporter system was well tested. As of the past two hundred years, it had been the primary method of mass transit.

Archer had initially been reluctant to leave the shuttle pods on *Enterprise,* as he hated lacking his own means of egress. He'd been convinced when Gaemes guilelessly offered to share their cultural database. T'Pol had perused it and confirmed that it matched the scans she'd taken, which showed a peaceful planet.

Gaemes, flanked by a man and a woman, came striding forward, a beaming grin on his face. "Captain Archer, it's a pleasure. Welcome to Nalyn." His two companions were equally blue, the woman with paler skin and much fairer blue hair. The other man had skin almost as dark as Gaemes's navy hair. His own short tresses were such a dark blue as to be almost black.

"Thank you," Archer found himself smiling as well. "Please, it's Jonathan." The other man's good humor seemed to be infectious. He introduced his communications officer and chief engineer who received equally warm greetings.

"Please, feel free to explore all you like," Gaemes said. "We'll be happy to answer any questions to the best of our ability. This is Elfys and Ralf." He indicated the man and woman, respectively.

"We're all with the Bureau of Offworld Affairs. But before we proceed, Captain, there is something you need to know."

Gaemes' voice grew intense, although not in a threatening way. "This world is only here for a day, as I told you. Then—from the perspective of anyone not actually on Nalyn—we vanish again. We won't reappear for five days, but that is five days *from our perspective* on the other side of the Curtain. From your perspective *here on this side* it will be over a century before we return. It's very important to watch the time, Captain. Otherwise you'll be returning home a hundred years in your future."

Not an engineer by profession, Elfys had always had an interest and was one by education. He and Trip strolled off in one direction, while Ralf suggested that Hoshi would enjoy seeing more of the sky gardens.

"Jonathan, I was giving some thought to what damaged your ship," Gaemes said as they wandered among the trees. "We'd always wondered what would happen when Nalyn appeared, if something were there at that precise moment. I think you've answered our question. The ion wave from the rift acted like a blast wave and cleared the area. You were tossed out of the space."

"That makes sense." It wasn't an event Archer cared to repeat. The crew had escaped with only bruises, but he didn't care to tempt fate any further. Fixing his mind on more pleasant things, he looked around the arborium. "Nalyn is beautiful. I wish we had more time."

"You, or your people, are welcome to return."

"Thank you, Gaemes. We might take you up on that. Or at least, someone from my future should."


"This is a waste of time and resources," James Kirk fumed, pacing in the small sickbay office. His chief medical officer, Leonard McCoy, regarded him with irritation.

"Would you sit down," McCoy snapped, "you're making me spacesick. You know, rest does a person good on occasion. This crew deserves a break. So do you."

Kirk pulled a face, then acquiesced and sat down opposite McCoy at his desk. "But chasing after a vanishing planet, Bones? Even resting, this crew has better things to do."

"Oh, come on." McCoy slid a glass of Romulan ale across the desk. "I know you're a skeptic, but the report wasn't from some fly-by-night freighter captain trying to explain a late delivery. It's from Jonathan Archer's logs. You know, captain of some starship called *Enterprise*. Went on to become President of the Federation. That guy."

Kirk's surliness didn't abate. "I know; and I'm sure it was accurate to the best of his ability. But I can't help it; I just can't shake the feeling that there was some misunderstanding. I don't believe we'll find a planet in the Nalyn System."

"Well, we'll find out soon enough." McCoy gulped down some of his own drink. "In the meantime, quit worrying."

The captain grunted and emptied his glass, then sat there contemplating it as he turned it round in both hands. "No, thanks," he said quickly, stopping the doctor just as he was about to pour a refill.

McCoy shrugged, added a little to his own glass then set the bottle down. "What's the problem, Jim? We've seen an amoeba eleven thousand kilometers long and met Apollo himself. Why shouldn't an entire planet vanish and reappear like Brigadoon?"

"Brigadoon?" Kirk frowned.

McCoy waved an impatient hand. "Never mind. Why shouldn't a planet cycle between two dimensions?"

"I don't know." Kirk shook his head and with the gesture seemed to shake off much of his foul mood. "Just sour grapes we're not at Eeixi Prime, I suppose. Spock would die before admitting it to anyone, but he was bitterly disappointed. He wanted to lead the science team studying the supernova as it collapsed into a black hole."

"Yeah. I was irritated on his behalf as well." McCoy finished his drink. "But don't you dare tell him I said so."

Kirk chuckled as he stood. "Your secret is safe with me, Doctor.

And you're right, we should be approaching the system now. Care to join me on the bridge?"

Spock vacated the captain's chair in a fluid motion and returned to his post at the science station as Kirk strode onto the bridge. McCoy took up his customary, albeit unofficial, position at Kirk's left shoulder.

"We are in-system, Captain, and scanning the area where Na-lyn is to appear. We are also safely out of range, to prevent a repeat of the damage Archer's *Enterprise* experienced."

"If their calculations are correct," McCoy muttered.

The first officer raised his eyebrow. "Indeed, Doctor. There is no reason to consider the data is anything less than reliable. Captain Archer's logs are a reputable source. And it is unlikely his science officer made a mathematical miscalculation."

McCoy snorted. "And why is that? After all, he was only human."

The eyebrow arched higher. "On the contrary, Doctor, she was Vulcan. I'm surprised you were not aware of that fact."

"Gentlemen, thank you for the history lesson." Kirk feigned severity as he regarded his two senior officers. "Mister Spock, what's the expected arrival time?"

"Precisely one day from now, Captain. Sensors are on highest resolution and are recording scans of the system. Thus far, there is no indication of any dimensional rift. But per Captain Archer's and Commander T'Pol's logs, there is no advance warning."

Nor was there any warning before the world appeared. The sensor probes they'd deployed registered nothing but stardust from the solar wind. Then came a rainbow burst of ionized energy, and a lovely blue-white-green planet swirled in the blackness of space.

*Just as Archer had said,* Kirk admitted. He imagined the energy storm hadn't had a good effect on that previous ship and gave silent thanks he'd been warned to stay out of the way.

Uhura turned from the control panel to face the captain. "Sir, we're receiving a hail from Nalyn. It's a general hail from someone named Gaemes to any ships in the area."

"On screen, Lieutenant." After she complied, he continued, "This is Captain Kirk of the Federation *Starship Enterprise*."

"A pleasure to meet you, Captain." The young blue-hued man smiled, but the expression didn't reach his eyes. A crease between his brows betrayed some concern. "We were very much hoping to encounter someone after meeting the Earth captain. Your ship is named after his?"

"Yes, Gaemes, it is. Good to meet you as well. Is it true you spoke to Captain Archer just last week? By your timeframe, that is."

"That's correct captain." But then Gaemes's smile faded and he didn't wait for a reply. "Captain, we're very glad you're here. We're in dire need of assistance. There has been a change in the dimensional transition. We're still investigating the cause. It might be cyclical, or a natural shift that won't reverse itself. We don't know.

"But it's affecting our technology like it never has before. Last time, it shut down half the planet for a whole day. This time was even worse—despite our taking precautions. Captain, if we can't find a way to block the effects, we'll be destroyed. Millions, if not tens of millions, will die. Our transportation, power, and communication grids will be shut down, we won't be able to distribute food, hospitals will be ineffective. Our whole infrastructure will crash.

"Our technology isn't designed to be shut off for one out of every six days. It can't work that way. We're implementing what changes we can, as fast as we can, but the death count by the time we can adapt . . . it will be staggering. And our culture will be thrown back to a pre-technological era."

The last thing Kirk had expected was such an entreaty from an "easy" diplomatic mission. "How can we help?" he asked.

"Our preparations were hasty, as you can no doubt imagine, but we have five science ships ready. Almost ready, that is. We intend to have them stay on your side of the curtain. That will give them plenty of time to solve the problem. We hope. But because the preparations were so rushed, any help you can provide would be very welcome. Plus, from our perspective, the astropolitical situation over there changes so rapidly, well, we have no idea where the ships would be safe. If you could suggest a location where we would not bother anyone, or be bothered, that would also be greatly appreciated."

"Of course. But Gaemes, anyone who stays, doesn't that mean . . . ? I don't know how long you live, but . . ." Kirk couldn't think of any nonpainful way to phrase the question.

"That's right, Captain. All of us who volunteered realize we'll be very old when we see home again, if we ever do."

"You'll be aboard?"

"That's right. Along with five hundred of our best young scientists. I'm proud to say we had many more volunteers than we could use. But we ran out of time to gather more ships or more equipment. And plenty of crisis management will be needed on Nalyn itself."

The five ships, each with its own distinct shape, arrayed themselves around the *Enterprise* and out of range when Nalyn disappeared. One reminded Kirk of a huge gray bat, another brown vessel was wedge-shaped. The largest, a blue disk twice the diameter of the *Enterprise*'s main hull, simply looked like a flying saucer. A silver ship looked like its little sister, and the last craft looked like green spheres that had been glopped haphazardly together.

Kirk felt like he was shepherding a rag-tag fleet.

"Captain, I have a reply from Admiral Stone. He concurred with your recommendation and says Starfleet can increase ship traffic in this sector to check in on the Nalynians." Uhura's voice sounded somber, no doubt out of empathy for those people willing to never see home again. "And he says they'll dispatch a science team to assist."

"Thank you, Lieutenant. Please send an acknowledgment."

The neighboring star system was two light-years away,

uninhabited, and appeared to be free of any dimensional tears or other natural hazards. Kirk had suggested to Gaemes that they could set up their research center there.

"The lead ship is hailing us, sir," Uhura said as she transferred Gaemes to the main viewer.

Although Kirk couldn't be sure due to the unusual complexion, he thought Gaemes looked paler than usual. Beneath the determined set to the other man's face, Kirk detected sadness.

"Thank you, Captain. We're setting course for the coordinates you provided. Hopefully we'll have a solution ready long before the rift reopens. Who knows? Maybe we'll even find a way to cross the barrier sooner, as you said."

Jean-Luc Picard sat at his desk perusing the report on the computer screen in front of him. Like most Starfleet officers, he'd never heard of the Brigadoon Project. Until now, he'd had no reason to be familiar with it. Starfleet was a huge organization; the Federation, even more extensive.

But the scientists had heard of him. Or—more accurately—they'd heard of two of his officers. It was Commanders LaForge and Data who had caught their attention with the follow-up work they'd done on metaphasic shielding. And now the Nalyn thought they could benefit from those advances.

The captain summoned the two officers to his ready room. "Well, what do you think?" he asked them both after giving them a brief summary of the report.

Geordi gave that tilt of his head that he did when he was hesitant. "I don't know, captain. Two months isn't a lot of time, and we haven't even looked at the data yet. It would have been better if they'd sent this a lot earlier."

"Agreed," Picard gave a brisk nod. "But they didn't come across your research until now, so that can't be helped. Relegate all your other duties until further notice. We've already set course for the Brigadoon Research Station. It'll take us a week to arrive. You can use that time to get up to speed on what they've done so far."

"Captain, have they found a way to breach the dimensional barrier?" Data asked. "That would greatly accelerate their investigation. It would allow a constant flow of information in both directions and increase . . ." He fell silent as Picard raised a hand.

"Yes, Data, they've continued to pursue that avenue as well, without success so far. Maybe you and LaForge will have better luck. Feel free to reassign any crewmembers you require to assist you. See Commander Riker or myself if there is anything else you need. Good luck. Dismissed."

LaForge leaned forward removed his VISOR and put his face in his hands, then rubbed his temples and tired eyes. VISOR or not, they still hurt at the moment. "We're not making any progress," he grumbled through his hands, knowing Data's acute hearing could discern his words regardless.

"That is not true, Geordi. We have already eliminated a large number of potential solutions as ineffective," Data replied from his seat on the other side of the workstation island in the science lab.

LaForge glared at him through splayed fingers.

Data refused to be discouraged. "I believe we can emulate the conditions that open the interdimensional gateway. That does not solve the problem of the temporal discrepancy, but it does mean that people on both sides can bridge the gap at will."

"Which doesn't mean much when you're talking six days, but makes a heck of a lot of difference with regard to a hundred years," LaForge said. "That's excellent, Data. From now on, that means the researchers can test their theories as they go, instead of having to wait, or rely on guesswork. Now all we have to do is test it."

"Perhaps we should ask the captain if he wishes us to test it before our rendezvous with the research station, or after."

"Engage." Picard gave the order to activate the deflector shield, altered to resonate at the frequency to open the door between dimensions.

Nothing happened. On any of the several attempts.

Disappointment filled the bridge like a dense fog. Picard felt it most keenly from LaForge but, ironically, his "unemotional" android crewmate seemed almost equally dejected.

"It was still good work, Data," Troi pointed out. "Perhaps the Nalynians will have some insight to add that will allow the final breakthrough."

"You made considerable progress just from their notes," Riker added. "Working together, you should be able to make the final step."

"We'll keep at it, Captain," LaForge said. "Maybe the scientists will see something we missed."

"They'll be aboard tomorrow. You can ask them then. Have you already transmitted your notes?"

"Yes, sir."

Picard had seen pictures of Gaemes, as well as of several of the other Nalynians. All had appeared vigorous and youthful. And while he could still see the vigor in the man before him, the youthfulness had long ago fled.

Deep lines creased his face, and his dark blue hair hair was streaked with white. Still, his handclasp was strong as he greeted the current *Enterprise* officers.

"We've gone over the reports from your Commander Data and Commander LaForge," Gaemes said after the niceties were dispensed with. "Very impressive." He and two others, along with several members of Picard's senior staff, were seated around a table in a conference room. "Perhaps working together we can find a way to amplify the frequency enough to actually open the gateway. Then we can test if the shielding works as it should."

From there the talk grew heavily technical, with Picard and Gaemes deferring to the scientists such as LaForge and Data, as well as the Nalynians—Ralf and Elfys.

When Picard noted that Gaemes was saying as little as he himself, the captain caught the Nalynian's eye and gave a slight nod toward the door. The two men rose in unison, not interrupting the conversation around them.

Once out in the hall, Picard said, "We do have a contingency plan to present to you. I have no idea if you've considered it or not. But with the temporal differential, well, it would be simple for us to evacuate your people. We could help you relocate."

"We have discussed that, Captain. And the offer is greatly appreciated. But surely you'll understand when I say that abandoning our home is not an option."

"I do understand. But if it should come to that . . ."

"It won't, Captain." Gaemes said firmly. At Picard's skeptical look, he elaborated, "Please forgive me, Captain. I don't mean to sound stubborn or ungrateful. Perhaps if I explain . . . It's our experience that, when a 'fall back' plan exists, it increases the tendency to, well, fall back. We aren't going to do that. We will find a solution to this problem."

Picard admired their tenacity even as he questioned their wisdom. Still, it wasn't for him to dictate. The decision ultimately rested with the Nalynians, and them alone. "I just thought you should know it is an option."

"Thank you. But, please understand. It really isn't an option. We have discussed it, and we won't be pursuing it. And I don't mean this is something our small group has decided for everyone. It was discussed on Nalyn by those still there. I doubt if they've changed their minds in six days. None of us here have, after much more time than that."

Back in the conference room, Picard listened with half an ear as they continued discussing variables and assigning tasks. The true test would come when the portal between dimensions opened. Picard could tell the Nalynians were both eager for the renewed contact with home, and fearful of what they would find after two more transitions.

Perhaps, Picard thought, exposure to the interdimensional

opening was what they needed to finally complete the research. If they could find a way to open the gap artificially, and keep it open, that would greatly accelerate the progress.

The *Enterprise* accompanied the largest of the Nalynian ships back to the other system where Nalyn itself appeared right on schedule.

Gaemes had opted to stay on the *Enterprise* with its more up-to-date technology, although scientists were busily working on his own ship as well. They kept an open comm line between the ships' labs, and the bridge was tapped in at the moment.

"Sensor readings coming in now," LaForge was saying. "Comparing the data against what's already in the computers." Then his voice grew heavy with disappointment. "Noting various discrepancies. We'll have to adjust our calculations for the shielding, and for opening the portal."

"What's the time frame, Geordi?" Picard asked.

"A few hours, or a few days. It depends on the cause of the differential. It could have been that the older instruments were less accurate, or perhaps the gateway itself has continued to change."

Picard turned to Gaemes, whose expression was so determinedly neutral as he stared at the image of his homeworld that Picard's heart went out to the man.

"We're not giving up," Picard told him, and received a sad smile in response.

"Thank you, Captain. Nor are we. If you'll excuse me, I'll get back to my ship."

"Of course." Picard watched him go, then exchanged a glance with ship's cousellor Deanna Troi. "I think he was hoping to return home."

Troi concurred with the observation. "Perhaps he still should. His leadership has no doubt been invaluable to them, but he's not a scientist. They can continue without him."

"I can't see him leaving a job undone." Picard gave a huge sigh. "We'll have to work faster. If a breakthrough comes fast enough, he can return home for his final years and take the solution with him."

Barely stifling a growl, Captain Benjamin Sisko glared at his commanding officer. "Admiral, don't you find this delay specious? It has nothing to do with the war effort."

Admiral Ross returned the glower full force. "Obviously you didn't grasp that billions of lives, an entire planet's population, are at stake. Otherwise you wouldn't have wasted my time with that question. Just what are we fighting to defend if we ignore such a plea for help?"

"Sir, with all due respect, the *Defiant* is a warship . . ."

"Captain," Ross's voice took on a sharper edge, "the war will survive just fine for a whole month without you. Those are your orders. Dismissed."

As it only took thirty seconds to beam from Starbase 13 back to the *Defiant,* Sisko's mood had not improved by the time he materialized in the small ship's transporter room.

He stalked onto the bridge.

"Coordinates laid in for Brigadoon," Commander Jadzia Dax informed him as she vacated the captain's chair and resumed her place at the helm.

"Best speed, Commander. Raise shields and the cloak." Sisko's voice still held the undertone of a growl. He motioned to the relief helmsman, a young Vulcan man, to wait a moment.

"Aye, sir." If her commanding officer's foul mood disconcerted her any, the Trill officer didn't show it. "Arrival in four days at warp nine." Dax noted the loitering Vulcan and got up again so he could resume that post.

Sisko handed her a data chip. "Have at it, Old Man. They seem to think that *Defiant*'s souped up shields will help solve the interference problem Nalyn has when traveling between the dimensions. And they think the cloaking harmonics might help open the rift."

"They knew about the cloak?" Dax couldn't keep the surprise out of her voice.

"They knew about the Romulan ships' cloaking abilities. Starfleet graciously volunteered the *Defiant.*" Sisko's grim tone showed how little he appreciated being loaned out.

"Ah. Well, I'll take a look at this," she tapped the data chip, "and get up to speed by the time we're there."

The five Nalynian ships still hovered in orbit around the previously uninhabited world. Over the preceding decades a research base had grown on the surface below. The *Defiant* took up a geosynchronous position with the rest of the science fleet.

As they'd arranged while enroute, Gaemes and two of the senior scientists, Elfys and Ralf, beamed aboard as soon as the *Defiant* arrived.

The eldest of the three, Gaemes moved carefully and deliberately, as if not wanting to overbalance and fall. His thick, short hair had gone completely white and age had added gravel to his voice. His two companions, although also not young, still had steadier gaits, straighter postures and more color in their hair.

"Captain Sisko." He gave a pleasant nod that included Sisko and Dax, then looked startled. "Commander Dax?"

"That's right," she gave a friendly smile.

"A pleasure to meet you both," he said, then added to Dax, "Forgive my staring. I'd been told you were over three hundred years old. I'm afraid I projected my own expectations."

"Don't worry about it. If you'll follow me, I'll show you to your quarters. We'll be in the Nalyn system in about two hours and can get started."

Dax maneuvered the *Defiant* to where Nalyn would next appear. Since that anticipated appearance would not be for more than a hundred years, the danger of accidentally running into the planet would be nonexistent.

"Captain, the modifications to the shields and the deflector dish are complete. We're ready to try to open a rift," Dax said.

Sisko stood and with a gentle hand and a nod, guided Gaemes

to the center seat. "Go ahead, Commander." He just stopped himself from calling his longtime friend "old man." No use creating confusion.

"Probe launched," Dax reported, her fingers flying gracefully across the science console. "Deflector shield emitting the beam."

As they watched on the viewscreen, the space before the probe seemed to bubble and roil. An eruption of multi-hued light appeared then vanished. The silver cylindrical probe was gone.

"I programmed the probe to emit a burst like our deflector shield did, and return after only two and a half seconds," Dax explained for the benefit of Elfys and Ralf. "I doubt they'll even notice it there, but if it worked, it'll return here in six hours. The next step should be to send a small uncrewed ship through, to make sure the passage is stable. Plus, we can send another probe with all our data, and we can send updates."

"So even if it takes us years to send data, they'll be getting it minutes apart. In plenty of time to help before Nalyn reappears on this side of the rift." Gaemes beamed with joy. "This is wonderful, Captain. You and your crew can't imagine how this helps us. There's no way we can ever thank you."

Six hours later, the probe returned. Barely. "The trip fried the circuitry, Captain," Dax said, frowning deeply as she read the telemetry coming in from the probe. "If the backup system hadn't activated, it wouldn't have made it."

"So we've solved half the problem." Sisko was determined to remain optimistic. "Now let's see about adopting the *Defiant*'s shield harmonics."

Over the next few days, Dax customized and sent a dozen more probes, none of which came back in any better condition than the first.

Sisko found himself using his engineering background as he helped review data and adapt the probes. It felt good to think of something besides the war, to be doing something constructive rather than defensive or destructive.

Then they waited a day the final probes to return. The last couple had included a microburst of the data accumulated thus far, in the hope it would help somewhat despite being incomplete.

"Benjamin! That last probe to return, I'm pretty sure it includes a message. A small magnetic box is attached. It didn't activate until this side of the barrier. Downloading the data now."

Sisko stopped what he was doing and moved closer to see. Gaemes, Ralf and Elfys crowded around as well. They could all see that the last transition had wreaked havoc on the planet. The people were scrambling—finding stopgap solutions to delay the inevitable—but the world's infrastructure was crumbling. The temporary patches would not hold for long.

In a month's time people would begin dying of things as basic as starvation and thirst, or from easily curable diseases or easily treatable injuries.

But that month on Nalyn gave those on the Federation's side of the rift over 450 years to figure it out.

"So, what do you want to do next?" Sisko asked the Nalynians.

"We were thinking," Ralf spoke up quickly, "we've done so much work here, including artificially triggering the portal. One of us who is familiar with the work needs to go back. We've all discussed it, Gaemes. We think you should go. You've done so much. You deserve to go back. And you can do a lot of good there."

A series of emotions flickered across Gaemes face and for a moment, Sisko couldn't tell if he wanted to strangle them or if he would cry. Likely, both feelings were competing.

"Go on, Gaemes," Elfys added. "We'll be right behind you."

"I can't quit now," he protested.

"You're not. We need someone to go back with the work we've done thus far. You can help get things ready for the next transition. We're close to a solution; I can feel it. You can help them prepare to implement it, whatever it is."

Gaemes looked back and forth between his colleagues, his countenance still conflicted.

"Go on, Gaemes," Ralf echoed. "We really will be right behind you."

Sisko could see the instant the man reached a decision, because all the tension left his face and carriage. In a moment's time he looked decades younger.

They made sure he had several copies of all the data so at least those on the other side could open a rift at will. He also had all the data that, although it had proven useful, hadn't yet led to an answer to the dilemma.

"All right." Dax leaned over the elderly man's shoulder and pointed to the controls. "Here is the emergency shutdown. That kills all power. Your ship doesn't have warp drive, so you don't have to worry about losing antimatter containment. Count to five after you open the rift, then hit that. Inertia will carry you through. Once on the other side, hit the switch again. That should reactivate everything. If power doesn't come back on." She patted the slim gray box on the copilot's seat beside him. "This is a distress beacon, with its own power source. It's off now, but it'll work just fine if you need it."

"Everything I need to know. Thank you so much." And with that, after over a century, Gaemes was finally returning home.

Admiral Kathryn Janeway stood quietly on *Voyager*'s bridge and watched the controlled chaos swirl around her. It felt good being there; she still took great pride in the achievements of her former crew. And the ship itself retained a special place in her heart.

It also felt odd. Not necessarily in a bad way. Just strange to see someone else in the captain's seat. Even if that person was Captain Chakotay. Even stranger, but more gratifying, was seeing Thomas Paris beside him as first officer.

Janeway folded her arms and leaned back against the wall, simply enjoying being there again. Then she felt a huge grin crease her face. Somehow she doubted the new chief engineer was as thrilled to have his predecessor B'Elanna Torres aboard. Torres could be intimidating enough even without the feeling of having to follow in her footsteps.

She saw Harry Kim casting glances in her direction and winked at him. They'd come up in the turbolift together, and he'd gone to his post, heeding her admonishment not to make a fuss. Janeway still expected to see Tuvok there, although she knew full well he'd been reassigned to the *Titan*.

She cleared her throat a little and stepped down to the lower level.

"Hello, Chakotay. Tom." She noted that Tom's head snapped around rather quickly, but Chakotay didn't looked startled.

"Good to see you, Admiral," Chakotay said, rising. He gave her an affectionate hug. Greetings followed from the rest of the bridge crew as well.

"You sure you don't mind chauffeuring around annoying flag officers" she asked, half-seriously.

"It's a pleasure," he replied, warmth in his voice and smile. Then he grew slightly more businesslike. "Sounds like you're back in science officer mode." He offered her the seat. Despite a sharp twinge of longing, she declined.

"Actually, Seven made the observation that led to the idea *Voyager's* bioneural gelpacks might help solve Nalyn's problem. She came across the Brigadoon Project during her work at the think tank. And she's the one who noted that, even though traveling through dimensions was wreaking havoc with technology, it wasn't hurting any of the life on the planet. That made me think that maybe we could adapt the gel packs."

"Let's hope it works. We're ready to break orbit whenever you give the order, Admiral."

"Thank you, Captain. In that case, let's get under way. Best speed to the Brigadoon Research Station."

"This should solve the problem of computers shutting down," B'Elanna said, glancing up from her work as Janeway and Chakotay strode into the science lab. "But it's not going to do much good with regard to protecting power sources."

"One step at a time, Commander," Janeway said, as encouragement rather than a rebuke. "I'm sure they'll take whatever victories they can get."

Chakotay looked from one woman to the other. "I didn't think power sources needed to be protected. Don't they just need to be managed? And if the bio-neural circuitry will do that . . ."

"Then it's just a matter of redesigning power management to be variable-flow instead of steady, or even just to add a pause. Once we get to the research station, we can see how well the gel-packs integrate into their systems. If that goes well—and that is a huge 'if'—then we can see about systems overhauls to accommodate the downtime. The actual transition time between dimensions is only a minute or two, right?"

"I believe it's less than that," Janeway said, thinking over all the data she'd reviewed. "Only a few seconds."

"Even better. So if the gel-packs aren't affected by the transition, and we can program a pause into them. . . ." Torres turned back to the engineering console where she sat, the other two officers already forgotten.

Exchanging a wry smile with the admiral, Chakotay slipped out of engineering and left them to work undisturbed.

"I'll send the specs on the gel-packs to the research station," Torres said. "They can start studying them. By the time we get there, they should have a good idea of how easy or difficult it will be to mesh them with their technology."

"That should be half the battle," Janeway said.

Torres shot her a sharp look. "I'll be pleasantly surprised if it's only half. But I certainly hope you're right."

"Approaching Brigadoon Station, Captain," Harry Kim announced.

Janeway had to stop herself from responding. Old habits died hard, after all. She saw Chakotay look quickly away, but not before she'd glimpsed a knowing smile.

"Hail them, Mister Kim. They should be expecting us."

An ancient dark-skinned man—with dark blue skin, that is—

and silver-white hair, appeared. "Greetings, Captain. I'm Elfys. We've been working with the data you sent. Thus far, combining the two systems is proving to be a bit problematic. But we'll keep at it."

"Commander Torres is the one who provided the data. She and Admiral Janeway have been continuing to work at it from our side. Perhaps it would help if they beamed over with some of the actual gel-packs. First hand is usually better than computer simulations."

"That sounds like a very practical idea."

Janeway and Torres materialized in a laboratory that looked remarkably similar to the one they'd just left. Each carried a box of several of the bio-neural gel-packs.

Elfys smiled in welcome, but his eyes betrayed exhaustion. "If only we could get the technologies to talk as easily as you and I can," he said.

"That might just work. Have you tried a translation matrix to link the two systems?" Janeway asked.

"Hmm, not yet," Elfys replied, and that got them all started.

"Got it!" Ralf shouted in jubilation. Everyone crowded around her workstation to watch the test run, then run again. The gel-pack was working in perfect concert with the rest of the controls.

"That is wonderful," Janeway beamed at their triumph. "We brought a supply of the gel-packs, and you're welcome to them, but that's only a thousand and I suspect you can easily use millions of them. And they can't be replicated."

"We can convert the most critical systems first," Elfys agreed, "But yes, we'll need many more than that. However, we can continue to use the temporal discrepancy to our advantage. After we arrange payment or trade for them, if you'd be so kind to send them as quickly as you can conveniently make them . . ."

"You'll still be receiving them every few minutes," Janeway said, finishing the sentence for him.

"Exactly. We may even have to ask you to slow down a little on delivery." He gave a huge sigh of bliss and pressed his eyes tightly closed for a moment. "After all this time . . ."

Then he took a deep breath. "Computer, communications to all the ships and planetside," he said. After the computer acknowledged the open channel, he continued. "May I have your attention please. Our latest experiment has been a complete success. All ships, prepare to return home. All personnel on the surface, gather up all equipment and personal items and report to your ships. Thank you all for your dedication."

Elfys turned to Janeway and Torres. "Thank you, and all your coworkers, so very much. You can't imagine what all your assistance has meant to us."

"I'm just sorry the problem took so long to solve," Janeway said.

Sorrow flickered across his face so quickly that Janeway wasn't sure if she'd imagined it or not. He certainly sounded sincere when he said, "But that's the beauty of it, Admiral. It's only been seven days. That strikes me as remarkably quick problem-solving."

She just nodded. They both knew that wasn't what she meant, but the last thing she wanted was to emphasize his sense of loss rather than of accomplishment. Still, she marveled at the fact that this man and all the original scientists with him were contemporaries of Jonathan Archer. No doubt the historians would have loved to spend time with them if the Nalynians' mission hadn't been so critical.

"Admiral, I realize it's unlikely any of your people will be interested, due to the time difference, but you are always welcome on Nalyn."

"That's very kind, Elfys," Janeway said, thinking even more of Archer's era. Back then, exploring did mean being gone for months, if not years at a time. Nowadays, *Titan* and the other *Luna*-class vessels notwithstanding, that was the exception rather than the rule. They'd grown accustomed to the immediacy of the Federation, far flung though it was. "I'll be sure to pass along your invitation. I'm sure some of the more adventurous types, particularly of the long-lived species, will be tempted."

"It would be a pleasure. If there is ever any way we can repay you, please let us know."

"Just make good use of your discoveries," Janeway said. "So all your hard work was worthwhile."

"Of that you can be sure," Elfys said. "And now it's time to finally go home."

Janeway knew the arduous task ahead didn't lessen his joy.

# Reborn

Jeremy Yoder

**Jeremy Yoder** is a computer programmer in Sioux Falls, South Dakota. During his spare time, he strives to turn his hobby of writing into a profession. In addition to his writing, he enjoys his wonderful three-year-old daughter and lovely wife. He extends special thanks to those who make *Strange New Worlds* possible, including the other writers in this volume. This is his second entry in *SNW,* with his first being "The Smallest Choices" in *SNW 9.*

Picard glanced up from the request on his ready room desk to Riker, who awaited his response. "Risa?" Picard asked. "Aren't you tired of taking shore leave there?" They smiled, knowing many would vacation at the so-called pleasure planet, now that the Dominion War had recently ended. But before Riker could reply, a flash of light near the center of the room blinded them. It disappeared just as quickly to reveal—

"Q!" Picard barked, standing upright. The alien entity lay on the floor in an apparently weakened state, but Picard wasn't buying it. He was so tired of Q's interruptions that he hardly noticed Riker requesting security. "I've tolerated your games," Picard hissed, "far longer than I—"

"Jean-Luc," Q gasped, struggling for breath. "No games. Too much. At stake. Space. Time. Everything."

Riker strode toward Q, gripped his arm, and hauled him to his feet. The door swished open and in stepped Data with phaser drawn. "I suggest," Riker said, "that you listen and—"

"Would you both shut up and listen!" Q ripped his arm away and staggered to Picard's desk. He leaned on it while gasping for breath. "You have to help. I'm depleted. They attacked. The Continuum had no idea. Beyond what even we can comprehend."

As Data stepped closer, Picard held up a hand, signaling for the android to wait. "You have one minute," Picard said. "If by then you can't convince me you're telling the truth—"

"The Pah-wraiths have been unleashed," Q blurted.

Picard's eyebrows shot up. To the Bajorans, the wormhole near their planet was the Celestial Temple, where benevolent aliens called the Prophets existed. According to myth, the Prophets had banished their rebellious brethren, the Pah-wraiths. From Captain Sisko's reports over the years, he knew such aliens existed, but didn't know where myth ended and fact began. "I know of them. But what do you—"

"We've watched what you call the 'wormhole aliens' for eons, curious they have so much power over space and time, but rarely use it. That was up until a few minutes ago, when Sisko fell with Dukat into the fire caves and unleashed the Pah-wraiths."

Picard held up a hand and shook his head. "I'm sorry. Fire caves? You need to back up. I don't understand."

Q dashed around the desk and gripped Picard's shoulders. "There's no *time* to back up! They're consuming all of time and space!" Q slumped into Picard's chair. "Dukat talked about them setting the heavens aflame. We thought it was just an expression, but the Pah-wraiths swarmed out, attacking the wormhole and Continuum. None of us had time to respond, except the so-called Prophets sent their beloved Emissary out at multiple light speeds toward the Delta Quadrant."

"Emissary?" Riker asked, stepping forward.

Before Q could respond with annoyance, Picard interjected. "A title the Bajorans use for Captain Sisko in their viewing him as a religious figure." He looked down at Q. "But how could they do that to Sisko? He's just a man."

Q shook his head. "Not anymore. I don't know what the Prophets changed him into after he fell into those fire caves. All I know is I barely escaped with my life, but not before the Pah-wraiths had siphoned off most of my energy. Now all I can do is teleport across space and time—while they last—until I'm spent. So I came here, hoping you'd help."

"But if there's nothing *you* can do, what can I offer?"

Q gazed off into the distance. "I don't know. I've never had to be fast-thinking when I was nearly omniscient." He stood. "So be my guide, Jean-Luc. Tell me where to go and I'll take us."

"This is madness," Picard said, starting to pace.

"How much time have we got?" Riker asked.

Red alert sirens blared all over the ship, making them jump.

Q took a deep breath. "My guess is, not long."

They rushed out to the bridge, where Data sat down at his console. "Data," Picard began, though the android was already working on it. "Locate the source and put it on screen." Picard turned to Q. "When you said the Pah-wraiths were setting the heavens aflame, what exactly did you . . ."

The viewscreen blinked on to maximum magnification. They stared in shock and silence at what appeared to be a wall of flame-like energy of every color, scorching across the cosmos in every direction.

"Unfortunately," Q said, "I meant exactly that."

Picard took a few hesitant steps closer to the viewscreen. "Data, what do you register beyond it?"

Data swiveled in his chair. If ever there was an odd time for the android to speak without emotion, it was then. "Nothing. No planets. No debris. No light. Not even space to measure."

Q stretched out his hands in a pleading motion. "Picard, where can we go? You need to decide."

"Shields up!" Picard barked. "Helm, turn about. Maximum—"

"Jean-Luc!" Q pointed at the viewscreen. "That crossed from Bajor to here in minutes, which would take you *days*. You can't outrun it. We need to act now!"

"Then teleport our ship to—"

"I told you. My power is diminished. Transporting that much matter will drain me, and I need to conserve what little I have. I can only take you at the moment, so make it count."

"Seventeen seconds until impact," Data said.

Picard stared at the advancing wave. In all his travels, nothing had come close to such devastation and magnitude. Without having time to consider if it was wise or foolish, he whispered, "*Voyager*. We know Janeway and her crew are trapped in the Delta Quadrant, where you say the Prophets sent Sisko." He turned to Q. "Take us to *Voyager*."

As light enveloped him, Picard couldn't help but tear up, knowing his beloved *Enterprise* crew was about to be destroyed.

Janeway shifted in her captain's chair and turned to her first officer, Chakotay. "At the risk of jinxing our recent good fortune," she said, "I have to say the past few uneventful days have felt like vacation."

"I know what you—" Chakotay began when a brilliant white light erupted over the bridge.

Janeway was about to sound a red alert when she saw Q and a Starfleet captain, who seemed vaguely familiar, standing before her. Q moaned and slouched, but the other man held him up.

"Captain Janeway?" the mystery captain asked.

Janeway stood. "What is the meaning of this?" Q had been an unwelcome visitor before, and she didn't want him around again. As she studied the captain, recognition came over her. "You're Jean-Luc Picard of the *Starship Enterprise*. Why—"

"We've very little time," Picard said as Chakotay stepped forward and helped support Q. "A horrible event has occurred that threatens the entire cosmos. We just came from the Alpha Quadrant, which is literally being destroyed."

Janeway stared open-mouthed at the newcomers. From behind Picard, Paris stood from his station. "I do believe," Paris said, "that you officially jinxed our 'vacation.' "

Just as Picard was about to continue, the ship shuddered, as if an energy wave had struck them. Picard turned to Q in alarm. "The Pah-wraiths already?"

"Soon," Q said. "That was an initial shockwave from their awesome power now devouring space-time. There will be more before the actual wave reaches us."

"Red alert! Shields up!" Janeway walked around Picard. The viewscreen only revealed silent stars as they journeyed at warp speed. "Now what exactly are the Pah-wraiths?"

"Fearsome aliens," Picard said. "Almost godlike in their abilities. They've escaped their prison and are on a rampage to destroy all of space-time." Picard cocked his head toward Q. "Even the Continuum has been neutralized by their onslaught. I saw their path of annihilation myself."

"What can we do to help?" Janeway asked.

Picard stepped closer. "We need to scan the entire Delta Quadrant to seek a certain entity. Once we find him, we need to bring him to us. Do you know of a way?"

After a few seconds of stunned silence, Janeway shook her head. "I'm sorry, but what you request is incredible." She looked to her science officer. "Tuvok, the only thing I can think of is the Caretaker's Array."

Before the stalwart Vulcan could reply, Picard interjected. "Then take us to—"

"It is not a question of capability," Tuvok interrupted. "But of existence. It brought us here to the Delta Quadrant, but was destroyed. And even so, it would need to be reconfigured by myself and our Chief Engineer, B'Elanna Torres."

Picard wiped sweat from his brow. Janeway tried to think of an alternative, but nothing came to mind.

"I told you, Jean-Luc," Q said, standing on his own. "I can take us anywhere across space *and* time." Another energy wave hit them. The viewscreen stars wavered as it passed. "In fact, I'd *highly* recommend we change our place in time, which will take the Pah-wraiths longer to reach."

"Very well, then," Picard said. "Take me, Janeway, Tuvok, and B'Elanna to this Array in the past."

"If I may make a suggestion," Janeway quickly added, "place us at a time when the Caretaker alien isn't present. He's quite formidable, and I can't imagine he'd assist us."

With a nod, Q closed his eyes and they vanished.

Upon their arrival at the Array, Picard and Janeway acted more like ensigns by obeying whatever requests Tuvok and B'Elanna gave them. Over the next few days, they worked hard while Q recovered from the teleport strain.

Picard squatted at a console near the Array's core, which had been shut down while Tuvok and B'Elanna reprogrammed it. Under the console, B'Elanna lay on her back, her feet sticking out the bottom. On the opposite side of the core, Tuvok and Janeway worked while Q paced.

"Blasted alien technology," B'Elanna muttered. She stuck her hand out of the opening. "Coilspanner."

Picard handed her the tool from several on the floor. His eyes were heavy after so little sleep; he and Janeway required more rest than the Vulcan and half-Klingon. During their time together, Picard had come to know his fellow Starfleet officers, yet still lamented the loss of his own crew.

Picard called out to Q. "Do you have *any* idea how much time we have?"

Q scowled. "How many times can I say I don't know? I'm sure the Pah-wraiths have begun marching into the past, but such a process is time-consuming . . . no pun intended."

Before Picard could ask another question, the Array core sprung to life. Various consoles and lights now blinked on it in an assortment of colors.

"That was it!" B'Elanna shouted while backing out. Janeway ran around from the other side, her hair frazzled. "I've kick-started the initialization process," B'Elanna continued, "which should now interface with our new configuration. Speaking of which . . ." She looked at Tuvok.

"From Q's input," Tuvok said while operating a console, "we should now be able to synchronize the Array to scan for non-corporeal entities outside of space-time, which is apparently where Captain Sisko now exists."

"Thereby allowing us," Q said, his eyes dancing, "to not only pinpoint his location—regardless that he was shot into this quadrant years ago in the future—but to draw him to us like a giant magnet."

With a grin, Janeway sidled alongside Picard, squeezed his arm, and whispered, "Did you understand any of that?"

Picard chuckled for the first time since this odyssey had begun. While Tuvok, B'Elanna, and Q talked amongst themselves and operated various instruments, Picard patted Janeway's hand and whispered back, "I never do."

"I think that's him!" B'Elanna pointed at a display, until her excitement faded to doubt. "But how do we know for sure?"

Q pushed a series of buttons. "Only one way to find out." Lights flickered all over the monolith of alien technology. The entire structure whined, growing in intensity.

A flash of light erupted nearby, leaving a man curled up on the floor. When the newcomer groaned, Picard stepped closer and offered a hand. "Though the situation leaves much to be desired," Picard said, "it's good to see you again, Captain." As Sisko blinked and took his hand, Picard noticed a golden glow radiating about Sisko. "Or should I say, Emissary of the Prophets?"

"What . . . ," Sisko began. "Where . . ."

In a flurry of words, Q described the situation, often in terms Picard didn't understand in regards to nonlinear time, Prophets, space-time, and Pah-wraiths. Yet throughout the monologue, Sisko simply nodded.

"I see," Sisko finally said. He rubbed his goatee in a thoughtful manner. "I remember tackling Dukat and tumbling over the precipice into the fire caves. After that, I found myself surrounded by infinite whiteness. At first I thought I had died, but then realized I'd entered the Celestial Temple."

"Celestial Temple?" Janeway asked.

Sisko began to pace. "Known to humans and most other races as the stable wormhole near Bajor."

"You make it sound as if you're no longer human," B'Elanna said.

Sisko paused and studied the glow about his body.

"He's not," Q muttered. "And I doubt he even knows what he's become."

Sisko acted as if he hadn't heard them as he gazed off into the distance. With a heavy sigh, he spoke in a deep, rumbling voice. "They're coming."

"We know that," Q spouted. "It's only a matter of—"

"I mean here. Specifically." Sisko studied them. "Returning to my corporeal self has alerted them to my location. Now they'll come quickly by ignoring the rest of space-time. Because to them, I'm the last possible hurdle in their plans."

"What exactly can you do?" Tuvok asked.

Sisko shrugged. "I've no idea."

"You've no idea?" Q strode about with arms waving. "Great. Just great! We take what little resources and time we have, throw it all in a gamble that finding you might save life as we know it, and you're saying there's nothing you can do?"

Janeway stepped closer to Sisko. "Think carefully, Captain. Why did the Prophets send you this way?"

"No reason. They just sent me away to keep me safe, hoping I could alter events." Sisko pinched the bridge of his nose and closed his eyes. "I'm trying to understand my abilities . . . trying to piece together all the threads. . . ."

"Could it have anything to do with your final moments with Dukat?" Picard asked, desperate to find an answer. "Something you maybe could have done differently. Or something you didn't—"

"The book!" Sisko gasped, his eyes wide. "That's what the Prophets tried to tell me, just before sending me away. I was supposed to destroy the book as well."

"The book?" B'Elanna asked.

Sisko continued, but more to himself than anyone else. "The Kosst Amojan that Kai Winn and Dukat used in the fire caves was the key. It wasn't enough that I stopped Dukat, since the door remained unlocked. But if I had also destroyed the key . . ." He shook his head. "I'm getting ahead of myself. All I know is if we can destroy the universe on our own terms, it would halt the Pah-wraiths' advance and obliterate them."

Janeway cocked an eyebrow and crossed her arms. "I don't pretend to know a fraction of what you're talking about, but I know enough to say that'd be a bit counterintuitive."

Sisko raised a finger. "Not necessarily. I'm still learning what I'm capable of, but I think . . ." His gaze drifted. "Yes. Yes, I can do it. But I can't wipe the existing slate clean."

Q flailed his arms. "Not even I could have done that!"

"But you can transport us anywhere into the past," Sisko said. "So we'd better think of someone who can do it and get to them before—" The Array shuddered from an energy shockwave. "Before they get any closer."

"Jean-Luc," Q said, "you've taken us this far. Where to now? Who in the past could do such a thing?"

"I don't know," Picard said. "But I can send us to someone who might. Someone much further back in time."

With a sigh, Janeway muttered, "James T. Kirk." After Picard nodded, she continued. "I doubt there's a single ship and crew in the entire fleet—past, present, or future—which saw more sights and experienced more bizarre scenarios."

"The trick will be convincing him," Sisko said. "And though I already met him once, he won't remember me." Everyone stared in confusion at Sisko, but he just shook his head. "It's a long story that got me into a lot of . . . trouble . . . with the Department of Temporal Investigations. Let's just hope Kirk knows something. The only question is when?"

"Just before his ship was decommissioned for the last time," Picard said. "That'd be after most of his career, giving Kirk his entire life experience to draw upon."

"Very well," Q said. The Array shook violently for several seconds. "But that far back, I can only send one person on alone. After that, I'll be spent."

"Then the choice is obvious." Picard stepped up to Sisko and shook his hand. "Consider the baton passed. It's up to you."

After a flash of light, Sisko vanished. Immediately after, Q collapsed and faded. Picard was surprised at finding himself saddened by the sight. He studied the three remaining Starfleet officers, thinking he should say something, but nothing came to mind. Shortly afterward, he realized it didn't matter, when a final wave struck.

Chekov turned in his chair. "Course heading, Keptin?"

Kirk sat straighter and studied the viewscreen. "Second star to the right. And straight on 'til morn—" A bright light erupted in the room. Kirk raised a hand, shielding his vision. When it had faded, it revealed a man with a golden hue about him. Kirk slowly stood. "Who are you? What—"

"I am the Sisko, from the future." The man spoke in a deep, rumbling voice. "A Starfleet captain, like yourself. Or at least, I used to be. What I'm about to tell you is incredible, but I've only a few minutes. They're on their way."

Kirk could only stare as Sisko spoke, going into selective details in a few minutes. When Sisko reached the end and said he needed to find a way to destroy the universe in order to preserve it, Kirk's eyebrows shot up. "You can't be serious."

"I'm afraid so. Or everything will be lost. By doing it ourselves, I'll have the chance to rectify everything."

Kirk glanced at his crew who appeared just as shocked and doubtful. "For all I know," Kirk said, "you could be insane. I can't think of any reason we should believe or trust you."

"Except that everything will be lost if you don't."

A rumble rippled throughout the ship.

"Vhat vas that?" Chekov asked.

"That's them," Sisko said. "Shockwaves pushing their way on ahead through time. I was quite serious when I said we only have a few minutes."

"Fascinating," Spock said while studying his instruments. "We just felt a displacement of space-time as it temporarily merged with unreality."

"That is not possible!" Scotty exclaimed.

Uhura operated her console. "The boards are lit up. Every space station, ship, and planet in the quadrant just experienced the same thing, all at once." She stared at Sisko in wonder. "Which should likewise be impossible."

"Jim!" McCoy stepped down beside Kirk. "Destroying everything to save it? This man's obviously deranged."

Kirk rubbed his jaw. "The problem is, Doctor, what if he's not? However, if his claim about the future is true, there may be a way to prove it. Uhura, patch me through to Research Base 19. Emergency Channel."

Uhura frowned, until enlightenment came over her face. "Aye, sir." As she operated her console, Kirk studied the newcomer, who gazed anxiously at the viewscreen. Finally, Uhura said, "I've got them."

The viewscreen changed from a field of stars to a frazzled admiral. "Kirk, you've caught us at a bad time. We're dealing with a bit of an emergency that started a few minutes before the spatial distortion that everyone just experienced. So I don't know how much time I can spare."

Kirk stood, as if he'd been shocked out of his chair. "You mean with the Guardian?"

"Well, yes, actually. But what made you guess that" The admiral frowned. "It just went dormant. We've always monitored it day and night, and for the first time, it's simply dead. No energy signature or anything."

"Spock?" Kirk asked, whirling about.

The Vulcan nodded. "The removal of time from the future would have an immediate effect on the Guardian, which claimed to be both the beginning and the end. If indeed the 'end' has been obliterated, it stands to reason that it could no longer exist."

The admiral raised his voice. "You know what's happening? Kirk, I demand to know—"

A stronger, second wave rocked the *Enterprise* and research station. "I would, but there's no time." Kirk pressed a button on his chair, reverting the viewscreen to stars. He turned to Sisko. "If what you say is true, how will destroying everything help?"

"As you said," Sisko said, "there's no time to explain."

"Jim!" McCoy cried. "You can't take a gamble like this!"

Kirk whirled on his friend. "In all the decades we've watched the Guardian, nothing like this has ever happened. I can't dismiss that, or these seismic, reality-distorting waves. Doing nothing is just as much of a gamble."

"Even so," McCoy began, "we've encountered things that could destroy entire solar systems, but a universe?" McCoy shook his head. "There's no such object."

"Not so much an *object*," Kirk said. "But a *who*." He glanced at Spock. As if they were of the same mind, they both spoke a single word—

"Lazarus."

"Who?" McCoy asked, until his eyes grew wide. "Oh, now wait a minute. That really *would* do the trick."

Sisko stepped closer. "Who is this Lazarus?"

"A bomb!" Scotty exclaimed as he gripped the railing. "A man, trapped in a dimensional corridor with an identical madman at his throat from an antimatter universe. If both men ever met outside of it—thereby bridging the gap between both universes—well, you can guess what would happen."

Uhura stood. "But we made that impossible by sealing them off for eternity." She placed a hand over her heart. "It was at Lazarus's request, but it was horrible."

Sisko raised a hand to his temple as the magnitude of it all seemed to strike him. "So we could do this, if we had to. I just don't know how else to stop the Pah-wraiths."

Kirk felt comforted that Sisko didn't actually want to pull the trigger on doomsday. "Spock, the dimensional corridor could only be reached from Lazarus's ship, but we vaporized it."

"More specifically," Spock replied, "the ship generated a trans-spatial dimensional frequency. One we recorded and can duplicate, but cannot breach as it requires a catalyst outside of time and space."

"I may be able to access it," Sisko said.

Another energy wave hit, only stronger. "Chekov, shields up,"

Kirk ordered. "Spock, start working on that frequency." He approached Sisko. "If there's anything you need to do beforehand, now's the time."

"Actually, there is." Sisko closed his eyes and took a deep breath. "I'll be back soon." Yet all he did was cup his hands together and open his eyes. "I'm back."

"You . . . you never left," Chekov muttered.

"It's because I can now exist outside linear time . . . but believe me, I'm trying to get used to it myself." Sisko peered down at his folded hands at something he apparently held.

A huge shockwave hit the *Enterprise,* jarring them all. "Shields down to twenty-three percent!" Chekov shouted.

"Whenever you're ready, Mr. Spock," Kirk said.

"I'm now radiating the trans-spatial pulse from our ship." Spock looked at Sisko and raised an eyebrow. "You may proceed."

Sisko closed his eyes. Beyond the ship, he sensed the strange signal that felt both unreal and incomplete. Yet now having been elevated to a being similar to the Prophets, he knew how to touch it, thereby acting as the key to a temporal doorway.

In the void of space, a dimensional corridor opened. Inside fought two ragged, bearded men. Both unable to die or age, with one of them mad in his hatred toward the other. They stared in shock at Sisko's arrival, which wasn't surprising, given they had been imprisoned in such torment for almost thirty years.

"Please leave," the sane one begged, staring past Sisko at the rift opening. "You don't know what you're doing."

Sisko glided past them before propelling them out into space amidst their screams. He shut the rift. In this existence outside of time and space, he neither saw nor heard anything. Yet his corporeal tether allowed him to sense the destruction of both universes, while feeling the death of the Pah-wraiths.

Sisko realized he was the only being in all of existence. A disconcerting feeling, even for one who had become a Prophet.

There remained no matter, future, present, or past. Simply nothingness all around him.

With great reverence, he opened his hands. There lay the pulsating glimmer of the beginning of time, which he had retrieved in order to start time all over again. Without intervention from him, existence would play out exactly the same. Every birth, death, and decision would converge into the same tapestry that had allowed the matter and antimatter universes to expand side by side.

Now all he had to do was wait for trillions and trillions of eons to pass. He found it curious that in his noncorporeal state outside of linear time, how quickly existence played out. Yet at the same time, he realized he shouldn't be surprised. After all, up until the moment of his existence, eternity was just starting.

He awaited two particular events. After the first occurred, he held the life energy of two beings, one in each hand. As the second event started, he watched his corporeal self, poised to attack Dukat. The Cardassian stood at the edge of the fire caves with the Kosst Amojan in hand.

The Sisko prepared to return to the confining body he once knew, but now with a simple message: "Include the book." But just before doing so, he deposited two similar individuals, each into their respective universes, on Bajor.

Sisko remained hunched over, held in place by Dukat's will, now that the Cardassian was possessed by the Pah-wraiths. He stared up into Dukat's blood red eyes, feeling helpless in the face of pure evil.

"Then I'll stop you!" a voice said to one side.

Sisko turned to see Kai Winn hold the Kosst Amojan above her head, until it was torn from her grasp and appeared in Dukat's hand. With a sneer, Dukat muttered, "Are you still here?"

"Emissary!" Kai Winn shouted. "The book!" Sisko could only watch as Dukat conjured up licks of flames from the fire caves to consume Kai Winn. She screamed in torment before dissolving to nothing.

"Farewell, Adami," Dukat hissed.

Sisko felt a brief lapse in Dukat's hold and lunged at his nemesis. Just then, he heard a voice in his head say, "Include the book." He hadn't considered how important Winn's plea may have been, but now he made sure to grab the text as he tackled Dukat and both men fell into the flames. . . .

Lazarus stared up at the Bajoran sky, feeling the hot sun on his face. He sat crouched over his garden, when his thoughts were interrupted by the sound of a transporter. He turned to see his dark-haired daughter materializing near the front of his modest country house. With a smile, he opened his arms and she ran into them. "Back from school already?"

"The teacher let us go early," the eight-year-old said. "But guess what I learned today?"

"Oh, I couldn't possibly guess," he said.

The door to their house opened to reveal his lovely wife, smiling as she approached. She was a Bajoran, who had passed on some of her nose wrinkles to their daughter.

The little girl spoke in an excited rush. "We learned that back on Earth they had a man named Lazarus too. And according to the story, he came back from the dead."

"Really?" Lazarus stroked his beard. "Well, I guess I can relate to that."

His daughter frowned, until he started tickling her. She giggled, dropped her books, and frolicked in the yard. When his wife drew near, they slid their arms around each other.

"What did you mean by that?" she asked. "Does it have to do with your past, which you refuse to share?"

"Possibly."

"Aren't you ever going to tell me?"

Lazarus's smile faded. "No. Recalling it means risking that I'll never forget." Before she could ask another question, he said, "Now let's get ready for services and let the Prophets know how much we appreciate them."

His little girl stopped running. "Ah, Dad. Do we have to? Can't we just stay home and play?"

Lazarus felt his wife tense at their daughter's reluctance, but his gentle squeeze relaxed her. "No, it's important we go." He looked back up at the sky and squinted against the sun's brightness. "We definitely need to go."